TONKE DRAGT

THE
LETTER
FOR THE
KING

TRANSLATED BY LAURA WATKINSON

PUSHKIN CHILDREN'S

the kingdom of Dagonaut
to the east of the great mountains

THE
LETTER
FOR THE
KING

Pushkin Children's Books
71–75 Shelton Street
London, WC2H 9JQ

The Letter for the King was first published in Dutch as *De brief voor de koning*

© 1962, *De brief voor de koning* by Tonke Dragt, Uitgeverij Leopold, Amsterdam

© Illustrations Tonke Dragt

English language translation © 2013 Laura Watkinson
First published by Pushkin Children's Books in 2013
This edition first published by Pushkin Children's Books in 2020

The publisher gratefully acknowledges the support of the Dutch Foundation
for Literature

N ederlands
letterenfonds
dutch foundation
for literature

9 8 7 6 5 4 3 2 1

ISBN 978-1-78269-259-1

Text designed and typeset by Tetragon, London
Printed and bound in the United States

www.pushkinpress.com

Dedicated to
the three stars in the west

Contents

Prologue

The Knights of King Dagonaut

This is a tale of long ago, when knights still roamed the land. It takes place in two kingdoms: the land of King Dagonaut, to the east of the Great Mountains, and the land of King Unauwen, to the west of the Great Mountains. The capital cities of these two realms also bear the name of their kings: the City of Dagonaut and the City of Unauwen. A third land also plays an important part in this tale, but now is not the time for stories of that place.

This account begins in the Kingdom of Dagonaut. But first you will need to know more about King Dagonaut and his knights and, with this in mind, I have transcribed a number of pages on the subject from an old, old book:

Our King Dagonaut is a mighty king; his reign is praised as wise and just, and his realm is large and beautiful, with hills and meadows, fertile fields, wide rivers and vast forests. There are mountains in the north and even higher mountains in the west. Beyond those mountains lies the land of King Unauwen, a realm of which our minstrels sing such beautiful songs. To the east and the south, the land is flatter, and enemies from those parts sometimes attempt to invade our country, jealous of the prosperity we enjoy. But no one has ever succeeded in conquering the realm, as the king's knights guard it well and defend it with courage. Within our borders, life is good, and all is safe and peaceful.

King Dagonaut is served by many knights, brave and bold men who help him to govern the kingdom and to maintain order. Many of these knights are famed throughout the land. Who among us has not heard of Sir Fantumar, and Tiuri the Valiant, and Ristridin of the South, to name but a few? The king has granted many of his knights land in fief, which they govern in his name. They are duty bound to come when he calls, and to aid him with their might and with their men.

Some knights, however, own no land; most of these men are still young but will succeed their fathers when they are older. And there are also knights-errant, men who have no desire for property and who travel around the land and offer their services wherever they go, patrolling the borders and even journeying beyond our kingdom to bring back news of distant lands.

The realm of King Dagonaut has many knights, and yet joining their ranks is no easy task. Any man who wishes to be knighted must prove himself worthy. He must undergo an arduous apprenticeship, first serving as a squire to an experienced knight and then joining the king's guards for another year. Not only must a knight be able to use weapons and prove himself knowledgeable in many fields, but above all he must prove that he is chivalrous and honest, brave and true. He must be knightly in every respect.

Once every four years, at midsummer, King Dagonaut summons all of the knights to his city, where they remain for seven days.

They inform him about the state of affairs in the various parts of the realm and give an account of their own activities and accomplishments.

And in that week, on midsummer's day, the young men who have been found worthy are ceremoniously knighted by the king. It is a great day! After the ceremony, there is a service in the cathedral, followed by a feast at the palace. Then comes a magnificent procession through the city, in which all of the knights ride, in full armour, with their shields and banners, and the newest young knights leading the way. Citizens of Dagonaut come from far and wide to see the spectacle. The celebration takes place not just in the palace, but all over the city. A fair is held in the marketplace, with musicians playing and people singing and dancing in every street, in daylight at first and later by the glow of hundreds of torches. The next day, the king calls his men together and the new knights are permitted to join their gathering for the first time. And the day after that, they take part in a great tournament, which many people view as the most thrilling part of the week. Nowhere else in the realm can such splendour and chivalry, such courage and agility, all be seen in one place.

But before those glorious days, the young knights have to pass one final test. They must fast for twenty-four hours before the knighting ceremony. They are not allowed to eat a morsel or drink a drop. And they have to spend the night in contemplation at a small chapel beyond the city walls. The young men lay their swords before the altar and, dressed in their white robes, they kneel down to reflect upon the great task that lies ahead. They undertake to serve their king loyally as knights of Dagonaut, and to protect his kingdom, their own homeland. They swear to themselves that they will always be honest and chivalrous, and fight for what is good. The knights remain awake and reflect all night, praying for strength for their task. They are not permitted *to sleep or to speak, or to pay any heed to those outside the chapel, until a delegation of the king's knights comes at seven o'clock in the morning to take them before the king.*

This story begins on such a night, in the small chapel on the hill outside the City of Dagonaut, where five young men were spending the night in reflection on the eve of their knighting ceremony. Their names were Wilmo, Foldo, Jussipo, Arman and Tiuri. Tiuri was the youngest of them; he was just sixteen years old.

PART ONE

—

A MYSTERIOUS MISSION

1 THE VIGIL IN THE CHAPEL

Tiuri knelt on the stone floor of the chapel, staring at the pale flame of the candle in front of him.

What time was it? He was supposed to be reflecting seriously upon the duties he would have to perform once he was a knight, but his mind kept wandering. And sometimes he found that he wasn't thinking about anything at all. He wondered if his friends felt the same.

He glanced across at Foldo and Arman, at Wilmo and Jussipo. Foldo and Wilmo were gazing at their candles, while Arman had buried his face in his hands. Jussipo was kneeling with a straight back and staring up at the ceiling, but then he changed position and looked Tiuri right in the eyes. Tiuri turned his head away and fixed his gaze on the candle again.

What was Jussipo thinking about?

Wilmo moved, scraping his shoe on the floor. The others all looked in his direction. Wilmo hung his head and looked a little embarrassed.

It's so quiet, thought Tiuri. *I've never known such quietness in my entire life. All I can hear is our breathing, and maybe, if I listen carefully, the beating of my own heart...*

The five young men were not permitted to say anything to one another, not even a word, all night long. They were also forbidden to have any contact at all with the outside world. They had locked the chapel door behind them and would not open it again until the next morning, at seven o'clock, when King Dagonaut's knights would come to fetch them.

Tomorrow morning! Tiuri could already picture the celebratory procession: the knights on their magnificently caparisoned horses, with their colourful shields and fluttering banners. He imagined himself among them, riding a fine steed, clad in shining armour, with a helmet and a waving plume. But then he shook his head to rid himself of that vision. He knew he should not be thinking about the external trappings of knighthood, but instead vowing to be chivalrous and honest, brave and true.

The candlelight made his eyes hurt. He looked at the altar, where the five swords lay waiting. The shields hung above the altar, gleaming in the flickering light of the candles.

Tomorrow there will be two knights bearing the same coat of arms, thought Tiuri. *Father and myself.* His father's name was also Tiuri and he was known as Tiuri the Valiant. Was he lying awake now, thinking about his son? Tiuri hoped he would become as worthy a knight as his father.

Then another thought occurred to him. What if someone were to knock at the door? He and his companions would not be permitted to open it. Tiuri remembered something that Sir Fantumar, whose squire he had been, had once told him. During his own vigil in the chapel, there had been a loud knocking at the door. Fantumar had been there with three other young men, and none of them had opened up. And it was just as well, because they later discovered that it had been one of the king's servants, who had wanted to put them to the test.

Tiuri looked again at his friends. They were still kneeling in the same position. He knew it must be after midnight. His candle had almost burnt down; it was the shortest of the five. Perhaps it was because he was sitting by a window. The chapel was a draughty place and he could feel a chilly gust of air. *When my candle goes out*, he thought, *I won't light another one*. The others wouldn't be able to see him in the dark, which was an appealing thought, and he wasn't worried that he might fall asleep.

Had Wilmo dozed off? No, he just shifted position, so he must be awake.

I'm not spending my vigil as I should, thought Tiuri. He clasped his hands together and rested his eyes on his sword, which he would be allowed to use only for a just cause. He repeated to himself the words that he would have to speak to King Dagonaut the following day: "I swear as a knight to serve you loyally, as I will all of your subjects and those who call upon my aid. I promise to..."

Then he heard a knock at the door. It was quiet, but there could be no doubt. The five young men held their breath, but stayed exactly where they were.

Then there was another knock.

They looked at one another, but no one said a word or moved a muscle.

The handle turned and rattled, but of course the door was locked. Then they heard the sound of footsteps slowly moving away.

All five of them sighed at the same time.

Good, thought Tiuri. *That's it over with.* It was strange, but he felt as though, all throughout his vigil, he had been waiting for such an interruption. His heart was pounding so loudly that he was sure the others must be able to hear it. *Come on, Tiuri, calm down*, he said to himself. *It was just a stranger who didn't know about our vigil, or someone who wanted to disturb us, or to put us to the test.*

But still, Tiuri waited anxiously for another sound. His candle flared brightly and then went out, with a quiet hiss, and he was surrounded by darkness.

He had no idea how much more time had passed when he heard a quiet noise above his head. It sounded like someone scratching at the window!

And then he heard a voice, as soft as a breath. "In the name of God, open the door!"

2 A Stranger's Request

Tiuri straightened his back and looked at the window. He could see nothing, not even a shadow, so he might almost have imagined it. If only that were true! He couldn't do as the voice had asked, no matter how urgent it had sounded. Tiuri hid his face in his hands and tried to banish every thought from his mind.

But again he heard the voice, very clearly, even though it was no more than a whisper. "In the name of God, open the door!"

It sounded even more urgent than before.

Tiuri looked at his friends. They didn't appear to have heard anything. But he had definitely heard the voice! "In the name of God, open the door!"

What should he do? He wasn't allowed to open the door... but what if it was someone who was in need of help, a fugitive in search of sanctuary?

He listened. All was silent again. But the voice was still echoing in his ears; he would never be able to forget it. Oh, why did this have to happen now of all times? Why did he have to be the one who heard the plea? He was not allowed to respond, but he knew that he would be unable to rest until he had done so.

Then Tiuri made a decision. Quietly, he stood up, stiff from kneeling on the cold floor for so long. Feeling his way along the wall, he tiptoed towards the door. He glanced at his friends and thought at first that they had not noticed anything, but then he saw Arman looking in his direction. He knew his friend would never betray him.

It seemed to take forever to reach the door of the chapel. Tiuri looked back one more time, at his friends, at the altar and the shields above it, at the light of the four candles, and at the dark shadows throughout the chapel, between the columns and around the vaulted ceiling. Then he headed to the door and put his hand on the key.

If I open this door, he thought, *I'll have broken the rules. And then the king will not knight me tomorrow.*

Tiuri turned the key, opened the door a crack and peered out into the night.

A man stood outside the door, dressed in a monk's habit, with the hood pulled down over his eyes. Tiuri could not see his face, as it was too dark. He opened the door a little wider and waited in silence for the man to speak.

"Thank you!" whispered the stranger.

Tiuri did not reply.

The stranger waited for a moment and then said, still in a whisper, "I need your help. It's a matter of life and death! Will you help me? Please." When Tiuri did not reply, he said, "My God, why won't you say something?"

"How can you expect me to help you?" whispered Tiuri. "Why have you come here? Don't you know that I am to be knighted tomorrow and that I may speak to no one?"

"I know that," answered the stranger. "That is why I came to this place."

"Well, you should have gone somewhere else," Tiuri said. "Now I've broken the rules and so I can't be knighted tomorrow."

"You will be knighted and you will have earned your knighthood," said the stranger. "A knight must help when his assistance is requested, must he not? Come outside, and I shall explain what I need you to do. Hurry, hurry, for there's little time!"

What do I have to lose now? thought Tiuri. *I've already spoken and I've opened the door, so why not leave the chapel too?*

The stranger took him by the hand and led him around the outside of the chapel. His hand felt bony and wrinkled. It was the hand of an old man. *His voice sounded old as well,* thought Tiuri. *Who could he be?*

The stranger stopped beside a small, dark alcove. "Let's hide here," he whispered, "and we must speak quietly, so that no one can hear us." Then he released Tiuri's hand and asked, "What is your name?"

"Tiuri," he answered.

"Ah, Tiuri. I know I shall be able to count on you."

"What do you want of me?" asked Tiuri.

The stranger leant close and whispered in his ear, "I have a letter here, with a message of vital importance. One might even say that the fate of an entire kingdom depends on it. It is a letter for King Unauwen."

King Unauwen! Tiuri had heard that name many times before. He reigned over the land to the west of the mountains, and was renowned as a noble and just ruler.

"This letter must be taken across the Great Mountains to the king in the City of Unauwen," said the stranger. "As quickly as possible."

"You don't expect me..." Tiuri began.

"No," said the stranger, interrupting him. "The man who shall deliver the letter is the Black Knight with the White Shield. At this moment, he is in the forest, at the Yikarvara

Inn. What I need you to do is to take this letter to him. I cannot do so myself, as I am old and there are enemies all around, who are pursuing me and who know my face."

"Why do you not ask someone else?" said Tiuri. "The city is full of knights right now, and there must be plenty of men you can trust."

"I cannot ask any of those knights," responded the stranger. "They would attract too much attention. Did I not tell you that there are enemies everywhere? Spies are lying in wait throughout the city, just looking for an opportunity to steal this letter. A famous knight is no good to me. I need someone who is unknown and who will go unnoticed. But at the same time I must be able to trust him with this letter. In other words, I am looking for someone who is a knight and yet not a knight! You are the one I need. You have been found worthy of being knighted tomorrow, but you are still young and have no reputation for your valiant deeds. And yet I know I can trust you."

Tiuri could find no argument to counter his words. He tried again to make out the stranger's features, but it was still too dark. "So this letter is of great importance?" he said.

"Of more importance than you could ever imagine!" whispered the stranger. "Come, you must hesitate no longer," he continued, his voice trembling. "We're wasting too much time! Near this place, behind the chapel, there is a horse in a meadow. If you take it, you can be at the inn within three hours – sooner if you ride quickly. It is about quarter past one now. You can be back by seven, when King Dagonaut's men will come to fetch you. Please, do as I ask!"

Tiuri knew he could not refuse. The rules that a future knight had to follow were important, but this appeal for his assistance seemed to matter even more.

"I will do it," he said. "Give me the letter and tell me how to find the inn."

"My thanks!" sighed the stranger. He quickly continued, in a whisper, "The place where he is to be found is called the Yikarvara Inn. Do you know King Dagonaut's hunting lodge? Behind it, there is a track that heads north-west. Ride along it until you reach a clearing in the forest. Two paths run on from there. Take the left-hand path and it will lead you to the inn. As for the letter, you must promise me on your honour as a knight that you will guard it as you would your own life and give it to no one other than the Black Knight with the White Shield."

"I am not yet a knight," said Tiuri, "but if I were, I would promise it on my honour as a knight."

"Good. If someone tries to steal the letter, you must destroy it, but only if it is absolutely necessary. Understood?"

"Understood," said Tiuri.

"And mark this well: when you find the Black Knight with the White Shield, you must ask him: Why is your shield white? And he will respond: Because white contains every colour. Then he will ask you: Where do you come from? You must answer: I come from afar. Only after that exchange should you hand over the letter."

"Like a password," said Tiuri.

"Exactly. A password. Do you understand exactly what you need to do?"

"Yes," said Tiuri. "Please give me the letter."

"One last thing," said the stranger. "Be careful. You must make sure that you are not followed. Here is the letter; guard it well."

Tiuri took the letter. It was small and flat and he could feel, in the darkness, that there were seals on it. He slipped it under his shirt, close to his chest.

"You won't lose it if you keep it there, will you?" asked the stranger.

"No," Tiuri replied. "That's the safest place."

The stranger grasped his hands and shook them firmly. "Then go," he said. "And God bless you!" He let go of Tiuri's hands, turned around and slipped back into the darkness.

Tiuri waited for a moment and then walked, quickly and quietly, in the opposite direction. He looked over at the dimly lit windows of the chapel, where his friends were still keeping their vigil before the altar. "Come on," he whispered to himself, "You have to hurry."

And he went in search of the meadow where the stranger had told him he would find a horse waiting.

3   THE RIDE TO THE INN

It was a beautiful summer's night and the sky was full of stars. Tiuri found the horse behind the chapel, as the stranger had said he would. It was tied to a fence, but it had neither bridle nor saddle.

It's just as well I've ridden bareback before, he thought, as he undid the rope, his fingers trembling slightly. The rope was tightly fastened with lots of knots and he wished he had brought his knife. In fact, he had no weapons with him at all, as he had left everything behind in the chapel.

The horse whinnied quietly, but it sounded so loud in the stillness of the night. Tiuri glanced around. His eyes had become accustomed to the darkness and he could see a building nearby, probably the house of the farmer who owned the meadow.

Finally, Tiuri managed to get the rope untied.

"Come on, horse," he whispered. "Come with me."

The animal whinnied again. A dog barked and a light shone out from the farmhouse. Tiuri climbed up onto the horse and clicked his tongue. "Come on!" The horse slowly started walking.

"Hey!" someone shouted. "Who's there?"

Tiuri wasn't about to answer him.

The barking grew loud and fierce, as a man dashed out of the farmhouse with a lantern in his hand. "Thief!" he shouted. "Stop right there! Jian, Marten, get out here! A thief's making off with my horse!"

Tiuri gasped. A thief? He hadn't meant to steal anything. But there was no time to lose. He leant forward and urged the horse on. The animal started trotting.

"Faster!" Tiuri whispered urgently. "Faster!"

Behind them, there was a commotion of shouting, yelling and furious barking. The horse flattened its ears and ran off as fast as the wind.

I'm sorry I had to borrow your horse, Tiuri imagined himself saying to the poor farmer, who was still shouting after him. *I'm not really stealing it. I promise to bring it back soon.*

When he looked back, the farmhouse was already a long way behind him and there was no sign of anyone following. All the same, he kept racing onwards at the same speed.

Tiuri thought the stranger really should have mentioned that the horse belonged to someone else, no matter how important the letter was and how secret its contents were. He reined in the horse and checked that the precious document was safe. Yes, there it was, still in the same place. He looked around cautiously, remembering that the stranger had mentioned that enemies might be on the lookout. But Tiuri saw no one. He gazed back towards the city, which was almost completely in darkness, and looked up at the chapel, dimly visible on the hillside, small and white.

Then he rode towards the forest.

The forest was not far from the City of Dagonaut. It covered a large area and there were places within it where no human had ever set foot. Tiuri knew the way to the lodge, as he had hunted in the king's retinue on many occasions.

It was much darker in the forest, but the road was wide, so he could keep riding at a quick pace. Now and then, he slowed the horse and took a good look around. He saw no one, but he felt as if the forest was full of men lurking and spying on him, just waiting to attack.

He reached the hunting lodge without incident and had no trouble finding the track that the stranger had mentioned. It was narrow and winding, which forced him to ride more slowly.

I hope I'll be back in time, he thought. *Just imagine not being there when the king's knights come to fetch us for the ceremony! But the stranger said I should be able to reach the inn in three hours.*

He thought about the Black Knight with the White Shield, the man to whom he was supposed to give the letter. He had never heard that knight's name before. Who was he? Where did he come from? None of King Dagonaut's knights wore those colours, so he was probably one of King Unauwen's men. Why he was here, so far from his own country, was a mystery. Tiuri had heard stories from travellers who had met Unauwen's knights. They sometimes rode along the Great Southern Road on their way to Eviellan, the hostile land on the other side of the Grey River, where one of Unauwen's sons ruled.

Tiuri wondered how long he had been riding. An hour? That would make it quarter past two. Maybe it was even later than that – it seemed such a long time since he'd been kneeling in the chapel and had heard the voice asking him to open the door.

There were more hills now and the track went up and down. The horse seemed able to see better in the dark than Tiuri. Sure of foot, it kept on going.

The forest was quiet at night, but not as quiet as the chapel. Tiuri could hear all sorts of strange, soft noises, probably animals. There was the sound of leaves rustling, and the steps of the horse, and dry twigs and branches snapping as he rode by. Something flew into his face and gave him a fright, but it was just a moth or some other insect.

The track led uphill again, and the sky was growing lighter. The trees and undergrowth became less dense. *I must be close to the clearing now*, Tiuri thought.

And indeed, he soon came to a treeless glade. It had to be the place that the stranger had mentioned. Tiuri knew he should take the path to the left.

As he rode across the clearing, he heard more noises, noises that were unlike anything he'd heard so far during his ride. Horses neighing and the clatter of hoofs!

From his high vantage point, he could see out over the forest and, in the distance, he made out dark figures and the gleam of weapons. A group of horsemen was passing swiftly through the forest.

Tiuri retreated to the trees, wondering who the horsemen were and what they were doing in the forest in the middle of the night. When he finally ventured back out into the clearing, there was neither sight nor sound of the riders. It was as though he had been dreaming. However, he did not stay there puzzling about it for long, but took the path to the left, which led down from the clearing.

The path was not a clear track, but more like an overgrown trail. Tiuri sighed, because it was going to slow him down even more. He was soon forced to dismount and lead the horse on foot, following the path one hesitant step at a time and constantly worrying that he would lose his way altogether. Branches whipped at Tiuri's face, and the dew on the long grass soaked his feet and legs.

Tiuri kept wondering about the time. The path was so tricky to navigate that he feared he would not get back to the chapel by seven o'clock.

By then, the sky was much lighter and, here and there, birds were starting to sing.

Tiuri was relieved when the path finally improved and he could climb back onto his horse.

In the grey moment just before daybreak, he came upon another clearing. A small wooden building stood in the middle – it had to be the inn.

4 THE YIKARVARA INN

T iuri climbed down from his horse, tied it to a tree, and ran to the inn. It was silent and dark, and all of the doors and windows were closed. He rapped the knocker on the front door; it made a loud, resounding bang that was sure to wake up everyone within. But no one answered. He rattled the door, but it was locked. Impatiently, he banged the knocker again. This time, a window opened upstairs. A man wearing a nightcap leant out and asked in a sleepy voice what Tiuri wanted.

"Is this the Yikarvara Inn?" asked Tiuri.

"Yes, this is it," the man replied. "Did you really need to wake me to ask that, and probably my guests too? We've had little enough rest tonight!"

"Are you the innkeeper?" asked Tiuri. "I'd like to speak to one of your guests."

"In the middle of the night?" spluttered the man. "I'm afraid that won't be possible, young man! You'll have to come back tomorrow."

"This is important!" Tiuri said in an urgent tone. "Please... don't close the window."

The man leant out further. "Who are you?" he asked. "And who do you want to speak to?"

"It doesn't matter who I am," Tiuri said. "I'm looking for the Black Knight with the White Shield."

The man made a strange noise. Tiuri couldn't quite tell whether it was anger or surprise. Either way, all traces of sleepiness had gone from his voice when he answered. "Wait there a moment, I'm coming down." The head disappeared from the window, and soon Tiuri heard the bolts of the door sliding aside. Then the door opened and the man was standing there, wearing a nightshirt and carrying a candle.

"Well, then," he said, looking Tiuri up and down. "Yes, I'm the innkeeper. And now you can tell me why you've got me out of bed."

"I've come to see the Black Knight with the White Shield," answered Tiuri. "I have to speak to him immediately."

"You're the second one tonight," said the innkeeper. "But you won't be able to speak to him right now."

"Can't you wake him up?" said Tiuri.

"I'm afraid that won't be possible," the innkeeper said

again. "The Black Knight with the White Shield isn't here. He left earlier tonight."

Tiuri gasped. "No!" he said. "He can't have done!"

"And why not?" the innkeeper responded calmly.

"Where did he go? Quickly, tell me!" said Tiuri.

"If I knew, I'd tell you," replied the innkeeper. "But I don't have a clue." He seemed to have realized how anxious Tiuri was, because he added, "He should be back before long, at least if he's as good a knight as he seems to be. What is it that you need to say to him so urgently?"

"I can't tell you that," said Tiuri. "But it's urgent. Do you know when he'll be back?"

"Again, if I knew, I'd tell you," said the innkeeper, "but I don't know that either. In fact, I don't know anything at all about that knight. It's a strange business." He scratched his head so hard that his nightcap fell off.

"You must know something!" said Tiuri. "When did he leave and why? And which way did he go?"

"That's too many questions at once," said the innkeeper. He slowly stooped to pick up his cap. "Come in," he said. "I'm not keen on this damp morning air. It's not good for my stiff joints."

When they were inside, he placed his candle on the table and put his nightcap back on. Tiuri asked impatiently, "So which way did the Black Knight go?"

"He got here yesterday morning," said the innkeeper. "Bit of a peculiar fellow. Not that I doubt he's a brave knight, oh no. In fact, he was most impressive. He was all alone. Didn't even have a squire with him! He was wearing a pitch-black suit of armour, but the shield on his arm was as white as snow. He'd lowered his black visor and he didn't raise it when he asked me for a room, or when he came into the inn. Well, I gave him a room, of course, and later in the day I took some food to the room, as he'd requested. I thought I'd see his face then, but no! He'd taken off his armour, including his helmet, but he was wearing a black silk mask, and all I could see were his eyes. Don't you think that's strange? He must have taken some kind of vow. Would you know anything about that?"

"Which way did he go?" Tiuri asked again.

The innkeeper looked a little irritated, but he continued. "I was just coming to that," he said. "At about one or two in the morning, when I was already in bed, there was a loud knocking at the door. I looked out of the window and saw another black knight! 'Open the door!' he shouted. 'Is the Black Knight with the White Shield within?' Well, I told him that he was here, but I said it was a little late. And then this knight yelled at me to open the door or he said he'd knock it down. So I flew downstairs and opened the door. The knight was dressed in a pitch-black suit of armour too, but he had a shield that was as red as blood. Then he just barked at me! 'Where is the Black Knight with the White Shield?' he said. I told him he was asleep and he ordered me to wake him up. Said he had to speak to him and that I should be quick about it! Well, to be honest, he gave me a bit of a fright. But my guest was already coming down the stairs. He was dressed in his black armour and his helmet, and his visor was down. He was carrying his weapons and had the white shield on his arm. The Black Knight with the Red Shield walked towards him and then stopped, and they stood there, facing each other, right here in this very room. The Knight with the Red Shield pulled off his glove and tossed it onto the floor at the other man's feet. The Knight with the White Shield picked it up and said, 'When?' And the Knight with the Red Shield said, 'Now!'"

The innkeeper stopped to catch his breath before finishing his tale, "And then, without saying another word, the two of them marched out of here and rode off together, into the forest."

"To fight a duel," said Tiuri.

"Yes, that's what I thought too," said the innkeeper. "And neither of them has returned as yet."

"So they left at about two?" asked Tiuri. "And what time is it now?"

"Half four, or thereabouts," said the innkeeper. "The sun's coming up."

"Which direction did they ride in?" asked Tiuri.

The innkeeper went outside with Tiuri and pointed out the path they had taken. "But I don't know where exactly they were going," he said.

"I'll try to follow their trail," said Tiuri. "Thank you!" And before the innkeeper could ask any questions, Tiuri had run to his horse, jumped on and ridden away.

5 THE BLACK KNIGHT WITH THE WHITE SHIELD

The sky in the east glowed pink and orange; the sun was about to come up. The birds were chirping and whistling and twittering away, as if they were delighted to greet the beautiful day that was dawning. Tiuri, however, was not at all happy. He was annoyed because it was so late and he still had not delivered the letter. How was he ever going to get back to the chapel in time? But he carried on riding along the trail that the two Black Knights had left. He had promised to take the letter and he did not want to break that promise. But that didn't stop him from grumbling and muttering to himself. He cursed the Black Knight with the Red Shield for challenging the Black Knight with the White Shield, and he resented the Knight with the White Shield for accepting the challenge. And he cursed both of them for riding straight through the forest instead of leaving clear tracks on a proper path.

It must be five by now, he thought. *It's already light. Where on earth have they got to?*

He thought about how surprised Dagonaut's knights would be when they arrived at the chapel to find he wasn't there. And what would the king think when he found out Tiuri had run away on the night before the ceremony? And what about his friends and his parents, and everyone else? But he remembered the stranger's words and sighed; he knew there was no other way he could have reacted. Then, with a jolt, he realized that he had lost the trail.

He was in a clearing. The sandy ground was churned up with hoofmarks and footprints... but which ones belonged to the two knights?

Tiuri quickly glanced all around. It seemed as if an entire troop of horsemen had passed this way, perhaps the men he had seen earlier that night. They had raced through the forest, trampling plants and snapping branches. The trail of the two knights was lost.

He decided to go in the direction that the troop of riders had come from, as they'd left a clearly visible path. As he rode on, Tiuri wondered if these horsemen had anything to do with the two Black Knights. Although it was light now, he shivered. He felt more anxious than he'd been at any point in his adventure so far.

Tiuri continued on his way for a while before hearing a sound, a quiet, anxious whinny. Then he spotted a horse tied to a tree. It was a beautiful black horse, with a simple harness, and it looked at him with sad dark eyes and whinnied once again.

Tiuri gently stroked the horse's nose and whispered, "You just wait there and I'll go and see where your master is. I think he must be somewhere nearby. Is that right?"

He rode on and then, between the trees, he spotted something lying on the pale green grass. Something that was black and white and red... His breath caught in his throat, but he leapt quickly from his horse and ran over to take a look.

A man was lying on the ground, clad in a black suit of armour that was damaged and dented. The shield beside him was white, and the red that Tiuri had seen was blood. Tiuri had found the Black Knight with the White Shield, but the man was wounded... or worse.

Tiuri knelt down beside him. Although the knight was clearly injured, he was still breathing. He was not wearing a helmet now, but his face was covered with a black mask. Tiuri felt himself trembling as he stared down at him, but then he pulled himself together. He had to do something, to find out the extent of his injuries, to stop the bleeding somehow.

Then the knight moved and whispered, "Who are you?"

Tiuri leant over him. "Please do not move, sir knight," he said. "I am here to help. Are you in pain?"

He could see that the knight was looking at him through his mask. "I do not know you," he said in a weak voice, "but I am glad someone has found me before I die. Do not worry about my wounds; there is nothing that can be done."

"You must not say that," said Tiuri, and he carefully started to remove the knight's armour.

"Do not trouble yourself," whispered the knight. "I know that I am dying."

Tiuri feared he was right. Yet he continued with his attempts to alleviate the injured man's suffering, tearing a strip of fabric from his robe and bandaging the wounds as well as he could.

"Thank you," whispered the knight. "Who are you and what has brought you to this place?"

"My name is Tiuri. Shall I fetch some water for you? Perhaps you would like something to drink."

"There is no need," said the knight. "Tiuri... I know that name. Are you related to Tiuri the Valiant?"

"He is my father," said Tiuri.

"And what are you doing here?" asked the knight.

"I... I came here to find you... I am so sorry that..."

"You came to find me?" said the Black Knight. "You are here on my account? Thank the Lord! Then perhaps it is not too late..." He looked at Tiuri with eyes that gleamed behind his black mask and said, "Do you have something for me?"

"Yes, sir knight," Tiuri replied. "A letter."

"I knew my squire would find a messenger," said the knight with a sigh. "Wait a moment," he continued, as Tiuri reached for the letter. "Is there not a question that you wish to ask me?"

Tiuri remembered the words he needed to say. "Why... Why is your shield white?" he stammered.

"Because white contains every colour," the knight responded. His voice sounded much stronger. It was a voice that inspired Tiuri with great confidence. Then the knight asked, "Where do you come from?"

"I come from afar," answered Tiuri.

"Now show me the letter," the knight ordered. "But first make sure no one is spying on us."

Tiuri looked around the area. "I see no one nearby," he said. "Just our horses." He took out the letter and showed it to the knight. "Oh, sir knight," he blurted out, "I am so sorry you were defeated in the duel!"

"Duel?" said the injured man. "That was no duel! I remain unvanquished by any one man. The Black Knight with the Red Shield lured me into an ambush. His Red Riders leapt out and attacked me in large numbers."

Tiuri gasped. "That is disgraceful!" he said.

"But they did not find what they were looking for," said the knight. "They wanted to destroy not only me, but also the letter, the one you just showed me! Conceal it well – and then I will tell you what you must do with it. But first tell me, Tiuri, how did you come to have this letter?"

Tiuri told him all that happened.

"Good," whispered the knight. He fell silent for a few moments. "Do not look so worried," he said kindly. Tiuri could tell that he was smiling beneath his mask and he wished he knew what the knight's face looked like.

"Listen to me," the knight said. "I must keep this brief, because I have little time. This letter is for King Unauwen and it is of the utmost importance. Now that I can no longer deliver it, you must do so!"

"Me?" whispered Tiuri.

"Yes, I know of no one who could do it better. You are perfectly capable and I have every faith in you. You must leave immediately. Enough time has been lost already. Journey westwards, first through the forest, and then along the Blue River, until you reach its source. There is a hermit who lives there, Menaures. Take this ring from my finger. When you show it to Menaures, he will know it was I who sent you. He will help you to cross the mountains, because you will not be able to do it alone. Once you are on the other side of the mountains, the road will lead you to Unauwen." The knight raised his hand and said, "Here, take my ring. I know I am asking much of you, but I am sure you are the right person for this task."

Tiuri carefully removed the ring from the knight's finger. "I want to do it," he said, "but I do not know..."

"You *must* do it," said the knight. "But I do not deny that it will be difficult. You already know I have enemies who are after this letter. Many dangers will threaten you along the way. So you must keep your mission secret. Tell no one about it. And give this letter to King Unauwen alone."

"What... what does the letter say?" asked Tiuri, as he slowly slipped the ring onto his own finger.

"That is a secret," answered the knight. "You must not open the letter. But if you fear that you will lose the letter, then – and only then – you may open it and commit its message to memory, so that you may pass it on to King Unauwen. Then you must destroy the letter itself. But do so only as a final resort." The knight gasped and fell silent. Then, in a much weaker voice, he asked, "Will you take the letter?"

"Yes, sir knight," Tiuri replied.

"Promise me this on your honour as a knight," he whispered.

"I swear on my honour as a knight," said Tiuri. "Except," he added, "I am not yet a knight."

"But you will become one," said the knight. "Please, would you remove my mask? A knight must always face Death with an open visor."

Hands shaking, Tiuri did as he was asked. And when he saw the Black Knight's calm and noble face, he felt moved to grasp his hand and swore to deliver the letter safely. "And," he said, "I shall find your murderers and take vengeance on them!"

"That is not your task," whispered the knight. "You have only to serve as my messenger."

The knight closed his eyes. His fingers twitched in Tiuri's hand and then were still. Tiuri looked at him and gently released his hand. He knew the knight was dead and he was deeply saddened, even though they had only just met. Tiuri buried his face in his hands and prayed for the man's soul.

6 RED RIDERS

Tiuri stood up and took one last look at the peaceful face of the Black Knight with the White Shield, before turning around and walking slowly back to his horse. Now he had to carry out the task that the knight had given him, and deliver the letter to King Unauwen in the land to the west of the Great Mountains.

He stopped beside the horse and considered his course of action. He could not return to the City of Dagonaut, because that would take too long. He would also have to explain what had happened and that would not be possible, as his mission had to remain a secret. And yet somehow he had to send a message to the city, to his parents, so that they would not be worried and go in search of him. He also had to ensure that the Knight with the White Shield had a decent burial and that everyone knew who had murdered him. *The best thing I can do*, he thought, *is ride back to the inn. I can tell the innkeeper that the Knight with the White Shield is dead and ask him to send word to the city.*

And soon, he was on his way, feeling a lot older and more serious than he had just a short time before. After a while, he heard someone approaching, and a man on horseback appeared, travelling towards him. He was equipped for battle, with helmet and chainmail, lance and sword. His tabard, shield and the feathers on his helmet were as red as blood. *One of the Red Riders!* thought Tiuri. He remembered then that he was unarmed. Even so, he rode on calmly and acted as though everything was normal.

The Red Rider moved aside to let Tiuri pass. Tiuri rode by, his heart pounding, and as he came alongside the horseman, the man spoke. "Ho, friend," he said. "What are you doing so early in the forest? Where did you come from and where are you bound?"

"That is my concern," Tiuri answered brusquely. "I bid you good morning."

Tiuri rode on, expecting to feel a weapon in his back at any moment. However, nothing happened. He breathed out again, but dared not look around or quicken his pace. Then he heard the man shout something, but he could not make out what he said. Tiuri looked around to see that a second Red Rider had joined the first. Both men were looking at him. One of them gave another shout. Tiuri heard an answer, far away. He was growing uneasy and he made his horse go faster.

Soon he realized that the Red Riders were following him!

He urged his tired horse to go even faster, as he knew the inn could not be far. But then another Red Rider appeared on his right and barked at him to stop. Before Tiuri could respond, a fourth horseman came up on the other side, and Tiuri had to pull hard on his horse's reins to avoid him.

Tiuri knew he was going to have to make a run for it. Suddenly, the entire forest seemed to be full of Red Riders, and they were all after him. They chased Tiuri, yelling at him to stop. But of course Tiuri did nothing of the kind. He swerved from the path and raced into a dense part of the forest, in a desperate attempt to shake off his pursuers.

Tiuri had no idea how long he raced onwards, uphill and downhill, ploughing through bushes and thorny undergrowth, with the shouts and yells following after him. He only knew that he didn't want to be murdered like the Black Knight with the White Shield.

After some time, he looked back and saw that he had gained a lead, but he knew he could not keep it for long. His horse was tired, the forest was difficult to ride through, and there were so many pursuers. But then he had a bright idea. He jumped off his horse and slapped its hindquarters. As the horse ran off one way, Tiuri raced in the opposite direction and shinned up a tree as fast as he could. He sat high up in the branches, safely hidden among the leaves, panting and trying to catch his breath as he waited to see what would happen.

A group of men rode past beneath the tree, but they did not notice him. Then he heard more shouts, but the voices were in the distance, so he dared to move into a more comfortable position. However, he still did not climb down the tree, because he was scared they might come back.

Tiuri stayed up in his tree for a good while, but the Red Riders did not return. The forest seemed so calm and peaceful and it was almost impossible to believe that the past few hours had been so eventful.

Tiuri looked around and then carefully took out the letter so that he could take a closer look. There was nothing remarkable about the letter: it was small, white and flat, and there were no words written on the outside. He studied the three seals; each had a crown on it, but there was nothing else to indicate the importance of the letter. As he tucked it away again, he realized that it must be around seven o'clock. He leant back against the trunk and closed his eyes. *Dagonaut's knights must be blowing their horns outside the chapel door right at this very moment*, he thought. *And Arman, Foldo, Wilmo and Jussipo are standing up and going over to open the door*. He pictured the knights standing outside the chapel and heard them say, "Good morning. King Dagonaut requires your presence. Take up your swords and your shields and come with us." He tried to imagine what would happen after that, but his thoughts wandered. The next image that came into his mind was the Black Knight with the White Shield saying to him, "You have only to serve as my messenger."

Tiuri opened his eyes. The chapel seemed so far away and the vigil long ago. It had nothing to do with him now. He looked down. *It must be safe by now*, he thought. He climbed down the tree and cautiously made his way through the forest, glancing around at every unexpected sound.

Soon, he had a pleasant surprise: he came across his horse, quietly grazing.

"Good horse," he said, climbing onto its back. "Let's head back to the inn and you can eat your fill." Then he gasped as he remembered that the horse did not belong to him. He had to return it to its owner somehow.

Tiuri started riding and, before long, without any further adventures, he arrived back at the inn.

7 A CLOSE SHAVE

The innkeeper was busily sweeping the floor. He was dressed now, but he still had his nightcap on. Two men were eating breakfast at one of the tables, beside an open window. When Tiuri came in, they all turned to stare.

"My goodness me!" exclaimed the innkeeper. "Whatever have you been up to?"

Tiuri realized how dishevelled he must look. His white robe was stained and torn from his adventures of the previous night, and his hair was wild and unkempt. He realized, too, that he was covered in scratches and cuts after his escape from the Red Riders.

"Did you find the Black Knight?" asked the innkeeper.

"Yes. I found him," Tiuri replied sombrely.

The innkeeper looked him up and down. Then his eyes rested on Tiuri's left hand and the surprise on his face slowly gave way to suspicion.

Tiuri followed the man's gaze and saw what he was staring at. The knight's ring!

"Isn't that ring..." the innkeeper began.

Tiuri interrupted the innkeeper. "The Black Knight with the White Shield is dead," he said quietly.

"What's that?" the innkeeper gasped. "Dead? So the Knight with the Red Shield won the duel?"

"There was no duel," said Tiuri. "The Knight with the White Shield was murdered."

"Oh, my goodness!" cried the innkeeper. "Murdered!"

"Please listen!" said Tiuri. "I have little time and what I have to say is of the greatest importance."

The men at the table had stopped eating and were staring at Tiuri. One of them got up and said, "Has something happened to the Black Knight? The one who was here yesterday?"

Before Tiuri could reply, the door flew open and a voice yelled, "Whose is that horse in front of the inn?!"

Tiuri turned around. In the doorway stood a burly man with a red face, who glared angrily at each of them in turn. Tiuri did not recognize the man, but his voice sounded familiar.

"It belongs to this young man here," said the man who was sitting at the table. "He just arrived on that horse."

"That's right," said Tiuri. "It's mine. Well, actually, it's..." He fell silent. Suddenly he knew who the man in the doorway was. That voice... It was the horse's owner!

The man came right up to Tiuri and roared in his face. "No, it most definitely isn't yours! That horse is mine! And you are the thief who stole it last night!"

"Good sir," said Tiuri, "I did not steal it! I only borrowed it for a while! Please forgive me, I was..."

But the man was too angry to listen. He grabbed Tiuri by the arm and growled, "Well, I've got you now, thief!" He turned to the others and said, "Followed his trail half the night, but then I lost it. I get to the inn and what do I see? My horse – and the thief along with it!"

Tiuri pulled himself free. "I am not a thief!" he shouted. "I was planning to return your property to you, as any honest man would. Listen. I can explain everything!"

"Fine words!" scoffed the man. "But I believe none of them!"

"But, my good sir..." began Tiuri.

"I'm not your good sir," the man spat. "And I don't like fine stories like the one you're spinning now! You're one of those lads who are all mouth and no morals!"

"Just let me explain!" cried Tiuri.

"You can explain to the sheriff," said the man. "You're coming with me to the city."

To the city? Tiuri couldn't do that! He had no time to waste. And anyway, he knew he really couldn't explain anything about his mission. The task itself was a secret and that meant keeping quiet about the events that had led up to it. He stepped back and said, "I cannot go with you to the city. But I am no thief. I assure you on my word of honour!"

"Ha, it gets better!" cried the man. "Word of honour! How dare you say that, you villain?!"

"And how dare you call me a villain?!" shouted Tiuri. He was furious that anyone would call him that. If everything had gone to plan, he would have been a knight by now, and treated with respect by everyone he met. A villain? Tiuri, who had been chosen for such an important task?!

"I don't understand what's going on!" cried the innkeeper. "Did he steal your horse? He arrived here in the middle of the night and he just came back and told me the Knight with the White Shield has been murdered. And he's wearing his ring. What is the meaning of this?"

"I can explain everything," said Tiuri once again, "but you're not giving me the chance." He spoke calmly but he felt so anxious inside. The men looked so angry and threatening. "I took your horse," he continued, "because I had to deliver an urgent message."

"Poppycock!" said the horse's owner. "You could have just asked me if you needed to borrow it, couldn't you? How much time would that have taken? Now you can hold your tongue and come with me. I've had enough of your prattling!"

"No, wait a moment!" said the innkeeper. "There's still something I need him to explain! Whatever happened to the Black Knight with the White Shield?"

"The Knight with the White Shield is dead," said Tiuri, "and I would ask you to ensure that he receives a burial befitting a noble knight. You will find him not far from here." He explained where the knight was to be found.

"But who killed him?" asked the innkeeper.

"The Red Riders," answered Tiuri. "It was an ambush."

"Red Riders!" exclaimed the man at the table. "I saw them. They rode past here early this morning when I..."

"What are you talking about?" shouted the horse's owner. "This boy is a thief and I want him punished."

"But there's been a murder!" shouted the innkeeper.

"Then he can tell that to the sheriff as well, can't he?" said the man, grabbing hold of Tiuri again. "But one thing's certain. There's no way I'm letting this young man escape."

"The Red Riders..." began the man at the table.

"The Black Knight..." said the innkeeper.

But Tiuri didn't wait to hear what they had to say. He tore himself free and ran outside. They would just have to think he was a thief, because he couldn't allow himself to be dragged back to the city! The four men followed him, shouting and yelling as Tiuri raced into the forest. He soon had a lead on his pursuers, but he knew it wouldn't last. He could feel his heart pounding in his throat and saw black spots before his eyes. He slowed down and looked over his shoulder. Then, for the second time, he gathered all of his strength and climbed into a tree.

His ruse worked this time as well. The men soon ran past beneath the tree without noticing him. *But I mustn't do it a third time*, he thought, as he was getting his breath back. *They say, try a trick thrice and tempt the devil!*

Tiuri was exhausted. But, fortunately, he was able to rest for a short while, as he had to wait until the coast was clear. After some time, he saw the innkeeper and the horse's owner walk by, with gloomy faces. The innkeeper had lost his nightcap and Tiuri couldn't help but grin, even though the situation was so serious.

Things were not looking good for Tiuri! He had to travel to a distant land to deliver an important letter, and all he had was the clothes on his back. And his tattered robe was far from suitable for such a long journey. He had no weapons, no money and no horse. People thought he was a thief. And what was more, he had dangerous enemies: the Red Riders and their leader, the Black Knight with the Red Shield.

Tiuri sighed. He knew the task ahead of him would not be an easy one. *And I haven't even been able to send word to the city*, he thought. He would have to do so, one way or another. The horse's owner was sure to report him to the sheriff. Would they realize in the city that the so-called thief was the same boy who had escaped from the chapel on the night before he was due to become a knight? *Father, Mother and my friends won't believe I am a thief*, thought Tiuri, *and I don't think the king will either. But they're sure to be worried about me.* He sighed again. "Come on," he said sternly to himself. "There's just one thing you should be thinking about. You have to deliver the letter. That's what you promised the knight." Tiuri looked down at the beautiful ring on his finger and the large stone in it, which sparkled like a diamond. Perhaps it was not such a good idea to wear it on his hand – in fact, it was a really foolish idea. He pulled out the cord that fastened his robe at the neck and slipped it through the ring. Then he hung it around his neck, beneath his shirt, where no one would be able to see it.

And then he had to be on his way. He thought it must be safe by now and perhaps he would somehow manage to find weapons and a horse.

Oh, I am such a fool! he suddenly thought. *The knight's horse. I can take him!*

Tiuri jumped down from the tree. He knew now what he needed to do. First get the horse, and then set off on his journey!

Part Two

The Journey through the Forest

1 RIDING A BLACK HORSE

Tiuri warily started to make his way through the forest again, towards the spot where he had found the Black Knight with the White Shield. Then he heard someone nearby, whistling a tune. He crept along, following the sound, and found a boy of his own age, who was making bundles of branches and twigs. He was whistling away happily and didn't notice Tiuri.

Tiuri watched him for a while. Then he came to a decision. He stepped out from his hiding place in the bushes and said, "Good morning!"

The boy was startled. He stopped whistling and stared at Tiuri. "Good morning," Tiuri repeated. "Could I ask you to do me a favour?"

"Not likely!" the boy said. "You're the one they're looking for, aren't you? The horse thief!"

"Sssh!" whispered Tiuri. "Keep your voice down!"

The boy took a step backwards and glanced at his axe.

"There's no need to be frightened of me," said Tiuri. "In fact, I have more reason to fear you, because I have no weapon at all. And you're right. I'm the one they're looking for, but I'm not a thief. I swear it on my word of honour."

"So what are you doing here?" asked the boy. "And what do you want from me?"

"I need your help," replied Tiuri. "Would you go to the city for me and take someone a message?"

"A message?" said the boy. "Why? Why should I help you?"

"I'm only asking," said Tiuri. "If you don't want to do it, I can't force you. But I would be very grateful. And truly, I am not a thief!"

"Hm," said the boy, frowning. "So what is it that you want me to do? Not that I'm promising to help, mind you! In fact, I'm not at all sure about this."

"Go to the City of Dagonaut, to Sir Tiuri the Valiant, and tell him that his son is fine, but that he cannot yet return to the city. Say that his son is well and that he should not go in search of him."

"Can't you do it yourself?" asked the boy. "The city's a long way from here and I have a lot of work to do."

"I can't go myself," said Tiuri. "People are after me. As you already know! Please, do this for me. I need you to leave right away."

"Sir Tiuri the Valiant? What could I say to such a powerful lord? He won't listen to me!"

"He will listen to you, because you are bringing him a message from his son. Or you can go to my... go to his wife and tell her instead. Wait, can I have a piece of that rope?"

"Erm... yes," said the boy, handing him a length of the rope he was holding.

Tiuri took off his belt and tied the rope around his waist. He handed the belt to the boy. It was a very fine belt. His mother had embroidered it and his father had bought the golden buckle from the best smith in the city.

"Look," he said, "give this to Sir Tiuri, or to his wife, and then they will know that I sent you. And you may keep the buckle as a reward."

Hesitantly, the boy took the belt. "What am I to say?" he asked.

Tiuri repeated the message. "Do not forget it," he added. "And go right now! One last request: tell no one that you saw me!"

"Except for Sir Tiuri," said the boy with a smile.

"So you'll do it?" asked Tiuri.

"Yes," said the boy, carefully rolling up the belt.

"Promise me you will not forget."

"If I were a knight," said the boy, smiling again, "I would swear on my honour as a knight."

"Thank you!" said Tiuri.

The boy gave him a searching look. "I'll set off immediately," he said, "and I won't tell anyone I saw you. I don't believe you're a thief, even though I don't understand what exactly is going on."

"Again, I thank you," said Tiuri.

The boy gave him a shy grin, turned around and headed into the trees.

Good, thought Tiuri, as he walked on. *That's that taken care of.* The boy would keep his promise. He was sure of it. And Tiuri could devote himself to his task with an easy mind.

He was soon back at the clearing where the soil had been churned up by hoofs. Quietly, he moved towards the place where the Black Knight lay. As he came closer, he heard the sound of voices. Was it the men from the inn? He thought he recognized the innkeeper's voice, even though all he could make out was "Oh!" and "Woe!" and "Murder!" The black horse was still there, tied to a tree. Tiuri untied the horse in an instant and climbed onto its back. As Tiuri sat in the saddle, it started to rear up.

"Calm down!" he whispered. "You must obey me! I have a task to perform for your master!"

The horse tossed back its head and whinnied. It was difficult to gain control of the animal, but Tiuri succeeded.

Then he heard a shout. "Hey, who's that?"

Tiuri dug his heels into the horse's flanks, slapped its neck and hissed, "Run!" The horse obeyed. It raced away, galloping straight through the forest, leaping over bushes and ploughing through the undergrowth, pushing leaves aside and snapping branches. Tiuri had to hold on tight. He thought he heard a man shouting, but it could have been his imagination. Soon he had left the grim place far behind.

The horse was fast and fiery, a steed that was worthy of the Black Knight. Could it sense that it was carrying out its master's final orders by bearing Tiuri as quickly as possible to the west, to the land of King Unauwen? If it was actually heading westwards... Tiuri had not been paying attention. How could he when they were racing so quickly through the dense forest?

He let the horse run on until they reached a wide, straight road. At that point, he stopped to take a good look around and work out the right direction. He was fortunate; he could tell from the position of the sun that the road ran roughly east to west. *This must be the First Great Road*, he thought.

Two major roads ran from Dagonaut's land to the Kingdom of Unauwen: the First Great Road, which passed through the forest, and the Third Great Road, which ran along the border to the south of the forest. There had once been a Second Great Road, but the final section of that road had been impassable for years, as it was overgrown by the Wild Wood. In bygone days, the three roads had been busy and many travellers had passed between the Kingdom of Unauwen and the Kingdom of Dagonaut. Later, the contact between the two lands had lessened and the Second Great Road had fallen into disuse.

Tiuri had heard, however, that more travellers and knights were now heading along the southern road from the Kingdom of Unauwen to Dagonaut's land. The Black Knight with the White Shield had probably been one of them.

Tiuri looked along the road in both directions. There was no one in sight. He thought it could not hurt to ride along it for some way. It would certainly be quicker and easier than travelling off road through the forest. And so he began his journey westwards.

The horse galloped along smoothly and seemed tireless, but Tiuri found to his frustration that he could barely stay upright in his saddle. The sound of the hoofs thudded away inside his head until he felt like it might burst, and a haze descended in front of his eyes so that it seemed as if he were looking at everything through a fog. It eventually became so bad that he feared he would fall from the horse. He pulled at the reins, turned left, and rode a short way into the trees, where he stopped the horse, slipped from its back, and sank down onto the ground. The branches above his head seemed to be moving and changing shape, and the fog grew darker. Tiuri lay on his stomach with his face in the cool grass.

After a while, he began to feel better, but then he became aware of another sensation: he was hungry – and thirsty! He remembered that he had not had anything to eat or drink since the morning of the previous day and he realized why he was feeling so weak. He sat up and looked around. He needed to eat something to keep his strength up, but where was he to get food? Perhaps he could find some fruit. He looked at the horse, which was grazing quietly beside him. His eye fell on the bag that was hanging from the saddle... maybe there was something he could eat in there. He stood up and opened the saddlebag. The horse briefly lifted its head, but it let him look inside. There was not much in there: two pieces of stale bread, a small parcel wrapped in leather, and a horse comb. Tiuri was delighted to see the bread, and he quickly took a bite. The horse looked at him as though it was expecting some, too. "Yes, I'm sure this bread was meant for you," said Tiuri, "but you don't mind if I eat it, do you? You can eat grass and I can't."

The horse looked at him with understanding eyes, or at least he thought it did. He took another bite and realized that he was more thirsty than hungry. He pulled the horse's reins and said, "Come on, let's go and look for water. There might be a spring or a stream nearby."

He walked through the forest for a while, leading the horse, but soon their positions reversed, with Tiuri trudging behind and the horse pulling him along. Finally, they came to a narrow stream, babbling along between tall ferns. Tiuri lay down beside it and drank. Then he sat up and looked at the horse. "Horse," he said. "You are a miracle-worker! You are the kind of horse that great knights rode and minstrels praised, a steed that understands everything and has the intelligence of a human. You have led me to water and I thank you for your kindness!"

He took out the bread and ate some more. He also gave a little to the horse this time. He broke the remaining bread into two pieces and put them back in the bag. *One for this evening and one for tomorrow morning*, he thought. *Then I'll have to find something else.*

He carefully unwrapped the small parcel and found three flints inside. "These will come in handy if I need to make a fire," he said to himself. "And I'll make use of the horse comb too," he said to the horse. "I don't know your name, but I shall call you Trusted Ally, and Ebony Steed, and Good Companion.

I am glad that you have accepted me as your rider and I shall try to be worthy of your former master."

Tiuri lay down again and thought about the Black Knight with the White Shield. What was his name? Who was he? Why had he come to the Kingdom of Dagonaut? And what was in the letter? He ran his hand over the place where it was hidden. He must not lose the letter! Then he thought about the road that lay ahead of him: through the forest, along the Blue River, and over the mountains to the west. He had to set off again soon. But not along the road. That might attract too much attention. He would stay in the forest, travelling alongside the road and checking often to make sure he was heading in the right direction.

And so Tiuri resumed his journey. The water and bread had done him good, although more would have been nice. For a while, he stayed parallel to the road, sometimes riding, sometimes on foot, depending on the terrain. At times, he came close to the road and he looked at it longingly. He would be able to make much faster progress on that smooth surface! However, it didn't seem like a good idea, particularly when he saw various people walking by later that day, woodcutters with axes and people on horses. None of those who went by looked like enemies, but they might see him and tell his pursuers.

In the afternoon, Tiuri came upon a wild apple tree, but sadly most of the apples were unripe. He picked a few, putting three in the saddlebag and eating one, even though it was hard and sour.

When the sun was just above the trees in the west, he moved away from the road to find a place to sleep for the night. He tied the horse in a small grassy clearing, removed the saddle and harness and rubbed the animal's coat with a piece of his tattered robe. Then he had his evening meal: half of the bread and an apple. It was becoming rather chilly. He took the blanket that had been beneath the horse's saddle, wrapped himself in it and lay down. Then he mumbled, "Goodnight, Trusted Ally. Wake me if there's any danger."

Tiuri closed his eyes and, exhausted after a day of emotion and exertion, he immediately fell asleep.

2 THE FOOL

At first, Tiuri slept very soundly, but then he awoke with a start. It took him a moment to remember where he was. All around him, the forest was pitch black and very quiet. For a while, he lay motionless on his back, staring up at the sky. He couldn't see a thing. There was just stillness and darkness, so intense that it took his breath away. Tiuri realized that he was scared. He didn't dare to move a muscle and he felt himself breaking out in a cold sweat...

A faint sound made him gasp, but then he calmed down a little. He was still scared, but no longer so petrified that he couldn't move. The sound he'd heard was probably completely innocent. In fact, he realized what it had been. The horse had snorted.

Tiuri smiled. At least he was not alone; he had a companion, a living creature that belonged with him. But why had he woken up? Purely by chance? Or was he being watched?

That's nonsense, he thought. *No one can see me in this darkness.*

Tiuri closed his eyes and then opened them again, finding that it made little difference. He touched the letter through his shirt. His task seemed impossible. The Black Knight with the White Shield had been murdered by the Red Riders. How could he, so young and inexperienced, achieve something that had brought about the defeat of such a valiant knight? The horse snorted again. Tiuri wanted to say something to the animal, but he didn't dare, because someone or something might hear him. Then he looked up again and spotted a star. It was just a small star, but it gave him light... and hope. It didn't entirely banish his fear, but he felt his courage returning. Slowly, his eyes became accustomed to the darkness. He saw branches and leaves, vaguely silhouetted against the sky, and the pale trunk of a tree.

He tried to think about other things than his task and his enemies, attempting to fill his mind with thoughts of his friends, his parents, King Dagonaut and the celebrations in the city. He wondered what had happened in his absence. Had the ceremony seemed strange after one of the future knights had run away from the chapel? That had surely never happened before. Had the owner of the horse reported him to the sheriff? Had the woodcutter's boy delivered the message? Had the friends who were keeping vigil with him in the chapel also heard the stranger's request? He thought not. Arman had seen him slip away, but he hadn't said a word.

Tiuri relived the moment in the chapel... the scratching on the window, the whispering voice... If only none of it had happened, he would be a knight by now. *This is so peculiar,* he thought. *I'm lying here, and I still haven't been knighted, but I have a task ahead of me that would be a challenge for a seasoned adventurer...*

He sighed. "You are still young and have no reputation for your valiant deeds," the stranger had said. "And yet I know I can trust you."

Tiuri's thoughts became muddled and leapt from one thing to another, although they kept returning to the same problems and events. It was exhausting. And all the while, he remained alert, fearing danger.

I must sleep, he thought. *I have a long way to travel tomorrow.* But still he couldn't fall asleep, even though he'd often slept outside before, in the woods near Tehuri, his father's castle. But that forest was a peaceful, friendly place, and there had been no enemies to fear.

He changed position and closed his eyes again. When sleep finally came, it was uneasy and full of troubled dreams.

It was light when Tiuri awoke, and the trees were alive with birdsong. He yawned and stretched. He felt weary and stiff and his hair was damp with dew. The black horse, however, seemed bright and fresh and looked at him with alert eyes.

"Good morning," said Tiuri. "We need to get going, eh? I can't say I'm itching to set off again. But I must admit that everything looks very different in the morning light." He looked around. His fears of the previous night had been unfounded. There was no one else nearby.

He was soon back in the saddle, after a meagre breakfast that had consisted of the last of the bread and an apple. When he reached the Great Road, it seemed to be deserted. It was still early in the morning, probably not much later than seven o'clock, but still Tiuri did not travel on the road, instead keeping parallel to it, as he had the previous day. The journey went fairly quickly, as the trees were widely spaced and there was little undergrowth.

Tiuri rode on for a while without meeting anyone or seeing anything of note. His tiredness disappeared and he was feeling quite cheerful. It was a beautiful day; the sun shone through the trees, lending the leaves a golden glow.

The journey to Unauwen's kingdom no longer seemed quite so long and dangerous.

When Tiuri spotted some bushes with red berries growing on them, he dismounted to pick as many as he could. As he was picking the berries, he heard a familiar sound. The click-clack of horses' hoofs! He crouched behind the bushes and peered through the leaves. As the horsemen came by, his cheerful mood evaporated. Two Red Riders!

They were riding quickly westwards and looked neither right nor left. Tiuri stayed perfectly still until the sound of the hoofs had died away. Then he walked to the road and looked in both directions. There was no one in sight, but danger had come so close. It was lucky he had not chosen to ride along the road!

Tiuri climbed back onto the horse and thought: *I need to get away from the road. Those two riders weren't paying attention, but if they'd been looking they'd have seen me, or at least my trail. I should go more to the south and ride through the forest.*

So he did just that, but he soon realized that it was not going to be easy to keep heading in the right direction.

Around midday, he came to a narrow path, which he decided to follow. A little later, he ate his last apple. He had already finished the berries, so he had nothing left to eat. Tiuri was starving but he knew that he could not spare the time to go looking for food.

When he came to a fork in the path, Tiuri stopped, uncertain which way to go.

"Ho, there, fine horse and rider!" came a voice from behind him. "Where are you going? Don't go straight on. No, not straight on. Come this way instead!"

Tiuri was startled. He looked around to see a man, who appeared to have stepped out from the undergrowth. The man walked up to him and repeated his words, "Don't go straight on, stranger, traveller. No, not straight on. Come this way instead. The way to my house! Have you come to visit me, fine black horse and strange rider?"

The man was a peculiar sight. He was short and stocky, with wild dark hair and a curly beard, and dressed in ragged brown trousers and a grey sheepskin. He stood there, barefoot, with his hands on his hips. "Why do you not wish me a good day, stranger on your fine black horse?" he asked. "Why do you not greet me, rider, traveller? Why not wish me a good day? I am the Fool in the Forest." He came closer and held out a hand to the horse. "You see, your horse has wished me a good day," he said. "Why not you, strange rider? You may call me the Fool in the Forest. That's what everyone calls me. Everyone but my mother. She calls me Marius."

"Ah, good day," said Tiuri, pulling on the reins.

"No, do not ride away!" cried the bearded man. "Do not ride away! Talk to me, stranger, traveller. And come with me to my cabin!"

Tiuri saw that the man had round, bright blue eyes, and a childlike expression. He did not seem at all dangerous. He just looked disappointed that Tiuri was leaving.

"What do you want me to say?" he asked.

"I want you to talk to me. Tell me where you came from," said the man. "And where you are going, and who you are. I am the Fool in the Forest – that's what they all call me, the woodcutters and the charcoal burners, and my father and my brothers call me the same. But my mother calls me Marius." He took hold of the reins and looked up pleadingly at Tiuri.

"Dear Marius," said Tiuri. "I have wished you a good day, but I really cannot stay to talk. I am in a hurry and I must keep on going."

"Why are you in a hurry? Why? You really can call me 'Fool', you know. I don't mind. I am never in a hurry. And the trees are never in a hurry to grow. Some animals may hurry, but they never have to keep on going like you do, except perhaps for the birds that move on in winter. So why are you in a hurry? Why do you need to keep on going? Come with me to my cabin. And I shall tell my father and my mother that you have come to see me and to talk with me."

"Another time," said Tiuri, gently pulling the reins away from the man. "I cannot talk to you now. I have to move on."

"Move on, and on, and then on some more?"

"That's right," said Tiuri.

"Where to?" asked the Fool. "Where are you going in such a hurry, strange rider on your fine black horse, rider with your odd clothing?"

Tiuri was growing rather impatient. "Truly," he said, "I have no time. Let me travel onwards."

"But where to, where to?" shouted the Fool.

"Far away," answered Tiuri.

"Are you following the sun? The beautiful white and yellow and orange sun, the golden ball?"

"That's it," said Tiuri. "I'm following the sun." Why was the Fool shouting? Every Red Rider for miles around would hear him!

"There's no one else around here," said the Fool, as though he had guessed Tiuri's thoughts. "Mother is spinning in the cabin and Father will be home soon, with my brothers. They're chopping wood in the valley over there." He pointed to the east. "Hardly anyone ever comes here," he continued. "And they never come to see the Fool in the Forest. They pass through sometimes, but they never come here for me." He looked sadly at Tiuri.

Tiuri sighed. He was actually starting to feel a little sorry for the man. "If I had time, I would talk to you," he said. "But I really must be going."

"Following the sun."

"Yes, and I have already spoken to you for quite a long time now."

"No, no, not a long time at all," said the Fool, reaching up into his thick mop of hair to scratch his head. "Not long at all, strange traveller. And you're following the sun. Sometimes I wish I could follow the sun, but my father says it just goes down, and my mother cries whenever I leave. Will you come back and tell me where the sun sets? Where the sun lives? Or is the place where the sun sets not the same place where the sun lives? Will you come back and tell me?"

"Yes," said Tiuri. "I'll come back and I'll talk to you and tell you all about it."

"Tell me everything!" cried the Fool happily. "Every single thing! And will you come with me to the cabin?"

"Sssh!" whispered Tiuri.

"Are you scared of the forest, strange traveller? The forest will not hurt you, and neither will the foxes or the birds. And neither will I."

"Ah, but there might be other things out there," said Tiuri quietly.

"Sssh," said the Fool. "Like what? Creatures that creep and snakes that slither? Who is after you, stranger?"

"Have you seen someone?" asked Tiuri.

"No, I've seen nothing," said the Fool. He ruffled his hair and wrinkled his forehead. "But I felt things... I felt things that were creeping and slithering. But they are not here. They are not here yet."

"I have to get on," said Tiuri anxiously.

"They are not here yet," repeated the Fool, looking at Tiuri. "You are a strange stranger, young rider on your fine black horse. Are you hungry?"

Tiuri looked around and did not reply.

"Are you hungry?" repeated the Fool, taking hold of the reins again.

"Yes," replied Tiuri.

"Then come to the cabin, and my mother will give you some food."

"Thank you," said Tiuri. "But I have to go."

"Fine, fine," whispered the Fool. "You are following the sun. What is your name, stranger?"

"I cannot tell you that," answered Tiuri. "Not now."

"A secret?" asked the Fool. "You're a man with a secret, strange traveller?"

"Why would you think that?" asked Tiuri.

"I do not think. I do not think – that's what people say about me – and that is why I am a Fool. But I know... I know many things that no one wishes to know."

"So tell me, what do you know?"

The Fool chuckled and smiled at Tiuri. "You are asking me, stranger," he said. "No one ever asks me anything. You shall see what I know. Just ride on. You do not need to come with me. Ride on, very slowly, and then I'll bring you food."

Food! Tiuri's stomach rumbled. "But, dear Fool," he said. "You must tell no one you have seen me."

"Not even my mother?"

"Not even your mother."

"Then I shall not tell anyone, not even my mother."

"Promise me," said Tiuri.

The Fool frowned. "I always do as I say," he said. "Will you come back to talk with me and tell me everything?"

"I always do as I say too," said Tiuri, smiling at the Fool.

The Fool turned around and loped down the path on the left. Tiuri watched him until he disappeared from sight. Then he rode slowly onwards, wondering if he should have insisted more strongly that the Fool not mention him to anyone. Would he really bring him some food? Tiuri stopped the horse and looked back, but could not see anyone. He waited for a while before riding on. But then he heard rapid footsteps behind him and the Fool came running up, with his hands full.

"Ride on, ride on, anxious stranger," he panted. "You can stop to eat soon." He caught up with Tiuri and walked ahead of him, humming quietly. "Here," he said after a while. "The grass is soft and the water is fresh. Can you hear it?"

Tiuri could indeed hear the babbling of water. A narrow stream ran alongside the path. The Fool knelt down and laid out the food on the grass, carefully, as if it were precious treasure. When Tiuri had climbed down from his horse and sat down beside the Fool, he saw what food he had brought: two large pieces of brown bread, half a ham pancake and a hunk of cheese. Precious treasure indeed!

"It's all for you," said the Fool proudly. "From my mother's pantry. But she doesn't know. I sneaked in and took it and she doesn't know."

"Will she mind?" asked Tiuri.

"You said I'm not allowed to tell her," said the Fool. "I told no one and I said nothing. This is a secret."

"When I return, I shall tell her and I shall pay her," said Tiuri. "You won't get into trouble, will you?"

"Trouble? You don't have to pay for anything. I have enough and my mother won't mind, even if she doesn't know. Now eat, stranger with a secret."

Tiuri didn't protest. He was far too hungry. He thanked the Fool and started eating. For the first time in some days, he enjoyed a good meal. He didn't eat everything, though, because there was enough for him to save a little for his journey. The Fool happily watched him eat, twirling the curls in his beard and nodding at every bite Tiuri took.

"Would you like some?" asked Tiuri, who thought the Fool looked peckish.

"N-no, no," said the Fool. "This is for you. Oh, but go on. Just a piece of cheese."

He happily ate the chunk that Tiuri gave him, but refused to accept anything else.

"That was delicious," sighed Tiuri when he'd had enough. "I'm very grateful to you."

"You haven't finished it all!" said the Fool. "There's a piece of bread left, and some pancake."

"May I take it with me? I have a long way to go and I need food for the journey."

"Of course," said the Fool. "You have a long way to go, a long way. This is not enough food. But you can eat berries too. There are lots of them along the way, blue berries, sweet ones, sour ones. And those plants with the ragged leaves have roots, tasty roots." He stood up and pulled a plant out of the ground. There was a large root attached. He brushed off the dirt and bit a chunk out of it. "Good root," he said, chewing. He walked over to the horse and offered it the rest, which was eagerly accepted.

"I'll remember that," said Tiuri. "My thanks once again! And now I have a question for you: does this road lead to the west?"

The Fool wrinkled his forehead. "What do you mean?" he asked.

"Does this road lead westwards... to the place where the sun goes down?"

"Oh, where the sun goes down," said the Fool. "Yes, for a while. But then it stops, at the bare place with the tree trunks. But you can ride on without a road, stranger, on and on and on some more. But don't go that way," he said, pointing south, "because there's danger out there."

"Then I shall go straight on," said Tiuri. "And you'll remember not to tell anyone, won't you? There may be dangerous things coming after me too, things that would like to catch me and kill me."

"It is a secret, strange rider and traveller. I shall tell no one that you have eaten my food and that you are following the sun. Sometimes I find birds' nests, with eggs inside them, but I don't tell my brothers, because they'll want to suck the eggs dry. It's the birds' secret. I shall tell no one your secret. But you must come back and talk with me!"

"I promise," said Tiuri, and he meant it.

"How long will you be gone, traveller?"

Tiuri sighed. "I don't know," he said. "A long time, I fear. But I will return. At least, that is my hope and my wish." He slowly rose to his feet.

"You will return," said the Fool, looking at Tiuri with his bright eyes. "Ride on now, stranger. Ride straight on, fine black horse. But do not drink from the dark pool that you will soon pass, because that belongs to the forest spirits."

Tiuri put the rest of the food in his saddlebag, shook the Fool by the hand, climbed onto the horse and rode away. He looked back a couple of times and waved. The forest dweller stood in the middle of the path, with his arms hanging by his sides, watching Tiuri go. But when Tiuri looked around for the third time, he had disappeared.

He was a good man, thought Tiuri, *and he may be different, but I don't think he's really all that foolish.* Having spoken to him, Tiuri felt stronger somehow and full of fresh courage.

The road did indeed come to a dead end at a clearing, where piles of tree trunks were stacked up. Tiuri carried on, straight through the forest. He came to a dark pool, which was surrounded by very tall, old trees. That must be the pool that the Fool had warned him about. Tiuri was thirsty again, but he followed the Fool's advice. He didn't like the look of the still, dark water, with its surface untouched by the slightest ripple. The place could easily be enchanted... It certainly felt strange and hostile to humans. Tiuri rode on quickly and was glad when he had left the pool far behind.

Gradually, the landscape became wilder and hillier, with twisted trees and dense undergrowth. Tiuri saw ferns that were the height of a man and curtains of creepers hanging from branches.

It was hard to make any progress through this landscape and sometimes he wondered whether he was riding in a straight line and still heading in the right direction.

When it started to get dark, Tiuri found a place to sleep in a bushy hollow, where he decided to spend the night and travel on in the morning.

3   THE SOUND OF A HORN

The first thing Tiuri did the next morning was climb as high as possible into a tree, so that he could work out the right direction from the position of the sun.

He soon set off again, wondering how long the journey

through the forest would take and how close he would be to the Blue River when he emerged.

The Blue River also flowed through the City of Dagonaut and past Castle Tehuri, Tiuri's home. Its source was in the Great Mountains, and it flowed eastwards before curving to the north, around the Blue Forest, and then to the southeast, through the City of Dagonaut, and finally along the country's eastern border. Tiuri had heard that the First Great Road ran alongside the river for some way close near the mountains, but he did not know where the river's source was, the exact point where the river began. From the City of Dagonaut to the mountains in the west was a journey of around eight to ten days along the Great Road. Tiuri had never been all the way along the road himself, but he heard about it from travellers and knights-errant. His journey was sure to take longer, and still he would only have travelled as far as the mountains. The way was long and the letter was important, and the Black Knight had said there was little time to lose. The Black Knight might have dared to take the Great Road himself, but he had been armed.

The journey through the forest proved hard and slow. Sometimes he had to lead the horse and, to make it easier to fight his way through the undergrowth, Tiuri tore off a large strip from the bottom of his robe. He had eaten the last of the Fool's bread that morning and so he had to survive on whatever he could find: fruit and roots, as he had no weapons to catch game and no time to make traps. He encountered no one all day. It seemed as if no one ever set foot in the forest.

On the fourth day of his journey, however, events took a different turn. Tiuri heard the sound of voices and of people making their way through the undergrowth. He quickly hid and waited to see what would happen. The voices moved away, but soon after that a young man walked by, close to Tiuri's hiding place. He was dressed in grey and was leading a horse. Tiuri could see that he was armed. He kept stopping and looking around, but he didn't spot Tiuri or his black horse. He soon disappeared, but Tiuri could hear him speaking to someone.

"Where have they all got to?"

"They're hunting further to the north," said another voice. "Have you seen anything?"

"Nothing. And no tracks either. But it's hard to say. This part of the forest is so wild. You could search for days here without ever finding anyone. But he has to be somewhere."

"All I can see is trees, trees and more trees!" grumbled the other voice. "And thorns and creepers to trip you up! This forest is the perfect hiding place for a person who does not wish to be found."

The voices grew fainter until Tiuri could no longer understand what they were saying. Then, in the distance, he heard the clear sound of a hunting horn.

"Come on!" Tiuri heard someone shout.

And then he was alone again. Tiuri put his arm around the horse's neck and whispered, "So who were they? A hunting party? But what are they hunting?"

The horse didn't answer, but Tiuri felt that it could understand him and that it had its own thoughts about the men who were roaming the forest.

If I'm careful, they won't see me, thought Tiuri. He sighed. Would it always be like this, having to be suspicious of everyone, scared that they might be enemies? He travelled on, even more warily, and saw no one else, although he did hear the distant sound of the horn a few times.

Sir Fantumar had a famous horn, which he had once used to summon his men to battle, a long time ago, when enemies from the east had invaded the country. When Tiuri had been Sir Fantumar's squire, he had listened breathlessly as the knight told of his adventures. Now he was in the middle of an adventure himself. *Perhaps one day*, he thought, *my squire will listen as I tell him my tale... If I ever get out of this in one piece... and if I ever become a knight...*

That afternoon, the forest changed once again. It became less dense and the trees were tall, with straight, thin trunks. Tiuri could see a long way ahead. It looked almost like a vast great hall with an undulating, mossy floor and lots of wooden pillars. It was easy enough to ride through, but that also meant that anyone could see him from a long way off, which wasn't a comforting thought, particularly when he heard the distant sound of the horn again.

After a while, Tiuri came to a shallow valley, with a stream running through it, one of so many streams crisscrossing the forest. He decided to stop there and rest until evening. Then he would travel on in darkness, which felt safer.

Tiuri crawled beneath a bush and fell asleep. When he awoke, it was completely dark. He felt his way to the stream and leant forward to drink. Then he spotted something strange: a glowing dot darting around beneath his head. For a moment, he thought it was a firefly and he reached out to grab it. But when he caught it, he found that it was hard and round. To his surprise, he realized it was the Black Knight's ring, which was hanging on the cord around his neck. He studied it carefully. Yes, the stone was glowing in the dark! It was a weak light, like a distant star, but still clearly visible. It felt like a final farewell from the Knight with the White Shield, a reminder of the promise he had made. Tiuri's eyes welled with tears. He untied the cord and slipped the ring onto his finger.

This ring will protect me and guide me, he thought. *And I shall keep my promise, no matter how difficult that may be!*

Tiuri covered plenty of distance that night and he feared neither darkness nor mysterious noises. Sometimes he spotted a star shining between the trees, like a sister of the stone in the ring on his finger. He rode on in the grey light of dawn as the birds began to sing and did not stop until it was entirely light.

After a brief rest, he went in search of food and then carried on riding. There was no one around, but he could not see any good places to shelter. Tiuri noticed that the land to his left, to the south, was starting to rise and the wooded hills were becoming higher and higher. He crossed a path that led northwards from the hills, perhaps to the Great Road. A path meant there might be people around.

I'll look for somewhere to hide nearby, he thought. *There's sure to be a good spot in the hills. It's time to rest, especially for my companion. We'll travel onwards tonight.*

Tiuri found a place to rest and, unable to find anything to eat, he pulled the rope more tightly around his waist, lay down and tried to sleep. As he dozed off, he heard the sound of the horn again.

Onwards tonight, he thought, and he fell asleep.

4 AN UNWELCOME ENCOUNTER

Tiuri resumed his journey just before sunset. He had broken a branch from a tree and was holding it in his hand as his only weapon. He rode on through a forest that glowed brightly in the light of the setting sun.

"Following the sun..." the Fool had said.

Slowly, it grew darker. The ring on his finger started to shine again. Not enough to light his way, but enough to keep his spirits up. All he could hear were the normal sounds of a forest at night, to which he had grown accustomed. The horse moved on, fast and sure of foot. After a while, Tiuri realized they were following a path. It twisted and turned, but it seemed to lead to the west.

Tiuri rode onwards, but then he heard something: whispering, and it was not the sound of the wind in the trees... And the cracking of branches, but it was not animals moving through the forest... Suddenly they leapt out, on both sides of the road. One of them even dropped out of a tree! A gang of men – there must have been a dozen of them – surrounded Tiuri's horse and ordered him to stop. One of the men held up a lantern and Tiuri could see them by its light: rough, bearded men, armed with sticks, swords and daggers.

"Stop!" they cried. "Your money or your life!"

Robbers!

Tiuri was terrified and felt himself shaking all over, but he was brave enough not to show his fear. He looked at their threatening faces and said, "I have no money. I have nothing!"

"Ha!" cried the robber with the lantern, as he shone its light on Tiuri's face. "You don't look like a wealthy man, but that's a fine horse you have!"

"And look, he's wearing a fancy ring," said one of the others, grabbing Tiuri's hand.

Tiuri pulled his hand away and raised his stick.

"I spotted that ring in the distance when he was riding along," said a third robber. "Look how it glows!"

"Let me pass," Tiuri growled. His voice sounded steady, but his heart was racing.

The robbers were so surprised that they stepped back a little.

"Well, well!" one of the robbers said. "The lad's got nerve!"

"We won't let you go until you hand over all of your belongings," said the man who claimed he had spotted the ring in the distance. He stepped closer and took hold of the horse's reins. The horse raised its head and snorted angrily.

It occurred to Tiuri that a quick escape might yet save him, but then the other robbers closed in on him with raised weapons.

"Come, come, you know you can't take on all of us," said the robber who was holding the horse's reins. "Your life's not much good to us, but we could certainly use your money." He turned to the others and issued an order: "Take that stick from him before he whacks you on the head!" He seemed to be their leader.

Tiuri grasped the stick more firmly and said, "I have nothing. Not a brass farthing. I'm not going to fill your pockets. Let me go!"

One of the robbers sneered at him and another yelled, "Let's shut his trap for him! Pull him off his horse!"

The black horse lifted its head again and whinnied.

The leader let go of the reins and said gruffly, "You look poor enough, but that's a very fine ring on your finger. And I'd like it for myself!"

Tiuri gazed steadily at the man and said, "You will never take this ring!"

"What in the blazes...?!" cried the leader of the robbers. "Get down from that horse! Now!"

Rough hands grabbed hold of Tiuri, snatched away his stick and dragged him from the horse. The horse reared up and whinnied; it took three robbers to hold him. The men crowded around Tiuri, but the leader pushed them aside and shouted, "Hands off! I saw the ring first. It was shining like a star."

The robbers did as they were told, but they remained standing around Tiuri and glared at him threateningly. He took a deep breath, clasped one hand around the other and said, "I will never give you this ring! Never!"

"You won't? Well, I'm going to take it," said the leader, "and you'd have to be a clever boy to stop me. Why are you riding around here in the dead of night anyway?"

Tiuri's courage sank into his shoes. He couldn't lose the ring. He had to show it to the hermit at the source of the Blue River, so that he would agree to take him over the mountains. No, he couldn't lose that ring!

He looked at the leader of the robbers. "I am defenceless against you," he said. "I have no weapons and I am alone. But I cannot hand over this ring. I would rather die than give it away."

He knew it was probably a foolish thing to say and he couldn't dare to hope that it would do any good.

"Ah, stop your blethering!" said one of the robbers.

"Chop off his finger!" sneered another. "And be done with it!"

"I am powerless," said Tiuri to the leader, "but I beg you, let me keep this ring. It belonged to someone who died and it means a great deal to me."

The man came up very close to Tiuri and grabbed his hand. "I see," he said, "this ring means a great deal to you, does it? But I would think your fingers probably mean a great deal to you too. So how about I chop one of them off, eh?"

Tiuri desperately tried to pull his hand away.

"But in return... I'll let you keep the ring. What do you say to that?"

Tiuri stared blankly at the robber. "What do you mean?" he stammered.

"I'll chop off a finger instead of taking the ring. A finger in exchange for your ring. Do we have a deal?"

Tiuri started shaking. Let them chop off his finger? But what about the ring? The ring that had belonged to the brave Knight with the White Shield? The ring that he had to show to the hermit?

"All right. Do it, then," he said, with the courage of despair. "I'll still have four fingers left." He heard his voice as if it were someone else speaking, and was surprised at his own words.

The leader released his hand. "Fine, then," he growled.

Another robber came and stood beside him, with a sword in his hand. "Can I do it?" he said gleefully. "My sword's nice and sharp."

Tiuri closed his eyes, but he did not take back his words.

"Let me do it!" pleaded the robber.

Tiuri opened his eyes again in time to see the leader snatch the man's sword from him and cuff him around the ear.

"There!" he said. "That's all you're getting. Keep your hands off this boy!" He looked around at the gang of men before continuing. "He has more courage in one finger than you lot have in your entire bodies put together!"

Then he turned to Tiuri and said, "You can keep your ring. You've defended it bravely. But make sure you hide it well, because we're not the only thieves in this forest."

Tiuri could hardly believe it. He felt a great weight lift from him.

"Now go," the robber ordered. "And I'd advise you to leave this area. I'll hold on to your horse. I need to come away with something, after all."

His trusted ally, his good companion!

"But..." Tiuri began, "I can't..."

"Enough talking!" roared the leader of the robbers. "Make yourself scarce before I regret it!" He raised his dagger and glared angrily at Tiuri. The other men muttered and growled.

Tiuri hesitated for a moment but realized he had no choice. He turned around and walked away. He heard the robbers protesting as he went, but then the leader's angry voice ordered them to be quiet and to do as they were told. The horse whinnied and Tiuri looked back sadly over his shoulder.

The robbers were leaving, with the horse in their midst. Within seconds, they had disappeared into the forest. The light of the lantern glinted briefly among the trees and then that too was gone.

Tiuri stumbled on and then fell to the ground, sobbing. He cried because of his terrifying encounter and because he'd lost his friend and companion, the black horse.

5 GREY KNIGHTS

When Tiuri had calmed down a little, he took the ring from his finger and hung it around his neck again. Then he stood up and walked on, feeling his way through the dark forest. He had wandered away from the path and the land had become hilly and scattered with rocks and stones. Finally, he could go no further. He sank to the ground and fell into a sleep so deep that it was like being unconscious.

Early the next morning, he awoke and realized he was lying close to a path, probably the same path where he had encountered the robbers. He followed it for some way. On his left, the hills were becoming steeper and steeper and were sprinkled with spindly pine trees. The sun shone down on the path.

After a while, he heard a babbling brook and spotted the dark opening to a small cave halfway up one of the hills. It would be a good place to rest. But first, he needed water. Tiuri walked to the stream, which crossed the path, and after he had drunk his fill, he spotted the same kind of plant that the Fool had pulled out of the ground. With a few big black roots in his hands, Tiuri retraced his footsteps, climbed the hill and went into the cave. The cave was small and snug, but no animals appeared to have made it their home. Tiuri sat down, with his back against the wall of rock, and ate one of the roots. Then, in spite of his uncomfortable position, he fell asleep for a while.

The sound of voices startled him awake. Cautiously, he peered outside. Three men were talking on the path at the foot of the hill. With a shock, he recognized them as three of the robbers!

"Where's the boss got to?" one of them grumbled.

"He's trying to ride that new horse of his," another sneered. "He's already fallen off twice."

"Fallen off? More like thrown off," said the third one, clearly enjoying the thought.

All three of them laughed, but then one of them hissed, "Hush!"

Two more men were approaching. One was the leader of the robbers.

"You lot keep your mouths shut and take cover," he told the three men. "He'll be here any minute."

They followed his orders. The robbers and their leader left the path and hid behind the rocks and in the bushes. Tiuri was sure they were up to no good. Who was going to be here soon? He picked up some stones from the cave floor and piled them by the entrance. Then he lay on his stomach beside the stones, looking down the path and waiting to see what would happen.

He did not have to wait for long.

In the distance, he heard the sound of hoofs approaching – clip-clop, clip-clop – and then a knight appeared, coming from the east on a dapple-grey horse. He was riding very slowly, so Tiuri was able to take a good look at him. The knight was dressed in dark-grey chainmail and had a grey shield on his arm. His helmet with its lowered visor was grey, as was the cloak he wore. But around his neck something hung glinting in the sunlight: a large horn that seemed to be made of silver.

Tiuri saw the bushes moving and he held his breath. The robbers were planning to attack this lonely knight! He looked like a warrior, but it was unlikely that he would be able to take on five men. *I must help the knight*, thought Tiuri, *and warn him somehow...*

At that moment, the robbers yelled and leapt out from their hiding places. "Stop!" they shouted at the knight. "Your money or your life!"

The knight reined in his horse. Tiuri stood up and armed himself with a stone. The knight lifted his visor, put the horn to his lips and gave it a mighty blow. Then he dropped his visor and drew his sword.

The sound of the horn seemed to startle the robbers for a moment. Then they repeated their command: "Your money or your life!"

"You shall have neither," said the knight, raising his sword, as the sound of more voices and hoofs came from along the path.

The robbers looked at one another and it seemed that they were about to make a run for it. The knight urged on his horse and rode past them a little way, but then he turned and stopped. "Do not flee, you cowards!" he cried. "Come on! Attack, as you were planning to!"

"Attack him, you cowards!" cried the leader of the robbers, rushing towards the knight with his sword in his hand.

But the four other men yelled out in fear as seven riders came charging down the path, all of them on grey horses and dressed in grey. There were three knights, with helmets and swords, and four younger men, probably their squires.

Tiuri was still hidden inside his cave. His help was no longer needed, so he contented himself with watching the scene unfold. In an instant, four of the robbers, including their leader, were disarmed and tied up. The fifth fled and was pursued by two of the knights. The other knights gathered at the foot of Tiuri's hill and the knight with the silver horn spoke to the captives.

Those are the men I heard in the forest the day before yesterday, thought Tiuri. *I saw one of their squires. But who are they?*

None of the knights had raised their visors and they had no crests on their shields. The one with the horn, who seemed to be their leader, spoke sternly, "You shall pay for your misdeeds! Highway robbery is forbidden in the Kingdom of Dagonaut, as it is in every realm where order reigns."

"Have mercy!" begged one of the robbers.

"And you are cowards too! You dare to attack lonely travellers, but you flee from larger companies. You shall hang from a tree before the sun goes down."

"Sir knight," said the leader, "I am a thief. I cannot deny that. But I have never killed any man. So why should you wish to kill me?"

Tiuri felt a little sympathy for him. After all, the man had let him keep his ring.

Now the two knights returned. One of them held the

robber who had tried to escape, and the other was leading two horses: his own, and one that Tiuri would have recognized among hundreds of other horses. It was the black horse that had belonged to the Knight with the White Shield.

When the Grey Knight with the horn saw them approaching, he dismounted and walked to meet them. They stood for a while, talking quietly and studying the black horse. Then they went to join the others.

The knight with the horn turned to the robbers and barked, "Whose is this horse?"

"His," answered one of the robbers, nodding in the leader's direction.

"I see," said the knight. "And how did you come to have this horse? From whom did you steal it?"

"That horse belongs to me," said the leader gruffly.

"That is a lie! You stole it. I know this horse, you scoundrel!"

"There are plenty of black horses in the world," said the leader.

"You know nothing about horses," said the Grey Knight. "No horse is like another. I would recognize this horse anywhere and I know its name too. Ardanwen is his name, or Night Wind, and it is shameful that a man like you would dare to ride upon his back!"

Tiuri listened to all of this with increasing amazement. These knights knew the horse, so they must also know the Black Knight with the White Shield! He thought about stepping out of the cave and speaking to them, but something was stopping him, even though he could not have explained what it was. He stayed silent and kept listening.

The leader bowed his head and said nothing.

"From whom did you steal this horse?" the Grey Knight repeated.

"From a young man who passed through here last night," one of the robbers replied.

"And that's the truth," muttered the leader.

The knight stood right in front of the man, staring at him. "A young man who passed through last night? What did he look like? No older than seventeen? With dark hair and blue-grey eyes and dressed in a white robe?"

"His clothes didn't look very white," replied the leader, "but the rest sounds right enough. I reckon his eyes could have been blue-grey..."

"And his hair was dark," interjected one of the other men. "And on his finger he was wearing a..."

"A ring," said the Grey Knight, "that gleamed like a star!"

"That's right, sir knight," said the leader. "It was a very fine ring and it was shining away on his left hand."

This news clearly meant something to the Grey Knights.

"Where is he?" one of them cried.

"Where is the ring?" cried another.

"I did him no harm, knights!" said the leader. "And I let him keep the ring."

"Another lie," barked the knight with the horn. "Why would you steal the horse and neglect to take such a valuable jewel? Give it to me!"

"I don't have it!" cried the leader. "I swear it to you. He seemed very attached to it, so I let him keep the thing and go on his way in peace."

"It's true," said the other robbers, backing him up.

The Grey Knights conferred. Tiuri could not hear what they were saying.

"It would have been better if you had not let him go," the knight with the horn finally announced.

"Better?" said the leader.

"You are a thief and a scoundrel, but I think that young man is an even worse villain than you. If you had killed him, it would have been his just deserts."

The leader seemed surprised to hear this. But Tiuri was even more surprised. In fact, he was stunned!

"Where did he go?" barked one of the other knights. "Quick, tell us which way he went!"

"Into the forest, in that direction," said the leader, with a nod. "But I didn't watch to see where he was heading."

"He can't have gone very far," said another of the robbers. "He was on foot."

"Why are you looking for him?" asked the leader.

"That is none of your business," said the knight with the silver horn. "But I am so grateful to you for this news that I am inclined to allow you your life and your freedom. On one condition: you must look out for this young man and bring him to us if you find him. Dead or alive, but preferably alive. And be aware that he is dangerous!"

"I'm not at all surprised," said one of the robbers. It was the one who had wanted to chop off Tiuri's finger.

"Untie them," the knight ordered the squires. "I will grant them mercy. But," he continued, "I will return to this place and hunt down and hang any of you who remain robbers! Order and security must be maintained in this kingdom."

"One day we will rid this forest of every criminal," said the knight who stood beside him. "But now we have a more important task to perform. Find that boy for us, robbers!"

Then all of the men moved on, one group following the other: first the Grey Knights and their retinue, taking the black horse with them, and then the robbers, quietly talking among themselves. Both groups headed towards the west.

*

Tiuri sat in his cave, still stunned. He was the one the Grey Knights were seeking. And they wanted him dead or alive! Why? They weren't with the Red Riders, were they? Whatever the case, they were enemies – and formidable ones. He thanked his lucky stars that he had not left his hiding place.

But then he was overcome by a feeling of despair. He needed to travel on to the west, but the Grey Knights were after him and now the robbers were keeping an eye out for him too. The Red Riders were most probably still following him or lying in wait. And maybe other things were after him too, creatures that creep, as the Fool had said. How was he ever going to carry out his mission, alone, on foot and unarmed?

Tiuri took out the letter and turned it over and over in his hands. Such a small thing, but such an important message... What could be in the letter that mattered enough to risk his life for? Should he open it and read it? "Do so only as a final resort," the Knight with the White Shield had said. A final resort? Had that time come? The time to read the letter, commit its message to memory and then destroy it? Why should he risk his life when he had no idea what was in the letter and how important it was? That surely made no sense at all...

With trembling fingers, he stroked the seals on the letter. "If you fear that you will lose the letter, then, and only then..." There were no enemies nearby now. And the Grey Knights had not mentioned the letter. No, of course they hadn't. They knew better than that.

The Black Knight with the White Shield had surely not anticipated so many dangers. Or had he?

I can't do it, thought Tiuri. *This is impossible.*

Then, in his mind, he heard the words he had spoken when he had promised to deliver the letter: "I swear on my honour as a knight."

Tiuri's doubts evaporated. He hid the letter again. This was not yet the moment to open it. And he said to himself, "I must travel on and attempt to deliver the letter, as that is the promise I made. Onwards, to King Unauwen in the land to the west of the Great Mountains!"

6 SANCTUARY

All that day, Tiuri hid in the cave. The Grey Knights were searching elsewhere for him. He had to be sure that there was as much distance between him and the knights as possible. Only once did he venture outside, to drink some water from the stream.

The wait was long and dull. He tried to sleep, but that was not easy on the hard and stony ground. For a while, he entertained himself by watching two squirrels playing in a nearby tree. He missed them when they scampered off somewhere else.

Towards the evening, he set off on his way again. He kept parallel to the path as well as he could, always remaining alert and watchful. The night seemed endless and he made slow progress. But he did not encounter any enemies.

In the early morning, Tiuri stopped to rest behind some bushes. He worked out that he had been travelling for six days. When would he finally be out of the forest? He wondered if he should keep moving or wait for nightfall. He decided to push on – he could see more in the daytime and move faster. There was always danger, whether it was night or day.

Suddenly, Tiuri froze. Footsteps! He peered through the leaves at the nearby path. Some people were approaching. He soon saw that they were not robbers, knights or Red Riders, but two friendly-looking monks in brown habits.

I'm sure I can trust these men, thought Tiuri. *I wonder if they'll let me travel with them. Their company might offer me some protection.*

He stood up, stepped out onto the path and said, "Good morning."

The monks stopped. "God be with you," one of them replied. They didn't seem surprised to see him or, if they were, they didn't show it, even though, after all his adventures, Tiuri looked dishevelled enough to cause some alarm.

Tiuri looked more closely at the two monks. They both seemed trustworthy. One was old, tall and lean, with a brown face and grey hair. The other was short and fairly young, with freckles and penetrating grey eyes.

"You are out early, reverend brothers," he said. Then he fell silent, not knowing quite how to continue.

"As are you, my son," said the elder of the two monks.

"Are you heading westwards?" asked Tiuri.

"Yes," said the other monk, pointing down the path. "We are on our way home to our monastery."

"Might I walk with you?" asked Tiuri.

"Of course, my son," said the elder monk. "We do not walk quickly, but we walk steadily, and you may accompany us for as long as you wish."

"Thank you," said Tiuri.

"Then we should introduce ourselves," the elder monk said. "This is Brother Martin, and I am Brother Laurentius. And we live at the Brown Monastery, beside the Green River."

Tiuri nodded his greeting. Did he dare say his name? Not that he feared these monks, but they might mention his name to other people... He hesitated.

"Your name does not matter, my son," said Brother Laurentius. "Come, let us travel on."

"Oh, you are welcome to know my name," said Tiuri. "It's just that I can't... It's hard to explain, but..."

The old monk smiled. "Ah, be still, my son," he said. "Tell us or do not. It is all the same to us."

The three of them walked on for a while without speaking.

It was Tiuri who broke the silence. "Is your monastery far from here?" he asked.

"We hope to reach it before this evening," replied Brother Martin.

"Where is it?" asked Tiuri.

"At the end of this path," said the monk. "By the edge of the forest."

"And it's beside the Green River, you say? Is that close to the Blue River?"

"The Blue River lies more to the north," said Brother Laurentius. "By the Great Road to the west."

So I've strayed off course, thought Tiuri.

"Is that far from the monastery?" he asked.

"Not too distant," said Brother Laurentius. "A day's journey, I believe. Is that not so, Brother Martin?"

"It can't be much more than that," replied the other monk, looking thoughtfully at Tiuri.

The path was wide and pleasant to walk along. *Anyone would think we were out for a stroll*, thought Tiuri. The forest seemed so peaceful. It was like a completely different place now. Was that because of the monks? However, Tiuri still remained alert and he kept glancing back over his shoulder.

He noticed that Brother Martin was looking at him again.

"Where are you travelling from, Brother Martin?" Tiuri asked.

"A village back there, in the south, on the other side of the hills," the monk answered, pointing over his shoulder with his thumb. "There was sickness in the village and they needed our help."

"Are you not scared to travel through the forest?" asked Tiuri. "There are robbers hereabouts."

"We know," said Brother Laurentius sadly. "And their presence pains us. But we do not fear them. What could they steal from us?"

"But there is something that you fear, is there not?" said Brother Martin. "I have seen you look around a few times, as though you were afraid something might pounce on you. What are you so concerned about?"

Tiuri felt himself blushing and did not answer immediately. "Those robbers. They attacked me last night," he said finally.

"Oh dear," replied Brother Martin. "Did they hurt you?"

"They robbed me," replied Tiuri.

"Yes, I can see that, my son," said Brother Laurentius kindly.

Tiuri let him believe that his tattered appearance was the result of his encounter with the robbers.

"Something really must be done about those men," said Brother Martin with a frown. "I believe you have nothing to fear. The robbers never dare to come so close to the edge of the forest. And besides, you probably have little left for them to steal now."

Oh, if you only knew! thought Tiuri, but he said nothing.

"But it is not only the robbers that you are scared of," said Brother Martin. "There is something else, is there not?"

"Why would you think that?" asked Tiuri.

"You do not seem like a lad who would frighten easily," said Brother Martin, "and you have little reason to fear robbers now, particularly not in broad daylight. So there must be something else."

"Is your conscience clear?" asked Brother Laurentius.

"Yes," said Tiuri, "I believe it is. In fact, I am certain."

"Then you have nothing to fear," said the old monk.

"At least forget about your troubles for a moment," said the younger monk. He smiled and added, "The forest's beautiful. The weather's fine. It's a lovely day."

As they walked on, Tiuri's anxiety finally lifted, but he remained as alert as ever.

After about an hour, Brother Martin asked if he was hungry.

Tiuri was starving! But he said politely, "Yes, Brother Martin."

"It should have occurred to us sooner," said Brother Laurentius. "This young man has lost all of his possessions, and that must include his food."

They sat down by the roadside and the monks shared their food with Tiuri. Then they continued their journey.

The monks sometimes conversed as they walked along, talking about their work in nearby villages or about plants they saw growing alongside the path. They included Tiuri in their conversation, but they did not pry. In the afternoon, they paused to rest and to eat again.

"We'll be home in good time," said Brother Laurentius with a smile, when they continued their journey.

"Where are you heading?" Brother Martin asked Tiuri.

"The Blue River," replied Tiuri.

"The Blue River... There's a hermit who lives at its source," said Brother Laurentius pensively. "His name is Menaures, isn't it, Brother Martin?"

"Yes. That's it. Menaures," he replied. "He's very wise and very old. Pilgrims used to travel to his cabin in the mountains."

"Do you know him?" asked Tiuri keenly.

The monks shook their heads. "But Father Hyronimus does," said Brother Laurentius. "Our abbot."

"Ah," said Tiuri.

"You may spend the night at our monastery if you like," said Brother Martin.

"Oh yes, please. If I may," said Tiuri gratefully.

"Weary travellers are always welcome," said Brother Laurentius.

"My name is Tiuri," he said, on an impulse.

Brother Martin smiled and Brother Laurentius gave him a friendly nod. Then Tiuri asked the monks if they had encountered any other people in the forest. No, they told him, they had seen no one. But they had heard the sound of a horn in the distance.

By then, the sun had completed much of its daily journey. It hung above the end of the road to the west and the three travellers felt as if they were walking along a corridor of twilight. Ahead of them, they saw a slice of golden sky, framed by dark trees.

"We are almost there," said Brother Martin.

They soon reached the edge of the forest. Before them lay a rolling landscape, with cultivated fields, a sprinkling of white cottages and green copses, and blue mountains in the dim distance. To the south, the forest continued and in front of the trees stood a small church and a larger building, both built from wood and brown stone. A winding path led the way there.

"That is our monastery," said Brother Laurentius, pointing down the path. "And there's the road to the north. It meets the Great Road that leads to the west, up at the Blue River. You can't see the Green River from here. It runs through the forest, behind the monastery."

As they made their way to the monastery, Tiuri looked back over his shoulder at the forest. He was glad to have left the trees; that part of his journey was over now.

Brother Laurentius knocked at the gate of the monastery. The gatekeeper, a small man with a ruddy complexion, came to open up. He greeted them warmly and led them through the gate and into a small cloistered courtyard. It was a very pleasant place, full of blossoming flowers and with a well at its centre.

"Your garden's looking fine, Brother Julius," said Brother Laurentius.

"It's beautiful," said Tiuri with a contented sigh.

The gatekeeper beamed at him.

"This is Tiuri," said Brother Martin. "We met him along the way and he's staying here tonight. The peace and quiet will do him some good. He was just attacked by robbers who took all of his belongings."

"How awful!" exclaimed the gatekeeper. "Thank goodness he escaped in one piece. And your health is worth a great deal, my boy. Let it be a consolation to you." He looked Tiuri up and down and then said, "Did you travel from the east, through the forest?"

"Yes, Brother," replied Tiuri.

"I'm sure there are many young men who travel through the forest from the east," continued the gatekeeper, "but it could be... Yes, indeed it could."

"What is it?" asked Tiuri, suddenly a little worried.

"Someone came to the gate this morning," said the gate-keeper, "and asked me if I'd seen a young man... of around your age. He spoke in a very loud voice and he said... Now what was it again?"

"What did he say?" asked Tiuri. "And what did he look like?"

"It was a knight, a knight in grey. He had a squire with him too. I was working in the garden when he knocked at the gate. I opened up and there he stood. He asked me about a young man. A young man with blue-grey eyes, I believe... Yes, like yours." The gatekeeper shook his head. "He was rather impatient, but I said to him, 'Would you raise your visor, sir knight, and tell me who you are?' I prefer to talk to a face, you see. And he did so. I mean, he lifted his visor. But he still didn't tell me his name."

"What did he look like?" asked Tiuri.

"He was a rather fierce-looking gentleman, very dark and bearded. And I said I hadn't seen a young man who looked like that. Well, I hadn't at that point. Then he rode away, in a great hurry. I watched him go and saw him disappear into the forest. And I heard a horn. It was very loud and clear."

Tiuri felt the colour drain from his face. His enemy had even been here, to this peaceful monastery. The three monks looked at him curiously.

"Do you know this knight?" asked Brother Martin.

"No," said Tiuri, truthfully. "I don't know any of them. There are four knights, and their four squires. And they are looking for me."

"But why?" exclaimed the gatekeeper.

"I don't know," said Tiuri. "Or rather, I think I do know, but I'm not allowed to say. If they find me, they'll kill me."

It felt as though a dark shadow moved across the pleasant courtyard.

Brother Martin laid his hand on Tiuri's shoulder. Tiuri looked at him and said, "I do not know these knights. I have done them no harm. But they are pursuing me and they wish me dead."

"There is something mysterious about you," said the monk, "and I understand that there are things you are unwilling or unable to tell us. But you should know that you are safe in this monastery. No knight in grey will be able to harm you here."

"A sanctuary," said Tiuri.

"Exactly. This place is a sanctuary," replied Brother Martin.

"My thanks for your trust in me," said Tiuri. "I am grateful to you for allowing me to stay here."

"You may stay for as long as you wish," said Brother Laurentius.

"Just until tomorrow," said Tiuri. "Then I must move on." He sighed. The outside world seemed so hostile and full of dangers.

"Do not worry about tomorrow, for tomorrow will worry about itself," said Brother Martin. "First you must rest."

"If that knight returns, I shall say nothing," promised the gatekeeper. "Imagine you being the very boy he was looking for! Oh, now I remember something else. He mentioned a ring. You don't have a ring, do you?"

"Yes, I have a ring," said Tiuri, placing his hand on his chest.

"Come," said Brother Martin. "Brother Julius, would you show Tiuri to his bed? Brother Laurentius and I must go to see the abbot."

"Follow me," said the gatekeeper to Tiuri. "We'll be eating in half an hour, so you have arrived just at the right time."

"We shall see you later," said Brother Martin. He and Brother Laurentius left with a friendly nod.

Tiuri followed the gatekeeper around the cloister and up a flight of stairs. They came to a long corridor with lots of doors. When they reached the very end of the corridor, the gatekeeper stopped and opened a door.

"You may sleep in this room," he told Tiuri and then he left.

Tiuri stepped through the door. He found himself in a small, whitewashed cell, which was furnished with a narrow bed and a small bench. A few rays of sun peeped in through the high window. Tiuri sat down on the bed and looked up at the crucifix on the wall.

Then there was a sound of hurried footsteps and the gatekeeper returned, carrying a faded brown habit.

"Here," he said, "you can wear this. It'll be better than your torn clothes."

A little later, Tiuri, dressed in the habit, went for a walk in the garden. The gatekeeper proudly pointed out some of the more unusual flowers to him. Then he said he had something to do and he left Tiuri on his own. Tiuri wandered around the deserted cloister. In one corner he saw an open door with another courtyard beyond. On the far side of that courtyard, a few steps led up into the church. Quietly, he entered the building. There were some monks kneeling at prayer and a candle burning on the altar. The evening light streamed in through the stained-glass windows, bathing everything in a mysterious glow. Tiuri knelt and put his hands together.

After a while, he stood up and returned to the first courtyard, where Brother Martin came towards him, followed by a tall, dark-haired monk. The monk introduced himself as Father Hyronimus, the abbot, and he welcomed Tiuri to the monastery. Then a bell rang, indicating that it was time for dinner.

In the refectory, Tiuri sat at a long table between Brother Martin and the gatekeeper and enjoyed a simple meal with them.

After dinner, the abbot beckoned Tiuri to go with him and he followed him to his cell.

"Brother Laurentius and Brother Martin have told me all about you," said the abbot. "Or at least everything that they know. They say you intend to remain as our guest until tomorrow and then travel on to the Blue River."

"Yes, Father Hyronimus," said Tiuri.

"Will it be a dangerous journey for you?" asked the abbot.

"Yes, Father Hyronimus," replied Tiuri.

"Brother Martin told me there is much that is mysterious about you," said the abbot. "You are very young to be undertaking a journey that is so fraught with peril."

"I'm sixteen," said Tiuri.

The abbot smiled. "Where are you from?" he asked. "And where are you going?"

"I come from the City of Dagonaut," replied Tiuri, "and I am on my way to the source of the Blue River... to Menaures the hermit."

"Menaures the hermit! It is such a long time since I last saw him. Do give him my best wishes. And is your visit to him the reason for your journey?"

"N-no," said Tiuri. "I'm not actually allowed to tell anyone where I am going."

"If your path is taking you to Menaures, it is a good path," said the abbot. "And your eyes and your voice tell me the same thing. I shall not enquire about your destination or your mission. I should only like to ask if there is any assistance I can offer."

"My thanks, Father Hyronimus," said Tiuri. "Would you please tell no one that I have been here and that I am going to the Blue River?"

"I promise," said the abbot. Then he frowned and said, half to himself, "But you're going to need some protection." He fell silent for a moment and then said, "You must keep the habit you are wearing. If you pull the hood up, it will offer some disguise."

"Thank you, Father Hyronimus," said Tiuri.

"And now you must sleep," said the abbot. "May the peace of this place lend you new strength."

Tiuri thanked him again and returned to his cell. He slept peacefully that night, and had no dreams.

The next morning, Tiuri said farewell to the monastery and to the monks, to Brothers Laurentius, Martin and Julius the gatekeeper in particular. Then he knelt in front of the abbot and said, "Father, please give me your blessing."

The abbot laid his hand on Tiuri's head and blessed him.

"May God be with you, my son," he said, "on your long and arduous journey."

PART THREE

CASTLE MISTRINAUT

1   A Pilgrim

Feeling refreshed and in good spirits, Tiuri set off for the Blue River. He felt safer now. In the brown habit, with the hood pulled up over his head and a staff in his hand, he could pass for a pilgrim. His enemies would be far less likely to recognize him as the boy they were looking for. He walked briskly along the road that led northwards through the rolling fields. On his right was the dark forest he had left the previous day. Tiuri could see no sign of the Grey Knights, and he did not hear the sound of the horn either. The people out working in the fields greeted him cheerfully as he walked by. Tiuri nodded and waved back at them.

Halfway through the morning, a donkey cart came up behind him. The suntanned farmer sitting up front asked Tiuri if he wanted to travel with him for a while, and Tiuri gratefully accepted. He hopped up beside the man and told him he was on his way to the Blue River.

"I'm not going that far," said the farmer. "But you're welcome to ride with me for some way, brother. It'll save your legs. You've come from the Brown Monastery, haven't you?"

"I have indeed," replied Tiuri.

"On a pilgrimage?" asked the farmer.

"Yes," said Tiuri. "You could call it that." He realized then that it was true: in some ways, his journey was like a pilgrimage.

"Lots of pilgrims used to go to the Blue River in my younger days," said the farmer. "They travelled upstream to the spring at the source of the river. A hermit lived up there, in the mountains. I can't remember his name, but he may even live there still. You know, some people don't understand why anyone would want to go on a pilgrimage, but I always say that it can be of great benefit, even if that benefit is not immediately obvious. One man might stay at home and do his work, while another wanders afar and yet also finds favour in heaven. I always say: you never know what good it might do! Don't you agree, brother?" He did not wait for an answer, but continued, "In the past, people around these parts had great respect for pilgrims, hermits and the like. My father – God rest his soul – used to talk about them. Times were hard back then and, when people can't get by on their own, they hope for help from heaven. I remember very little about those days myself and, of course, you won't remember them at all. But I'm sure you've heard about the evil that ruled at Castle Mistrinaut in those days."

It was the first Tiuri had heard about any evil power at Mistrinaut, so he remained silent. The farmer didn't seem to notice and just went on talking.

"But now, thank the Lord, this land is peaceful and prosperous," he said. "And perhaps that's why there are fewer pilgrims. Have you ever been to the Blue River before?"

"No, not this part of the river anyway," Tiuri replied. "I'll be able to get there by this evening, won't I?"

"Oh, yes. No trouble," said the farmer. "You can sleep at Castle Mistrinaut tonight. It's on the opposite bank of the Blue River, where this road meets the Great Road. You can see it from a long way off."

"Castle Mistrinaut?" said Tiuri, thinking about what the farmer had just said about the evil that had dwelt there.

"Yes, you do know there's nothing to fear now, don't you? The present lord of the castle drove out the evil years ago.

Haven't you heard the story? He came here from another land and boldly defeated the previous resident of the castle and routed the evil spirits. The king himself gave him his thanks. Now Mistrinaut is a very hospitable place. The drawbridge is always down, everyone is welcome, and they will give you a bed and as much food as you can eat. I've stayed there a few times myself, when I've been to visit my brother who lives on the other side of the river..." And so he went on, telling Tiuri stories about his brother, and then about his wife, his children and his farm.

The farmer talked and talked, and Tiuri did not mind in the slightest. It meant all he had to do was listen and there was no need for him to talk about himself.

Towards the end of the morning, they came to the village that the farmer was travelling to. But the friendly farmer didn't want to say farewell until he and Tiuri had eaten together.

"Safe travels, brother," he said when Tiuri left. "Remember me in your prayers. I hope it's not late when you reach the castle and the Blue River. I think we're in for some bad weather."

The day was warm and sunny as Tiuri continued his journey on foot, but later that afternoon the farmer was proved right. The sky became overcast and a cold wind blew up. Tiuri started to walk faster. He could see a castle ahead, outlined sharply against the dark sky. It had to be Castle Mistrinaut, and so the Blue River and the Great Road must also be nearby.

As Tiuri stepped onto the Great Road, the rain came pouring down. The Blue River was not blue at all, but as grey as lead. The river was narrower here than when it flowed through the City of Dagonaut, and the current seemed much stronger. The castle stood on the opposite bank.

Tiuri had never heard of Mistrinaut before, although he knew the names of most of the castles in Dagonaut's kingdom. But this part of the country was somewhat isolated, as it lay beyond the forest, and it had not often played a role in the legends and history of the land. Tiuri stood in the rain, looking at the river and the castle. An open drawbridge led to the gate, which was positioned between two large towers. Even though the drawbridge was down, Tiuri thought the castle didn't look at all friendly or welcoming. It was big and dark and mysterious, with grim walls and forbidding towers.

He looked around, but there was nowhere to shelter nearby. *So why not cross the bridge*, he thought, *and ask for a place to sleep in the castle?* He was safe in his disguise and preferred not to sleep out in the fields that night if he didn't have to. Someone was lighting a lamp at one of the windows. It'd be dry and comfortable inside.

Tiuri crossed the drawbridge and banged the heavy knocker on the gate. The door in the gate opened immediately.

"Come in, come in!" said the guard. "What dreadful weather! Are you very wet, reverend brother?"

"Not too bad," said Tiuri. "I wish you a good evening. Might I be able to spend the night here?"

"Of course," said the guard. "Were you invited by the lord of the castle?"

"Erm... No, I'm afraid not," replied Tiuri.

"Oh, you are still most welcome in any case," the guard replied. "The question was merely a matter of form. Everyone who passes this way may stay the night here. Would you please come with me?"

Tiuri followed him to a small round room in one of the towers beside the gate, where another guard was sitting at a table, gazing thoughtfully at the pieces on the chessboard in front of him.

"We have a guest," said the first guard. "Will you sign him in?"

"Wait a moment," said the other guard. He moved one of the pieces and announced with satisfaction, "Your castle's in danger!" Then he stood up, walked over to a cupboard and took out a big book, a quill and an inkwell. He sat down again, opened the book and said to Tiuri, "And what is your name, brother?"

"Tarmin," said Tiuri. It was the first name that occurred to him.

"Brother Tarmin," repeated the guard. He dipped the quill into the ink and slowly wrote down the name. "From the Brown Monastery?" he asked.

Tiuri nodded.

That answer was carefully noted as well. The guard blew on the ink and closed the book. "There," he said, "now that's taken care of. Our master likes the names of all of his guests to be written in this book. It's getting to be quite a long list."

Then he looked at his fellow guard. "It's your turn to make a move," he said, pointing at the chessboard.

"You'll just have to wait," he replied. "First I'm going to show Brother Tarmin where he needs to go. And you should mind your manners! You haven't even welcomed our guest yet."

"Greetings, Brother Tarmin," said the guard, rising to his feet. He tucked the book under his arm and bowed. "Pray for me, poor sinner. Don't keep my friend here talking too long. He's slow enough as it is. And tell him he should guard his castle better. I don't mean Mistrinaut, where our drawbridge is always down, but that black rook of his on the chessboard."

The first guard shook his head. "Please come with me," he said to Tiuri. "There's no talking to that one. The only thing he's good for is chess."

He led Tiuri into the courtyard, where there was another gate in an inner wall. The two of them dashed across the courtyard, as the rain was still coming down. The guard unlocked the door with a large key. "If you carry on through there," he said, "you'll find someone who'll direct you to the great hall and a place to sleep for the night."

Tiuri thanked him and did as he was told. He came to another courtyard, bigger and more beautiful than the first, but it was gloomy and deserted in the rain. On the other side of the courtyard was a covered gallery with people hurrying to and fro. As Tiuri headed across to join them, a man in blue came to meet him.

"Blessed be your evening," said Tiuri with a bow. "I am a pilgrim and I ask you kindly to grant me shelter."

"Be welcome, pilgrim," said the man. "Just go through that door and you will come to the great hall. There's a fire in there, so you can dry your wet clothes while you wait for dinner."

"Thank you," said Tiuri.

The great hall looked a little like the hall at Castle Tehuri, his home, but it was older and much darker. The beams were blackened with smoke, and the walls were grey and worn. Long benches and trestle tables filled the room. At one end of the hall was a platform with a table on it, which was covered with a white cloth. That was of course where the lord of the castle sat, along with his family. It was also the place where the minstrels and the musicians would perform on festive occasions. A servant in blue stood beside the large open fireplace, turning a large piece of meat on a spit. It smelled delicious. Tiuri walked over to the fire to dry himself off a little.

The servant smiled. "Good evening, brother," he said. "You are early. Are you very hungry? You're not fasting, are you?"

"Not today," Tiuri said, smiling back at him.

Other servants came in, carrying pitchers and bowls of bread, which they put down on the tables. One of the servants lit the torches that hung in metal rings around the walls. The light completely changed the dark hall, bathing everything in a warm, reddish glow.

Tiuri's gaze rested on a tapestry on the wall above the high table. The image on the cloth almost seemed to come to life. The tapestry had the strangest figures on it: soldiers with winged helmets were fighting a monster that looked like a dragon, but had many vicious-looking heads and sinuous necks. In the shifting light of the torches, the scene looked beautiful and mysterious, but also a little eerie.

Then one of the servants banged a gong. More people came into the hall, castle residents and guests, and sat down at the long tables. Tiuri found a seat too, in a dark corner. The people who joined him at the table said good evening, but then mostly ignored him. They were more interested in another guest, a pedlar who was showing his wares and chattering away about what he had to sell.

Last of all, the lord of the castle entered. He was a tall and strong-looking man with a pale, stern face and red hair and beard. He was accompanied by two ladies and a priest. When they were seated and the priest had said a prayer, everyone started to eat.

Tiuri tucked in. There was plenty of white and brown bread, roast meat, fruit and ale. He sat quietly in his dark corner, eating, watching and listening. His thoughts turned to Castle Fantumar, where he had lived as a squire, and to Castle Tehuri, his home, where he had spent his carefree childhood years. *Not that long ago*, he thought, *I was sitting at the high table in a castle too, as part of the lord's family*. There were always lots of guests at Tehuri as well, passing travellers who were given shelter. He thought about his parents, who were probably wondering where he was and worrying about him.

After dinner, a servant showed the guests to their sleeping places. He led them along lots of corridors and up and down flights of stairs. Tiuri realized that the castle was very large and had a complex layout. He was sharing a room with the pedlar and a farmer who said very little. The room was small and basic, but clean, and had three beds. Tiuri and the farmer both wanted to go straight to bed, but the pedlar said he was going back to the great hall, because he might be able to do some business there.

"Perhaps the lord would like to buy something," he said. "I have some lovely jewellery for his wife and daughter: necklaces and hairbands and clasps for their cloaks."

"What's the lord of Mistrinaut actually called?" asked Tiuri.

"Now you're asking!" said the pedlar. "I did know, but I've forgotten. It's one of those impossibly long foreign names, a real tongue-twister. So most people just call him the lord of Mistrinaut. Well, that's what he is, after all. You know he's not from these parts, don't you?"

"Where does he come from?" asked Tiuri.

"He's from the north. They say all the people up there have red hair like him. But he's been living here for a long time now. He's a powerful lord, and a good man too." The pedlar gathered up his goods, wished them goodnight and left.

Tiuri was soon in bed, and he lay there listening to the rain. The farmer soon fell asleep, as Tiuri could hear from his steady breathing. But Tiuri was wide awake. That surprised him; he had every reason to be sleepy and he was in a comfortable bed, instead of on the hard ground somewhere outside.

He had no idea how long he lay awake, but he heard people talking outside and then the castle growing quieter and later he heard the pedlar return and climb into bed… and in all that time he had not slept a wink. Finally, the castle was silent and he realized that everyone must have gone to bed. Even the sound of the rain had stopped.

Why can't you get to sleep? Tiuri thought to himself. *You don't deserve a nice, dry bed! Come on, go to sleep!*

But beneath those thoughts another feeling was lurking, a feeling he didn't want to give in to. It was… a sense of foreboding. Quietly, Tiuri got up and opened the door, which led onto a small courtyard. It was dry now, but still cloudy; he couldn't see a single star in the sky. A cold wind was blowing and he shivered as he returned to bed.

Finally, Tiuri managed to fall asleep, but soon he was awakened by the sound of many hoofs clattering over the drawbridge. *Who could that be, so late at night?* he wondered, but he was too sleepy to think about it for long. He went back to sleep and did not wake again until the next morning.

The farmer and the pedlar were still asleep. Tiuri reached for the letter, which was the first thing he did every morning. Then he got up and went outside. It was still dry, but the sky was grey. He could tell that more rain would fall before long. Tiuri washed at the pump in the courtyard and headed to the great hall. The servants were already up and busy at work in the large courtyard. One of the men was chasing a white chicken, which flew into the great hall with a loud cackling, just as Tiuri arrived. He bent down and scooped up the agitated bird in his arms.

"Thank you, brother," said the man, taking the chicken from him. "She's such a pampered little beast. She thinks she can do whatever she likes. You're up at an early hour, aren't you?"

"Well, I want to make an early start today," said Tiuri. "Might I be able to get something to eat yet?"

"Oh yes, of course," came the answer. "Everything's ready for breakfast. Many of us have already eaten, including our master. But I'm afraid you won't be able to leave right away; the drawbridge is up."

"Oh, is it?" said Tiuri. "When will they lower it?"

"Well, it's usually down by now. By six at the latest, in the summer. Generally they don't even bother to raise it at all. But the boss's orders are that the drawbridge can't go down until he says so. I'm sure it won't be long, though. There are other guests who want to leave and some of us have work to do outside the castle."

"Then I shall wait," said Tiuri. "Do you know why the drawbridge is up this morning?"

"No idea," said the man. "They say some unexpected guests arrived in the middle of the night and the drawbridge went up soon after that. But go and eat. I'm sure you'll be able to leave after breakfast."

Tiuri had a strange feeling in his stomach as he started his breakfast. He didn't like the drawbridge being up. But he thought to himself, *Don't go jumping at shadows, Tiuri! You mustn't fear danger wherever you go. And the monk's habit is a good disguise. Just make sure you don't show how keen you are to get away...*

After breakfast, he walked out into the courtyard, where he caught snatches of conversations: "Strange knights..." "In the middle of the night... The lord's friends..."

Tiuri was becoming more and more worried, so he made his way to the gate. One of the guards was sitting on a bench in the passageway, stringing his bow.

"Good morning," said Tiuri.

"Morning," replied the guard.

The other guard called through the doorway. "Your move! Your king's in check!"

"Blast it!" said the first guard. "Just leave me in peace for once!" He lowered the bow and said to Tiuri, "So, Brother Tarmin, you're leaving us, are you? You'll have to wait, I'm afraid. The drawbridge isn't down yet."

"When will I be able to go?" asked Tiuri.

"Oh, I don't really know. The bridge is usually down by now," replied the guard and he began to tinker with his bow again.

Tiuri gave an impatient sigh.

"Eager to leave, reverend brother?" came a voice from behind him.

Startled, Tiuri turned around to see the lord of the castle. He must have walked up behind him very quietly. The guard was about to stand up, but the lord raised his hand and said, "Please do not get up. Carry on with your work." Then he turned to Tiuri and said, "My other guests are still at breakfast. I shall soon give the order to open the gate and let down the drawbridge."

Tiuri noticed that he spoke with an accent.

"Where have you come from, brother?" asked the lord of Mistrinaut. "And where are you going?"

Tiuri answered only his first question. "I have come from the Brown Monastery," he said. "And now that you are here, my lord, I should like to thank you for your kind and gracious hospitality."

"You are most welcome," the lord replied.

Tiuri thought the man was eyeing him suspiciously, but he could not tell for certain, as it was dark in the passageway and the lord of Mistrinaut was standing with his back to the light. But he was glad that he had pulled up his hood.

The lord turned and started walking towards the courtyard. "So, brother," he called back over his shoulder. "You have come from the Brown Monastery. But there is another question I would like to ask you."

Tiuri followed him. They stopped just outside the passageway. The lord looked up at the grey sky and said, "There is another storm on the way." Then he turned to Tiuri, who could finally take a good look at him. Tiuri saw that his skin was not so much pale as very fair, and that his eyes were light green and penetrating, beneath bushy eyebrows.

"Did you by any chance encounter a young man on your travels, brother?" he asked. "A young man of about sixteen, with dark hair and blue-grey eyes?"

It felt as though an ice-cold hand was closing around Tiuri's heart.

"A young man..." he repeated. "I can't remember seeing anyone who looked like that. But I wasn't paying too much attention to my fellow travellers." He wondered if his words sounded convincing or if the man had noticed how anxious he was. The gaze of those pale eyes was so intense! "One sees so many people on the road," he added.

"But you would have noticed this young man," said the lord. "He is wearing torn and ragged clothing, most probably a robe that was once white, but on his finger he has a valuable ring with a sparkling, white stone."

Tiuri shook his head. "No, my lord," he said slowly. "I didn't see that young man. I am certain of it."

"Well, there was a chance you might have done, was there not?" said the lord. "After all, you are travelling from the same direction. But he has had a longer journey, from the east."

"I am sorry I cannot help you," said Tiuri, as calmly as he

could. "Who is this young man?" he added after a moment's thought. "A friend of yours?"

"No, I have never met him," replied the lord and then he fell silent.

Tiuri waited in silence too, not knowing what else to say. He looked out at the quiet courtyard and wondered if the lord was still studying him. Then he heard the second guard's voice again, "Come and see! Your king's in check, I tell you!"

"What is your name, brother?" asked the lord.

"Tarmin," replied Tiuri.

"You have a young voice, Brother Tarmin. How old are you, in fact? Sixteen, seventeen? Have you already taken orders?" He leant over to Tiuri. "I should like to see your face more clearly," he said. "Would you lower your hood?" And before Tiuri could react, the lord had reached out and done it himself.

"Aha!" He frowned. "Dark hair, blue-grey eyes! I believe you are also the right age."

Tiuri took a step backwards and said, with as much surprise as he could muster, "You surely don't think I'm the young man you're looking for, do you?"

"I know there are many people who match the description," replied the lord, "but you are the only one among my guests. So I would like you to accompany me for a moment."

"But why?" said Tiuri, still acting astounded. "I don't know what you want from me! I am Brother Tarmin from the Brown Monastery and I..."

"You have nothing to fear. At least if you are who you say you are. I only want you to come and meet a few friends of mine, who arrived here last night. If you are not the one they are seeking, there will be no consequences."

"But no one is looking for me!" shouted Tiuri. "I don't understand what you want from me."

"I do not want anything from you," said the lord abruptly. He put his hand on Tiuri's shoulder and ordered him to go with him.

Tiuri obeyed. If he kept resisting, he would only make the lord even more suspicious, and escape was not an option, not with the closed gate and the raised drawbridge. His heart was pounding. He was afraid that he knew who the lord's friends were. But he planned to maintain his new identity for as long as he could. They walked across the courtyard and through the second gate. The lord did not remove his hand from Tiuri's shoulder. He seemed concerned that Tiuri might run away. As they passed through the second courtyard, Tiuri saw something that almost stopped him in his tracks.

Two grooms were rubbing down a black horse, which was reluctantly submitting to the treatment. Other servants were standing around and making comments like, "Full of fire, that one!" and "What a beautiful creature!"

Tiuri recognized the horse immediately. It was his trusted ally, the ebony steed of the Knight with the White Shield. And now he knew the horse's real name: Ardanwen, or Night Wind. There was no need to wonder how the animal had come to be there.

When the horse saw him, it raised its head and whinnied.

"That horse would appear to be greeting you," said the lord. "Do you know the creature?"

"No," said Tiuri. He was sorry that he had to deny knowing his good companion, but he knew he had no choice.

The lord glanced sideways at him, but said nothing. They walked on, through the covered gallery and the great hall, and then through a door and up a flight of stairs to another door, which the lord opened. He released his hold on Tiuri and stopped in the doorway, blocking Tiuri's view of the room.

"I have only one guest who matches the description," said the lord. "Do you wish to speak to him?"

A voice called out, "Wait a moment..." And then, "Send him in."

The lord turned to Tiuri. "Go on," he ordered.

Tiuri did as he was told. He heard the door close and found himself in a low-ceilinged room with a large table that was covered with the remains of a meal. Around that table, standing and seated, were the men he had expected to see. The four Grey Knights and their squires. They were all wearing their helmets, with their visors down.

"He calls himself Brother Tarmin," came the lord's voice, "but he answers to the description you gave."

Tiuri glanced over his shoulder. His host was leaning with his back against the door and looking at the Grey Knights with a frown on his face. The men had all stood up by then and Tiuri could see that their eyes, gleaming through the slits in their helmets, were focused on him.

"Is he the one you are looking for?" asked the lord.

"I don't know," answered one of the knights. "Does he have the ring?"

Don't let them see you're scared, thought Tiuri. He feigned astonishment as he addressed the knights, "What do you want from me? Who are you? I don't know you!"

"Do you have the ring?" said another of the knights, in a gruff voice.

"Ring? What ring? I don't know what you're talking about!" Tiuri exclaimed.

The Grey Knights and their squires said nothing. They stood motionlessly, staring at Tiuri.

"So he is not the one you are seeking?" asked the lord.

"We do not know," said the knight who had spoken first.

Tiuri recognized him by his voice. It was the knight with the silver horn.

"But we intend to find out," added the second.

"Indeed we do," replied the first. He turned to Tiuri and said, "Have you fled here from the east, from the Royal Forest?"

"I have come from the Brown Monastery," replied Tiuri.

"Do you have the ring?" asked the second.

"I don't know anything about any ring," said Tiuri.

"We will know if you are telling the truth," said the first Grey Knight. "You may well have concealed it beneath your habit."

"I do not understand why you are treating me this way," said Tiuri, feigning anger. "You really should raise your visors and say who you are!"

"This is not the attitude of a meek and obedient lay brother!" said a third knight.

"Search his clothes," the first knight ordered the squires. "Then we shall know for certain."

The squires walked towards Tiuri, who backed away until he bumped into the lord.

"I will not permit you to treat me like this!" he cried. "I do not know you and I know nothing about any ring!"

The squires hesitated for a moment, but one of the Grey Knights barked, "Search through his clothes to see if he has the ring."

But Tiuri could not allow that to happen. He felt the letter on his chest, the letter that no one must know about. If they searched him, they would find it. So he would just have to tell them about the ring and perhaps there was a chance that they would not discover the letter...

He raised his hand and pulled out the cord from around his neck. "There is no need for you to search me," he said. "I have a ring. Here it is."

2 HANDS TIED

The squires stood aside for the Grey Knights, who came over to Tiuri and looked at the ring, which lay in his palm, still attached to the cord.

"It's the ring!" one of them gasped.

"He's the one..." another whispered.

The third knight snatched the ring from Tiuri's hand, so roughly that the cord snapped.

"That ring is mine!" said Tiuri. "Give it back!"

"Yours?" sneered the knight. "Shame on you, shame on you for standing before us in the guise of a monk!"

"He is the one we are looking for," said the first knight to the lord. "And we shall treat him as he deserves. He is our prisoner."

Tiuri looked at the lord of Mistrinaut. "Let me go!" he said. "I do not know these knights and I have done nothing to deserve imprisonment."

The lord was still leaning against the door. He eyed Tiuri sharply, but did not respond.

"I am your guest!" cried Tiuri. "Why would you allow these knights to capture me and take me prisoner? They have not told me their names or even raised their visors. This is a violation of the sacred laws of hospitality! They must return my ring and let me go!"

The lord looked away and said nothing.

"Seize him," said one of the Grey Knights.

"At least tell me why you are taking me prisoner!" cried Tiuri, as several hands grabbed hold of him.

But the Grey Knights said nothing. The lord stepped aside and opened the door. Tiuri was led away by two knights and two squires, down a corridor and up a long flight of stairs. As they walked, they did not say a single word, and neither did Tiuri, because he knew it would do no good.

Finally, they reached a door that opened into a small room. They pushed Tiuri into the room and slammed the door behind him. He was a prisoner at Castle Mistrinaut.

The room was octagonal, with a single window, which was open. Tiuri walked over to the window and looked out. He realized that he was in a tower and he gazed down at the empty courtyard, so far below. Opposite was another tower and a sheer wall without windows. Tiuri sighed and turned away from the window. It would be impossible to escape.

He looked around the room. There were a few pieces of heavy furniture: a large table, a smaller table and two chairs with cushions. A rug lay on the floor and there was a tablecloth on the larger of the two tables, tapestries on the wall and a beautifully crafted brass lamp hanging from the ceiling. It was a finely furnished prison, but it was still a prison!

Tiuri sat down on one of the chairs and started to think.

One thing was puzzling him. Why had the Grey Knights asked about the ring and not about the letter? Didn't they want the lord to know about it? Would they soon come and take the letter from him, too? At that thought, he leapt to his feet and started anxiously pacing the small room. Then he stopped. And listened.

He heard footsteps outside the room and a metallic sound, as if someone had rested a spear on the floor. Was there a guard outside the door? Was someone about to come in? Men were murmuring outside, but he couldn't make out what they were saying. He put his ear to the keyhole and caught a few words.

"...locked up good and proper."

"...get the same treatment he doled out..."

"He seems very young to..."

"...do not agree... evil everywhere... escape... But now we should..."

Tiuri could make little sense of what he heard.

When the key turned in the lock, Tiuri backed away. The door opened and one of the Grey Knights, still with his visor down, looked into the room. He did not speak and he soon left, locking the door behind him. Tiuri heard more footsteps and mumbling.

Fingers trembling, he pulled the letter from its hiding place and thought, *Now is surely the time to read the letter and destroy it – before it ends up in their hands! Why else would they have taken me prisoner?*

Tiuri broke one of the letter's three seals but was startled by the sound of the key in the lock again. Quickly, he lifted up the tablecloth and slid the letter beneath it. When another knight looked into the room, Tiuri was sitting quietly in a chair. It was a different knight, the one with the gruff voice and the fiery temper. Maybe he was the knight who had asked about Tiuri at the monastery. The knight came in and glanced around the room, without even deigning to look at Tiuri. Tiuri waited, his heart thumping. Was the knight just checking that the prison was suitable, or was he looking for something?

But then he left. *I'm going to have to be careful*, thought Tiuri. *I don't want them to see the letter if they come in when I'm not expecting it.*

It was a pity there were no locks on the inside of the door. Tiuri wondered if all four of the knights meant to take turns to come and inspect the room. It seemed he was going to have to get rid of the letter...

He could still hear noises on the other side of the door. Had the entire company of Grey Knights and their squires gathered outside the room? Tiuri took the letter from beneath the tablecloth and thought frantically. He needed to read the letter and destroy it, but how? If only there was a fire in the room!

He was going to have to tear the letter into a thousand tiny pieces – and swallow them if necessary. But first he had to read it... And quickly! He broke the second seal. *I need to commit the message to memory*, he thought. *But what if someone comes? Then it's all over... Oh, I can hear something! Is the third knight on his way?*

But no one came. Tiuri looked thoughtfully at the furniture in the room. What if he pushed a heavy chair in front of the door? Then no one would be able to burst into the room unexpectedly, and he'd have time to get rid of the letter.

He set to work immediately. It wasn't easy. The chair was very heavy and he knew he mustn't make a sound. He kept stopping to listen; he could still hear voices, but no one came in. Finally, the chair was in position. Tiuri lifted the small table onto the chair and tested the stack of furniture to find out how easy it would be to move. He feared it wouldn't keep anyone out for long, but he didn't dare waste any more time. He sat down on the floor and leant against the chair. Then he got ready to break the third seal.

Before he could do so, the key turned in the lock again. The handle moved and someone shouted, "It won't open!"

Too late! thought Tiuri.

"Hey, you in there!" the same voice cried. "Open this door!" Then the man shouted to someone else, "He's barred the door!"

The people outside started banging and pushing at the door. The chair shook. They'd be in the room at any moment!

It was going to be impossible to read the letter, memorize its contents and destroy the paper quickly enough. Tiuri slid the letter beneath the rug this time, silently praying that the knights wouldn't think to look there.

Then he stood up, with his feet on the spot where the letter was hidden, and waited to see what would happen.

The door burst open. The table fell off the chair with a bang, and a knight and two squires barged into the room.

"What is the meaning..." the knight began and then he fell silent, as though he regretted having spoken. It was the knight with the gruff voice. Tiuri could recognize two of the Grey Knights by now: he had dubbed them the Knight with the Gruff Voice and the Knight with the Silver Horn. The knight turned on his heels and left, but the squires stayed where they were, with their hands on their swords.

"Oh, don't worry. I'm not going to run away!" said Tiuri. "I know it's impossible to escape. I just want to know why I'm here!"

The squires did not respond.

The knight soon came back with some rope, which he threw to the squires. Then he pushed the chair back to the large table, grabbed Tiuri and pushed him down onto it. With a movement of his head, the knight signalled to the squires to come closer. The three of them tied Tiuri to the chair, all in complete silence. Tiuri didn't try to resist; he knew there was no point. He couldn't fight these silent grey enemies – he couldn't even speak to them!

Soon he was alone once again, tied up and powerless. The letter was out of reach, beneath the rug on the floor. But the knights hadn't asked about it, and they hadn't looked for it. The longer he thought about this, the stranger it seemed. He tried to move, but it was impossible. His enemies had done their job well. So he sat there, idly, and all the while time was passing.

"Enough time has been lost already," the Knight with the White Shield had said.

Tiuri sat in the chair, staring at the spot on the rug where the letter was hidden, a prisoner in an unfamiliar castle, not knowing what fate awaited him.

Tiuri would never forget that day in the tower room and would always shiver at the memory. Sitting there, all alone, unable to do anything except think, think, think... His back was to the window, but he could tell by the changes in the light that hours were passing. Sometimes it rained outside; he could hear it pouring down. No one came to the room for hours and he heard no more voices on the other side of the door. The same thought kept whirling around inside his head: the letter, the letter... Being tied up in one position for so long was becoming more and more painful as the rope cut into his wrists and ankles.

An eternity seemed to pass until, finally, Tiuri lost all sense of time. He could see only part of the room, but the details of what he saw became etched into his memory. As the day progressed, the light grew weak and pale and the tapestries seemed to come to life. They were like the tapestry in the great hall downstairs, with knights and monsters, but these figures were stranger and more brutal. When Tiuri closed his tired eyes, his overwrought imagination conjured up a wild dance of knights and monsters on the wall. Then he opened his eyes again to see the figures had just stopped moving.

He listened to the rain, which seemed to whisper words of endless sorrow and unutterable despair...

3 THE LORD AND LAVINIA

When Tiuri heard noises outside the room again, it was late in the day. The door opened and a man came in. It was not a Grey Knight, or one of their squires, but one of the blue-clad castle servants. He was carrying a tray of food, which he placed on the table.

He shook his head as he looked at Tiuri and said, "I'm just going to untie your hands for a moment. Otherwise I've just climbed up all those stairs for nothing."

Undoing the ropes was not easy, but eventually he managed it. Tiuri rubbed his wrists. The blood in his arms and hands could flow properly now, but it hurt. In fact, it was so painful that it brought tears to Tiuri's eyes. He didn't want the man to see him crying though, so he hung his head and bit his bottom lip.

The servant had stepped away and was standing by the door. He must have been told to wait until the prisoner had finished eating. After a while, Tiuri felt a little better and could start his meal. It consisted of bread and water, but that was enough for Tiuri, because he was starving. He ate in silence. He'd decided that he wouldn't say another word or ask any questions, and to bear his captivity with pride and dignity. When Tiuri had finished eating, the servant said, almost apologetically, "I'm going to have to tie you back up again."

Tiuri didn't reply, but allowed the servant to tie him to the chair. He noticed that the man had tied the rope far less securely than the knight and his squires had done. As soon as he was alone again, he decided to see if he could free himself. He hoped he might manage to release his hands and he knew that, once his hands were free, the rest would be easy. It seemed to take forever, and involved lots of tugging and twisting. But, finally, he did it! The ropes fell to the floor.

Tiuri sat there for a while, gently shaking his arms and legs. Then he stood up and quietly paced the room until the worst of the stiffness had gone. He looked out of the window. The day was coming to an end. It had stopped raining, but what little he could see out there looked dark and gloomy.

So now Tiuri was untied, but he still wasn't free. He felt better, though – calmer and more courageous. At least he would be able to read the letter before it got too dark.

But it didn't seem that he was going to get the chance!

The sound of footsteps and voices on the other side of the door sent Tiuri dashing back to the chair, where he wrapped the ropes back around himself to make it look like he was still tied up.

The lord of Mistrinaut entered the room. He frowned at Tiuri and said, "So they had to tie you up, did they?"

Tiuri maintained an aloof silence and hoped the man would not think to inspect the ropes. He came a little closer, put his hands on his hips, looked intently at Tiuri and then said, "What is your name?"

Tiuri met his gaze, but said nothing.

"As you will. Do not reply!" barked the lord. "It is what I would expect from you!"

Tiuri hesitated before responding. "They never spoke either," he said finally. "You and those knights have taken me prisoner without even accusing me of anything."

"I am sure you know why you are here," said the lord, also after a brief pause. "You had the ring, didn't you?"

"The ring!" cried Tiuri, his hand moving towards the place where it had been. "What do you know about the ring?"

"To whom did that ring belong?" came the response.

Again, Tiuri hesitated before answering. Could he tell the truth? *What does it matter?* Tiuri thought. *I think he knows the answer anyway.* But he still didn't understand why they kept asking about the ring and not about the letter. And he said, "It belonged to the Black Knight with the White Shield."

"The Black Knight with the White Shield," repeated the lord slowly. "So you admit it yourself. In that case, why were you wearing it?"

"Why was I wearing it?"

"Yes. That ring – as you have yourself admitted – belongs to the Black Knight with the White Shield. So why were you wearing it?"

"But the Knight with the White Shield is dead!" cried Tiuri.

The lord studied Tiuri. He seemed to be trying to read his mind.

"Did you know him?" asked Tiuri.

The lord came a step closer and leant over Tiuri. He poked Tiuri's chest with his finger and said, "You're right. The Black Knight with the White Shield is dead. And do you know how he met his death?"

"Yes," said Tiuri.

"He was murdered."

"Yes," said Tiuri. "I know." The lord's words and behaviour had surprised him; he didn't know what to think.

"You know. You know?!"

The lord stood up straight, looked at Tiuri one more time, and then turned and strode out of the room.

Tiuri sat there, staring at the door, even after the man was long gone. What had just happened? What had the lord of Mistrinaut meant? He had the peculiar feeling that they had been talking at cross purposes.

And why had he asked about the ring? Was there something

special about it? Did they not want him to take the ring to Menaures? Were they keeping him captive so that he couldn't complete his task? But then it would have been simpler to take the letter from him. Perhaps they thought he already knew what the message was, but then they would have been better off killing him. After all, the Knight with the White Shield had been murdered.

But then Tiuri realized that the lord must have seen that his ropes were loose. He *must* have noticed! And he hadn't done anything about it...

Tiuri knelt down to take the letter from beneath the rug. But then he heard a strange sound. A footstep, rustling, shuffling, a soft click. It wasn't coming from behind the door, or through the window...

Tiuri held his breath. For a moment he thought the tapestry he had spent so long staring at during his captivity had truly come to life! Then he realized that the cloth actually was moving. He leapt to his feet and ran over to take a look. There was a grinding noise, and then the tapestry shook and slid aside. Where it had been hanging, there was now a dark opening in the wall and a young woman stood with her finger on her lips.

Tiuri stared at her in amazement. She was about his own age, and she had long black plaits. He recognized her as one of the ladies who had eaten at the high table the night before.

"Who are you?" he whispered.

"Shh!" she said. "They mustn't hear me. Wait a moment." She disappeared into the dark doorway, which Tiuri realized must lead to a secret staircase. He heard another grating sound and he stepped closer and peered into the darkness. She reappeared, this time carrying a large bundle. "Here," she whispered. "Take this."

Tiuri did as he was told and laid the bundle on the table. The young woman disappeared again, but returned a moment later, holding in each hand something that gleamed in the evening light: a sword and a dagger. She placed both of the weapons beside the bundle on the table and said, still whispering, "Hide them beneath your habit. Quick, before somebody comes!"

She opened up the bundle. Tiuri saw that there was chainmail inside.

"Why have you brought this for me?" he whispered. "And who are you?"

"I am Lavinia," she answered. "The lord of this castle is my father. I'm not supposed to know anything about this, but I heard some of the things they were saying. They mean to do you harm."

"The Grey Knights?"

She nodded. "Yes, the Grey Knights. They're about to come and fetch you."

"But why? Who are they?"

"I don't know, I don't know! But they are bitterly angry. What did you do to them to make them so furious?"

"Nothing!" said Tiuri. "I don't know anything about them! I have never met them before! Or not as far as I know, because they have never raised their visors in my presence."

The young woman looked over her shoulder. "Quick!" she said. "I took these things from my father's armoury. Perhaps you can use them to protect yourself. Put on the chainmail and arm yourself!"

"Why are you helping me?" asked Tiuri.

"No matter what you've done," she said, "I couldn't bear the thought of you facing their vengeance with no defence."

"Their vengeance?"

"Yes, I overheard one of them saying that word. Someone from the castle said they call themselves the Avengers of the Four Winds. But I must go. Father mustn't find out that I'm here."

"I am very grateful to you," said Tiuri.

Lavinia suddenly looked startled. "Listen," she whispered. Tiuri heard the same grinding sound again.

"Someone's coming up the secret staircase," she said. "It could only be a member of my family. It's probably Father! We must hide these things!"

She quickly helped Tiuri to conceal the chainmail and the weapons beneath the big table. The sound of footsteps on the secret staircase came closer and closer. Then the lord appeared in the secret doorway.

When he saw his daughter, he frowned and said angrily, "Lavinia! What are you doing here?"

She stared back at her father, with a mixture of fear and defiance on her face.

"Father," she began, "I..."

He did not let her finish. "Go to your room," he said sternly. "I shall speak to you later. Go!"

Lavinia promptly did as her father said. Then the lord turned his attention to Tiuri, who had positioned himself in front of the table, hoping to hide what was beneath it. They eyed each other in silence.

"Well," he said, finally. "I came here to bring you something..." He hesitated, cleared his throat and then said gruffly, "Wait a moment."

He disappeared through the dark doorway and returned a moment later with a large package, which he placed at Tiuri's feet. "Inside this bundle," he said, "you'll find chainmail, a dagger and a sword. You must put on the chainmail and arm yourself."

Tiuri stared in astonishment, first at the man and then at the bundle. He certainly hadn't been expecting this! Then he saw the funny side of the situation. First the man shouted at his daughter and sent her to her room, and then he presented Tiuri with exactly the same items. He could not help but smile. If the lord of Mistrinaut could see what was beneath the table!

"Thank you, my lord," he said. "But why have you brought me these things?"

He did not answer immediately. Tiuri could see a mixture of emotions chasing across his face. "You are not my prisoner," he replied finally. "I am not the one to judge you. But you were my guest and, whatever you have done, I want you to be able to defend yourself should that become necessary."

"Defend myself? Against what?" cried Tiuri.

"Quiet! You'll find out soon enough," said the lord. He turned away from Tiuri and looked around the room. Then his gaze fell on what was beneath the table and he looked surprised, but he said nothing.

"How am I to defend myself if I don't know what I'm defending myself against?" said Tiuri quietly. "How can I clear my name if I don't know why I have been imprisoned here? Who are these knights you call your friends? Do you believe that I have been unjustly imprisoned?"

"I can answer none of those questions," said the lord abruptly. "You will be able to ask the Grey Knights soon, when you are summoned to appear before them. I am giving you the chance to defend yourself not only with your words, but also with your deeds."

He turned to go, but Tiuri took his arm and said, "You do not believe that I have done anything wrong! So I would ask you: give me the chance to escape! You are the master of this castle, so allow me to escape from it."

The lord pulled his arm away. "Ah, I see you're a coward!" he said angrily. "You want to run away! Only a man with a guilty conscience would attempt to flee. Do not ask me that again, or I will regret bringing weapons for you."

"I am no coward," began Tiuri and then he fell silent. There was no way he could explain that he had a very good reason for wanting to escape.

"Silence!" said the lord, looking at the door. "It is nearly time. I must go."

And then he left, without saying another word, and the secret door closed silently behind him. Tiuri inspected the door and tried to open it again, but it proved impossible. Finally, he turned away and looked around the room, which was almost in complete darkness.

"It is nearly time," the lord of Mistrinaut had said.

So it seemed he was about to be called before the mysterious Grey Knights, and the letter would have to remain unread.

What good is it for me to know the message, Tiuri thought, *when they are most likely going to kill me? There are four of them and I am alone.*

But the thought of the weapons gave him courage. He was not entirely alone. Two people had wanted to help him. He would defend himself to the last. He would convince the lord that he was worthy of his help!

Tiuri quickly removed his habit and chose his armour and his weapon. He took the dagger and the chainmail that Lavinia had given him, but the sword from her father. It was the better weapon, sharp and light. Tiuri was soon ready. He pulled on his habit to conceal what was beneath, and then slid the other chainmail and weapons back underneath the table. He took the letter from beneath the rug and hid it under his shirt again. Then he sat down and waited.

He did not have to wait for long. Footsteps soon sounded outside his prison, and then the key turned in the lock and the door swung open. Two of the squires entered, one with a torch in his hand, the other with a spear. Both men had their visors down. Still in silence, they motioned that Tiuri should go with them.

4 SWORDS DRAWN

Flanked by the two squires, Tiuri walked all the way down a seemingly endless number of steps, and through lots of different rooms and corridors. It was very quiet; the castle seemed to be deserted.

Finally they came to a courtyard that Tiuri did not recognize. There was a covered gallery all around it, with torches burning here and there. The four Grey Knights were lined up in the middle of the courtyard, waiting for him. The other two squires stood off to one side, with drums hanging around their necks. As Tiuri entered the courtyard, one of the knights gave a signal and quietly started beating a rhythm.

Everything seemed quite unreal to Tiuri: the hushed castle, the gloom of the courtyard, where a fine drizzle was falling, the silent knights, and the eerie sound of the drums, growing louder and louder.

The squires led Tiuri to a spot just in front of the Grey Knights. Then they stepped back to guard the gate to the courtyard.

Tiuri stood and looked at the four knights. They were wearing full suits of armour, with visors down, shields on their arms, hands on the hilts of their swords.

"You sent for me," said Tiuri. "What do you want from me?"

He had to speak loudly to make himself heard above the drums. The Grey Knights remained silent.

"What do you want from me?" Tiuri repeated.

The Grey Knights said nothing, but the drumming became louder.

"What do you want from me?!" Tiuri shouted for the third time, but the drumming was so loud by then that he could barely hear his own voice.

The Grey Knights stood motionlessly, staring at him. Tiuri felt his courage fading. His will was paralysed. He tried to say something else, but the words died on his lips. His feet seemed to be nailed to the ground. And the din of the drumming droned louder and louder, echoing off the high, dark walls around them.

Then one of the knights drew his sword and raised it above his head. The other three did the same and the first one stepped closer, like some nightmarish spectre. But then Tiuri snapped into action. He stepped backwards, turned and ran, as quickly as he could in his long habit and the chainmail he was wearing beneath it. He ran across the courtyard, with the knights following him, their feet thudding on the wet ground. Tiuri saw one of the squires running to stop him. But he did not intend to escape; he knew that was impossible. As he ran, he untied the rope around his waist and let his habit fall. Then he stopped, turned and drew his sword.

The Grey Knights were close behind him. Three of them also stopped, but the fourth came charging onwards at Tiuri, his weapon ready to strike. But when he struck, the blow was parried! Tiuri had taken him by surprise. He slashed at the knight so viciously that he made him stumble. The knight was soon back on his feet, but he staggered. Tiuri braced himself, sword in one hand, dagger in the other. He was no longer thinking about his fear and felt only a burning desire to fight. The other knights stood there for a moment; they appeared to be hesitating. Then one of the others came closer and attacked Tiuri. Their swords clashed fiercely. Tiuri fought like a man possessed. He was fighting for the letter – and for his life. Not only that, he was furious at the way the knights had treated him. He beat back his opponent, but he saw the next one waiting to take him on and he thought: *They're going to keep on fighting until I'm defeated… dead!*

But the knights seemed to be hesitating again. They were standing close together and looking at one another. Tiuri realized the drumming had stopped.

And then, once again, he shouted, "What do you want from me? Speak! Challenge me if you must, but tell me why!"

For a few moments, it was so silent in the courtyard that he could hear the gentle sound of the rain falling. Then one of the knights whispered something to his fellows.

"Are you truly knights?" called Tiuri. "Or just cowards who conceal yourselves behind closed visors? Tell me who you are!"

One of the knights turned to Tiuri and said, "And who are you?" Tiuri recognized it as the voice of the knight with the silver horn. "Because one thing is certain: you are not Brother Tarmin of the Brown Monastery."

"I do not need to tell you who I am," said Tiuri. "I do not know you. I have done nothing to you and I am nothing to you."

"No, you do not know us," the knight replied.

"We call ourselves the Grey Knights," said another, the knight with the gruff voice. "Grey is the colour of mourning, as you are surely aware. We are the four Grey Knights, the Avengers of the Four Winds. And we are seeking a young man who fled through the forest with a sparkling ring on his finger."

"Why?" Tiuri cried out. "What are your names? You are not Red Riders, are you?"

These words seemed to take the knights by surprise. The one who had spoken last took a step closer, as if he was about to attack again. But the knight with the silver horn held him back and said to Tiuri, "You are right about one thing: we should show you our faces, even if you have never met us before." He opened his visor and the others did the same.

Tiuri could not see their faces very clearly in the darkness of the courtyard, but he was fairly certain that he did not recognize the men. The two knights who had spoken to him were middle-aged, with dark hair and beards. The other two looked younger.

"We are knights-errant," said the knight with the silver horn. "This is Sir Bendu, and my other two companions are Sir Arwaut and Sir Evan, who is from the west. I am Ristridin of the South."

Sir Ristridin of the South!

Tiuri had often heard that name. It was a name of great renown, borne by a famous wandering knight, who travelled the land and fought evil and injustice wherever he found it. And it was the last name he had expected to hear!

"But who are you?" barked Sir Bendu. He was the darkest and gruffest of the four knights.

Tiuri spoke up, loud and proud. "My name is Tiuri, son of Tiuri."

"So it is true," said Sir Bendu. He leant forward and said, "Tiuri, son of Tiuri, why did you run from the chapel on the eve of your knighting?"

His words took Tiuri by surprise. "W-what..." he faltered, but then he regained his composure. And he countered with another question. "What business is that of yours, Sir Bendu?"

"Well, I'll..." growled Sir Bendu.

But Sir Ristridin intervened. "Tiuri," he said calmly. "It is true, is it not, that you ran from the chapel on the eve of the ceremony?"

"Yes," said Tiuri. "That is true."

"Such a thing has never happened before, at least as long as anyone can remember. A knight-to-be running away from his vigil! It is a most serious business. Why did you do such a thing, Tiuri, son of Tiuri? You surely must have had some reason."

"I had a reason," said Tiuri. "Of course I did! But I cannot tell you what it was."

"So can you explain to us why you stole a horse and rode off on it?" asked Sir Bendu. "Can you tell us why you fled into the forest to hide?"

"And, above all, can you tell us why you were wearing that ring?" added Sir Evan, "and why you were riding the horse Ardanwen, which did not belong to you and which has, until now, obeyed only one master?"

The Grey Knights looked at Tiuri and waited for his response.

"Do you know whose ring it was?" asked Sir Ristridin, when no response came. "Do you know who was the black horse's master?"

"Of course I do," said Tiuri. "It was the Black Knight with the White Shield."

"That is right," said Sir Bendu. "The Black Knight with the White Shield!"

The knights fell silent again and looked at one another.

"Why are you asking me all these questions?" Tiuri asked. "Why have you pursued me, aiming to capture me, dead or alive? And what is so special about the ring? It belongs to me..."

"The ring belongs to you?!" exclaimed Sir Evan. "How, in heaven's name, did you come to have it?"

"It... it was given to me," replied Tiuri.

"Given to you?" came the incredulous response.

Tiuri hesitated for a moment and then continued. He knew he couldn't tell them too much. But so far the conversation had taken a most unexpected course. "The Black Knight gave it to me," he said.

This time it was Sir Ristridin who came closer and leant over him. "He gave it to you?" he repeated. "But what happened to him?"

"He was murdered," said Tiuri.

"Indeed! Murdered!" said Sir Bendu. "Not defeated, not fallen, but murdered!" Then he checked himself and fell silent.

"Tiuri, son of Tiuri," said Sir Ristridin, "you were about to become a knight, like your renowned father, but you ran away and forsook your duty. You say you cannot tell us the reason. But can you tell us how the Black Knight with the White Shield met his end?"

"He was lured into an ambush," replied Tiuri. Then something occurred to him. A thought lit up his mind like a flash of lightning.

"You knew him!" he cried. "He was a friend of yours!"

"Continue," said Sir Ristridin.

Tiuri paused to absorb his insight. He was sure he had guessed correctly.

"The Black Knight with the Red Shield challenged him," he continued, "but it was a trap. His men, the Red Riders, attacked your friend in large numbers, and that is how he died. He was never defeated in a duel."

The knights said nothing, but Tiuri could feel that their attitude towards him was changing. And he went on, more quietly. "He asked me to remove his mask because he said a knight must always face Death with an open visor."

The silence weighed heavily.

"So you were there," Sir Evan said finally.

"Yes," said Tiuri. "But I arrived too late."

"You say the Red Riders murdered him?" said Sir Bendu. "But what about the ring?"

"He gave it to me," said Tiuri.

"Why?"

Tiuri did not respond. "He gave it to me," he repeated, "and now I would like it back." And when the Grey Knights did not move, he continued, "I would also like to know why you have asked me all these questions, and why you have treated me this way."

"Yes, you owe him an answer," said a voice, and the lord of the castle stepped from the shadows.

"You are the one who gave him the weapons!" exclaimed Sir Ristridin.

"Of course," answered the lord of Mistrinaut calmly. "And it is just as well I did! How would you feel now, Sir Ristridin, if, in your blind lust for revenge, you and your fellow knights had defeated this boy, without even listening to him? How would you have felt, Sir Ristridin of the South, champion of peace and justice, if you had committed such an act, dishonouring your chivalry and staining your reputation? How would you all have felt, you, Sir Bendu, and Sir Arwaut, and Sir Evan? Of course I gave him weapons and I stood ready to intervene. I have doubted your suspicions from the start."

"So you believe him," said Sir Bendu, nodding at Tiuri.

"And you do not, Sir Bendu?" came the lord's response.

"It would make sense for us to believe him," said Sir Bendu. "He is young and brave and he has an honest face. He also bears a name of renown. He is the son of Tiuri the Valiant. But most of us know that such things are not always to be trusted."

"Well, it was either him... or the Knight with the Red Shield," said Sir Evan. "And the latter seems more likely."

Tiuri looked with increasing astonishment from one knight to the other.

"I believe him," said Sir Ristridin, loud and clear.

But Tiuri was growing impatient. "Sir knights," he said, "you still have not answered my question."

The Grey Knights said nothing. Ristridin cleared his throat.

"Speak, Ristridin," said the lord. "You owe this to him! You are unhappy about the situation, and you no longer believe in his guilt, but still: you believed he was guilty and you acted accordingly. So, speak your accusation! Let him hear it!" He walked up to one of the squires and took the torch from his hand. Then he let the light fall on Tiuri's face.

Sir Ristridin hesitated for just a moment before speaking. "Tiuri," he said, "this is why we were looking for you: we believed it was you who had murdered the Black Knight with the White Shield, stolen the ring, and fled on his horse. But, as heaven is my witness, I now believe this accusation to be false."

5 A Web of Suspicion

So that was it! Tiuri recoiled as though he had been slapped in the face. Sir Ristridin's final words were not enough to soften the vile accusation. He, Tiuri, the murderer of the Black Knight with the White Shield! Actually, it was more ridiculous than vile. And that was the first word Tiuri said as soon as he found his voice again.

"Ridiculous!" he whispered.

Now he had some understanding of the Grey Knights' actions, but he still didn't see how they could have made such an accusation.

"Well, then," said the lord of Mistrinaut. "I think it's about time we went inside. There's no need for us to become even more soaked." He walked up to Tiuri, placed his hand on his shoulder, and led him into the castle.

Tiuri meekly allowed himself to be guided. The Grey Knights and their squires followed them inside. The castle was not entirely deserted; now and then, Tiuri caught a glimpse of a curious face peeping around a corner. Before long, they were back in the room where he had met the Grey Knights for the first time. The table was laid and candles lit up the room.

The lord guided Tiuri to a chair and filled a cup, which he put down in front of him. "Here," he said in a tone that was brisk, but not unfriendly. "Drink this."

But Tiuri looked at the four Grey Knights, who sat down at the table with him, one by one, and he pushed the cup aside. The knights had taken off their helmets and opened their gorgets. Finally he could see them properly. The lord also filled their cups and said, "I suspected my guests might enjoy something to eat after all that has happened. Call it a meal of reconciliation."

The Grey Knights did not touch their cups. They all looked at Tiuri as though they were waiting for him to speak.

Tiuri responded by looking at each of them in turn. He saw Ristridin, sitting opposite him; tall and lean, with a weathered, angular face. His curly black hair was already rather grey, but his blue eyes were young and bright. Beside him sat Bendu, large and strong, with dark hair and eyes and thick, menacing eyebrows. Sir Arwaut, beside Sir Bendu, resembled him; he was also sturdy and dark-haired, but he was young, less than twenty-five years old, and his eyes were lighter and friendlier. Sir Evan, who was sitting on the other side of Ristridin, was also young, with pale skin and eyes and very blond hair.

When Tiuri began to speak, he directed most of his words at Ristridin, who seemed to be their leader. "A meal of reconciliation," he repeated. "You have treated me like a criminal! How did you come to make this accusation? And do you all now believe that it is false?"

Sir Ristridin nodded and Arwaut and Evan spoke as one: "Yes."

But Bendu said, "What I *believe* does not matter. I want to *know*, not merely believe. You may very well be innocent, Tiuri, son of Tiuri, but treachery and deceit are often concealed behind an innocent face. And before I follow my friends and say yes, I would like to know who it was that murdered the Knight with the White Shield. You say it was the Red Riders, on the orders of the Black Knight with the Red Shield. But how do you know that?"

"He told me so himself," answered Tiuri.

"Who did?"

"The Black Knight with the White Shield."

"So you spoke to him?"

"I found him in the forest and I was with him when he died."

"And how did that happen?"

Tiuri rose to his feet. He stood before the table and glared at Bendu, his expression both proud and a little angry. "Sir Bendu," he said, "I ran away from the chapel where I was to spend my vigil on the eve of the ceremony that would make me a knight. I took a horse that did not belong to me and I rode away on it. I found the Knight with the White Shield and I was with him when he died. He told me who had murdered him and he gave me his ring. Soon after that, I encountered the Red Riders and they tried to murder me too, but I escaped. Then I rode through the forest to the west on the horse that had belonged to the Knight with the White Shield. That is all I can tell you. But I swear to you that my conscience is clear. Had I been knighted, I would swear it on my honour as a knight. Your accusation is as false as it is ridiculous!"

Bendu looked at him with a frown. "I see," he growled. "So now we know. You may sit down."

But Tiuri remained standing, even though he could feel his legs shaking. "I will not sit down," he said, "until every one of you believes me! I am sorry I cannot give you a better explanation, but that is not possible."

"We believe you," said Sir Ristridin.

"Yes," muttered Bendu. "We believe you."

Tiuri was about to sit down, but then he remembered something. "In that case, give me back the ring," he said. "The ring that belonged to the Knight with the White Shield."

Sir Ristridin slowly took the ring from a pouch on his belt. "Here you are," he said. "Please take it."

Tiuri took the ring and clasped it in his hand. Then he sank back into his chair. A dreadful weariness washed over him. The fear and the tension of the past day had been too much for him. He picked up his cup in his shaking hand and took a large gulp. It was wine, which burned in his throat and then warmed his stomach. He looked again at the knights, who were all watching him and seemed rather ill at ease.

"We know the Red Riders were enemies of the Knight with the White Shield," said Sir Ristridin, "as was their master, the

Knight with the Red Shield. We also know about the challenge. But we had heard that the duel had a very different outcome."

"There never was any duel," said Tiuri.

"You need to know what we were told," said Ristridin.

"I went looking for him, for the Knight with the Red Shield," said Bendu. "The Knight with the White Shield had been found murdered and we knew who his enemy was. And I found the Knight with the Red Shield in the Royal Forest, to the south of the hunting lodge, together with half a dozen of his Red Riders. I asked him to lift his visor and to tell me what he had done to his opponent, the Knight with the White Shield. He removed his helmet, but he was wearing a black mask."

"Another mask," murmured Tiuri.

"He was wearing a black mask," Bendu continued. "And he said, 'I am sorry, sir knight, but I cannot remove my mask. As for the Knight with the White Shield, I challenged him to a duel. There's no law against that! But I have to confess that he defeated me. I fell flat on my face! And for the second time. But when I meet him a third time, I shall defeat him!' And then I said, 'But the Knight with the White Shield is dead!' He looked at me, but the mask hid his expression. 'Dead?' he replied. 'I cannot say that the news saddens me. You know he was my enemy.' And so I said, 'He was murdered! And I would like to know where your Red Riders were last night and what they know about this.' But he became angry. 'They are here!' he shouted. 'And they have been by my side constantly.' So I said I believed he had other men in his company, but then he yelled, 'Do you dare to suggest that I or my men had a hand in this murder? Do you dare to say that I would dishonour my knighthood? The Knight with the White Shield was my enemy and I would have killed him if I could, but in an honest fight!' And his Red Riders closed ranks and stood around him with threatening expressions. But I said, 'A brave knight has been slain and everyone, friend or foe, must grieve for the way it happened. As for you, sir knight with the mask, I cannot judge you, because I do not know you. But I do not like that you have brought your feud to the Kingdom of Dagonaut! Return to the land of Eviellan, whence you came, and fight on your own soil or in the Kingdom of Unauwen!' He laughed and said, 'Should the same not apply to the Knight with the White Shield? He too was a stranger in your land and had no business here. I shall depart now. But one last thing: my Red Riders should not be your only suspects! A man like the Knight with the White Shield has many enemies. He knew too much about many things. Danger lurked wherever he went, even in the most innocent of forms. I was far from the only man who wished him dead! And finally, remember this: he was my enemy, but I respected and admired him, and you may write that on his gravestone.'"

Bendu paused before concluding, "And the Knight with the Red Shield rode away with his men and I could not stop him, as I had no one with me but Sir Arwaut and my squire. But I was not pleased! I did not know who he was, but I distrusted him, although I did not believe at the time that he had killed his enemy in such a treacherous way."

"I met another group of Red Riders," said Ristridin, "and they, too, strongly denied knowing anything about the murder. But then one of them came after me and confided that he had more to say. This, in short, is his story: their master, the Knight with the Red Shield, lost the duel and left, but he told a number of the Red Riders to keep an eye on his enemy. It was those men who found the Knight with the White Shield murdered. However, they were afraid that they would be accused, so they fled. The Red Rider also informed me of a young traveller who had been spying on the Knight with the White Shield for a while; apparently, for some reason this fellow wanted the ring that the knight wore. The young man had been in the area on that fateful night, and they had all seen him and even tried to apprehend him, but he had fled. Then, at the Yikarvara Inn, we heard about a young man who had stolen a horse, who had been acting strangely and who was indeed wearing the ring on his finger. He had fled and had most likely taken the horse Ardanwen with him."

"Then later, in the city, there was talk of a young man who had run away from the chapel," said Sir Bendu. "People thought it a most peculiar affair, but his friends and his father, and even the king, did not believe he was capable of any wrongdoing. For my part, I still believe it was outrageous behaviour and broke every rule. I was sure this son of Tiuri could easily be the same individual as the horse thief who had made off with the ring."

"Whereas I found it hard to believe," said Ristridin. "The son of Tiuri had been found worthy of being a knight, which was at odds with these stories about a thief and a murderer."

"But we agreed that the young man who was on the run, whoever he was, must be the murderer," said Bendu.

"Our story would be too long if we told you our other reasons," said Ristridin. "The real murderers and their accomplices have cunningly spun a web of suspicion around you."

Tiuri had listened closely to their words. The Red Riders and their master had indeed been cunning! They had ensured that others were also pursuing him, while shifting suspicion from themselves. They were probably still lying in ambush for him. He had seen some of them riding to the west, and maybe they were waiting for him somewhere along the way.

"And now you know why we suspected you," said Ristridin. "I hope you do not intend to remain angry with us. You are still young and you have not seen the things we have seen. As Bendu says, treachery can lurk behind the most innocent of faces."

"No," said Tiuri quietly. "I am not angry." He didn't even know if that was true; his feelings were so confused. He stared at the ring that had belonged to the Knight with the White Shield and slid it onto his finger.

"So, let us eat and drink," said the lord.

Tiuri emptied his cup of wine, but he couldn't swallow a morsel of food. He was thinking about everything Ristridin and Bendu had told him and he realized there were still many things he didn't know. Who was the Black Knight with the White Shield? The Grey Knights had known him. They wanted to avenge his death. He would have liked to ask them, but he didn't dare. His ignorance might surprise the knights and arouse their suspicions once again. They didn't seem to know anything about the letter and he couldn't say anything that might alert them to his mission. So he remained silent and leant back in his chair. He really was very tired.

The lord of Mistrinaut stood up and walked over to him. "Young man," he said, "perhaps it would be wise for you to withdraw to your sleeping quarters. Tomorrow, after a good night's rest, there will be more time for talking and for questions. Come with me."

As if in a dream, Tiuri stood up and followed him. The knights also got up and wished him goodnight. The lord led him to another part of the castle and up many stairs.

"I have made you do a lot of climbing," said the lord as he opened a door for Tiuri, "but this is my son's room. I thought you might like it. He is not at home now, but serving as a squire with one of Dagonaut's knights. How old are you, Tiuri?"

"Sixteen," he replied.

"My son is only fourteen, but I hope he will grow up to be as brave as you. Sleep well, young man!"

And, with those words, he left Tiuri.

The room was cosy and welcoming. The bed, with its clean white sheets, had been turned down. Two candles illuminated the room; one on the table beside the bed and one on the washstand, where two jugs of water stood waiting beside the basin, one hot and one cold. As Tiuri was exploring the room, there was a knock at the door and a woman came in.

"I have come to see if everything is to your liking," she said. "This is our son Sigirdiwarth's room."

Tiuri bowed and thanked her. As she smiled, he realized how much Lavinia resembled her mother. Then she kindly wished him goodnight and left the room.

Tiuri removed his clothes and had a wash. He had been in bed for less than a minute when he fell into a deep, deep sleep.

6 SECRETS AND REVELATIONS

When Tiuri awoke, it took him a moment to remember where he was. Slowly, everything that had happened the previous day came back to him. He lay there for a while, enjoying the cosy bed and the pleasant room, before getting up and putting on his faded habit. He left the chainmail on a chair, even though he would have gladly kept it, along with the weapons. When he was dressed, he looked up at the only window in the room. It was high in the wall, but there was a bench beneath it, so he climbed up and looked out. What he saw through the window made him sigh with admiration. He was in one of the outer towers of Mistrinaut, which had a magnificent view over the countryside to the west.

The weather was beautiful now, with sunlight gleaming on the wet fields and meadows. The Blue River looked truly blue, a sparkling azure, with the First Great Road running alongside it like a brown ribbon, all the way to the mountains. He could see the mountains, grey, blue and purple, with their snowy tops sharply silhouetted against the bright sky. That was where he would be heading soon!

He gazed out at the view for a while and then he heard a knock at the door.

He turned and called, "Come in!"

It was Sir Ristridin. He stood in the doorway and seemed to be hesitating. He was wearing his grey chainmail and cloak, but his head was bare.

"Good morning," he said. "I see you're up and dressed."

"Good morning, Sir Ristridin," said Tiuri. He was not quite sure how to respond to this man, who had treated him so harshly before, but was now smiling warmly at him.

Ristridin walked over and, when he looked up at Tiuri, his expression had become serious. He was very tall, but Tiuri, standing on the bench, was slightly higher than him.

"Tiuri," he said, "I have come to tell you something – or rather, to ask you something. Now, seeing you again, my mistake seems even more foolish. I would ask your forgiveness for the way I have treated you. I was furious and blinded by my desire for revenge, but that is no excuse. Please forgive me!"

"Oh, of course!" said Tiuri immediately, jumping down. His face flushed. He felt almost embarrassed that this famous knight, who was so many years older than him, was speaking to him in this way.

Sir Ristridin held out his hand and Tiuri shook it firmly. It was strange perhaps, but he felt that he liked the leader of the Grey Knights. He actually found it hard to see him as one of the band of men who had been pursuing him. Neither of them spoke for a moment. Then Ristridin asked if Tiuri was ready for breakfast.

"Definitely," said Tiuri, who suddenly felt very hungry. "What time is it?"

"About half past seven," replied Ristridin. "My friends and I have already eaten. Bendu and Arwaut have ridden out, hoping to find some sign of the Red Riders."

"Really? Have they been spotted?" asked Tiuri.

"We have heard from various residents of the castle that a number of men in red rode past a few days ago, heading west. They could still be nearby. Or there may at least be other people who have seen them."

"I saw two of them myself," said Tiuri. "About a week ago. They were also riding down the Great Road to the west." He thought it quite likely that a few of their number might still be in the area. They had good reason to want to capture him...

Sir Ristridin uttered Tiuri's own thoughts when he said, "After all their efforts to bring about your downfall, they are sure to want to know if they have succeeded."

"I agree," said Tiuri.

Ristridin's hand was already on the door handle, but he paused and asked, "What are you going to do now, Tiuri?"

"Now? I'm going to have breakfast," the young man replied.

But the knight's expression remained serious. "And then?" he asked.

"Then I will continue my journey... I... I have to travel onwards."

"Where to?"

"Along the Blue River."

Sir Ristridin came a little closer. "You have a secret," he said quietly.

"Yes, sir knight," said Tiuri.

"I shall not ask what it is," continued Ristridin, "but I suspect that the Knight with the White Shield charged you with a task. You do not have to tell me anything. I am only speaking my thoughts aloud. You are on your way to the west, and your destination lies over the mountains, perhaps even in the Kingdom of Unauwen. And the Red Riders do not want you to succeed, just as they did not want Sir Edwinem to succeed."

Sir Edwinem! So that was the name of the Black Knight with the White Shield!

Ristridin did not wait for an answer, but opened the door. "Come," he said, "let us go to the great hall."

They walked in silence. Now and then, Tiuri glanced at Ristridin. The knight had guessed much of his secret. But perhaps he knew more than Tiuri; he had known the Knight with the White Shield – Sir Edwinem. Tiuri was burning to ask questions, but he did not have the opportunity, as the lord of Mistrinaut and Sir Evan came towards them. The two men wished them both good morning and the lord asked if he had slept well.

"You are still wearing your habit," he said. "I have clothes that will fit you better."

"Thank you," said Tiuri. "But perhaps this clothing will attract least attention."

"So you need a disguise?" asked the lord. "Do not forget that everyone in this castle is already aware that you are not a monk. In any event, you can wear chainmail beneath it. Or do you think that will be unnecessary?"

"Oh, that would be most helpful," said Tiuri.

"So you are planning to leave us and travel onwards?" continued the lord. "When?"

"As soon as possible," replied Tiuri. "Right away."

"Don't be too hasty," said the lord. "At least wait until Sir Bendu and his nephew have returned. Perhaps they will have some news that could be of benefit to you."

"Do you fear the Red Riders?" asked Sir Evan.

"Yes, sir knight," said Tiuri. "With good reason."

"I have no doubt of that," said the young knight. "They may of course have travelled on to the west, through the pass and over the mountains, but I think not. They will certainly not be welcome in the land of my king."

"Are you... Do you hail from the Kingdom of Unauwen?" asked Tiuri, surprised.

"Yes, I am a knight of King Unauwen."

"Did you know the Knight with... Sir Edwinem well?"

"I served under him," answered Evan, "before I was a knight. I was in his retinue when he was sent out to secure the Forest of Vorgóta. Sir Ristridin was also with us."

"The Forest of Vorgóta?" repeated Tiuri. He had never heard that name before. "I know little of King Unauwen's land," he added.

"The same is true of many of your compatriots," said Evan. "It is a pity. Maybe this will change, now that more people from our land are travelling to the Kingdom of Dagonaut. I was sent by King Unauwen to bring a message of friendship to your king." He turned to Ristridin and the lord of Mistrinaut. "You are among the few people in this land who know us better," he said. "You are our friends and you fear the same enemy."

"Which enemy?" asked Tiuri. "Not... Eviellan?"

The land of Eviellan lay to the south and bordered on the Kingdoms of both Dagonaut and Unauwen. In the past, attacks had often been led from Eviellan into Dagonaut's land, but since one of Unauwen's sons had reigned there, there had been fewer raids. Tiuri had heard there was conflict between Eviellan and the Kingdom of Unauwen, but he had always thought this strange, because Unauwen's son had caused Eviellan to prosper. Generally, discord between Eviellan and the kingdom to the west was regarded as something that did not concern the inhabitants of Dagonaut's land.

"Yes, the land of Eviellan," said Sir Evan.

"The Black Knight with the Red Shield comes from Eviellan," said Ristridin. "All the knights of the King of Eviellan carry red or black shields. The King of Eviellan is the younger son of King Unauwen and also his greatest enemy. At least, that was always the case."

"There were rumours that he was going to make peace with his father," said Sir Evan, "to the joy of many people, including myself. But now I'm no longer sure if I should believe it."

Tiuri listened with great interest. He had little or no knowledge of these matters. Might the letter be connected to the feud between the Kingdom of Unauwen and Eviellan? The Knight with the White Shield had been one of Unauwen's knights, but Tiuri still knew nothing about him other than his name. The Grey Knights could surely tell him more about the knight. If only they would!

"What will you do now?" he asked Ristridin and Evan. "Are you going to look for the Red Riders?"

"Yes," replied Ristridin. "And the Knight with the Red Shield. We shall not rest until we have found them."

By then, they had reached the great hall.

"Go and eat, Tiuri," said the lord. "You may travel onwards whenever you wish, but please wait until I have found better clothes for you. And you may keep the weapons I gave you... unless you prefer the ones from my daughter."

Tiuri thanked him warmly. Then he said, "The black horse is here – Ardanwen, the steed of the Knight with the White Shield. I should like to ride him again."

"Robbers stole the horse from you, didn't they?" said Ristridin. "We took it back from them."

"I know," replied Tiuri. "I was hiding in a cave and I saw and heard everything."

"Oh, really?" exclaimed Ristridin.

"Is there anything else you need?" asked the lord.

"No, thank you," said Tiuri. "Oh, actually, yes. A length of cord. I'd like to hang the ring around my neck again. It seems wiser than wearing it on my finger."

"That sounds like a fine plan," said Ristridin. "Why did the robbers not take the ring from you?"

"They wanted to," said Tiuri, "but..." He paused. He wasn't keen to talk about his encounter with the robbers.

The knights and the lord waited for him to continue. "And?" asked Ristridin.

"They let me keep it," was all that Tiuri said.

The others asked no more questions.

"This is a precious ring," said Evan. "Only a chosen few of our knights wear such a ring. King Unauwen gives them to his most faithful paladins. Some say there are only twelve of these rings in existence. Others claim there are only seven."

Tiuri looked at the ring with even more admiration than before. So that was another reason not to wear it on his finger. After all, he had been given the ring only so that he could show it to the hermit Menaures as proof of who had sent him. He would have to return it to King Unauwen later.

Tiuri walked alone into the great hall. The others had already eaten and they all had things to do. The hall was not very busy. It seemed that people ate at whatever time suited them.

Lavinia was sitting at the high table, on her own. Tiuri greeted her with a bow and a smile. He sat at one of the other tables, but a servant came over with a message from Lady Lavinia asking him to join her. Tiuri got up and walked to the high table. He could feel the servant watching him. He was surely amazed – along with the other residents of the castle – that someone who had been a prisoner one day could be an honoured guest the next.

"Eat with me," said Lavinia. "It's terribly impolite of you to leave me sitting here alone. And it's such a strange day. Everyone is so restless... as if all manner of things were about to happen. How are you feeling now?"

"Very well, thank you," said Tiuri, as he sat down. "And how are you, Lady Lavinia? I should like to thank you once again for what you did for me yesterday."

"Oh, it was nothing!" said Lavinia. "I am just happy to have you sitting here beside me now, safe and sound. Even though I understand very little about the matter. And Father gives me answers of one syllable... or no answers at all. So tell me... Who are you, what are you doing, where did you come from, where are you going, and why did they take you prisoner?"

Tiuri laughed. "What a lot of questions all at once!" he said. "And," he added in a more serious tone, "I'm afraid I can't give you many answers."

"Oh, Father already told me not to ask you anything! But I do know one thing. Your name! It's Tiuri, isn't it? Is Tiuri the Valiant truly your father?"

"Yes, milady," answered Tiuri, feeling rather proud. "Do you know him?"

"No, but I have heard of him. He is one of the knights the minstrels sing about. There's Tiuri the Valiant, and Sir Edwinem, and Ristridin of the South..."

"Sir Edwinem," said Tiuri. "Did you know him?"

"No, I didn't know him either. The only famous knight I know is Sir Ristridin – I used to ride on his back when I was a little girl, and now he's suddenly refusing to tell me what's going on. I was so surprised when I heard that he was one of the Grey Knights! He seemed so angry and sombre. I'd never seen him like that before. But you were asking about Sir Edwinem. Did you ever meet him?"

"Only once," said Tiuri.

"My father knew him, when he was in the Kingdom of Unauwen. We once had a minstrel here who sang a beautiful song about him. It started like this." And Lavinia sang softly:

Sir Edwinem the brave rode out
from Forèstèrra in the west.
Of all the knights of Unauwen,
he surely was the best.

His heart though stayed in Forèstèrra,
by the forest, by the shore.
Edwinem rode like the wind,
so that evil would be no more.

He rode south with the north wind,
up mountains topped with snow.
And as he passed, the bells rang out,
to let the people know.

Here comes the lord of Forèstèrra,
by the forest, by the shore.
Now he has come to fight for us,
and evil will be no more.

Greetings to you, oh Edwinem,
with your shield so white.
Your name shines like the rainbow.
You fight for what is right.

You have left your home in Forèstèrra,
by the forest, by the shore,
and ridden out to fight for us.
Now evil is no more!

Lavinia stopped. "I can't remember how it went after that," she said. "It was very long, full of brave deeds, a story from the Kingdom of Unauwen. I have also heard Sir Ristridin talk about Sir Edwinem... Why exactly was Sir Ristridin so angry with you?" She paused and then said with a smile, "I am asking too many questions again. I can tell from your face. Father says I'm too curious and that I talk too much. But," she said in a whisper, "I also know when to be silent. Secrets are safe with me."

"Do you think I have a secret?" asked Tiuri.

"Of course," answered Lavinia. "Tell me. What is it? You really can trust me."

"I believe you, milady," said Tiuri. "But my secret is not mine alone, and I cannot tell it to you. It would be better if no one even knew I had a secret."

Lavinia looked disappointed. But then she smiled and said, "I can take a hint. Never fear, I promise that I shall not speak about the mysterious pilgrim who was our guest. Will that do?"

"Thank you, Lavinia," said Tiuri.

Then they spoke about other things, but not for long, because Lavinia's father arrived and asked Tiuri to accompany him. Tiuri took his leave of Lady Lavinia and followed his host to the room with the low ceiling, where the Grey Knights were waiting for him.

"Sir Bendu and Sir Arwaut have just returned," said the lord. "They did not find the Red Riders, but they did find their trail."

"Yes," said Bendu, "they were certainly nearby. Several people saw them. But they are no longer in this area, or they are hiding very well."

"We believe they have travelled onwards to the west," added Arwaut.

"So we too shall head westwards," said Bendu.

"Along the Blue River."

"That is our plan," said Sir Ristridin to Tiuri. "And as you also have to travel in that direction, would you like to ride with our company, at least for some of the way?"

"The company will make quick progress," said the lord. "You shall ride the horse Ardanwen, of course, and I will provide equipment for you."

Tiuri thought for a moment. The idea was an appealing one. He would be able to travel quickly and safely and he might also find out more about the Black Knight with the White Shield, Edwinem, the lord of Forèstèrra. "Yes, knights, I would like to journey some of the way with you," he said.

"And I suppose we are not allowed to ask how far you will travel with us, and what your destination is," said Bendu.

But Ristridin said, "You may travel with us for as long as you please. We do not know how far we will go. We are to follow the First Great Road and the trail of the Red Riders. Your destination may lie beyond that."

"And why would that be?" asked Bendu, looking at Ristridin, then Tiuri.

"I intend to follow the Blue River," said Tiuri. He paused briefly and added, "To its source."

"To Menaures?" asked the lord.

"Yes," replied Tiuri. "To Menaures."

"The hermit Menaures," said the lord. "So that's where your road is taking you! Then it is a good road," he continued, looking at Bendu, the only one of the Grey Knights who still seemed not to trust Tiuri entirely. "Give him my regards," he said to Tiuri. "I have not seen him for a long time, and that is wrong of me, as I have much to thank him for. It is about time I visited the mountains again. Please do give him my greetings!"

"I shall do so," Tiuri promised.

"Then we shall make ourselves ready," said Ristridin. "We wish to leave as soon as possible."

"As do I," said Tiuri. "As do I."

PART FOUR

ALONG THE BLUE RIVER

1   BACK ON THE ROAD

Half an hour later, a large company rode over the drawbridge. The group was made up of Tiuri, the four Grey Knights, their squires and three of Mistrinaut's men-at-arms. Tiuri rode on the black horse Ardanwen and he wore the same chainmail and blue tunic as the men from Castle Mistrinaut. He still had his monk's habit with him, though, rolled up in his saddlebag. He had said a fond farewell to the lord of the castle and his wife, and to Lavinia. Riding alongside Sir Ristridin, he set out on the next part of his journey.

The guards stared in astonishment as the group passed by. Perhaps they even forgot their game of chess for a moment as they wondered how someone could be first a monk and then a prisoner, before becoming a person of importance, riding away on a fine horse, in the company of the mysterious Grey Knights.

The First Great Road followed the course of the Blue River, sometimes meandering, but always leading westwards. Tiuri looked back once again at the castle. It still seemed forbidding, but he knew now that the people who lived there were his friends. He could see someone standing at the top of one of the towers, waving. Could it be Lavinia? He waved back and then turned to Ristridin.

"Sir Ristridin," he said, "This is rather strange, but I still do not know the name of my host. What is the lord of Mistrinaut called?"

"His name is an unusual one," Ristridin replied. "He is called Sigirdiwarth Rafox of Azular Northa. Long ago, he was the knight of a king in the north. War and civil strife forced him to flee his homeland. After long wanderings, he found himself here. At that time – almost twenty years ago now – a wicked lord ruled Castle Mistrinaut, and he was the terror of these parts. Sigirdiwarth Rafox took up the fight against him and defeated him, liberating the region from a great evil. King Dagonaut was most grateful to him and he granted the castle and its lands to him in fief and gave him leave to call himself lord of Mistrinaut. Rafox has been living here for a long time now and he has become one of our own."

"He knew the Knight with the White Shield, didn't he? Sir Edwinem?" asked Tiuri.

"Yes, he met him long ago in the Kingdom of Unauwen."

Tiuri hesitated before asking his next question, "Sir Ristridin, could you tell me more about the Black Knight with the White Shield?"

"What do you want to know?" asked Ristridin.

Tiuri rode closer to him. "Everything," he said quietly.

"Well, that is more than I can tell," said Ristridin with a smile.

"I know hardly anything about him," said Tiuri. "Little more than his name, and I heard that for the first time from you."

The knight gave him a searching look, but showed no surprise. "He had many names," he replied. "Sir Edwinem, lord of Forèstèrra by the Sea, the Invincible, Paladin of King Unauwen. He performed many great deeds, always battling against evil. He was a good and noble man. It is rare indeed to meet a man like him."

"Did you know him well?" asked Tiuri.

"He was my friend," Ristridin replied. He fell silent for a time and then said, "Look, Sir Bendu is indicating that we should go faster. We shall ride at some speed for a while. Later, when we stop to rest or are going more slowly, I'll tell you how I met Sir Edwinem, and how we fought side by side, even though he was a knight of Unauwen and I a knight of King Dagonaut."

The riders urged on their horses and raced along. People at the roadside watched in surprise as they went by; they were probably wondering where they were riding so quickly, those four Grey Knights and their grey squires and the four men in blue from Castle Mistrinaut. Tiuri's horse was the fastest of all. He sometimes had to rein it in or it would have flown past the others. They rode on quickly, not stopping for rest until the sun was high overhead. Then they stopped, rubbed down their horses and allowed them to graze. The men sat down by the side of the road to eat their own lunch. However, Bendu and Ristridin did not rest with the others. They walked away from the group and stood on the riverbank for some time, talking quietly. Then they returned to the company and Ristridin sat down beside Tiuri.

"It is strange how little most people here know about the Kingdom of Unauwen," he said, "even though that country borders on our own. Perhaps it is because the Great Mountains are so high and forbidding. I am a knight-errant and so have travelled a great deal. And yet I have been to the Kingdom of Unauwen only once, even though my ancestral castle is not far from that land."

"You are from the south," said Tiuri.

"Yes, as you can tell from my name. I come from Castle Ristridin, on the Grey River, close to the border."

"Castle Ristridin," repeated Tiuri. "How is it that you are a knight-errant when you own a castle and estates?"

"I chose instead to wander," Ristridin replied. "And so I renounced my possessions. My brother, Arturin, is now lord of those lands in my stead. I have travelled the realm for many years, and I shall continue to travel, even though I am no longer a young man. That is what I am best suited for. But I was going to tell you how I met Sir Edwinem. Of course you have heard of the land of Eviellan. It lies to the south, on the other side of the Grey River. It is an inhospitable land, with wild forests and barren plains. There are many stone castles throughout the land, inhabited by lords who would constantly do battle with one another or go on raids across the border. We often had to fight them back.

"Seven years ago, the younger son of King Unauwen went to Eviellan, conquered the country, and declared himself king. Since then he has ruled with an iron fist, putting an end to feuds and pillaging.

"However, there has still been much fighting because of a rift between Eviellan and the Kingdom of Unauwen. Soldiers passed along our Third Great Road from both directions, Eviellan and Unauwen. They often came to blows, destroying our property and setting fire to our villages. And, of course, we inhabitants of the Kingdom of Dagonaut could not accept such behaviour. Knights rode out to make it clear to these disturbers of the peace that they must resolve their feuds on their own soil.

"And that is how I and a handful of stalwart men came to be pursuing a troop of warriors from Eviellan along the Third Great Road into the Kingdom of Unauwen. There they fled into the Forest of Vorgóta. I went after them, but I lost their trail. For a long time, I wandered through that forest with my men, until we encountered an enemy troop, which attacked us. We defended ourselves as well as we could, but we knew we were lost, as we were few against many, and we were in unfamiliar territory.

"But lo and behold, a knight came riding up, followed by many men on white horses. He was on a black horse himself and his chainmail was silvery white. The shield on his arm was also white. And he raised his flashing sword and let his battle cry ring throughout the forest. That is how Edwinem, the lord of Forèstèrra, came to our aid."

"And did he win?" asked Tiuri.

"There is a reason why his nickname was the Invincible," said Ristridin.

"You said his armour was white," said Tiuri. "So he did not wear a black suit of armour at that time?"

"The knights of King Unauwen wear every colour, but they never wore black... until recently, when Sir Edwinem donned his black armour," replied Ristridin. "The white shield is the sign of all of the knights of Unauwen. The heraldic colours of the kingdom are white and the many-coloured rainbow. Sir Edwinem had been sent by Unauwen to drive bands of wicked men from the Forest of Vorgóta. Those men came from Eviellan."

"Why is Eviellan the enemy of Unauwen?" asked Tiuri. "The King of Eviellan is the son of the King of Unauwen, is he not?"

"That is a long story," said Ristridin. "Perhaps Evan had better tell you that tale. The Kingdom of Unauwen is his homeland, as you know. Evan served as one of Edwinem's companions before he became a knight."

"Was he Sir Edwinem's squire?" asked Tiuri.

"No. There are many young men who would have liked to be Edwinem's squire but, strangely enough, the man who served him as squire was an old fellow, who was lean and weather-beaten."

Tiuri thought back to the stranger who had called him out of the chapel. The man must, of course, have been Sir Edwinem's squire. And he asked, "What was his name?"

"The squire? His name was Vokia," answered Ristridin. Then he stood up and said it was time to move on.

"It is strange to see you on that horse," he said, when Tiuri had climbed up onto Ardanwen. "Edwinem never rode another. The horse is worthy of its name: Ardanwen means Night Wind in the old tongue of the Kingdom of Unauwen. I have seldom met a faster horse."

Soon they were back on the road. Ristridin and his squire led the way, while Tiuri rode beside one of the men from Mistrinaut. Sometimes they stopped at a village or a house to ask if anyone had seen the Red Riders. But they found no leads.

"Not a single sighting," said Bendu. "And that wretched rain we had yesterday has wiped out any traces."

Ristridin looked at the opposite bank of the river. "They may have ridden along the other side of the river," he commented.

"That is true," said Bendu. "We will cross as soon as possible and see if we can discover anything over there."

Later that afternoon, they came to a ford. Ristridin and Bendu crossed the river, while the rest of the company waited for them. They returned after half an hour. They had found no traces, but a shepherd had told them that he had seen riders go by two nights ago, heading westwards. However, he had not been able to see if they were dressed in red.

"He says it was no more than a dozen," said Bendu. "There's a forest nearby, where they could be hiding."

They continued their journey. When they slowed for a while to rest the horses, Ristridin came to ride with Tiuri again and told him the tale of how he and Sir Edwinem had secured the Forest of Vorgóta and routed the bands of wicked men. For a long time, they shared dangers, joys and sorrows, and they became great friends.

"We were both sorry when the day came for us to say farewell," said Ristridin, "but I had to go back to my own land, because King Dagonaut was awaiting my return. Edwinem gave me a silver horn as a parting gift, the horn I always carry with me. That was four years ago now."

"Did you see him again?" asked Tiuri.

"Yes, I did," said Ristridin.

"And what about Sir Bendu," asked Tiuri. "Was he also a friend of Edwinem's?"

"Did I hear my name?" said Sir Bendu. He caught up with Ristridin and Tiuri and rode between them. "Of course I was his friend," he said. "What have you been telling him, Ristridin?" He turned to Tiuri and added, "I could tell you a thing or two as well, if you tell me a few things in exchange."

"What do you want to know?" asked Tiuri.

"A great deal! I know nothing about you."

"I have told you all I can," said Tiuri.

"Well, that was precious little!" said Bendu. "You do not happen to know the name of the Knight with the Red Shield, do you?"

"I am sorry, Sir Bendu," Tiuri replied. "I really have no idea."

Bendu grunted something into his beard. Then he turned to Ristridin. "We'll be coming to a village soon," he said, "but I would suggest we do not spend the night there. We would do better to keep on riding as long as it is still light, and then sleep in the open air."

"That is not necessary," said Ristridin. "I know an inn not too far from here with the illustrious name of the Setting Sun. I am certain we can reach it before dark."

"Fine, let us make that our aim for today," said Bendu. "We can ask again in the village about the Red Riders and then ride on at a gallop."

He urged on his horse and rode ahead; he seemed keen to resume his questioning.

Tiuri watched him go and thought to himself: *I believe, even now, Sir Bendu still does not trust me.*

2   THE INN OF THE SETTING SUN

The sun was just above the mountains to the west when they reached the inn. The four Grey Knights lowered their visors before going inside.

"We wish to remain anonymous," said Bendu to Tiuri. "Our identity does not matter. We are simply avengers, servants of justice."

The innkeeper was most impressed by his fine guests. When Ristridin asked if the company could dine privately, he said there were no other guests at the inn, so they were welcome to use the main room. It was small and poorly furnished, but it had one special attraction: all of the windows, with their small leaded panes, faced westwards, and they gleamed with a beautiful, rich light as the setting sun illuminated them. That was how the inn had earned its name.

Bendu asked the innkeeper about the Red Riders, but he had seen no sign of them. "But," he said, "perhaps my manservant can tell you something. He always knows what's going on." He raised his voice and called, "Leor!"

A door opened at the back of the room and a gaunt-looking man entered. When he saw the Grey Knights, he seemed taken aback. The innkeeper beckoned him over and he shuffled closer and stood before the knights, his head bowed. But his eyes were wandering around and he took a good look at every member of the party. Tiuri noticed his piercing gaze and thought to himself, *I have never met a man who looked quite so unpleasant and deceitful.* He wondered if the others were thinking the same.

"Leor," said the innkeeper, "these knights would like to know if you've seen some riders dressed in red pass through. Wait a second... Now that I'm thinking about it... Didn't you mention something about horsemen earlier?"

"Horsemen?" said the man slowly. "Horsemen? No, not I! I've not seen any riders, not a red one, nor a black one. I saw a few fellows riding along in grey and blue, but that was these gentlemen here." He grinned at the company and then looked down at the floor again. Perhaps he was afraid that he had said too much. But Tiuri could see that his eyes were still spying at them.

"Are you certain you have seen no other riders?" asked Ristridin.

"No," mumbled the man. "I mean yes. Yes, I'm certain."

"Look at me," Ristridin commanded, "and answer me truthfully. Have you seen any men on horseback around here, riders in red, perhaps at night?"

The manservant stared at him, with a mixture of fear and defiance on his face.

"No," he said, "I've not seen them. And if they'd been here, I'd know about it."

"Fine," said Ristridin. "You may go. And would you ensure that our horses are fed?"

"He will," said the innkeeper. "Go on, Leor, off you go." Then he turned to his guests and asked what they would like to eat.

"We do not mind," said Bendu, "as long as it is cooked well and there is enough for all of us. And we do not wish to be disturbed while we are eating."

The innkeeper gave them a bow and left the room. Tiuri went with one of the men from Mistrinaut to make sure that the horses were being taken care of. The manservant Leor was already getting down to work. He seemed more at ease in the stable than he had been inside the inn.

"Such fine horses," he said. "I'm sure they can gallop for a while without tiring. You've come from Castle Mistrinaut, haven't you?"

"We have indeed," said the man from Mistrinaut.

"When did you set off?"

"This morning."

"Then you've ridden quickly. Riders in grey and blue. Those men in grey, the knights, who are they?"

"No idea," said Tiuri and the man-at-arms at the same time.

"We're just servants," added Tiuri. It had been agreed that he would pass himself off as one of Mistrinaut's men.

"Oh yes, I know all about that," said Leor, emptying a sack of oats into one of the troughs. "The fine gentlemen don't tell us much, do they? They think their affairs are beyond our understanding." He turned his attention to the horses. "This black beast is the finest of the lot," he said, "and yet it's not ridden by one of the knights, is it?" He looked at Tiuri, but did not ask him a direct question.

The horse Ardanwen stamped his hoof on the ground and shook his mane.

"He's a wild one," said Leor and then he looked at Tiuri again, with a sly grin on his face.

The more Tiuri saw of the man, the less he liked him. He was glad to leave the stable.

Back inside the inn, the candles had been lit and the innkeeper had laid the table. He and Leor soon brought in the food. Ristridin thanked him and said he would call if they needed anything else. Then he and the other knights made themselves comfortable, removing their helmets and gorgets and unbuckling their weapons.

Bendu slid the bolt on the door and said, "There. Now we are alone."

As they were eating, Tiuri said, "Perhaps I am being overly suspicious, but I do not trust that Leor."

"You don't? Well, neither do I," said Bendu. "But we shall keep an eye on him. We will find the Red Riders in any case, whether he wishes to tell us the truth or not."

Sir Ristridin looked thoughtfully at Tiuri. "Would everyone please remember," he said, "that Tiuri is supposed to be passing as a man from Castle Mistrinaut?" He did not explain why he was reminding them, but Tiuri understood very well. The Red Riders would surely want to know where he was; Tiuri himself was the only member of the company who knew exactly why. With a shock, he realized that the Grey Knights might not even need to go in search of the Red Riders. *If I stay with them, they'll come to us*, he thought. *They'll try to take the letter from me.* As long as the knights were with him, he was relatively safe, even if his enemies did find out who he was. They would probably know soon enough; he was disguised as a man-at-arms, but he was once again riding the horse that had belonged to Sir Edwinem, the Black Knight with the White Shield.

He did not speak his thoughts aloud; there was no point. Instead, he turned to Evan.

"Sir Evan," he said, "would you tell me why the King of Eviellan is the enemy of King Unauwen?"

"That is a long story," Evan replied. "But I would be happy to tell you."

"Just as long as you remember that we should not be too late to bed," said Bendu. "We shall be up with the sun tomorrow."

"Where can a man find better rest than sitting with his companions, drinking wine and listening to stories?" said Ristridin. And he ordered his squire to go in search of the innkeeper and ask for more bottles of wine.

After they had finished their meal, they filled their glasses again, pushed back their chairs and sat comfortably to listen with Tiuri to the tale that Evan told.

"The land I come from," spoke Evan, "is said to be the most beautiful in the world. Our king, Unauwen, has ruled for many, many years, and he is wise and just. For century after century, peace has reigned in our land. Only in recent years have we come to know war and discord. But that discord was born in the heart of the kingdom itself.

"King Unauwen has two sons. As is customary, the elder son is the crown prince and since his eighteenth year he has served as vice-regent and governor of the realm. But the two princes were born on the same day, and the younger son was never content with his position. He found it unfair that his brother, who was only minutes older, was the heir to the throne. You need to know that the two princes are each other's double in terms of appearance and intellect. This made the difference in their position even more unacceptable to the younger son. And yet their characters are very different, and that became more and more obvious as they grew older. The crown prince is like his father; he cares deeply about the welfare of the kingdom and of his future subjects. His brother, however, is domineering, and longs for power.

"The contrast between the two brothers grew with the years. The younger brother began to hate the elder brother, and so a rift developed between the two. King Unauwen tried in many different ways to reconcile the two brothers and to help his younger son accept his place. But he was unrelenting on one point: he would never split his kingdom in two. It had to remain intact as a single whole, under the rule of the rightful heir.

"The king did, however, appoint his younger son the governor of the Province of the Rushing Rivers in the south of the realm. At first it seemed to be a good move, but the prince became increasingly headstrong, sometimes even acting directly against his father's will. Finally he did something King Unauwen would never have done: he headed south and invaded the land of Eviellan. He conquered the country and made it a province of the Kingdom of Unauwen. The king, however, revoked this move, ordering his son to withdraw from Eviellan immediately. The prince responded by declaring himself King of Eviellan, and said that now he was a ruler and his father's equal he no longer owed him allegiance!

"This pained the king greatly and he removed his son from the position of governor. But the foolhardy prince refused to accept his dismissal. Sadly, many people in the Province of the Rushing Rivers were devoted to him and supported his rebellion. The crown prince took an army to reclaim the province, and there was a battle. Brother fought against brother!

Unauwen, represented by his elder son, was the victor. But since then, something has gone from our kingdom; peace and friendship no longer rule throughout the land.

"The younger prince, the King of Eviellan, sent bands of wild warriors to his father's land to cause turmoil. And although war was not officially declared, there was constant fighting on the border and in the south of our land."

"One of those bands of men," said Ristridin, "had hidden in the Forest of Vorgóta. King Unauwen sent Sir Edwinem to drive them out."

"I was there too," said Sir Evan, "as part of Edwinem's company. I was not yet a knight myself. Ristridin will have told you that we succeeded in routing that wicked crew. But still the evil had not been banished from our land. The crown prince tried a few times to make peace, but he did not succeed. It is said that he still loves his brother. The King of Eviellan, however, refused all such approaches and so, with heavy hearts, the knights of Unauwen took up their white shields, buckled on their swords and prepared themselves for more fighting.

"But recently, glad tidings started to spread throughout my land. It was said that the King of Eviellan finally wanted to make peace, even that he would surrender Eviellan and travel to the City of Unauwen to be reconciled with his father and his brother. It is true that he sent messengers to his father, the king, and that the king in turn sent envoys to Eviellan. It is also true that those envoys were sent to negotiate a peace, and that they went on their way with good wishes. One of those men was Sir Edwinem, the lord of Forèstèrra."

Evan stopped.

"And what happened?" asked Tiuri.

"I have told you all I know," said Evan. "I was in a joyous, hopeful mood when I left my country, to take a message from my king to King Dagonaut. I could never have expected that I would soon exchange my white shield for a grey one and that I would be travelling this land looking for vengeance."

The room was silent.

It is strange, thought Tiuri. *Here we are, sitting together, and we are embroiled in the affairs of a country that is not our own – all but for Evan, who comes from that land.*

Tiuri was about to say something but, to his surprise, Bendu raised a hand to silence him, then stood up, without making a sound, and walked to the door at the back of the room. Then, very quietly, he slid the bolt and whipped open the door.

A man came tumbling into the room. It was Leor, the manservant.

Bendu grabbed hold of him and dragged him to his feet. "Got you!" he cried. "Why were you listening to us?"

"Help! Ow!" wailed the manservant. "I wasn't... Ow, ow, let me go!"

Bendu grabbed him even more firmly. "Out with it, eavesdropper!" he barked. "Why were you spying on us? And who ordered you to do so?"

"No one!" said Leor. "I was just about to knock and ask if you needed anything."

"That is a lie!" said Bendu, shaking the manservant. "Come on, answer me!"

"Ow!" cried Leor. "You're hurting me! I don't know anything, I tell you. Ow, ow!"

He was wailing so loudly that the innkeeper came to see what all the noise was about.

"Sir knights," he cried in dismay. "What on earth is happening?"

"Did you tell your man to listen at the door?" asked Bendu.

"No, of course not!" said the innkeeper. "What do you want with Leor?"

"Let him go," said Ristridin to Bendu. Then he turned to the innkeeper and said, "Your manservant has been acting very suspiciously, Foram. I am sure you will not object if we ask him a few questions."

"Not at all, Sir Ristridin," replied the innkeeper, looking in astonishment at the knight, who now stood before him without a helmet.

Bendu released Leor, who started rubbing his sore arms. "I've done nothing. And I know nothing," he muttered.

"You had better answer these gentlemen, Leor," said the innkeeper sternly. "I am ashamed of you!"

"So, then," said Ristridin, "tell us what you know about the Red Riders. Because we know that you have seen them!"

Bendu said nothing, but he looked so fiercely at Leor that the manservant soon backed down. "Yes... yes, I saw some riders," he said reluctantly. "Night before last. But they weren't in red."

"They were not in red?" cried Bendu.

"Not all of them, at any rate," said Leor. He seemed to have forgotten his pain and a grin appeared on his face. "The one who spoke to me was black – dressed in black, I mean – and there were others who weren't in red. I don't know what they looked like. It was dark."

"They spoke to you?" said Bendu. "What did they say? How many were there?"

"They rode by," said Leor. "I don't know how many there were. Ten, maybe twelve... I was awake and I saw them through my window. My room's at the front. They stopped a way past the inn, and I got up to take a look. I thought maybe they wanted to come in. So I went outside and then they saw me. They didn't want to spend the night, but they asked me to bring them some beer. So that's what I did."

"And what did they say?" asked Ristridin.

"Nothing much," replied Leor.

"So why were you so keen to find out what we were talking about?" asked Ristridin.

"And why, sir knight, are you so keen to find out what they said?" asked Leor. "Not that it's any of my business, but..."

"Answer the question!" shouted Bendu.

"The Red Riders have committed a murder," said Ristridin. "We are knights of King Dagonaut and we must punish them."

"Oh, really?" said Leor. Ristridin's words seemed to have made quite an impression on him. "Please forgive me, sir knight," he continued. "Well, they asked about you. They wanted to know if I had seen four Grey Knights and their squires, travelling from the direction of Castle Mistrinaut. I hadn't and that's what I told them. They asked about..." He paused for a moment and glanced at Tiuri. "About a young man with a beautiful ring on his finger. I haven't seen a young man matching that description as yet."

"And?" said Ristridin. Tall and stern, he stood before Leor, who was unable to resist the knight's piercing gaze.

"They said I should watch for the Grey Knights and the young man," he continued. "And that I should let them know if I saw them."

"And how were you to let them know?" asked Ristridin. "How were you to contact them? Where are they now?"

"I don't know. I truly don't. They said they would return here, to ask me."

"Is that the truth?"

"Yes, sir knight," replied Leor. "That's the truth."

Now the innkeeper chimed in. "You must believe him, Sir Ristridin," he said. "Of course it was wrong of him to listen in on your conversation. His curiosity will be the end of him. But he wasn't to know that the Red Riders are murderers."

"Of course I didn't know," said Leor indignantly.

"It is a pity you cannot tell us where they are," said Ristridin. "But we shall find them anyway. Go, Leor. But one last thing: you must alert us if they should return."

"Yes, sir knight," said Leor meekly, as he shuffled away.

"Is there anything else I can do for you?" asked the innkeeper.

"Yes, Foram," said Ristridin. "Please do not use my name again, as long as I am wearing this grey armour."

"As you wish, sir knight," said the innkeeper. "I shall keep a close eye on Leor, although I do not believe that he knows any more than he has told us."

"Good, Foram," said Ristridin. "We shall retire to bed. We intend to depart early tomorrow morning."

After the innkeeper had left, the members of the company sat together for a while, discussing the situation.

"I for one believe this Leor knows more than he has told," said Bendu.

"That is possible," said Ristridin thoughtfully.

"And is the innkeeper to be trusted?" asked Arwaut.

"If he knew anything, I am sure he would have told me," answered Ristridin. "I know him. He is a good man, but not very bright."

"What do we do now?" asked Evan.

"Nothing," replied Bendu. "Let us go to bed. But I think we should take it in turns to keep watch, so that no one may enter or leave the inn without our knowledge."

"That sounds like a good plan," said Ristridin.

They divided the watch, with Ristridin taking first turn, along with Tiuri, at Ristridin's request. They were to stay in the main room and occasionally patrol the inn. When an hour had passed, they would wake two of the others.

Soon Tiuri was alone with Ristridin. With only one candle burning, the room was in almost complete darkness.

"I asked to keep watch with you," said the knight, "because it gives me a good opportunity to talk to you about something."

"Are you not concerned that someone might be listening in?" asked Tiuri.

"Leor? What I have to tell you is no secret. Leor is welcome to hear it, even if he is a spy for the Red Riders."

"Do you think the Red Riders are nearby?" asked Tiuri. "And that they plan to return here?"

Ristridin shrugged. "I am certain they are nearby," he replied.

Tiuri fell silent for a few moments. "I think they are looking for me," he said quietly. "And if they know I am in your company, they will probably come to us."

"Let them come," said Ristridin. "The sooner, the better. As long as you are with us, you are under our protection." He stood up, walked over to the door and looked outside. Then he returned and sat beside Tiuri, but left the door open.

The hour passed quickly, as Ristridin told stories about Sir Edwinem.

Tiuri listened. Later, he would often think back to this night. And he would picture the quiet room once again, by the flickering light of the single candle, and the darkness through the open door, and hear the sound of the river and the soft voice of Sir Ristridin as he told his story. And he would see Sir Edwinem, not dying and defeated as he had been in the forest, but riding proudly and valiantly through the world on his black horse, with the sunlight glinting on his white shield.

3   EDWINEM

Sir Ristridin spoke about his friend, Edwinem of Forèstèrra. He told a tale of adventure and great deeds, a story whose end Tiuri already knew. But now Tiuri heard more about Edwinem's last adventure, even though Ristridin's story was incomplete. He made no mention of the letter for King Unauwen, and yet that was most surely the cause of Sir Edwinem's flight – and his demise.

This is what Ristridin told Tiuri.

"In the spring of this year," he said, "I was with my brother at Castle Ristridin by the Grey River. Bendu and Edwinem had also promised to come; the three of us were to go together to the Wild Wood, where we had never ventured before.

"One day, messengers arrived with news that knights of Unauwen were approaching. I set out to meet them. They were few in number, but the small procession looked very fine. All of the knights were in full armour, in white plate, with white shields and rainbow-coloured cloaks. At the front, on his black horse, rode Edwinem of Forèstèrra, who owned a magnificent estate in the Kingdom of Unauwen, but who, like me, was a knight-errant. The other knights also bore names of renown; I shall mention only Andomar of Ingewel, Argarath of Fardale, Marcian, and Darowin. They were on their way to Eviellan as envoys of King Unauwen. At Sir Edwinem's request, they were passing through our land, so that he could tell me in person that he would not be able to join us on our expedition for some time. His king had given him a more important task. As you know, the King of Eviellan had sent messages to his father and his brother, expressing the wish that they might make peace. That is why King Unauwen had sent the best of his knights to Eviellan.

"The knights stayed for one day and one night as guests at my brother's castle. They were full of joy and hope... all but one of them. Sir Edwinem was silent and withdrawn. That afternoon I stood with him on the tallest tower of the castle and we looked out over the plains of Eviellan, on the other side of the Grey River. Then I asked him why he was unhappy. At first he would not say anything, but finally he sighed and said, 'I do not know! Everyone is joyful and hopes for peace with Eviellan. But my heart is held captive by a dark foreboding. Sometimes I grow angry with myself and wonder if I have become too suspicious and distrustful. But I have never felt this way before, not even in moments of danger.'

"I told him he had no reason to fear, but he replied, 'I know that as well as you, Ristridin! And yet still I cannot shake off this feeling.'

"Then he turned his face to the west and said, 'Far from here, by the forest and by the shore, lies my castle, Forèstèrra. I love my home and, when I wander far, my heart is gladdened by the thought that one day I will be there again. But now I am only sad when I think of it, and I believe I shall never see my home again.'

"I asked him if he feared treachery.

"'Do not speak that word aloud,' he replied. 'The King of Eviellan has long been my enemy. I have fought against many of his knights and never has one of them been able to defeat me. But none of them has ever behaved towards me in an unknightly manner. So I cannot imagine that treachery is afoot. And yet – and it is only to you that I would say this, Ristridin – I do not believe that the King of Eviellan truly desires peace. I know him; he is a wicked man.'

"'But he may have changed,' I objected.

"'God grant it,' replied Edwinem. 'I certainly hope so. Yes, I hope so, Ristridin! Perhaps, when I see him, I will forget my misgivings. The King of Eviellan has a most winning way; he looks so like his brother, the crown prince, that all who meet him find it hard to believe in his wickedness. And that is precisely why he is so dangerous.' Then he shook his head and said with a smile, 'And now I shall remain silent on this subject, Ristridin! Do not concern yourself about me; let me go where I must. And you must do as you have planned: head into the Wild Wood. The idea is a sound one, for very few people have ventured there before, and a knight should know his own land.'

"The next morning, he and the other knights took their leave and rode on to Eviellan. Edwinem's squire, Vokia, stayed behind at Castle Ristridin, although it had taken considerable effort for his master to persuade him. The journey would have been too arduous for the old man, who was not in good health. The knights intended to stop off on their return journey and take him with them.

"After their departure, I found that Edwinem's fear had infected me. So I decided not to leave for the Wild Wood until they had returned. Bendu arrived and he waited with me, as he did not wish to travel without my company. We crossed the Grey River and entered into Eviellan, but we heard nothing of interest. There were rumours of peace and reconciliation there, too, but we also heard that the armies of

Eviellan had greatly increased in number and that they were closely watching the border of the Kingdom of Unauwen.

"Summer was approaching by then. It would soon be time to leave for the City of Dagonaut for the four-yearly gathering. We knew we would not be able to go to the Wild Wood as planned.

"Then came the day when I saw Sir Edwinem for the last time. It was a peculiar day: it was raining and yet the sun was shining at the same time, and old Vokia was anxiously pacing, muttering about a dream he had had, and lamenting that he was not with his master. As the sun set, a strange knight knocked at the gates of Castle Ristridin. He wanted to speak to me, but would not give his name. The gatekeeper believed it was a knight from Eviellan. I went to the gates, followed by Vokia, who was convinced that the unknown visitor had something to do with his master. There stood the knight; black was his armour, black was his shield, and black was his horse. But even without that horse, I would have known who he was, although he did not raise his visor and acted as if he did not know me. I let him in, but I did not speak his name. Only later, when we were alone, was our greeting warmer.

"'What has happened, Edwinem,' I asked, 'that you have come here alone, and clad all in black, like a knight of Eviellan?'

"'It was the only way to escape from that land,' he replied. 'I detest this black, but the white is concealed beneath it and soon it will reappear.'

"He was unable or unwilling to say what was going on, and his arrival had to remain secret. I gathered that he had fled for some reason and that he was in a hurry. If it had not been essential for him and his horse to rest, he would not even have come. He wanted to ride on after a few hours, and travel along the Third Great Road to his homeland. However, when I told him there were more troops on the border, he abandoned that plan.

"'They will be watching the border,' he said. 'Much of the south of the Kingdom of Unauwen is in their power. The Forest of Vorgóta is safe, but Eviellan's warriors are lying in wait in the Southerly Mountains and there are sure to be more men there now than a couple of months ago. No, I shall take a detour to reach the Kingdom of Unauwen; first to the north and then along the First Great Road.'

"I asked if I could help him, but he shook his head, 'This matter concerns my kingdom and my king alone. But that may not always be the case.' Then he smiled and added, 'This must be the most peculiar of all my adventures! I am travelling in deepest secrecy, fleeing as though death itself were on my heels, dressed in black like some servant of the night. But it may well be the most important mission of my life. God grant that I may reach my goal!'

"And that was all he said. A few hours later, he rode away, but he was no longer alone; his old squire went with him.

"I remained behind, full of fear, worry and doubt. The next day, a group of riders in red crossed the river, heading northwards. My brother and I stopped them and asked what business they had in the Kingdom of Dagonaut. They replied that they had been sent by their king to pay homage to King Dagonaut in honour of the festival on midsummer's day. We could do nothing but let them go; after all, recent relations between our kingdom and Eviellan had been good. Back at the castle, I consulted with Bendu and my brother. I knew what I wanted to do: follow the Red Riders and keep an eye on them. Bendu wanted to come with me, and Arturin, my brother, would remain at Ristridin to keep an eye on the border. We quickly made ready, and Bendu and I left that same day.

"As we travelled, we heard that a strange knight had joined the Red Riders; he wore a black suit of armour and a red shield.

"Oh, that journey to the north, in hot pursuit! We were following the Red Riders, and we feared that they were following the lord of Forèstèrra. We heard news of them in a village by the Green River. Two black knights had come to blows there, one with a red shield and one with a white shield. So we realized then that Edwinem had taken the black from his shield. The Knight with the White Shield had defeated his opponent, but he had not killed him. A band of Red Riders had arrived and chased the victor into the forest, after which they had all disappeared. Later, however, the old man who had accompanied the victorious knight had returned and ridden at full tilt towards the City of Dagonaut.

"When we heard that, we decided to split up. Bendu rode to the city and I headed into the forest. But I found no trace of any riders or of the Black Knight with the White Shield. Finally, I went to the city too, and I arrived just after the knighting ceremony. There was, of course, a great deal of discussion about the young man who had run away, but at that time I thought it was of little import. I was thinking about Edwinem and the Red Riders. I met up again with Bendu, who had been unable to find the old squire. I also learnt that only a few of the Red Riders had come to pay their respects to King Dagonaut and that no Black Knight had arrived in the city. The king gave us leave to investigate the matter. Sir Evan, who happened to be in the city at that time, joined us, as did Arwaut, Bendu's nephew.

"But we did not have to search long for Sir Edwinem. That same day, we heard that the Black Knight with the White Shield had been found murdered in the forest, not far from the Yikarvara Inn, where he had briefly stayed.

"He, one of the most valiant of Unauwen's knights, one of his most noble and true paladins, he, the Invincible, had been defeated, not in a fair and honest duel, but through cowardly deceit. His premonition had come true: never again would he see his land, or his beloved Forèstèrra by the sea."

This, and more, was what Sir Ristridin told Tiuri, as they shared the watch. In and around the inn, all was quiet, and they were not disturbed.

4   A Shock

Tiuri was riding again with the Grey Knights along the Blue River; only it was not the Red Riders that they were following, but Sir Edwinem with the White Shield. Tiuri could see him riding in the distance, on the black horse Ardanwen, but he could not catch up with him and that made him very sad.

"He has gone too far ahead," said the knight who was riding alongside him. He thought at first that it was Ristridin, but then he realized the lord of Mistrinaut had taken his place. "Ristridin has gone to the Wild Wood," the man said. "He could not ride on with us."

Tiuri was shocked to see Leor standing by the roadside, with a dagger in his hand and a mean grin on his face. He gasped and heard Bendu cry out, "There they are, the Red Riders! They are attacking! This is your fault, Tiuri. You brought them here!" Then Bendu rode up beside him and shook him angrily.

Tiuri woke up. Ristridin's squire was standing over him, shaking his shoulder.

"Don't be alarmed," he said, laughing. "It's time to get up."

Tiuri groaned as he sat up and rubbed his eyes. It took him a moment to separate his dreams from reality.

He had sat for a long time with Sir Ristridin the previous evening. Neither of them had noticed the hourglass showing that their watch was over. When Tiuri finally went to bed, he immediately fell fast asleep, even though he had not expected to. But now he felt as though he had been riding all night.

He got out of bed. Ristridin and Bendu's squires, with whom he was sharing a room, were almost ready to leave. It was still dark outside and rather chilly.

When he went downstairs, he found the Grey Knights already there; Ristridin and Bendu were talking to a pale and grumpy Leor.

"So they did not say when they would return?" Tiuri heard Bendu say.

"No, sir knight," replied Leor. "I am certain they did not. And maybe they never will come back. If they know you've been here..."

"How could they know that?" asked Ristridin.

The manservant looked surprised by the question. "How?" he said. "A company like yours does not go unnoticed! Everyone along the Blue River must be talking about you. And when the Red Riders hear, they'll be sure to make themselves scarce. Or at least I imagine they will."

"Indeed," growled Bendu. "I've heard enough. You can go."

Then the knights discussed their plans. Should they ride onwards, or wait at the inn?

"I think we should ride on," said Bendu. "I do not trust that Leor at all. If necessary, we can leave one or two of our party here."

Tiuri hoped the others would agree with Bendu's proposal. Whatever they decided, Tiuri would have to ride on and it would be good not to have to travel alone, as the Red Riders would be sure to come looking for him.

"Sir Bendu," he said. "I agree that it would be best for you to ride on..."

"Is that right?" snapped Bendu. "Well, it's certainly best for you, eh? You will be able to travel quickly and with a strong escort."

Tiuri fell silent after this harsh response. Sir Bendu seemed not to trust him or to like him. At least Ristridin knew why Tiuri thought it was a good idea for the knights to accompany him.

As they ate breakfast, Tiuri kept glancing over at the leader of the Grey Knights. It was strange that he, Tiuri, was the one who was now carrying Sir Edwinem's letter... even though he had never known Edwinem and had nothing to do with the daring deeds of the knights-errant. It would have been more obvious for Sir Ristridin to take on Edwinem's task, as surely would have happened if he had been the one to find Edwinem. But, thanks to a peculiar set of circumstances, it was Tiuri who was carrying the important message close to his chest. What if he were to tell Ristridin? But Sir Edwinem had made him promise not to tell anyone. And yet, when he had said that, he would hardly have been thinking of his friend Ristridin.

Tiuri sighed. He knew he would say nothing. Ristridin had not asked him about his secret, even though he probably suspected much. Sir Edwinem had entrusted Tiuri with the task, and he would have to carry it out, even if someone else seemed better suited.

Then he felt a nudge in his ribs. "Hey, what are you daydreaming about?" said Sir Arwaut. "Are you ready? It's time to go."

The landscape became hillier. Tiuri knew the mountains must be much closer now, although it was hard to see in the early morning mist.

Tiuri rode beside Ilmar, Ristridin's squire, a friendly boy of about his own age, who talked a lot about his master as they travelled along. He had not been serving Ristridin for long, but he was already full of admiration for him.

They made fast progress, in spite of occasional stops to ask about the Red Riders or to search for their trail. Later that morning, the clouds cleared a little and a watery sun emerged. The road became stony and there were boulders lying here and there on the verge. The river had narrowed by that point and it too was full of rocks and stones, with white water splashing all around them.

In the afternoon, they rode between rocky crags to their left and a dark pine forest on the right, on the opposite bank of the river. *That forest would make a fine hiding place for Red Riders*, thought Tiuri. Alert and tense, he was constantly on the lookout. The road was quiet and they met no one coming in the other direction. Sometimes they heard the echo of their horses' hoofs. No one spoke. They all seemed to be on their guard.

It was late in the afternoon when it finally happened. Suddenly, loud shouts came from the forest on the right.

"This is it," cried Bendu, reining in his horse and reaching for his sword. The others did the same.

"Look!" cried Arwaut. "Up in the tree! I think it's a man in red!"

"And I can see men moving among the trees," said Evan.

Bendu urged on his horse and rode into the river. It was shallow and easy to ford, although the current was rather strong. Arwaut and their squires followed. Arrows flew at them from the forest, but none found a target.

Before Tiuri knew what was happening, a man leapt down from the crags to the left of the road. Tiuri felt a sudden weight on his back and two hands around his throat. As Ardanwen reared up, whinnying, Tiuri tried to shake off the attacker. There was more shouting in the background, and other men jumped down from the rocks. Tiuri fell to the ground, his attacker on top of him.

Later, he could never recall exactly what occurred in those seconds of confusion, which seemed to last for hours. But in a flash he understood the attacker was after both the letter and his life! They wrestled. Neither had the chance to reach for a weapon. All around were the sounds of hoofs stamping, men shouting, and weapons clashing.

Finally, Tiuri overpowered his opponent, pinning him to the ground. For the first time, he saw the man's face. It was wicked and cruel, and his mouth opened wide and cried out. Tiuri sensed danger and leapt to his feet, drawing his sword.

Then someone seized him from behind, but this time he was ready, and, when he felt hands closing around his neck again, Tiuri fell backwards and took his second attacker by surprise. The man stayed on the ground where he had fallen, and did not move again. But then the first man stood up and launched himself at Tiuri. And he was followed by another man! One grabbed at his hands, while the other tugged at his clothes. Tiuri desperately tried to defend himself. The letter! These men wanted the letter! Ristridin's horn sounded, and Tiuri shouted for help. At that moment he felt a sharp pain at the top of his left arm. One of them had stabbed him!

Everything was fading to black, but Tiuri kept on fighting. More men seemed to arrive; there was so much shouting and whinnying, and all the while he went on struggling, even as he felt his strength ebbing away. But they did not have the letter – no, not yet! Just as his attackers finally let go of him, he lost consciousness.

Tiuri came to as someone took hold of him again. He shot up with a scream, his hand on the place where he had hidden the letter.

"Calm yourself," said Sir Ristridin. "It's only me! Just lie there."

Tiuri sank back down. To his utter relief, the letter was still there. With a sigh, he closed his eyes. The noise of the fight had stopped; he could hear only a few distant shouts. He opened his eyes again and looked up into Ristridin's concerned face.

"How do you feel?" asked the knight. "You're wounded, but I do not think it is too serious."

"Oh, it's nothing," mumbled Tiuri, as he struggled to sit up and then looked around, feeling rather dizzy. The fight was apparently over. Two Red Riders lay close to him, both dead. Another man lay motionless nearby. He was not dressed in red, but he was not a member of the company of the Grey Knights either. Ristridin's squire, Ilmar, was trying to calm an agitated group of horses. No one else was around. "Where are the others?" Tiuri asked.

"They went after the Red Riders," replied Ristridin, "who have fled into the forest." He examined Tiuri's wound with quick, capable hands. "The wound is indeed not too bad," he said. "Wait a moment." He fetched his bag and took out some bandages. Ilmar brought over a helmet full of water. Ristridin washed and bandaged Tiuri's arm and said, "We shall have to find a better spot for you. This is not the most comfortable of places." Without waiting for a response, he picked up Tiuri like a little boy and put him down by the side of the road, where he could lean against a rock. Then he made him drink a few sips from a bottle of spiced wine. "Now sit and rest quietly," he said. "And you will soon feel better."

The horse Ardanwen walked over, lowered his head and nuzzled Tiuri.

"That animal saved your life," said Ristridin. "One of the riders was about to attack you with an axe, but Ardanwen gave him a good kick, and now he's lying over there, dead."

Tiuri stroked the loyal creature's head. "What actually happened?" he asked. "Everything's still so confused."

"A gang of men attacked you all at once," Ristridin replied. "You were already fighting two men, but then more of them came. We were able to come to your aid just in time, but if Ardanwen had not been there, we would probably have been too late." He shaded his eyes with his hand and looked over at the opposite riverbank. Twilight was approaching and it was already dark among the trees. "I need to leave you on your own for a short while," he said. "Here is my horn. Blow it if danger threatens."

Then he left, followed by his squire. Tiuri leant against the rock and looked down at the horn on his knees. He was tired and his wound was painful, but he was thankful that things had not turned out worse. Although... he didn't yet know how the rest of the company had fared. Were they out there somewhere, fighting the Red Riders? Tiuri looked around. The dead bodies were not a pretty sight, so he focused his gaze on the forest instead. But he could see nothing among the dark trees. Tiuri took out the letter and looked at it. Then he heard footsteps, so he quickly tucked it away.

It was Ristridin and Ilmar coming back. "We went to see if anyone was still hiding among the rocks," said Ristridin, "but we found no one." He turned to his squire. "Let us first take care of the dead," he said. "We can bury them away from the road or build a cairn of stones over their bodies."

"Can I help?" asked Tiuri.

"No, you just sit and rest," said the knight. "You have already had enough exertion. Wait, I shall lay out a blanket for you and you can try to sleep a little."

Soon Tiuri was wrapped up in two blankets, with a saddle as a pillow. He could not imagine sleeping, however; he felt far too restless. Ristridin came and sat beside him, as Ilmar gathered wood and made a fire. It was almost completely dark by then.

"Do you not need to go after the others?" asked Tiuri. "There seemed to be so many riders out there."

"There were no more than twenty," said Ristridin. "And five of them are dead. No, I shall remain here, with you. You are the member of our company who is in the greatest danger. You were right when you said the riders would come for you. They may be running from us now, but I would still prefer not to leave you on your own."

"My thanks," said Tiuri quietly. "But what about the others? Are there enough of them to take on the riders?"

"For certain," said Ristridin with a smile. "They have faced more fearsome foes. My only concern is whether they will catch up with them. When the riders realized they could not defeat you, they ran like rabbits."

"It was all so fast," said Tiuri. "That man jumped on top of me. And then... I'm still not sure exactly what happened."

"The men who were shouting in the forest were intended

as a distraction," Ristridin told him. "And it worked at first. Some of our company had already crossed the river when the rest of the gang leapt down from the rocks. And they went straight for you. They merely tried to prevent us from coming to your aid. When they did not succeed, they fled across the river and into the forest. I wonder how they knew you were the one they were seeking."

"Ardanwen," murmured Tiuri.

"Because you were riding Sir Edwinem's horse? Yes, that is possible," said Ristridin.

"Leor kept looking at Ardanwen," said Tiuri, "and he mentioned the horse a few times. I think he must somehow have alerted the Red Riders."

"You could be right," Ristridin agreed. "I am sure they have their spies." He stood up. "We must remain patient until the others return," he said. "And in the meantime, we should have something to eat. Don't you think?"

It was more than an hour before the sound of voices and hoofs announced the return of the rest of the party. Tiuri, who had dozed off after all, woke up with a start. When they came into view, he quickly counted them: all nine of them were there, and they had another man with them, whose hands were tied behind his back.

Ristridin walked to meet them. "Well? How did it go?" he asked.

"Killed six. Took one prisoner," said Bendu, jumping down from his horse and throwing the reins to Ilmar. "The others fled." He strode over to Tiuri. "How's the lad?" he said.

"A flesh wound in his arm," Ristridin replied. "Nothing serious."

"You were lucky," said Bendu to Tiuri. "I was afraid it was worse. Those riders were out to get you; it is good that you were not travelling alone." His voice sounded as gruff as ever, but Tiuri could hear that his tone was different now.

Sir Bendu finally believes I am to be trusted, he thought.

"And how did you all fare?" asked Ristridin.

"Oh, not too badly," said Bendu. "Arwaut has a cut on his scalp and Evan's squire has some bruising on his arm, but nothing too serious."

Ristridin looked at the prisoner. He was a squat and muscular man with a furious face. He was not dressed in red, but wore chainmail over his ragged clothes.

"Was he with them?" he asked.

"Yes," replied Bendu. "They were not only Red Riders. I noticed that two of the company were wearing the black armour of Eviellan's soldiers. We killed one of them. And there were a few rogues like him. I would rather have captured a Red Rider to interrogate instead. This one swears he knows nothing."

"We shall question him again later," said Ristridin.

For a while, there was much to be done. The men unsaddled the horses and rubbed them down, bandaged and tended to the injuries, and prepared food. As they worked, Bendu told them what had happened.

The Red Riders had clearly wished to avoid a confrontation; they had only stopped to fight when the knights had caught up with them. However, some of them had taken advantage of the commotion to flee. When darkness fell, it had become impossible to find them, so Bendu and his companions had returned. "But we will track down those men as well," he concluded.

After eating, they questioned the prisoner again. At first he refused to speak, but the threatening gazes of the Grey Knights soon loosened his tongue.

"Where are you from?" asked Ristridin. "Are you a man of Eviellan?"

"No," said the man. "I'm from over there, in the forest."

"How did you come to join the Red Riders? And why did you attack us?"

"I don't know."

"Answer the question!"

"I really don't know," the man insisted. "It was no business of mine. I was just doing as I was told."

"So you are a man who fights for money, and who does evil on command?"

"A man has to earn a living, doesn't he? What do I know about good and evil? Yes, I served the Red Riders and they paid me for my services. But precious little, the scoundrels!"

"Who was your commander?"

"What do you mean?"

"Who gave the orders?"

"Don't know."

"You know very well!"

"No, I've no idea. The captain, I suppose, the leader of the Red Riders."

"And what is his name?"

"Don't know. We just called him the captain."

"We? Who do you mean?"

"All of us."

"Were there others who came from the forest?"

"Yes. My mate, Udan, and Asgar, but he's dead now."

"How did you come to be working for the Red Riders?"

"They rode by and asked if we wanted to work for them. They gave us weapons and chainmail. And so we went with them."

"I see. What were you doing before that?"

"What business is that of yours?"

"Answer the question!"

"This and that. We used to chop wood sometimes."

"And I'm sure you were robbers too," growled Bendu. "I can't imagine you were doing honest work."

The man muttered something under his breath.

"Who gave the orders?" Ristridin asked for the second time.

"I told you that already. The captain."

"Not the Black Knight with the Red Shield?"

"Knight?" said the man, with what seemed to be a genuine look of surprise. "I never saw any knight!"

The prisoner was able to provide little information. The Red Riders had not mentioned what they were doing in the Kingdom of Dagonaut. Most of them, he told the knights, did indeed come from Eviellan, but he had not known them for long, no more than a week. So he had entered into their service after the murder of Sir Edwinem. He had met five of the men in the forest; others had joined them later, but not until they were near Castle Mistrinaut. He had never seen the Knight with the Red Shield, but he believed that the captain had received his orders from another man. He was also able to tell them that the Red Riders had various spies. Leor, the manservant at the Inn of the Setting Sun, was indeed one of their informants. He had passed on the message, via another spy, that the Grey Knights were approaching, together with the young man the Red Riders had been seeking, who was on a black horse. He did not know why they were after this young man, but he did say that the captain had been very angry when he heard the Grey Knights were accompanying him. He could not tell them anything about what other plans the Red Riders might have.

"You understand that you will be punished for your actions," said Ristridin sternly. "Assaulting travellers on the road is a serious offence. We shall hand you over to the lord who governs this region and he will deal with you as you deserve."

"Who is the local lord?" asked Arwaut.

"The lord of Castle Westenaut," replied Ristridin. "I suggest that a number of us ride to the castle to hand over the prisoner and to request some men and horses to assist us."

"That is not necessary," said Bendu. "We can handle those few riders on our own."

"I am sure we can," said Ristridin. "But they may spread out over the area and go into hiding. So we need to ensure that everyone in this region is informed and is on the lookout. There may also be others out there, who are not dressed in red – their spies and accomplices. They should not be given any chance to escape."

"You make a good point," said Bendu.

"It is now about ten o'clock, maybe half past," Ristridin continued. "The horses need to rest for at least an hour. Then three of our company can ride to Castle Westenaut, with the prisoner. It is around five hours from here, so they should be there by four."

"I know where it is," said Sir Evan. "I spent the night there on my way to the City of Dagonaut."

It was decided that Sir Evan should go, accompanied by Arwaut's squire and one of the men from Castle Mistrinaut. They would meet the rest of the company the following day at the place where the First Great Road left the Blue River.

"We shall set off early tomorrow morning," said Ristridin, "so we should be there around midday. We shall wait for you."

Tiuri watched his companions in silence. He wondered what they would do next. They would go after the Red Riders, of course. In that case, Tiuri could no longer stay with them; he had to travel onwards, along the Blue River. His task suddenly seemed very difficult again, but that was probably because he was feeling the effects of his injury.

The company did not talk for much longer. They divided the watch between the uninjured men who were not travelling to Castle Westenaut, and then all was quiet in the camp.

5 SAYING FAREWELL

When Tiuri awoke the next morning, he felt much better. It was early, and most of the men were still asleep. Arwaut was lying beside him; the white bandage had slipped down his forehead. Ilmar was hanging a pot over the fire, but Ristridin and Bendu were nowhere to be seen. Tiuri closed his eyes again; he could sleep a little longer. But sleep would not come. His mind was far too active and there was so much to think about.

After a while, he sat up and looked around. He realized just how close the mountains were. They were already in the foothills, in fact. It was a beautiful, cold, dewy morning, with a crisp breeze and a sun that made the snowy peaks glisten. Tiuri stood up, went over to the river and washed himself in the icy water. As he was washing, Ristridin and Bendu returned from their search in the forest.

"Good morning. Are you feeling better?" asked Bendu, smiling at Tiuri for the first time.

"I'll play the physician again soon and take another look at your wound," said Ristridin. "I have a good salve in my saddlebag. That should help. Arwaut and Marvin, Evan's squire, will have to submit to my ministrations too."

Later, as they were eating breakfast, Tiuri said, "What are your plans?"

"We will start by riding on to the point where the Great Road leaves the Blue River," Ristridin replied. "That's where we intend to meet Evan, with the reinforcements from Westenaut."

"In that case," said Tiuri, "the time has come for us to part company. You mean to hunt down and capture the Red Riders, while I shall travel onwards, along the Blue River."

"Surely you do not wish to travel on alone!" exclaimed Bendu.

"I cannot stay with you," Tiuri replied. "I am very grateful that I have been able to travel so far in your company. If you had not been with me yesterday, I would not be here now. But I must travel onwards, as quickly as possible." He paused. "You will have guessed that my goal lies beyond the source of the Blue River. I must cross the mountains, to the Kingdom of Unauwen. That is my mission."

For a few moments, there was silence.

"To the west," said Arwaut finally. "But why not travel along the Great Road?"

"There are other ways over the mountains," said Ristridin, "although they are known to few. The hermit Menaures knows the mountains well; he is sure to be aware of a path that is steeper and more difficult, but far quicker. And, more importantly, one that is unknown to the enemy."

"And the enemy will not pursue Tiuri," said Bendu. "That is where we come in. We shall take care of the Red Riders, so that Tiuri may travel on in safety and in peace."

"This is true," said Ristridin. "But I must say, Tiuri, it saddens me to say farewell."

"I am sorry too," said Tiuri, "but it has to be this way.

And you have said yourself that I no longer need fear the Red Riders."

"I will vouch for that," said Bendu firmly.

But Ristridin said, "Do not underestimate your enemies, Tiuri! I do not wish to scare you and I agree with your decision, but you must remember that the Red Riders may have many spies. The Riders themselves are conspicuous, but their accomplices might be watching you in secret, in the guise of ordinary people... a shepherd, a traveller, anyone! You must steal away from us quietly, so that you are long gone before they realize."

Tiuri could feel his courage beginning to falter. He had to admit that he was not looking forward to taking leave of the knights and travelling on alone. But he also knew that it could not be avoided. He had his job to do, and the Grey Knights had theirs.

They talked for a little longer and then decided to travel on together to the spot where they would meet Evan and his companions. Then Tiuri had a thought.

"What about Ardanwen?" he asked. "Could I cross the mountains on horseback?"

Ristridin shook his head. "That's not possible," he said. "Not along the paths you will be taking. You could if you were travelling along the Great Road, but that too can be hard going."

Tiuri sighed. "Then I must leave Ardanwen behind," he said.

"We shall take care of him," Ristridin promised. "He can stay at Castle Mistrinaut until you return to claim him."

"But he does not belong to me!" said Tiuri. "He is Sir Edwinem's horse."

"But he has accepted you as his master," said Ristridin. "Did I not tell you that he would not allow anyone on his back but Sir Edwinem? He would only take another rider if Edwinem ordered him to. I think you must be his master now. But that is a matter for later. You may be sure, however, that Ardanwen will be waiting for you on your return."

"I have an idea!" said Ilmar, who had been sitting and pondering. "One of us must exchange clothes with Tiuri. I can do that. And I will ride Ardanwen, if the horse does not object. Then, if they are spying on us, the riders will follow me and, in the meantime, Tiuri can slip away unnoticed and be on his way."

"That's a very generous offer," said Tiuri, "but I don't want you to do it. I do not wish to endanger others more than I already have."

"I think it is a fine suggestion," said Ristridin, "and Ilmar must do it! What matter if it is dangerous? We have all set out to defy danger! I believe that Ilmar's offer is most befitting of a future knight, and you, Tiuri, must allow him the opportunity to assist you."

Ilmar glowed with pleasure at Ristridin's words and Tiuri reluctantly agreed. Ilmar leapt to his feet. "Now you must tell Ardanwen to allow me on his back, Tiuri," he said. "And let's change our clothes right now, behind that rock, so that no spies see us."

"A fine idea," said Ristridin.

The First Great Road followed the Blue River to the point where it met a narrow tributary, which was called the Little Blue River. There, the road turned to the south, following the smaller river into the mountains. The company arrived around midday and found the other men already waiting. Sir Evan told them that the lord of Westenaut was equipping his men, and that they would arrive before nightfall. One of the men from Mistrinaut was sent back to warn his lord in case the Red Riders should head in that direction.

For a moment, Evan mistook Ilmar for Tiuri, so the ruse seemed to have worked. There was no reason to put off their farewell any longer.

"But let us first eat together," said Ristridin. "How is your arm now, Tiuri?"

"Oh, the wound is no longer troubling me," replied Tiuri, which was not entirely true.

The Grey Knights had made their plans as they were riding. They were going to divide the company. Ristridin, Evan, and their squires would travel on for some way along the Great Road to throw any spies off the scent. The others would cross the Blue River and head back into the forest. At the end of the afternoon, the two groups would meet up again at the point they had set out from. Tiuri would accompany the second group for a while before going his own way.

The meal was soon over. Tiuri said farewell to Ardanwen, who seemed to understand that he would have to be parted from his new master again; he gave a quiet whinny and looked at Tiuri with sad eyes. Then Tiuri shook each member of the company by the hand and thanked them for their help.

"May your road ahead be blessed," said Evan. "Perhaps we shall see each other again in the Kingdom of Unauwen."

"I wish you a successful journey," said Ilmar, who had climbed onto Ardanwen with Tiuri's help, "and I am sure it will be so."

"Goodbye for now," said Ristridin. "Soon you will hear from me again. At the first bend in the road, I will blow my horn twice to mark our parting. Farewell until we meet again!"

They parted company, without looking back. Tiuri rode on Ilmar's horse. Before long, he dismounted at a sheltered spot in the forest and took his leave of Bendu and his companions. "May you find the Red Riders, Sir Bendu," he said.

"Edwinem's death shall be avenged," said Bendu. "And my wish is for you to carry out his task as it should be done. And you will succeed; I have no doubt. Perhaps you will be a knight next time I see you, as by rights you should be already. Now leave. The coast is clear."

And then Tiuri was alone. The sound of hoofs died away and he felt lonely and vulnerable. But he moved on at a brisk pace, staying among the trees for as long as possible. Then he followed a rocky path that ran to the right of the Blue River. It went uphill and downhill, sometimes next to the river, sometimes on the slope above. The rocks on both sides became higher and higher, but to the left he occasionally had a beautiful view over the Little Blue River and the First Great Road.

After an hour or so, he paused as he heard the distant sound of a horn, the silver horn of Sir Ristridin, bidding him farewell.

Tiuri walked on and saw a section of the Great Road down below, and a few distant figures. They were already so far away!

The horn sounded once again, with echoes repeating its silvery note.

"Farewell, Grey Knights," Tiuri whispered. "Farewell, Ristridin of the South. Until we meet again!"

PART FIVE

—

IN THE MOUNTAINS

1 A Travelling Companion

When the sound of Ristridin's horn had died away, Tiuri walked on. He realized that he was now setting off on the final part of the road that the Knight with the White Shield had told him to follow. Once he was over the mountains, he would have to find his own way. It was now nearly two weeks since he'd left the chapel outside the City of Dagonaut. How much longer would he have to travel before he had completed his mission and could give the letter to King Unauwen in the land to the west of the Great Mountains?

He had to get used to being alone again, after travelling in the company of the Grey Knights. But he was now far better equipped than on his lonely journey through the forest; he had weapons, food and even some gold and silver coins. The threat also appeared to have passed. The Red Riders had been routed and the Grey Knights would soon take them prisoner. It seemed unlikely that they would find Tiuri now. So, even though at times it was narrow and winding, the path along the Blue River did not seem as arduous as the roads he had followed before.

After a few hours, the path veered away from the river and headed to the right. But Tiuri realized that he would be able to continue along the other side of the river. There was a small crucifix attached to the rock face there, with words carved in uneven letters on the stone beneath it:

Pilgrim climbing to the heights above,
may you travel with God's love.
And, dear friend, as you go,
pray for us in the valleys below.

Tiuri knelt there for a short while. *How many pilgrims have passed this way before me?* he wondered, as he set off. Once again he felt like a pilgrim, a pilgrim with an important but mysterious task.

A sudden noise disturbed his reflections: footsteps behind him. They could have been coming from some way off, but they sounded loud and clear on the stony ground. Tiuri looked around. There was no one in sight. *Oh, of course there must be other people wandering around these mountains,* he thought to himself. But, even so, he started walking faster. He could still hear the footsteps; in fact, they seemed to be coming closer.

After a while, Tiuri stopped to rest. He heard the other walker pause and then hurry onwards. He thought for a moment and took out the habit that the monks at the Brown Monastery had given him. He put it on over his grey chainmail and tied the rope around his waist. Anyone who saw him would think he was a pilgrim, on his way to the hermit Menaures, the kind of person who would be less conspicuous in these surroundings than a squire in chainmail.

He did not rest for long. A little later, he looked back again and saw a man appear around a bend in the path. The man looked tired and wearily raised his hand in greeting. Tiuri waved back, but did not slow his pace. Then he heard the man call out.

"Ho, traveller! Pilgrim!"

Tiuri wanted to act as if he hadn't heard, but the shout had been so urgent that he had to stop. Panting for breath, the man caught up with him.

"Greetings, pilgrim," he gasped. "What a climb! Wait a moment." He sat down at the side of the path, dipped his hands in the river and splashed his face. "That's better," he said, turning to look at Tiuri. "Hello, pilgrim. I am pleased to see you."

Tiuri didn't feel the same way. He didn't like the look of the man at all. But that was unfair, he told himself; he was probably just an innocent traveller. He was a stocky, dark-haired man, but the first thing Tiuri noticed about him was his hard, pale grey eyes beneath thick eyebrows that met in the middle. His mouth, however, curled into a friendly smile.

"I am pleased to see you," he repeated. "I'm not really at home in the mountains, you see, and I'd appreciate some company. I imagine you're off to see the hermit Menaures, eh?"

"That's right," Tiuri replied.

The man stood up and said, "I have an even longer journey – all the way over the mountains – and I heard the hermit knows the mountain paths. Would you mind if I travel with you?"

"Well," said Tiuri slowly, "I can hardly say no, because this path doesn't belong to me. But, to be honest, I prefer to travel alone and I want to walk quickly."

"Oh, I beg your pardon," said the man. "I did not wish to impose. Please do not think that, worthy pilgrim! It is true that one travels faster on one's own and we weren't put on this earth to help one another, after all." The man sighed and trudged onwards.

Tiuri suddenly felt ashamed at his own lack of courtesy. "My good man!" he called out, as he ran after him. "Come back! I didn't mean it. Please, come back."

The man went on for a few steps before stopping. "I truly don't wish to impose," he said.

Tiuri blushed. "Oh, please forget what I said," he said. "Of course you may travel with me."

The man didn't need to be asked again. "Well, if you're asking," he said.

"Yes, I'm asking," said Tiuri. "And I apologize for being so unfriendly."

"Ah, I understand," said the man, walking alongside him. "A pilgrim likes to contemplate. That's the right word, isn't it? And to reflect upon higher things. I promise I won't be a nuisance."

As he looked at Tiuri, his mouth smiled, but his eyes did not. Instead, they were studying him sharply and inquisitively. Tiuri felt as if those eyes could see right through his habit to the armour beneath... and that they were looking for what Tiuri had hidden there.

Nonsense! he thought to himself angrily. He was still ashamed of his rudeness and annoyed by his lack of trust. Suddenly he hated the letter, for making him see every stranger as a potential enemy. Sir Ristridin had warned him about spies who might look like ordinary people. Did that mean he had to reject every request for help and shun all company?

Then he realized that his unexpected travelling companion was speaking to him. "Forgive me, what did you say?" Tiuri asked.

"I was just telling you my name," the man replied. "Jaro is my name. Jaro, son of Janos. I come from the valley over there."

Tiuri knew he was also expected to introduce himself, but he couldn't use his own name or even the name of Tarmin, because the enemy probably knew it already. So he gave the name of one of the monks from the Brown Monastery. "My name is Martin," he said.

"Ah, Brother Martin," repeated Jaro. "You are a monk, aren't you?"

"I have not yet taken orders," said Tiuri.

"Oh, I see," said Jaro.

The two of them walked on in silence. Tiuri went more slowly than before, but soon realized that Jaro was easily keeping up with him. He quickened his pace and told Jaro to say if it was too fast for him.

"Oh, I'm fine," said Jaro. "I'm not as old as all that. It's just that I never travel up here. I don't like it. But I'm going to visit my son who lives on the other side of the mountains. He left us five years ago. He said goodbye and off he went! I haven't seen him since. Five years is a long time! So now I've finally set off to go and see him. I didn't want to wait until I was too old and stiff to climb such a long way uphill and back down again. I may even stay there. There's not a living soul to keep me here. My wife's dead and I have no other family. There are paths over the mountains, aren't there? I hope the hermit can show me a way through. I don't dare to just go climbing without any guidance. So many people have died up there, falling off mountains, tumbling into ravines..."

Jaro went on talking and Tiuri gave the occasional nod or a brief reply.

"Oh dear," Jaro said eventually. "I've been talking too much after all. You should have stopped me, pilgrim. I really don't want to be a bother."

"Oh, you're not bothering me at all," said Tiuri with a smile he didn't mean. He kept telling himself there was no good reason for it, but still he did not like his travelling companion.

*

Late that afternoon, they came to a cleft in the rocks, where Jaro suggested they should spend the night. Tiuri agreed.

Jaro chattered away happily as he made a fire and he insisted on sharing his food with Tiuri. "So," he said, when they had eaten, "it's time to sleep, don't you think? We have lots of climbing to do tomorrow. Do you know how far it is to the hermit's cabin from here?"

"I think we should be there before tomorrow evening," Tiuri replied. He had heard from Sir Ristridin and Lord Rafox that Menaures's cabin was around a day and a half's journey from the Little Blue River.

"That's not so bad," said Jaro, as he lay down and wrapped his cloak around him. "Sleep well, pilgrim. Remember me in your prayers."

But Tiuri didn't sleep well at all. First he waited for Jaro's breathing to become slow and steady, but even then he couldn't relax. His arm, which he'd barely thought about all day, was also starting to hurt again. He tossed and turned until he realized that Jaro was also moving. Then he lay still again and tried in vain to peer through the darkness. Was Jaro awake? Was he staring at Tiuri with those cold, piercing eyes? Jaro moved again and sighed, but he didn't say anything. Tiuri gazed up at the stars and the slim crescent moon. *Where will I be when this moon is full?* he wondered. Finally he dozed off, but slept lightly, constantly jolting awake to listen and to check for the letter on his chest. Nothing happened, but the next morning he awoke unrested and drowsy.

Jaro, on the other hand, was in high spirits. He praised the fine morning, the good weather, the beautiful landscape. Tiuri could hardly bear it. *I wish he'd shut up*, he thought irritably. *And I wish he'd stop laughing so much... His eyes never smile.*

Once they got moving, though, Tiuri's irritation lifted. It really was a very nice day and the views were magnificent. Even Jaro didn't seem quite so bad.

But then the river disappeared into a narrow gorge, where there was no path.

"What do we do now?" said Jaro. "We can't wade through the water, can we? And I think I can hear a waterfall. Are we going to have to climb up it?"

"No," said Tiuri. "Look, there's a path up the cliff on the left over there. I think we need to go that way. It looks like it runs onwards along the top of the gorge, high up above the river. Do you see the ledge?"

"Yes," said Jaro. "Not an easy path, by the looks of it. It's so narrow, and what a long drop!"

"There'll be trickier paths up in the mountains," replied Tiuri. "Or no paths at all."

They started the climb. Tiuri was right; the path first went very steeply upwards and then led up a gradual incline to the edge of the gorge. They looked down.

"Look how far away the river is already," Jaro said.

"I think we're going to come out above the waterfall," said Tiuri. "And then we'll be able to follow the river again."

For a while they walked on in silence, with Tiuri leading the way, as the path was so narrow that they could no longer walk next to each other. Jaro followed, puffing and panting. But he was a good walker, and when they stopped to rest for a moment, he did not seem at all tired. As they continued on their way, the path became narrower and the sound of the water grew louder. Tiuri, who was still in front, walked more slowly, so that he wouldn't stumble on the loose stones. He glanced down into the chasm, which was perilously deep, even though it was so narrow that a person could jump across it.

It all happened in an instant. Jaro stumbled, falling into Tiuri and grabbing on to him. Tiuri swayed; he kept his footing, but Jaro lost his hold and started screaming as stones went tumbling into the gorge. Tiuri turned around just as Jaro slipped and disappeared. Horrified, Tiuri stood nailed to the spot, his heart racing. Then he dropped to the ground and peered over the edge.

To his surprise and relief, he found himself looking into Jaro's face. The man had grabbed hold of a branch growing from the rocks just beneath the ledge, and was hanging on with both hands. But he was in a precarious position. Tiuri had never seen such fear in anyone's eyes before. Jaro was moving his lips, but no sound came out.

"Hold on!" said Tiuri. "Hold on tight. I'll help you."

He slid forward a little, reached out his hands and took hold of Jaro's wrists. "I'll pull you up," he gasped.

"It-it won't work," stammered Jaro. "I'm too heavy."

"It will work," said Tiuri. "It has to."

"No," groaned Jaro. "I don't dare let go."

Tiuri feared that Jaro was right and his plan wouldn't work. Jaro really was heavy, and it would be hard to brace himself on the narrow, uneven path. "You can help," he said. "Try to find a foothold."

Jaro tried, but his feet scrambled against the rock face. "No," he groaned. "I can't find anything to stand on. I'm done for."

Tiuri held firmly on to Jaro's wrists, but he was still too scared to let go of the branch, even though it was obvious he couldn't hold on for much longer.

Rope! thought Tiuri frantically. *If only I had some rope... Oh, but wait...* He untied the rope from around his waist, but as he was doing so he realized it would still be a difficult task. The rope was short and it looked old. What if it broke?

"I'm going to fall," said Jaro.

"No," said Tiuri. "Hold on... just for a moment. Let me think." And then he spotted something. "I've got it!" he exclaimed. A wide ledge ran along the rock face on the opposite side of the chasm, about five feet from the top. If he stood on that... "Hold on," he said. "I'm coming to help you."

First Tiuri had to jump over the chasm, and that required some willpower. He took off his habit, so that it wouldn't get in the way, and he jumped. He dropped down onto the ledge, and then turned with his back to the rock face and looked over at Jaro. "Nearly there," he said. "I'm coming!"

Tiuri avoided looking down as he fell forwards with his arms outstretched, until his hands were touching the opposite wall. Leaning there, he formed a bridge between the two sides of the chasm. Very carefully, he made his way towards Jaro. "I'm here, Jaro," he said. "Lift your feet and put them on my shoulders. Then you can push yourself up."

Jaro turned his head and looked at Tiuri with an expression of terror on his face. Tiuri moved a little closer and repeated what he had said.

"Can you take the weight?" mumbled Jaro.

"Yes," said Tiuri. "As long as you're careful. Now!"

"Now," repeated Jaro. He waved his legs around, and the branch he was hanging from creaked alarmingly. Then Tiuri felt a foot on his shoulder, swiftly followed by the other foot on his arm. The foot slipped and came down on his arm again. Tiuri clenched his teeth; it was his wounded arm. It felt like some kind of bad dream, but it worked! Jaro had something to rest on now, and with a great deal of struggling – and pain for Tiuri – he hauled himself up.

"Now help me up," said Tiuri.

But Jaro had collapsed onto the path, gasping for air, and didn't even seem to have heard his words.

Carefully, very carefully, Tiuri pushed himself back into position on the ledge. He wasn't sure how he did it, but he managed to pull himself back up and then jump across the chasm again. He landed beside Jaro, who had still not recovered from his exertions. Trembling, Tiuri dropped down to the ground beside him. They sat together for a while, without saying anything.

Tiuri was the first to recover. He stood up again, still shaking, and put his habit back on. He wondered if Jaro had seen his chainmail. No, he didn't seem to have noticed.

"Come on," he said, as he tied the rope around his waist again. "Shall we continue?"

Jaro bowed his head. "Just a minute," he whispered.

Tiuri would have liked to rest a little longer too, but a voice inside him told him that it would be better to get on their way. So he said again, "Come on. We can rest later, when we're away from this gorge."

Jaro raised his head and looked at Tiuri, with those peculiar, piercing eyes. There was an expression on his face that Tiuri did not understand.

"You saved my life," he said quietly.

Tiuri did not respond. "Come on," he said. "We'll walk very slowly and carefully."

Jaro started to get up. "You saved my life," he said again, a little more loudly.

"What was I supposed to do? Let you fall?" Tiuri answered, trying to make light of the situation. "It could just as easily have been me hanging there." Startled by the expression on Jaro's face, he fell silent.

Jaro was on his feet by then and he said briskly, "Let's be off, then." He turned and started walking slowly onwards along the path.

Bewildered, Tiuri followed him. He wouldn't easily forget the expression he'd seen on Jaro's face. What had it meant? Terror, surprise, gratitude? No, one thing: fury! But he must be mistaken. Why should Jaro be angry with him?

2   THE HERMIT

The path took them up above the waterfall and then alongside the Blue River, which was now a turbulent stream full of rapids. They rested for a short while and continued their journey through much gentler surroundings. The path wound its way over hills and along valleys, through pinewoods and across green mountain meadows.

They did not speak much. The day was growing warmer and they were both weary. Tiuri's arm was hurting, and his chainmail and his habit were slowing him down. They were not the most suitable clothes for climbing mountains. As the day went on, he noticed that Jaro's behaviour had changed since his fall into the gorge. He had become silent and surly.

What a strange man, Tiuri thought. *There's no need for him to be grateful, but why is he being so unfriendly now? Maybe it's the shock. I almost think I like him better this way, though. It seems more natural somehow.*

In the afternoon, Tiuri spotted a cabin on a hillside ahead of them. A cliff rose behind it, tall and dark, with snow-capped summits beyond.

"Look," he said to Jaro. "Do you think that's Menaures's cabin?"

Jaro just grunted. But the sight made Tiuri's spirits rise, like a horse that knows it's nearing the stable. As they followed the bends of the path, the cabin slipped in and out of sight. Then they heard music... a light, airy melody that perfectly suited the pine trees, the sun, and the fragrant grass on the mountain slopes.

A boy was playing the flute in a meadow above the path, with a black-and-white sheep grazing beside him. The boy did not stop playing as they approached, but he watched them curiously.

"Good afternoon!" said Tiuri.

The boy put down his flute, smiled and said, "And a good afternoon to you too."

"Is the river's source nearby?" asked Tiuri.

"Just head around that bend and you'll see it," said the boy, pointing. "You must be here to see Menaures."

"Indeed," replied Tiuri.

"Where have you travelled from?"

"From the east."

The boy grinned. "I know that much," he said. "I saw you coming." He was still studying them curiously.

Tiuri liked him immediately. In his mind, he named him the shepherd boy. He was wearing few clothes and his face and his bare arms and legs were sunburnt. His short, straight hair was dark and his eyes were bright and brown.

The boy smiled and said, "I shall let Menaures know you're coming." The boy put his flute to his lips again and played a few cheerful notes. When Jaro and Tiuri walked on, he leapt to his feet, climbed up the rocks above him and disappeared from sight.

They came to a small plateau, where the river's source welled up from between some stones. Above, on a grassy slope, stood the cabin, which was built from weathered wooden planks, with a roof of flat grey slates. It stood on low stilts and had wooden steps leading up to the open door. Tiuri and Jaro stopped for a moment to look at the water, and Tiuri marvelled at the fact that this tiny spring was the source of the largest river in the Kingdom of Dagonaut. As they made their way to the cabin, the shepherd boy came bounding from the opposite direction. He must have taken a shorter route and he reached the cabin before them. However, as the shepherd boy was about to climb the steps, a deep voice sounded from within. "It's fine, Piak. There's a young man who would like to speak to me. Please let him enter."

The shepherd boy took a step back and gestured to the travellers to step into the cabin. A thin old man appeared in the doorway, dressed in a robe of rough, blue-grey fabric. His long wavy hair and beard were as white as snow, and his face was kind, calm and wise.

"Ah, not one visitor, but two," he said. "Step closer and be welcome."

Tiuri and Jaro humbly greeted the hermit and climbed the rickety steps.

"Come inside," said the hermit. "Please be seated, travellers."

The cabin consisted of only one, humbly furnished room. The hermit sat down on a stool beside the table and pointed at a bench on the other side. "Be seated," he said again.

Jaro and Tiuri did as they were told. Side by side, they sat opposite the hermit, who studied them with interest.

He must be very old, thought Tiuri, looking into the deep, dark eyes of the hermit. *And wise. As wise as he is old, or even wiser*. It seemed to Tiuri as if that brief, searching look had told the hermit all he needed to know and that Tiuri had no need to explain anything to him.

Jaro shifted restlessly on the bench beside him.

"And what brings the two of you here?" asked the hermit. "What are you seeking? Is it something I can give you? All I can do is help you to search, you know; you'll have to find whatever it is yourself."

"You speak in riddles," said Jaro, clearly feeling ill at ease. "But, as for myself, I am looking for a path."

"A path that leads where?"

"Over the mountains."

"I see," said Menaures. "You wish to travel to the west."

"Indeed, wise man, and I have heard that you know the paths in these mountains."

"Yes, I know the paths. But I can no longer walk them myself. I am too old."

"I understand," said Jaro, after a moment's silence. "But could you tell me which path to take?"

The hermit shook his head. "No," he said slowly. "The secret paths over the mountains cannot be explained to one who is a stranger to these parts."

"That is a pity," said Jaro quietly. But he didn't actually sound very disappointed at all. Menaures's response had alarmed Tiuri, though. *But*, he thought, *perhaps his answer will be different when I show him Sir Edwinem's ring.*

"I could perhaps find a guide for you," said the hermit, looking at Jaro.

"Oh. That would be good. Most kind of you, holy man," replied Jaro.

"I am no holy man, traveller," said the hermit. "Just call me Menaures. And what is your name?"

"Jaro."

"And who are you, my son?" the hermit asked Tiuri.

"I... I am Martin."

"And what brought you here?"

"I would also like to ask you something," replied Tiuri. "But..." He looked at Jaro.

"Oh, I shall go," Jaro said, rising swiftly to his feet.

The hermit smiled. "Thank you, Jaro," he said. "We can talk later and I shall see what I can do for you."

"My thanks, Menaures," said Jaro. He gave an awkward bow and left the cabin.

The hermit stood up and closed the door behind Jaro. Then he turned to Tiuri. "Speak, Martin," he said. "No one can hear us now."

Tiuri also rose to his feet and said, "My name is not Martin. It is Tiuri, although my name is of no import. I am travelling over the mountains to the west. I was sent by Sir Edwinem with the White Shield. See, here is his ring. He told me to show it to you."

The hermit came closer and accepted the ring from Tiuri. "Sir Edwinem," he said softly. "Paladin of Unauwen, Bearer of the White Shield... And where is he?"

"He is dead," replied Tiuri.

The hermit looked at him. His expression showed no alarm, only great concern. Then he looked down at the ring. "Edwinem has met his end," he said. "Cut down in his constant battle against evil. This is sad news indeed, but it would have been even sadder if he had met his defeat in some other way."

"Oh, but he did not fall in battle," said Tiuri. "He was killed, treacherously murdered!"

"Then that is not as grave for him as it is for those who killed him," said the hermit. "But tell me, my son..." He took Tiuri by the arm and Tiuri could not help but flinch.

"Ah, you are wounded," said Menaures.

"It's nothing," mumbled Tiuri.

"Sit down," said the hermit, "and speak, my son."

"But," said Tiuri, "don't you already know everything? You weren't surprised to see me and you weren't shocked when you heard of Sir Edwinem's death."

"I don't actually know," replied the hermit, "but I suspect a great deal. Ah, it seems such a short time since Sir Edwinem first came to visit me here. He was about your age, newly knighted and burning with the desire to do great deeds. His wish has been fulfilled, yet perhaps not as he would have desired, although he could not have suspected that back then. Unauwen's sons were still young at that time, but I already feared that one of them would become a threat to his father and his brother. It feels like yesterday that young Edwinem was here, even though you were not yet born. And now here you are, ready to take his place and complete his mission. Or is that not the case?"

Then, for the first time, Tiuri spoke about the task with which Sir Edwinem had charged him. He told Menaures how he had met the Knight with the White Shield and had received the letter to take to King Unauwen in the land to the west of the Great Mountains.

The hermit listened closely and then said, "The tidings you bring are a matter of grave concern. The King of Eviellan and his followers are wicked men! But do not despair; evil will always be defeated in the end. Your task is to deliver the letter. I shall ensure that you cross the mountains quickly and safely."

"But... you can no longer show me the way yourself, can you?" said Tiuri.

"No, I am too old. But I will give you a guide you can trust as you would yourself. His name is Piak. You have already seen him outside."

"The shepherd boy?" asked Tiuri.

"Yes, the very same," replied the hermit with a smile.

"How old is he?"

"Younger than you, I believe. Fourteen years old. But he was born and raised in these mountains, and he comes from a long line of men who have climbing in their blood. He is the best guide you could have. You and Piak must leave tomorrow morning, at sunrise."

"Thank you, Menaures," said Tiuri. "But what about Jaro? He wants to cross the mountains too and I can hardly say I don't want him to come with me." He told the hermit how he had met Jaro and about their journey together to the source of the river.

"Hmm," said the hermit. "It is indeed possible that he lied and that he does not have a son on the other side of the mountains. He may be a spy. Do you know, I had a feeling that someone would come to see me today? I thought it would be a young man and that proved true. I did not foresee that man's arrival, however, so I do not believe he needs my help. But I could be wrong. There is a possibility that he is telling the truth. In that case, you cannot prevent him from travelling with you, because he will never get across the mountains on his own." He looked at Tiuri. "It is up to you," he said, "to decide what you wish to do."

"Then I have no choice but to let him travel with me," said Tiuri.

"I agree," replied the hermit. "And remember that there will be three of you. Keep a close eye on him, take it in turns to keep watch at night with Piak, and make sure Jaro never walks behind you. I do not believe you will have much to fear from him, however." Then he walked over to Tiuri and said, "Now take off your habit and let me take a look at your wound. Ah, I see you're wearing chainmail. You'd better leave that here. It is heavy and will be a hindrance as you climb higher into the mountains. Here, I have some clothes for you in this chest."

Menaures carried on talking as he undid the bandage around Tiuri's arm; the wound had opened up again and soaked it with blood. The hermit dabbed the wound with something from a bottle, which smelled of pine trees. It stung a little, but had a soothing effect. Then Menaures put a fresh bandage on the wound. As he did so, he asked Tiuri about his adventures.

Tiuri told him his tale and passed on greetings from Father Hyronimus and from the lord of Mistrinaut.

"Sigirdiwarth Rafox," said Menaures. "Yes, he has not been up here for a long time. But I do know that he governs his lands well."

"Have you known him long?" asked Tiuri.

"He came here twenty years ago, when he owned nothing more than his sword, which he wanted to use only for a righteous cause. I told him then that he should head down the mountain and follow the Blue River to Mistrinaut because there was a battle there that needed to be fought. And that is how he became lord of Mistrinaut."

The hermit opened the chest and said, "Choose some clothes and put them on. And here's the ring that Sir Edwinem gave you. Take it."

"Oh, but it doesn't belong to me," said Tiuri. "He gave it to me only so that I could show it to you."

"Carry it with you then," said the hermit, "and return it to King Unauwen, who gave it to Edwinem."

"I shall do so," said Tiuri, hanging the ring from the cord around his neck once again. He was pleased that he would be able to keep the ring with him; he had come to see it as a talisman and as a reminder of the promise he had made to Sir Edwinem.

"And I shall go and talk to Piak," said the hermit.

He left and closed the door behind him.

Tiuri laid his chainmail in the chest and instead put on a faded blue doublet. He kept his habit, though, and pulled it on over the top. Then he went to the door and looked outside. The view was astounding. He could see many miles to the east, over the Kingdom of Dagonaut. He saw the Blue River winding its way across the land and even thought he could make out the towers of Mistrinaut. Closer, he could see hills and farmland, villages, scattered houses and dark forests. The shadow of the mountains moved over the landscape.

Jaro was sitting on a rock beside the spring. His face was buried in his hands, as if he was sad or reflecting deeply about something. Menaures stood nearby, talking quietly to Piak, who smiled when he saw Tiuri on the steps of the cabin. Tiuri went to join them.

"This is Piak," said Menaures. "He will take you and Jaro over the mountains."

"And you are Martin; I already know that," said the boy. "I am at your service. We leave tomorrow morning."

"Go and make preparations, Piak," said the hermit. Then he raised his voice and called out, "Jaro!"

Jaro stood up and slowly came closer.

"You can travel over the mountains," the hermit told him. "Piak, my friend and helper, will be your guide."

"Ah..." said Jaro. He sounded surprised.

"Yes, Martin also wants to head to the west. So the three of you will share the journey. Piak knows the paths."

"That's... that's excellent," said Jaro. "Thank you."

"You should go and eat now," the hermit continued. "You have to set off early tomorrow, so you should get an early night."

As they ate, Jaro was still quiet, but Piak was very talkative. He told them that he came from a nearby village. He was an orphan and Menaures had taken charge of his upbringing. In return, Piak helped the hermit with all kinds of small chores: chopping wood, cooking food and suchlike. Tiuri asked the hermit how he would manage without his helper.

"I'll be fine," the hermit replied. "Piak isn't here all the time anyway. How do you think he learnt to be such a good climber?"

Piak had never travelled beyond the mountains and he asked the travellers what it was like out there, where the land was so flat. He said he wouldn't want to live there himself.

"But I would like to go down there some day," he added, "and see the land of King Dagonaut from close up. It looks so beautiful in the distance. And Menaures has told me so much about it."

"Well, you could go down and take a look, couldn't you?" said Tiuri.

"Yes, maybe. I wasn't allowed to go last year. I was too young."

"How old are you?" asked Jaro. It was the first thing he had said.

"I was born on midsummer's day," replied Piak. "Fifteen..." He paused and glanced at Menaures. "No, fourteen years ago."

"I see," said Jaro. "That's very young to be our guide, isn't it?"

"He is young," said Menaures, "but he is not too young. If he wished to do so, he would now be allowed to go down and take a closer look at all that he has seen from afar. And then, Piak, you will realize that everything looks very different indeed."

"Have you never visited the land of King Unauwen either?" asked Tiuri.

Piak shook his head. "I've never been beyond Filamen," he said. "That's a village on the other side of the mountains. Of course I've seen the Kingdom of Unauwen before. It looks even more beautiful than Dagonaut's land. There's even a city that you can see in the distance..."

"The City of Unauwen?"

"No, I don't think so."

"No, the City of Unauwen is more distant," said the hermit. "What you can see is Dangria, the City of the East."

"It has towers," said Piak. "Lots of them. And walls. When the weather's fine, you can see it quite clearly. I'd like to go and explore a place like that. And I think I've seen the Rainbow River too."

"But not the City of Unauwen?" asked Tiuri.

"You can't see the city from the mountains," said Menaures. "It's in the west of the country, on the White River, near the sea."

"Have you ever been to a city?" Piak asked Tiuri.

"Yes," he replied, "the City of Dagonaut. That too is far from here, on the Blue River, beside a large forest."

Piak asked Tiuri what the city looked like and Tiuri told him about the gates and the city walls, the houses and the narrow alleyways and the large square where the king's palace stood. On that square, he told Piak, there was often a market and sometimes tournaments were held there too. Piak was most interested to hear about the tournaments. He had always lapped up the stories about knights that Menaures had told him and he asked Tiuri question after question. Had he ever seen a tournament? What did he know about Dagonaut's knights? What did they look like, what were their names and their coats of arms, and what daring deeds had they performed?

Tiuri could have told him so many stories, but he did not dare to do so, because he might have revealed his true identity. So he answered Piak as though he'd occasionally seen knights from afar, not as someone who had spent a great deal of time in their company and had almost become a knight himself.

"Would you stop asking so many questions, Piak?" Menaures finally said with a smile. "You're not giving our guest a moment to eat."

When they had finished eating, Jaro and Tiuri helped Piak to pack for the journey. It would not be a long trip, but still they needed plenty of supplies: rope, blankets and food. The hermit sat quietly in a corner and watched as they packed.

"Fine. That's it," said Piak after a while. "This should be enough. Otherwise it'll be too much to carry."

"There's already such a lot," said Jaro. "Do we really need to take those blankets? We have our cloaks and jackets, and it's summer."

"It can get cold up there," said Piak, "particularly at night. We may have to walk across ice fields. Wait a moment..." He rummaged around in the chest and took out a couple of sheepskins.

"Here you are," he said, throwing one each to Tiuri and Jaro. Then he examined his travelling companions. "You need to hitch up that habit or take it off," he said to Tiuri. "And let me see your shoes. You'd better wear these boots. May we borrow yours too, Menaures?"

"But you're barefoot," said Tiuri.

"I'm used to it. And I'm carrying some boots for when we get up high. Good. I think we're ready."

"It would seem so," said Menaures. "Stack it all in the corner and lay some straw and blankets on the floor. Then you can get some sleep."

Soon, they were lying next to one another, with Piak between Jaro and Tiuri, and wishing one another goodnight. The hermit went outside and left the door ajar.

Piak quickly fell asleep and Jaro lay there very still, but Tiuri could not get to sleep. Quietly, he stood up and headed outside.

The hermit was sitting on the steps, gazing at the landscape to the east. The sun had disappeared behind the mountains, but it was still not entirely dark. In the east, a few stars were already shining in the greenish-blue sky. Tiuri sat down beside Menaures and silently contemplated the view. After a while, he turned to look at the hermit.

"Yes, my son?" the hermit said quietly, without moving.

There was something that Tiuri wanted to ask, but when he opened his mouth a different question came out. "Menaures, do you know the land of King Unauwen?"

"Yes," replied the hermit. "In fact, I know it very well indeed, because I was born there. I know your land too. Before I retreated to this place, many years ago, I travelled far around the world."

"Do you know King Unauwen, and his sons?"

"Yes, I know them."

"How far is it to the City of Unauwen, Menaures?"

"It takes about five days to get over the mountains," replied the hermit. "After that, you can reach Dangria in a day. From there, a good road leads straight to the City of Unauwen, over the Rainbow River, through the Forest of Ingewel and the Hills of the Moon. You'll have no trouble getting there from Dangria in about eight or nine days."

Then Tiuri asked what it was that he most dearly wanted to know, even though it was a secret.

"Do you know... do you know what's in the letter?" he whispered.

"No," said the hermit. "I have no more idea than you."

"Perhaps it was a foolish question," said Tiuri. "But you already knew and suspected so much."

"Even though I live so far away," said Menaures, "I still know the world at the foot of the mountains. I sometimes hear news from visiting pilgrims, and other things come to me during my silent contemplations. But as far as the letter is concerned, there is no need for you to guess at its contents. Your task is only to deliver it."

"You're right," said Tiuri quietly.

They sat in silence. The sky slowly grew darker and lights began to shine deep in the valley. Tiuri stayed with Menaures for some time, thinking about many things and listening to the chirping of the crickets in the grass and the gentle murmuring of the spring. Then he stood up and wished the hermit goodnight.

"Sleep well," said Menaures.

Tiuri fell asleep as soon as he lay down, and his sleep was calm and sound.

3   ANOTHER FAREWELL

The next morning, the two travellers and their guide were up early and ready to leave. The sun had just risen and the sky above the Kingdom of Dagonaut glowed pink and gold.

"It's so beautiful," Tiuri said to Piak, pointing to the east. "And you get to see that every day."

Piak looked a little surprised. "You're right," he replied. "But so often I don't even notice."

The hermit shook each of them by the hand and gave them his blessing. "Have a good journey," he said.

Then they picked up their bags and set off. Piak was in the lead, with Jaro and Tiuri following behind. They took a steep path that led upwards behind the cabin. To Tiuri's surprise, Piak walked very slowly, far more slowly than he and Jaro had walked the previous day. After quarter of an hour, they stopped for a moment to look down at the cabin beneath them. The hermit was standing on the hillside, waving at them. They waved back.

"Why are we going so slowly?" Tiuri asked Piak, once they were on their way again.

"Slowly?" exclaimed Piak. "This is how you have to walk. Otherwise there's no way you can go on climbing for hours and hours."

Tiuri realized that he was right. They were walking slowly but steadily and so they could keep going for a long time without having to rest. Even so, Tiuri felt himself tiring after a couple of hours and the sweat was streaming down his face. Jaro was puffing and panting too. Piak made it look easy; he climbed on upwards at the same pace, as casually as if he were walking along a level road, sometimes even singing quietly to himself. But eventually he stopped and announced that it was time for a short rest.

"Look," he said. "You can see the cabin one last time." They had reached the top of their climb and would have to go downhill for some way before they started to make their way up the next ridge.

"Phew," said Tiuri, throwing down his bag. "I'm so hot."

"It's going to get hotter soon," said Piak brightly. "There

are still trees at this height, but it's more exposed higher up. And when you get even higher, there's snow and ice."

"Oh, I could do with some snow right now," said Tiuri.

"You'll have plenty of chance to be cold later on," Piak cheerfully promised him. "Shall we get going?"

"We've barely had a minute's rest," grumbled Jaro.

"We'll take a rest later," said Piak. "When we stop to eat. Or are you really tired?"

"Hmm, tired," muttered Jaro. "No, I wouldn't say that. There's no need to stop on my account. This is a good path. Does it stay like this?"

"No," replied Piak. "This path leads up to a couple of cabins. After that, there's not an actual path as such... at least not for someone who doesn't know the way. But, honestly, it's really not going to be a difficult journey, and the weather's good."

Jaro opened his mouth as if to say something, but then seemed to think better of it.

They continued through a densely wooded valley with a brook babbling through it. Tiuri and Jaro quenched their thirst, but Piak warned them not to drink too much. Then they started climbing upwards again. By the time the sun was in the south, they had reached the second mountain ridge. The landscape was already much more wild and bare, but there was still a path. They sat down in the shade of a large rock, and unpacked their food.

"Wait," said Piak. "There are some berries growing near here; they'll be tasty. I'll go and pick a few." He dashed off.

"That boy never seems to get tired," remarked Jaro. "But then he's used to climbing."

"You're right," said Tiuri with a weary nod.

Jaro picked up a piece of bread and broke some off. He seemed distracted and, rather than eating it, he sat there, crumbling it between his fingers. Then he looked back at the path they'd followed and he frowned. Tiuri thought there was something troubling him, but he didn't know how to broach the subject, and so he remained silent.

Tiuri could hear Piak singing somewhere nearby, but then he must have moved, because his song became quieter and died away.

"Right then," said Jaro, so loudly and so suddenly that it startled Tiuri. Jaro took his bag, stood up and looked at Tiuri. "I'll be going, then," he announced.

Tiuri stared at him in amazement. "Going?" he repeated.

"Yes, I'm heading back," said Jaro, pointing eastwards. "I can find the way myself."

"But why?" said Tiuri, leaping to his feet.

"Don't you understand?" asked Jaro.

"But you wanted to cross the mountains!" said Tiuri.

"You think so? Did you believe me when I told you that?" said Jaro, staring right at him.

"Well, yes, I had no reason not to believe you," Tiuri began and then he fell silent. "That's not why..." he continued. "I mean, you don't think I don't want you here, do you?" Again he paused, as he searched for the right words. What he had said was not true. He had doubted Jaro, and he would have preferred not to have his company!

"You don't trust me," said Jaro with a grim smile.

"I trust you..." Tiuri began. "Look, Jaro, I have nothing against you! I wish I could explain it to you, but I can't. But you are welcome to travel with me."

"Ah, be quiet," said Jaro. He turned away and stared at the path again. "You were right not to trust me," he said, without looking at Tiuri.

"Why's that?" asked Tiuri after a moment's silence.

Jaro glanced at him. "Don't you understand?" he asked for the second time. "Do I have to spell it out? I knew very well that you didn't want my company, but I didn't care. I'd have followed you anyway. I had no idea why you called me back and asked me to travel with you. I wondered if you were a helpful fool or just very cunning. After all, it's better to have an enemy as a travelling companion, where you can keep an eye on him, than to have him sneaking after you, isn't it?" He looked again at Tiuri. "No matter," he said. "Whether it was folly or cunning, you've defeated me. I'm going back. You need fear me no longer."

"But why?" whispered Tiuri.

"Don't you understand?" asked Jaro for the third time.

Tiuri thought he understood, but he wanted to find out more, and to be certain. "Be straight with me, Jaro," he asked.

"Blast it," said Jaro, his eyes flashing. "If that's what you want! I have no business on the other side of the mountains. I was sent to kill you and to make sure that the letter you're carrying would never reach King Unauwen! But I can't do that now, can I? You saved my life! If you really didn't trust me, that was a foolish mistake, a mistake I would never make myself. And yet your folly has made me just as powerless as if you'd allowed me to fall into that gorge. I can't kill you. And I no longer want to."

Jaro bowed his head, and seemed ashamed.

Tiuri didn't know what to say. "Thank you," he said finally.

Jaro just laughed. "The fool gets even more foolish!" he cried. "You thank me for not murdering you!"

"No," said Tiuri. "That's not it. I'm thanking you because, because you..." He fell silent. It did seem foolish to thank Jaro. And yet, for some reason he felt gratitude towards the man. Why? Because he had overcome his wickedness?

Jaro interrupted his thoughts. "So now you know," he said. "And don't go thinking I'm any better than I am! Back there, by the gorge, I was planning to push you in, but I stumbled and I fell myself. It sounds like one of those stories with a moral, doesn't it? I thought I was a dead man, but then you..." He stopped. "So, anyway, that's it," he said calmly. "I've killed men before, but I can't murder you. Go on your way in peace. Perhaps you will reach your destination, but that is no concern of mine."

"So you were sent to murder me," said Tiuri. "Who sent you? Are you one of the Red Riders? Were you sent by the Black Knight with the Red Shield?"

"Yes, I am one of the Red Riders," replied Jaro, "and the Black Knight with the Red Shield is my master."

"Who is he?"

"And that is no concern of yours," said Jaro. "For your sake, I have disobeyed his orders for the first time. Let that be enough for you."

"But... do you intend to return to him?" asked Tiuri.

"I don't yet know what I mean to do," Jaro snapped. "But that is my business. And we shall never see each other again."

"I don't like the thought of you going back to him," said Tiuri.

"Ah, you're not going to start lecturing me, are you? Maybe I can't go back. He doesn't like servants who fail him. But, I repeat, that is my business alone."

"No," said Tiuri quietly. "Not entirely, Jaro! We may never see each other again, but each of us owes his life to the other, and that includes all that we might do in the future."

Jaro thought for a moment. "That may be so," he said. "Perhaps, if you put it that way, our affairs are somehow intertwined. But each of us will go his own way, even though my path may well be different from what I had always expected." Then he seemed to regret his words. "I'm leaving," he said. "And I wish you a good journey." Without waiting for an answer, he turned around and walked away.

"Farewell," said Tiuri.

Jaro walked for some way, but then stopped, hesitated, and came back. "It's not right of me to leave like this," he said. "There's something else I need to tell you."

"What?" asked Tiuri.

"I owe my life to you," replied Jaro, "and I cannot allow you to think that the danger is over now that I am leaving. I am not the only man who was sent to follow you."

"Not the only man?" repeated Tiuri.

"No. We saw your party split up. I was sent to follow your group, and another man went after the group that took the road to the west: two Grey Knights, a squire, and a young man on a black horse. We thought at first that he was the one we were after, but when we saw you setting off along the Blue River all by yourself, we began to have our doubts and so I went after you. When I saw you clearly, I knew you were the one we wanted."

"How?" said Tiuri, interrupting him.

"I recognized you. I was one of the Red Riders who went after you in King Dagonaut's forest."

"And were you with the...?" Tiuri bit his tongue. He had wanted to ask, "And were you with the men who murdered Sir Edwinem?", but it seemed wiser not to mention that subject.

Jaro, however, seemed to see the question in his eyes. He turned away and said, "You know that I am a wicked man, don't you?" Then he continued with his story. "The other man who came after you will soon realize that he's following a false trail," he said. "But that one won't give up and return. No, he'll keep on trying to find you, because that is his mission and his goal. Perhaps he will attempt to find and follow your trail. Or he might try to cross the mountains before you and wait for you on the other side. But he will not rest until he has you! He's not like me. If you'd pulled him out of the gorge, he'd have thrown you straight down into it without a second thought. He is the best of spies and the worst of men. He is crafty and cunning and nothing and nobody can stand in his way."

"Who is he?" whispered Tiuri.

"None of us know his true name, but we call him Slither. It seems to suit him. You must be on your guard against him!"

"What does he look like?"

Jaro shrugged his shoulders. "Sometimes he is a Red Rider," he replied, "and sometimes an ordinary soldier. But he usually works as a spy and then you might encounter him in any guise. What does he look like? Not big, not small, not short, not tall, not old not young, not dark nor blond. His eyes are the only thing that give him away; they're as mean as a snake's. We were all afraid of him. Sometimes we feared we might become as evil as him!" Jaro was silent for a moment and then he smiled and said, "So now I've not only defied my master's orders, I've done my best to scupper his plans! And that was all I wanted to tell you. Farewell."

Tiuri held out his hand. "Thank you, Jaro," he said. "If you don't know what to do now, speak to Menaures. I'm sure he will advise you and help you. He may already know more than you think. Farewell."

4 PIAK

Tiuri watched Jaro go until he had disappeared from sight. Then he sat down to think through what he had told him.

"Now we can eat," said Piak, suddenly reappearing. "Here you are." He held out a handful of berries to Tiuri.

Tiuri looked at him, feeling rather confused. The shepherd boy had slipped his mind for a moment. "Oh, thank you," he said.

Piak put the berries on a flat stone and squatted down. "So he's gone, then?" he said calmly.

"Yes," said Tiuri. "But how did you know that?"

"I saw him leave," replied Piak, popping a berry into his mouth.

"Oh," said Tiuri. He wondered if Piak had heard anything of their conversation.

Piak spat out a pip, picked up another berry and examined it. Then he turned his clear gaze on Tiuri.

"Who exactly are you?" he asked quietly.

"What do you mean?" Tiuri asked.

"Are you a knight on a quest?"

"However did you come up with that idea?" asked Tiuri.

"Oh, I already suspected you weren't an ordinary traveller. I saw your chainmail in the chest in Menaures's cabin, and..." Piak paused and ate the second berry. "And," he continued, "I heard every word the two of you said. I didn't do it on purpose! But sometimes up here you can hear voices from miles away. It's the echoes. I was going to walk away, but then I remembered what Menaures had said and thought it'd be better if I knew everything."

"Oh," said Tiuri again, not sure whether to be surprised, angry or worried.

"Yes," Piak continued. "At least I know what to look out for now. Like that Slither, for instance. He's not going to get his hands on us here, not up in the mountains, not if I have anything to do with it! He's more likely to take a tumble into a ravine himself."

"Really?" said Tiuri. "But now I want you to tell me exactly what..."

But Piak didn't let him finish. He leapt to his feet, grabbed their bags and said, "Come with me!"

"What's wrong?" asked Tiuri.

"Let's find somewhere else to sit. Think of the echoes!"

Soon they had found a safer spot and Piak resumed his story. "I don't understand everything that Jaro said to you, but I did get some of it," he said quietly. "You have a letter for King Unauwen, and some knight doesn't want the king to receive it. And so he sent Jaro to track you down. And he's sent a man called Slither after you as well, who's as sly as a snake." He paused. "You're not saying anything. Of course not! You don't trust me. I bet you're just like an uncle of mine, who always says: Trust only yourself! Well, you're right. But I know now and I think it's better that you know that I know. Then you know where you stand and I don't have to pretend not to know."

Tiuri laughed. "That's true enough," he said. "And there's something else that I know now: be careful when you're talking in the mountains. The echoes can give you away."

Piak laughed too. But then his expression became serious and he said, "There's no need to worry that I'll give you away, though. You really can trust me. You see, I have a task, too. Menaures gave it to me. 'You must be his guide,' he said to me. 'You must show him a short way that is as safe as possible. You must make sure no one follows him. You must remain awake when he sleeps and stay with him when he is awake.' And that is my task. That's why I stayed nearby and listened to your conversation. So I have the task of being a guide for someone with a task, and that somehow makes your task my task too."

Tiuri felt happy and relieved as he looked at Piak. Piak would be not only a guide and a travelling companion, but also a friend. He held out his hand. "I trust you completely," he said. "Here, let's shake on it. I do indeed have a task, but I'm not allowed to speak to anyone about it. There are enemies who want to stop me, as I know to my cost. I may tell you more about it later. But I would ask you this: never let anyone else see that you know."

"That goes without saying," said Piak, shaking Tiuri's hand. Then he gasped. "Oh, I'm such a fool!" he exclaimed. "I've left the berries behind! I'll fetch them. Actually, it's their fault that I found out your secret and they shall be eaten up as a punishment, so that they can never reveal it to anyone else."

"It's so beautiful up here," said Tiuri, as they went on their way. He seemed to be able to see everything so much better now that he was no longer burdened by weariness and pain, by worry and suspicion: the mighty mountains, the spindly pine trees scattered across the landscape, the constantly changing panoramas, the racing, splashing streams, and the clouds like veils on the mountain peaks.

"Do you think so, too?" asked Piak. "This is all I know, so I have no comparison, but I don't think I'd ever want to live anywhere else. I love to climb and climb and see where I end up. My father was just the same, and the people in my village said that he was mad. He fell into a ravine one day and they say I'm going to go the same way. Which is nonsense! One of my father's neighbours would never take a step outside the village and he died falling downstairs. You're better off going headfirst into a ravine, don't you think? Then at least you've seen something of the world."

Tiuri agreed with him.

Piak went on talking about his father. "They say I look like him," he said. "His name was Piak, too. Is your father still alive?"

"Yes," replied Tiuri. "We have the same name as well."

"So he's called Martin," said Piak.

"No," said Tiuri quietly. "His name is Tiuri, and that's my name as well."

"Ah," said Piak, staring at him with wide eyes.

"But you mustn't call me that when anyone else is around," added Tiuri.

"No, no, of course not," said Piak. It looked as if he wanted to ask Tiuri something, but he remained silent.

Around sunset, they reached the place that Piak had set as their goal for the day: the two mountain cabins he had mentioned. They were both empty and unused, but they would be a good shelter for the night. Tiuri realized that it was indeed becoming chilly now that the sun was going down, and he was glad he had the sheepskin to wear. They set up camp in one of the cabins and had something to eat. They did not make a fire, though, as the smoke might give away their position.

After they had finished eating, Piak took out a small bottle and said, "Menaures gave me this. He said I was to put it on your wound."

Tiuri smiled and bravely submitted to the treatment. "I don't know much about this kind of thing," said Piak, "but I think the wound's looking good. Menaures said to use the ointment if it starts to hurt again and to make sure the cold doesn't get into it."

"It's fine, you know," said Tiuri. "It's not bothering me anymore."

They rolled themselves up in their blankets to go to sleep.

"Tomorrow," said Piak, "we'll take a path where no one will follow us."

"How do you know that?" asked Tiuri, yawning.

"Nobody else knows about it. I don't think even my father ever discovered it. Menaures showed it to me and he only happened upon it by chance. Actually, someone else found it, someone who came from the other side of the mountains to visit the hermit."

"Oh yes?" said Tiuri sleepily. "So how did he find it?"

"It was a very long time ago, before I was born. A young knight of King Unauwen was travelling over the mountains; he got lost and found himself in a snowstorm. So he blew on his horn and Menaures heard it and went to look for him. And he found him on that path, which he'd never seen before. The knight had already crossed the pass and wasn't that far from his destination. Menaures said it had to be a miracle, because the knight didn't know his way through the mountains at all. He was a fine fellow and he later became a famous knight. His name was Sir Edwinem."

Tiuri was immediately wide awake. "Edwinem?" he repeated.

"Have you heard of him?"

"Yes," said Tiuri.

"Do you know him?" asked Piak.

Tiuri did not answer immediately. "Yes," he said after a while. "I once met him."

"Really? Did you speak to him?"

"Hm... yes," said Tiuri.

He heard Piak sit up. "Hey," he whispered, "your name's Tiuri, isn't it?"

"Yes," replied Tiuri, a little surprised at the question.

"I know a song about the knights of King Dagonaut. About the great battle in the east. Listen." And Piak quietly sang:

Oh, come and listen to my song,
and I shall sing to you
of deeds so brave and men so fine
and knights so brave and true.

And how our great king Dagonaut
roamed so far and wide
and fought against our enemies,
with his paladins at his side.

The king clad in his purple cloak
rode on his fiery steed
and battled for his people
in our hour of need.

And who rode upon his right
with shield azure and gold?
Sir Tiuri was his name,
a knight so brave and bold.

"You see, Sir Tiuri," said Piak, breaking off his song. "Tiuri the Valiant. Is he your father?"

"Why would you think..." Tiuri began, but then he changed his mind. "Yes, he's my father."

"So you *are* a knight, after all!" Piak whispered excitedly.

"No, I'm not," said Tiuri. "I'm... I was... just a squire."

"Oh, but you'll become a knight later, won't you? First a page, and then a squire. That's how it works, isn't it? Tell me all about it!"

"I was my mother's page and my father's squire," said Tiuri. He smiled in the darkness at the memory of those happy years at Castle Tehuri. For the first time in days, he wondered again how his parents were faring. Were they waiting for him in the City of Dagonaut, or had they returned to their castle?

"And when I was thirteen, I became Sir Fantumar's squire," he continued.

"Sir Fantumar," repeated Piak, his voice full of awe. "The song mentions him, too."

And who rode upon his left
with shield of red and white?
Sir Fantumar was his name,
that fine and worthy knight.

"And then I went into King Dagonaut's service," Tiuri told him. "As every prospective knight must do."

"And when will you be knighted?"

"I should already be a knight," replied Tiuri. "But now I don't know if I ever will be. I've broken the rules and the king is a strict man." He told Piak about the vigil in the chapel, and about the voice asking him to open the door and the stranger who gave him the letter for the Black Knight with the White Shield. He told him how he had found the knight dying and then taken on his task: to deliver the letter to King Unauwen.

"Ah," sighed Piak. "Then I would say that you're a knight on a quest. You did what had to be done, didn't you? You couldn't have reacted any differently, could you?"

"No," said Tiuri, "I couldn't."

"And what about the Black Knight with the White Shield. Who was he?"

"Sir Edwinem, lord of Forèstèrra. But I only found that out later."

"I'm glad you've told me," said Piak. "Maybe you'll tell me more stories about all the things you've done... You know, I'd really like to be your squire."

"But I'm not a knight," said Tiuri.

"Yes, you are!"

"I'd rather you were my companion and my friend."

"Would you? Then yes, let's be friends. I really want to hear more about your adventures, but I'm so tired now. So I'm just going to dream about what you've told me instead. Goodnight, Tiuri."

"Goodnight, Piak."

And then all was silent in the cabin.

5 MIST AND SNOW

The next morning, they both woke at the same time. Piak got up first, walked over to the door and looked outside. "Oh no! Mist!" he said. "I thought as much."

Tiuri went to look. The world outside had disappeared, and everything was enveloped in a thick grey cloud.

"I smelled it as soon as I woke up," said Piak.

"What do we do now?" said Tiuri, shivering with the cold.

"It might lift later," said Piak. "It's early and the sun's still low in the sky. We can get as far as the Green Shelf in any case. I know the way with my eyes closed."

Tiuri didn't reply. He wondered how anyone could ever find their way through such thick mist.

"Let's take our time over breakfast," said Piak. "At least we can make a fire now. No one's going to see it."

Tiuri thought that sounded like a fine idea. Before long, they were eating a hearty breakfast beside a fire that was merrily crackling away. When they'd finished, they looked outside again. It was a little lighter, but the mist was still just as thick.

"What do you think?" asked Tiuri. "Shall we wait a little longer or just set off?"

"What do you want to do?" asked Piak.

"I don't know. There's no way I could find my way through, but you're at home in the mountains. You're a better judge of the situation."

"If we wait, we could be here all morning," said Piak. "Let's get going. We'll just head for the Green Shelf for now. And then we'll see."

They put out the fire, picked up their bags and set off, with Piak leading and Tiuri following close behind. Piak had put on his boots and was carrying a walking stick that he'd cut from a tree.

As they slowly climbed on upwards, Tiuri realized that his life was entirely in Piak's hands. He could see no more than a few steps ahead and could only blindly follow his new friend. They did not speak much and whatever they said sounded strangely muffled. The mist seemed to deaden every sound, including their footsteps and the rushing water that they heard now and then. Sometimes Piak warned Tiuri about a steep incline or a sudden descent, or a fissure or a stream that they had to step over. Tiuri lost all sense of direction. He had no idea how long they'd been walking for or how far they'd come. Then Piak stopped and said, "Wait here. I'm going ahead to take a look. Don't move from this spot." Before Tiuri could respond, he was gone.

Tiuri sat down on a rock and tried again to peer through the mist. He felt so completely alone. It seemed like a really long wait and he started to wonder where Piak had got to. Perhaps he was lost; how would he ever find him again? But then he heard a reassuring cry, "Ho, there!" And his young guide emerged from the mist.

"Come on," Piak said cheerfully. "Let's get going. I think the weather's improving."

Tiuri couldn't see any signs that it was getting better. "Where were you?" he asked.

"I just wanted to check exactly where we are," replied Piak. "I recognized a big rock some way along the path. We're not far from the Green Shelf."

"Did you get lost?" asked Tiuri.

"No," said Piak, "I just wasn't sure how far we'd come, and I didn't want us to walk past the Green Shelf without noticing. It's hard to tell in this mist how far you've come," he added apologetically.

"I can see that," said Tiuri. "Wouldn't we have been better off waiting in the cabin?"

"I don't think so," said Piak. "You want to get over the mountains as quickly as possible, don't you? And we can at least get as far as the Green Shelf. After that, we'll need to be able to see more clearly, but I think the mist should lift soon."

"How can you tell?" said Tiuri.

"Can't you feel the wind getting up? And look, it's lighter in the east now."

They walked onwards, still one small step at a time. When they came to a large rock, Piak stopped. "This is where Menaures was sitting when he heard Sir Edwinem's horn," he said.

"Did Menaures often used to go up into the mountains?" asked Tiuri.

"Yes, in the old days. My father went on a lot of journeys with him. But Menaures would travel alone, as well. He'd sit thinking for hours and hours on a mountainside or a peak. Hey, look over there!"

Tiuri looked where Piak was pointing. The veil of mist parted to reveal the top of a mountain. It vanished again in an instant, but Piak smiled and said, "Perhaps we'll be walking in the sunshine before too long."

They decided to wait by the rock until the mist cleared a little. Piak said they could shelter there, as the Green Shelf was more exposed to wind and weather. The two boys sat for a while and ate some bread. The mist started to swirl, revealing sketchy fragments of the scenery around them. It was a wondrous, shifting spectacle. Piak was right about the mist lifting; about half an hour later, the sun appeared, small and pale. They decided to continue.

Tiuri and Piak soon reached the Green Shelf. Tiuri could make out two different paths leading onwards, but Piak said they were not taking either of them.

"One's a dead end," he told Tiuri. "The other goes in the right direction, but the route we're taking is one that no one else will follow."

He walked to the edge and looked down.

Tiuri did the same and found himself looking down into a ravine. He couldn't tell how deep it was, because it was still full of mist.

"Really? We need to go down there?" he asked incredulously.

"Yes, it's easier than it looks."

"I hope so," said Tiuri, taking a step back and looking around. He realized they were even higher up in the mountains; there were no trees, and the landscape was bare and desolate. To the west, he spotted a beautiful, conical mountain peak, and beside it a field of ice or snow, with claw-like fingers reaching out to the valley below.

"That's where the pass is," said Piak, pointing. "We're going over that glacier and on the other side of the ridge you'll be able to see the Kingdom of Unauwen."

"It doesn't even look all that far now," Tiuri remarked.

"We can reach the pass tomorrow morning," said Piak, as he roped the two of them together. "Come on," he said. "Let's go." But before they set off, he bent down and picked up something from the ground.

"For you," he said, holding out two flowers to Tiuri; one was white and greyish-green and looked like a star, and the other was like a small, blue bell.

"What? There are flowers growing up here?" Tiuri exclaimed.

"Yes, tuck them into your belt if you like. You'll need to keep your hands free."

Slowly and carefully, they began the descent. It was indeed easier than it looked, although they had to be careful because the surface was wet and slippery and strewn with loose stones. This time it was Tiuri who led the way, but Piak kept calling out to him to tell him the best places to put his feet. After a while, Tiuri became used to going downhill and he walked faster and more confidently.

But before long he slipped on a stone and went sliding down the slope. A tug on the rope brought him to a stop.

"Are you all right?" called Piak. "You haven't hurt yourself, have you?"

"N-no," said Tiuri. "I d-don't think so."

Piak was beside him in a second, helping him to his feet.

"It's all right," said Tiuri, "I'm fine."

"If you slip again, drop down," Piak advised him. "And try to keep as close to the ground as you can. Falling itself isn't so bad as long as you don't end up sliding."

"I see," said Tiuri, rather sheepishly. Only now did he truly understand that Piak, who was younger than him and who looked up to Tiuri as a brave knight, had so much to teach him about the mountains, and that he was a guide he could trust. "Don't you want to lead?" he asked.

"No, that's not how it's done," said Piak. "A guide has to lead while climbing, but follow during the descent."

It took a moment for Tiuri to realize why. As his guide, Piak was responsible for the lives of both of them; if Tiuri were to slip, Piak had to brace himself and stop him falling.

Tiuri heard rushing water, and soon they reached the bottom of the ravine. They waded through a stream, walked along the opposite bank for some way and then climbed back up again. By then, the sun was shining more brightly and there was a strong breeze.

"The weather really is nice now," said Tiuri when they stopped to rest for the second time.

Piak frowned and stared at the sky for a while. "What time do you think it is?" he asked. "Three o'clock, maybe half past? It's about an hour from here to the glacier, and then it takes another hour to cross it. We need to be past the Seven Crags before dark. Then we can reach the pass tomorrow morning and be within sight of the Kingdom of Unauwen by midday. We should get going."

Tiuri stood up and followed him. He would have preferred to rest for a little longer, but he knew that Piak must have good reasons for wanting to press on. They climbed a long way uphill on the other side of the ravine and after that they went up and down – more up than down – over increasingly difficult terrain. There was no sign of a path, but Piak headed onwards without hesitation and, whenever it was possible, he moved far more quickly than they had at the start of their trek. The higher they climbed, the more strongly the wind blew. It became colder and the sun disappeared into the clouds. After about an hour, they reached the glacier, a vast field of ice, furrowed with narrow, fast-flowing streams and treacherous crevasses.

"Just as well it hasn't been snowing," said Piak, as they stepped out onto the glacier. "But something's changed since I was last here. It looks like there are more cracks in the surface." He untied the rope between them, carefully coiled it back up, and then led the way over the ice. He didn't walk in a straight line, but seemed to be following a path, even though Tiuri could not see one.

The wind blasted across the landscape and it was icy cold.

"You're unlucky, Tiuri," said Piak. "When the sun's shining, you can sometimes walk around half-naked up here."

The walk across the glacier was an extraordinary experience for Tiuri. He had never seen anything quite like that ice field in the cold, grey light. They passed a strange and wonderful sight: some large boulders balancing on low, thin columns of ice. They looked like giant toadstools.

"They're glacier tables," said Piak. "That's where the mountain spirits sit when they come down from their peaks.

Sometimes they pick up the boulders and start hurling them at each other. It sounds like rumbling thunder. You can hear it for miles around."

"Is that true?" asked Tiuri, looking around as though he expected a giant mountain spirit to appear and fling a rock at him.

"I've never seen them myself," said Piak. "But I've heard them in the distance."

They jumped over a few crevasses and streams, but when they were about halfway across the glacier they came to a stream that was too wide for them to leap across. It had carved out a deep bed in the ice and its sides were as smooth as glass. All they could do was follow the course of the stream in the hope of finding a spot where they could cross.

"More bad luck," muttered Piak.

They walked quite some way before they dared to make the leap. And then they had to head back along the bank to a point where the path across the glacier was safer. As they walked, the wind grew colder and the sky became greyer.

Tiuri and Piak were chilled through by the time they reached the far side of the glacier. It had taken them much longer than an hour to cross. Piak looked up at the sky again. "Call me a goat if it's not about to snow," he said. "Come on, we need to hurry."

"How far do you want to get today?" asked Tiuri, when they stopped after a while to rope themselves together again.

"I want to get past the Seven Crags," replied Piak. "That's the most difficult part of the route. I just hope it doesn't get dark too soon."

But, once again, luck was not with them. The darkness rolled in at a frightening pace and the first snow soon began to fall. The wind picked up and their only good fortune was that it was at their back. The blizzard made it hard to see anything and the ground underfoot was even trickier than it had been before, because it was so slippery.

"First mist, then snow," grumbled Piak. "You know, the mountains could have given you a warmer welcome."

At that point, they were standing on a narrow ridge, with high rocks and cliffs to the right, and a ravine to the left.

"Where are the Seven Crags?" asked Tiuri.

"We're beneath the fourth crag now," Piak replied. "Let's keep going."

They scrambled onwards in the dwindling light. Tiuri's teeth were chattering and he had no sensation in his hands or feet. Worst of all, his arm was hurting again; it had become painful on the glacier and grew worse with every step he took. But he didn't mention it and ploughed on in silence.

Suddenly Piak stopped. "This isn't going to work!" he shouted back at Tiuri. "It'd be dangerous to continue. The path is even narrower and steeper further on and it'll be really dark soon."

"So what should we do?" Tiuri yelled back at him.

"We have to go back," replied Piak. "We can't stay here; it's too cold and exposed. There's a small cave by the third crag. We can shelter there. It's not the best of places, but we'll be able to cope for a night."

They started the walk back. Walking downhill proved to be even trickier than climbing upwards and the wind was against them now, so the blizzard was blinding. They made very slow progress, but they didn't dare to hurry, even though it was almost completely dark by that point. It was unlikely that they could have managed to walk any faster anyway. They took it in turns to lead and had to keep stopping to help each other. Neither of them said a word, until Piak gasped, "We're almost there! Do you remember this place?"

"I can hardly see anything," said Tiuri. "And it all looks the same!"

They continued the descent. *I can't keep this up for much longer*, thought Tiuri. *I'm going to collapse*. But then he recognized something. "Hey, Piak. Isn't that the third crag?"

"Yes!" shouted Piak. "Nearly there."

They reached their destination just in time. The cave was a very small one and the two of them could just squeeze in there, protected from the wind, but not the cold. They opened their bags and, shivering, wrapped their blankets around themselves.

"Well, then," said Piak, "here we are. But we mustn't fall asleep. We'd get too cold. We need to stand up and walk about once every so often, and stamp our feet. And just keep moving. How are you feeling, Tiuri?"

"Oh, I'm fine," he replied. "All things considered."

"Is your arm bothering you?"

"A little."

"I bet that means a lot," said Piak. "Wrap yourself up as well as you can. Wear your habit on top of the sheepskin and bundle yourself up in your blanket. There's nothing we can do about it now. We just have to concentrate on getting through the night. Let's make sure we have plenty to eat. That always helps. It's a shame we've got nothing to make a fire with," he added a while later. "But I think we'd have trouble getting a fire started in this weather, let alone keeping it going. You must be wondering what you've got yourself into, eh?"

"There's no way we could have seen this weather coming though, is there?" said Tiuri, shouting to make himself heard above the noise of the storm.

"No, I've only once seen this kind of weather at this time of year – and that was higher up! Believe it or not, I really didn't see this coming this morning. But later, I started to worry that it might snow, which is why I was in such a hurry. It would have been better if I'd looked for shelter for the night immediately after we crossed the glacier."

"You weren't to know it would get this bad," said Tiuri.

"No, I wasn't expecting it at all. But I'm sorry."

"There's no need to apologize," Tiuri replied. "You did what you thought was right." His teeth were chattering.

"Come on," said Piak. "We need to keep moving. Here, let's clap our hands. Like this." He started clapping and chanting a song, at the top of his voice:

In the mighty mountains, in the middle of the night,
A crashing and a flashing filled my heart with fright.
What a fearful shaking!
What a dreadful sound!
The spirits of the mountain were hurling rocks around!

The wind howled about the crags and in the distance they heard the rumble of thunder or of rolling boulders. Tiuri and Piak ate some food and huddled close together, trying desperately not to fall asleep.

It was a long night. Sometimes they stood up and cautiously walked up and down along the narrow ledge outside the cave, but the cold soon drove them back to their shelter. They sat up straight and tried to stamp their feet and rubbed each other's hands.

They kept themselves awake by telling stories. Tiuri told Piak about his adventures in the forest and at Castle Mistrinaut and, when he'd run out of things to say about that, he told

Piak about Castle Tehuri, the City of Dagonaut and the king's knights. He told Piak all of their names and described their shields and their banners.

Piak told Tiuri about the village where he was born, about the mountains and the hermit, and he sang all of the songs he knew. As the night passed, they became too tired to talk, so they sat in silence for long intervals. Sometimes, sleep got the better of them and they drowsed off, until one of them woke with a start and gave the other a shake.

But during the course of the night the wind slowly dropped and the snow stopped. And finally, finally, the pale light of dawn crested the horizon.

6   A Welcome Sight

"What I could really do with now is a bowl of hot bean soup," said Piak, as they nibbled on their hard bread. "But as there's none available, I shall just put in an order for plenty of sunshine instead."

Tiuri had come to admire his travelling companion's endless optimism and determination. But when he looked at Piak, he could see that the long, hard night had taken its toll. Piak's tanned face looked pale and grey and his lips were blue. Tiuri wondered how they were going to manage what Piak had said was the most difficult part of the journey. It had stopped snowing, but the path they had to follow was covered in snow and looked far from inviting. The sun was still low in the sky and they could feel little of its warmth. Tiuri thought it would take nothing less than a blazing fire now to drive the cold from his bones. But still, before long, he was packed and ready to go.

"How does your arm feel?" asked Piak.

"Oh, it's much better," Tiuri replied. He was exaggerating, but it really wasn't quite as painful as it had been.

"Good," said Piak. "Let's get going. But walk slowly. It'll be slippery underfoot."

For the second time, they made their way along the path beside the crags. Piak was right; it certainly was slippery. It was so cold and their frozen limbs were little use when it came to scrambling over the perilous rocks. What they had been unable to see clearly the previous day now served as a constant warning: deep ravines and chasms that seemed bottomless. The landscape around them was white and black and grey: the white of the snow and ice, the black of the rocks and crags, and the greys of the skies and distant mountain slopes. For a long time, they clambered on in silence, because they didn't have enough energy to speak. And then, after what seemed like hours, Piak announced, "This is the seventh crag. We need to climb up and onto the other side. It's the point I wanted to reach last night. There's a good place to shelter."

The climb up and over the seventh crag was the hardest of all. When they finally reached the top, everything was dancing before Tiuri's eyes and he was panting for breath. But Piak wasn't in much better shape. Still they pressed on, down the other side and then on downhill to a place where they would be less exposed. Then they sat down and rested for a while. Tiuri realized that he no longer felt quite as cold, but it was some time before he could pay much attention to their surroundings. To their right was a snow-covered ridge and, up above it, the sky was bright and blue. They still had some way to go before they would reach that point of the journey, but Piak said once they had climbed the ridge they would be at the pass and would be able to see the Kingdom of Unauwen. Tiuri gazed at the mountain to the right of the pass, with the conical peak that he had noticed before.

"I've been up on top of that one," said Piak. "But I wouldn't much like to be up there now," he added with a grimace. Then he stood up. "Shall we rest later in the sheltered spot I mentioned?" he suggested. "It'll be nicer there than here."

At the foot of the seventh crag was a cave that was much larger and deeper than the one where they'd spent the previous night. They had to scramble over piles of rocks and stones to reach the entrance.

"Maybe it wasn't such a bad thing, after all," said Piak to himself.

"What?" asked Tiuri.

"That the weather was so bad and we didn't manage to get here last night. These stones weren't here last time I came. It's quite possible that they fell down here last night. I wouldn't want a stone like that to fall on my head. Would you? But wait until you see what I've got here!"

Piak disappeared into the darkness at the back of the cave and emerged with an armful of branches. "What do you say to that?" he said triumphantly. "My supplies! I brought them here from Filamen last month. They're not even all that damp."

"That's wonderful!" said Tiuri.

"Now let's light a fire," said Piak. "I'm not as cold as I was this morning, but I'd like to be glowing with warmth before we set off again. And we're going to have some toast and I'm going to heat up some food in the ashes."

Piak was as good as his word, and by the time they set off again they were in a much better frame of mind and ready to resume their journey. The sun helped by shining more brightly, which made the last big climb almost enjoyable. By the time they reached the top, they were actually feeling warm. But, at that moment, neither of them was thinking too much about the cold or the heat. The Kingdom of Unauwen was in sight!

Tiuri gave a sigh. There, ahead of him, was his destination. He could see little more than one mountain ridge after another, vanishing into the mists, and could only guess at the flat land that lay beyond. They still had a long way to go; they had covered only half of the distance over the mountains.

"The air's a little hazy," said Piak. "And there's actually a better view later on, even though we'll be lower down. But just take a look around."

Tiuri realized what a beautiful spot they were standing in. They were surrounded by snow-covered mountain slopes and summits, which glowed in the glorious sunlight.

"Come on," said Piak, "I don't want to get cold again and that's what's going to happen if we stay here for much longer. And we've got so much time to make up."

Tiuri found the descent tricky. Up on the pass he had felt as though their difficulties were behind them, but the landscape here was still wild and barren. It was, however, much less cold, now that they could no longer feel the wind from the east. After a while, the craggy landscape around them blocked their view of the Kingdom of Unauwen.

The day grew longer and, as the sun in the west transformed the mountain tops into orange flames, Tiuri and Piak went looking for a place to sleep and found one beside a stream in a shallow valley. They were both too tired to eat much, but Piak took some time to treat Tiuri's arm with the ointment from Menaures's bottle. Then they lay down and fell fast asleep.

*

Morning came, bright and cold, but later in the day it warmed up. Piak pointed out a small, flattish peak to Tiuri and said, "That's my lookout tower. How about climbing up there and taking a quick look? It's not much of a detour. We'll be passing close by."

Tiuri didn't want to disappoint Piak and, when he was standing up on the peak, he didn't regret the short climb. Piak's lookout tower offered a fine view over the land to the west, and the clear weather meant they could see a long way. They saw fields and meadows and forests, and Dangria, like a city from a fairy tale, and small dots some way beyond the city that were probably villages, and a glistening ribbon that might be the Rainbow River. It seemed like a fantastically beautiful place to Tiuri and he thought how much he'd like to be a knight-errant, so that he could constantly travel to strange and distant lands and see new sights.

"How far is it from here to the foot of the mountains?" he wondered out loud.

"Shouldn't take us too long to get down there," said Piak. "Maybe two and a half days. I've never been far beyond Filamen, and we'll be there tomorrow evening."

So in two and a half days' time, I'll have to say goodbye to Piak, thought Tiuri. He didn't like that prospect. He was going to miss his companion. In fact, he was going to miss him more than Sir Ristridin and his company. He could be more himself with Piak and they had become good friends. And Piak's cheerful nature kept Tiuri's fears at bay.

"Is something wrong?" asked Piak.

"No," said Tiuri. "Why do you ask?"

"You look so terribly serious. You're not thinking about spending the night in Filamen, are you?"

"Why? Oh yes... No, we'd better not."

"That's right," said Piak. "We need to travel without leaving any trail. We're sure to be noticed in a place as small as Filamen. But I have another idea. An uncle and aunt of mine live up in the hills above Filamen. They're called Taki and Ilia, and they're both really nice. We can go there. They'll keep our visit a secret if I ask them to. And they'll feed us too. No one can cook like my aunt."

Tiuri smiled. "That does sound appealing," he said.

"Yes, and there's no need to worry. They won't say anything, and they live all on their own up there. Menaures knows them too. He sometimes used to visit them. So what do you think?"

"Lead the way," said Tiuri.

"Let's be quick about it, then," said Piak. "Maybe we can get there before dark."

The rest of the journey downhill went very quickly. Piak walked in front most of the way, to set the pace. Actually, it was more like falling forwards than walking, as he jumped from one rock to the next. Tiuri kept up with Piak, even though he felt a shooting pain in his arm with every step. By the afternoon, the landscape had become calmer and gentler and then they heard the tinkling of bells.

"Uncle Taki's sheep," said Piak.

They soon found the animals, which were grazing in a small meadow. When the sheep saw Tiuri and Piak, they ran up and started licking them.

"Hey, hey," said Piak. "Don't eat us!"

A man came walking from the other side of the meadow. "Well, look who's here!" he called. "It's our Piak!"

Piak greeted his uncle warmly and introduced him to Tiuri.

"This is my friend Martin," he said. "We were just on our way to see you."

Taki was a young man and he looked strong; his friendly face was just as brown as Piak's, but his hair was so bleached by the sun that it was more like straw. He took a good look at Tiuri and Piak and said, "You must be tired. Did you have bad weather up there?"

"We did indeed," said Piak. "Didn't you get any of it down here?"

"No, but we saw a nasty-looking sky over the mountains to the east and we heard the rumble of shifting stones." Taki chased the sheep away and continued, "But you can tell me all about it later. Let's get down to the house first, boys! I tell you what, I'll go ahead and tell Ilia to get some food on the fire."

Piak thought that sounded like an excellent plan, but he stopped his uncle for a moment and said in a hushed voice, "One more thing, Uncle Taki. Our visit has to remain a secret. I can't tell you why, but no one must know that we're here."

Taki showed no surprise. "That's fine by me," he said. "We have no other visitors and we lead a lonely life up here. So it'll be easy enough to do as you ask. See you down at the house." Then Taki strode off down a narrow track, with Piak and Tiuri following him more slowly.

"It's about another hour's walk from here," said Piak.

Taki ran on ahead and soon disappeared into a pinewood and out of their sight.

It was almost dark by the time they reached Taki's house, a wooden cabin with an adjoining barn. Light streamed from the windows and they could see the silhouette of a woman standing in the doorway. A dog came running towards them, barking, and it jumped up at Piak, wagging its tail.

"Hello, lad," Piak said to the dog. "How are you doing?"

"Welcome, boys!" called the woman. "Come on in and make yourselves at home."

7 Taki and Ilia

Piak's aunt Ilia was small and dark-haired, with a sweet, rosy face. She kissed Piak on both cheeks and warmly greeted Tiuri.

The cabin had only one room, which was small and simple, but Tiuri had never seen a cosier home. Two candles shone on a gleaming polished table, which was laid with wooden bowls of bread, cheese and fruit, and mugs of milk. A fire was burning in the hearth and water bubbled away in the large kettle hanging above it.

Taki came in through the opposite door, which connected the cabin to the barn. "Just drop your things on the floor," he said, "and pull off your boots. Then come with me into the barn. Your hunger will have to wait for a little longer." He picked up the kettle from the fire and walked ahead of them.

In the barn, a half-filled tub was waiting. Taki added the contents of the kettle. "There you go," he said, "now it should be warm enough. Get undressed and jump right in. There's nothing quite like a warm bath."

Tiuri and Piak did as they were told. Taki left them alone and closed the door as he left. A little later, Ilia came in and left them a couple of towels.

"I'll take your clothes," she said. "I can brush them down for you and hang them out for a while. Here's something to wear in the meantime."

After their bath, Piak bandaged Tiuri's wound again. "It's healing nicely now," he said, "which is just as well, because there's not much ointment left in Menaures's bottle."

When they were ready, Tiuri and Piak headed back into

the house, with damp hair and red cheeks. One was dressed in a long blue shirt and the other in a pair of patched red trousers, both of which belonged to Taki. Ilia was stirring the pot above the fire. Taki was sitting at the table and he invited them to join him.

"You can start eating," said Ilia. "But leave some room for the bean soup."

"Aunt Ilia!" said a delighted Piak. "You've actually made bean soup? Just what I wanted. But we won't start eating until you're sitting with us."

"It's only simple fare," Ilia said. "I didn't know you were coming."

"Well, it certainly looks like there'll be more than enough," said Taki. "They're never going to eat all that."

Piak and Tiuri nodded their agreement and tucked in. The dog sat beneath the table, gobbling up any scraps that were thrown in his direction. As they ate, they talked. Taki wanted to hear all about their journey and he asked Piak how their friends on the other side of the mountains were doing. Piak asked what his aunt and uncle had been up to lately and if there was any news from Filamen. Tiuri was the only one who listened more than he spoke.

"I've hardly asked you any questions, Martin," said Taki after a while, "but it isn't from a lack of courtesy. As it's supposed to be a secret that you're here, I thought questions might not be welcome."

"Thank you," said Tiuri with a smile.

"Yes, it's a secret," said Piak. "But Menaures knows all about it and he told me to be his guide. We may be able to tell you more another time."

"It's just as well I'm not the curious type," said Taki. "But Ilia is. She must be burning to know what's going on!"

"That's not true!" said Ilia. "I'm never nosy about things that are none of my business."

"In that case, there must be very many things in this world that *are* your business," said Taki, gently teasing his wife. "Well, well, I never knew you were so important!"

Then he gave her a wink and they all laughed, including Ilia.

It occurred to Tiuri that, now they'd gone over the pass, they must be in the Kingdom of Unauwen. He asked Taki if he'd got that right.

"Yes, indeed," Taki replied. "There are people who say the Great Mountains belong to no ruler. But I consider Unauwen to be my king."

"You've been to Dangria, haven't you?" asked Piak.

"Many a time, before I was married. It's a beautiful city, but I wouldn't like to live there."

"Why not?" asked Tiuri.

"Too crowded for me. I prefer a little cabin in the mountains, right up high in the fresh air. But Dangria's certainly beautiful, although I've heard it's nothing in comparison to the City of Unauwen. Is that where you're heading?"

"To Dangria? Yes," said Tiuri. "Is it far from here?"

"Well, you can reach the plateau near Filamen by tomorrow evening, and it'll take you a little more than a day to reach the foot of the mountains from there. Wait, I have an idea! A man I once worked for lives over there. His name's Ardoc. He's wealthy and has lots of horses and carts. If you mention my name, he might let you ride along with him to Dangria. He goes there to sell his produce at the market. I'm sure he won't mind. He's a nice fellow, although his manner can sometimes be a little gruff. But you'll have to be there early in the morning; he usually leaves before dawn so that he can get to Dangria by the afternoon."

"Thank you," said Piak. "We can certainly give it a try, don't you think... Martin? Where exactly does this Ardoc live, Uncle Taki?"

"I'll explain the route to you tomorrow," he replied. "I might even take you some of the way myself. The path has changed a bit, as there was a small landslide last month."

"Really?" said Piak. "Where? What happened?" And Taki had to tell him all about it.

After dinner, they went straight to bed. The young men refused the offer of Taki and Ilia's bed, so Taki made one up for them on the floor. Then they all said goodnight and slept soundly in that warm and welcoming home.

The next morning, Tiuri and Piak rose early and had a big breakfast. Ilia also put together a parcel of food for the journey. "This bread is fresh," she said. "Just leave your old bread here. I can use it to make some bread pudding for Taki."

Tiuri and Piak thanked her for her kindness and said goodbye. Taki and his dog accompanied them for some distance. They made their way over rocks and stones down a steep slope, along the dry bed of a stream, and finally down a beautiful path through flower-filled meadows. Around midday, Taki bade them farewell and gave them directions to Ardoc's farm. The young men thanked him and promised to visit on their way back.

"I hope Ardoc lets us travel with him," said Piak, as he and Tiuri walked on together. "I've never been on a cart before."

Tiuri stopped and looked at Piak. "What is it?" asked Piak.

"You were only supposed to take me over the mountains, weren't you?" said Tiuri. "Don't you have to go back to Menaures?"

"Can't I travel on with you?" asked Piak. "Menaures himself said, 'If you wish to accompany him beyond the mountains, you should do so.' And I would like to. That's if you don't mind."

"But... I do mind," said Tiuri.

"Why? Would you rather travel alone?" asked Piak.

Tiuri really wanted Piak to stay with him, but he said, "It could be dangerous. So, no, I don't want you to come."

"Oh, is that truly the reason?" said Piak. "I'm not worried about the danger. Go on, let me come with you to the City of Unauwen."

"No," said Tiuri. "It's... just better if I travel alone."

Piak looked disappointed. "Do you mean that?" he asked. "You think I'm going to slow you down, don't you?"

"No," said Tiuri, "that's not it at all! Thank you for the offer, but truly, it's..."

"...better if you travel alone!" said Piak, interrupting him. "You've already said that. You're scared it might be dangerous, but I already know that. Menaures knew that too, and he thought it was fine for me to go, if I wanted to. And I do want to! Or is there some other reason why you don't want me to come along?"

"No," said Tiuri. "But I think the danger is reason enough."

"Ha! That's no reason at all," said Piak. "I know all about the dangers, about the Red Riders and Slither the spy. You know two can keep watch better than one. You want to move quickly... and I'm quick. Come on, let me go with you. I shall be your squire and I shall obey your every command."

Tiuri hesitated. Could he accept Piak's offer?

"If you hesitate for too long, I'm going to walk away," Piak threatened. "But then I'll secretly follow you, and come sneaking after you like a spy."

Tiuri started to laugh. "Oh, in that case, all right," he said.

"I'd rather have an actual travelling companion than someone out there stalking me."

"Hoorah!" cried Piak. He broke into a run, but then stopped and waited for Tiuri to catch up with him. Then he bowed deeply. "I am your servant," he said solemnly.

"Don't be so silly," said Tiuri. "We are travelling companions, and equals."

"Friends!"

They walked on for a while in contented silence.

Then Piak said, "Hey, Tiuri, when you're a knight, could I really be your squire?"

"I'm not a knight yet," said Tiuri.

"But when you are a knight? Or can't boys like me become squires?"

"Of course they can!"

"So can I, then?"

Tiuri laughed. "If you really want to," he said, "I'm sure that you can. And I shall ensure that I am knighted, whatever it takes. Just to satisfy you!"

"That's very kind of you," said Piak with a grin.

The walk downhill went quickly and easily. They passed Filamen, and by the end of the day they had left the town some distance behind.

The next morning, Piak said, "I can't be your guide now, because I've never travelled beyond this point. You'll have to decide which way to go."

"I'm sure we'll find the way together," said Tiuri.

That wasn't difficult, as Taki had told them exactly which paths and roads to follow. By the afternoon, they'd left the mountains and were in the foothills. They saw villages and they passed people now too, who greeted them, but showed no surprise or curiosity. They were back in civilization.

Piak kept looking back over his shoulder. "Goodbye, mountains," he said finally.

"Do you regret coming with me?" asked Tiuri. "You know you can still go back."

"How can you say that?" said Piak. He sounded almost angry.

They went on walking after sunset. The night was clear and they wanted to reach Ardoc's by morning. It was late by the time they found a place to sleep, in a haystack.

"Right then," said Piak, "so that's that. And tomorrow I'll be starting something new, the next part of the journey, all the way across a flat land. Just imagine! I'm going to see cities, and big rivers! But, of course, you've seen it all before."

"That's not true," said Tiuri. "I don't know this country at all, like most people who live to the east of the mountains."

They both fell silent as they wondered what adventures awaited them in this strange land. And, still pondering, they fell asleep.

Part Six

—

To the East of the Rainbow River

I   The Road to Dangria

In the grey light of dawn, Tiuri and Piak walked along a small river. The slopes on the opposite bank were lined with vineyards.

"That must be Ardoc's land," said Tiuri.

A large stone house stood a short distance away, surrounded by wooden barns and stables. The two friends headed onto the bridge that led to the house and stopped for a moment to take a look. People were already up and about; there were lights in some of the windows and they could hear voices and horses whinnying. As they stood there, a large man came out of the building, holding a hammer in his right hand and a box under his left arm. He obviously noticed them, but he didn't acknowledge them. He just put the box down on the ground, rummaged around inside it and started repairing one of the windows.

Piak and Tiuri went up to him. "Good morning," they said.

The man was noisily hammering away, but he stopped and said, "What did you say?"

"Good morning," they repeated.

"Thank you, and the same to you," he said and then he went back to his hammering. The noise made any conversation impossible, but he soon returned the hammer to the box. Then he looked up at them and said, "You lads are out and about at an early hour, aren't you? I don't think I've seen you around here before."

"We've just walked down from the mountains," replied Piak.

"Oh, you've come from the other side, have you? We don't often see folk from those parts." The man hitched up his trousers and peered at them from beneath his bushy eyebrows. He was a striking figure, with long, wild yellowish-grey hair and a big beard.

"Is this Ardoc's house?" asked Tiuri.

"Indeed it is. This is Ardoc's house, in the shadow of the Great Mountains. Is that what you came here to ask?"

"We'd like to speak to Ardoc," said Tiuri.

"I see. You'd like to speak to Ardoc, would you? And what makes you think that gentleman's awake at such an early hour?"

"If he wasn't awake, I'm sure your hammering will have roused him," said Piak.

The man chuckled. "You're right," he said. "But do you think you can just ask to have a chat with him at this time in the morning?"

"Well, that's what we're asking you," said Tiuri.

"And why exactly do you want to speak to him?"

"Taki sent us," Tiuri replied. "He gave us Ardoc's name and told us where we could find him."

"Ah, Taki. How's the fool doing? He wanted to get married and go back to the mountains, instead of staying here and making a good living."

"He's married now," said Piak, "and he's very happy up in the mountains."

"Excellent. Just as it should be," said the man. "One man on the mountain, another on the plain. Everyone has his place... except for travellers who can find no peace anywhere and young folk with adventurous dispositions. I like to travel too, but I never go far from home these days. I have my duties here to take care of. I have to manage my lands and take care of the people who depend on me."

"Are you Ardoc?" exclaimed Piak.

"I am indeed. What did you think... that I'm some layabout who stays in bed and lets other people do the hard work? No. I'm always the first one up in the morning. Now, why don't you boys tell me what's on your minds?"

Tiuri and Piak made their request.

"You're in luck," said Ardoc. "I'm off to Dangria this very morning. My men are already loading up the cart. But it's so full of produce to sell at the market that there's barely enough room for a mouse up there. Never fear, though. I have horses that could do with some exercise. I'll be riding myself. My man Dieric is driving the cart. You lads can travel alongside on horseback. I generally take extra hands with me these days. Makes the road a safer place, you see. And when we get to the market, the two of you can help unload the produce. What do you say? Is it a deal? You do know how to ride, don't you?"

"N- no," said Piak uneasily.

"I've been on a horse before," said Tiuri.

"One of those mountain ponies, I'll warrant, with your feet dragging along the ground. But you'll be fine. I'll give you a couple of docile horses. So, does that sound good?"

Tiuri and Piak nodded, but Piak looked worried at the thought of having to ride a horse. Ardoc asked if they'd eaten yet. They had, but they didn't turn down the invitation to stock up on a little more breakfast.

They ate first and then got ready to leave. Carefully, Dieric drove two horses pulling a large covered cart over the bridge. Two stable boys brought horses for Tiuri and Piak.

"Go on, then, up you go," said Ardoc to Piak, with a wry grin.

Piak whispered to Tiuri, "I'll just have to give it a try. After all, I do want to be a squire one day." He found it difficult to climb onto the horse, but he didn't hesitate. Smiling nervously, he rode around the yard a few times.

Ardoc was too busy shouting instructions at Piak to pay any attention to Tiuri, who was climbing up onto the other horse. Tiuri was already sitting astride the horse by the time Ardoc looked over at him.

"No!" the farmer shouted at the stable boy. "Not Zéfilwen; she's too temperamental for an inexperienced rider. I told you to give him the chestnut mare."

"But he's already up there now," said the stable boy.

"Well, he'll have to get back down, won't he?" Ardoc began. But then he fell silent as he watched Tiuri trotting over to Piak. "Hm," he said. "No, you can leave him there."

The party set off, with Piak clinging on to the saddle and staring suspiciously at his horse's ears. After a while, he said, "Hey, it's not too bad. But I wouldn't call it comfortable. I prefer walking!"

Tiuri laughed. "You'll get used to it," he said.

Ardoc, who was riding on ahead, reined in his horse and waited for them to catch up. "So where are you from, Martin?" he asked Tiuri.

"A village on the other side of the mountains," he replied.

"I see. Well, you ride like an experienced horseman. I can tell you've ridden before."

"Yes," said Tiuri. "A few times."

"A few times?!" Ardoc exclaimed. "And what kind of horses were you riding? Zéfilwen is a beautiful animal, but she's not exactly docile."

I have ridden Ardanwen, Tiuri thought to himself. *Ardanwen, known as Night Wind, and Zéfilwen does not compare.* But he said, "Oh, I've ridden different kinds of horses, big ones and small."

"I see," said Ardoc and he left it at that.

"How far is it to Dangria?" asked Piak.

"I want to be there this afternoon," Ardoc replied. "We'll start moving more quickly later on, once you're more used to riding."

"There's still no sign of the city," said Piak, gazing to the west. "You can see it from up in the mountains, but it's all so flat down here."

Ardoc smiled. "You may call this flat," he said, "but I can still see plenty of hills. Up in the mountains, there's always some rock or peak or slope blocking your view. And don't you think this is a beautiful road?"

"That's true," said Piak. He looked back over his shoulder at the mighty mountains.

"Are you sure you wouldn't rather go back?" asked Tiuri.

"Oh no, no. Not at all."

"So, tell me, what is it that brings you to this land?" asked Ardoc.

"We want to see the Kingdom of Unauwen," said Tiuri.

"Well, you'll have to travel far and long... at least if you hope to see everything. And you really need to head to the west of the Rainbow River. That's the heart of the Kingdom of Unauwen."

"The king is the ruler here as well, isn't he?" asked Tiuri.

"Yes, but things to the east of the Rainbow River are not as they once were. Since the rift between Unauwen and Eviellan, fewer of the king's knights visit these parts. They're needed in the south, to defend the borders. But you wouldn't know about that, would you?"

"So why don't you tell us?" said Tiuri.

"No, you need to see things for yourselves and to form your own opinions. What I will say is that this road is not as safe as it once was. There are sometimes robbers lying in wait along the way!"

Tiuri and Piak looked at the quiver of arrows on Ardoc's back and understood now why he'd brought them.

"But it's a good idea for you to see what our country's like," the farmer said after a while. "More people should come over the mountains. We speak the same language, after all... even though this is the first time you're hearing it as it should be spoken."

"Why's that?" asked Tiuri.

"Well, we can understand one another, but you do hear the differences in our speech, don't you? The way we speak the language here is more melodic, more beautiful. It's how it should be spoken."

"Who says so?" said Piak indignantly.

"I say so, and it's the truth. Didn't you know that it was us who gave you people in the Kingdom of Dagonaut your language? Many centuries ago, our king's knights set off over the mountains to your land, and founded villages and built castles. They taught the people who lived there everything they knew, and they also gave them their language, the language of the Kingdom of Unauwen. It's even said that they founded the City of Dagonaut itself and that your kings and knights are descended from those men."

"I've never heard that story before," said Tiuri.

"Then it's about time you did. And, whether you believe it or not, it's true."

"Would you tell us more about the Kingdom of Unauwen?" asked Piak.

Ardoc thought for a moment and then shook his head. "No," he said. "I'm not going to do that. You have to look with your own eyes and discover things for yourselves. Come on, the sun's climbing higher and we're leaving the shadow of the mountains. Let's pick up the pace."

They all urged on their horses, except for Piak, who still didn't feel entirely safe. But his horse followed the others anyway and started to canter, with its rider clutching on to its mane. Piak managed to stay in the saddle, though, and before long he was smiling and looking proudly around.

"I think I'm starting to get the hang of this," he said.

From Piak's lookout tower in the mountains, Dangria had seemed like a dainty fairy-tale city. As they approached, however, it looked very different indeed. Its crenellated walls looked strong and impressive, with bastions built from huge blocks of stone. Towers jutted up above the walls, some thick and squat, others slim and pointed, with copper weathervanes on the roofs.

"There's the City of the East," said Ardoc.

"Is that really Dangria?" Piak asked. "I thought it would be... different."

"You seem disappointed," said Tiuri.

"I am. All those thick, high walls! Living there would be like being in prison. So do you think it's beautiful?"

"Hmm, beautiful," said Tiuri. "I wouldn't say that. But it does look like a real city."

"Is the City of Dagonaut the same, with walls all around?"

"Yes, I told you about them. It's different, and bigger, but it does look similar."

"You know the City of Dagonaut, do you?" Ardoc said to Tiuri.

"Yes, I've been there," he replied.

"Does the City of Unauwen look like this too?" Piak asked Ardoc.

"King Unauwen's city is like no other city," replied Ardoc.

"How many cities are there in this land?"

"Well, as you know, there's Dangria, the City of the East, and then there's the City of Unauwen, and two other cities besides: the City of the West, or the Harbour by the Sea; and the City of the South, between the great rivers, which is the seat of the crown prince."

They were approaching a large gate in the eastern city wall. Two pigeons flew over their heads, high above the wall, and landed on one of the towers.

"They've no need to worry about feeling imprisoned," said Piak.

"There are lots of pigeons in Dangria," said Ardoc. "Sometimes they bring news from far-off regions. That's how the mayor keeps informed about events throughout the land." He frowned and looked like he was about to add something, but then thought better of it.

"Do you come to Dangria very often?" asked Tiuri.

"Yes, often enough," replied the farmer. "But it depends how much produce I have to sell."

The city gate stood open, but there was a barrier and a number of armed guards. When they saw Ardoc and his companions, they raised the barrier and the captain of the guards came over to greet them.

"Good afternoon, Ardoc," he said. "And who are your companions?"

"Well, you know my man Dieric already," Ardoc replied, "and these two young fellows have come down from the mountains."

"Greetings," said the captain to Tiuri and Piak. "And what would your names be?"

"Piak Piakson and Martin Martinson," said Piak.

"From the mountains, eh?" he said. "What brought you here?"

"They want to see our land," said Ardoc.

"Excellent!" said the captain. "We don't have many visitors from foreign parts. You must go and see the mayor. I'm sure he'll give you a warm welcome and show you around."

"I think the mayor must have better things to do than show travellers around," said Ardoc.

"Oh, the mayor has time for everyone," said the captain. "How long are you young men staying here?"

"We don't know yet," replied Tiuri.

"Well, take your time," advised the captain. "Our city has a lot to offer."

He turned to Ardoc. "Where are you staying tonight?" he asked.

"The White Swan," Ardoc replied. "As usual."

"And how about these young men?"

"You'd have to ask them that, my good man."

"We haven't decided," said Tiuri. "We don't know our way around yet."

"Then go with Master Ardoc here; he knows where to find good food and drink. But I won't hold you up any longer. Welcome to our city."

They headed through the gate and into the city. Piak couldn't stop staring at all of the new sights: the rows of houses, the streets and the alleyways, the walls and the towers. He even forgot to hold anxiously on to his horse.

"Well," he said, "a city really is something special, after all."

When they reached the marketplace, they paused for a moment.

"Good gracious!" Piak exclaimed. "It's so big. And colourful!"

The marketplace was full of coloured tents and stalls, and people wearing every hue of the rainbow, all busily buying and selling. The sun streamed down on the bright and noisy spectacle. Flocks of doves flew through the air, swooping down and then taking off again.

"It really is very beautiful," said Piak.

But he couldn't look for long, because there was work to do. Ardoc's cart had to be unloaded and the horses unharnessed. Ardoc and Dieric left the horses in a nearby stable and turned the cart into a kind of stall, where they displayed the goods enticingly. Tiuri and Piak helped them and, when they were finished, Ardoc said, "Good. That's done. Now you're where you wanted to be and you're free to do as you please."

Tiuri and Piak thanked Ardoc warmly for allowing them to travel with him.

"No need to thank me," said Ardoc. "It was no trouble. I have business to attend to now, so let's say goodbye. You can find me this evening at the White Swan. I can reserve a bed for you there if you like."

"Thank you," said Tiuri. "But we're not sure of our plans yet."

Ardoc laughed. "Oh, it's not too expensive if that's what's worrying you," he said.

"Thanks, but don't book a bed for us," said Tiuri. "We may come, but we'll have to see."

They thanked Ardoc for his help and walked over to the fountain in the middle of the marketplace, where they sat down to eat.

"What's the plan?" asked Piak.

"We can rest here for a short while," said Tiuri, "but then we should travel on."

"So we're not staying here tonight?"

"No, there's still plenty of daylight left," said Tiuri. "The faster we travel, the better."

"That's true," said Piak. But then he added, "Can't we just go for a walk around first? Then at least we'll get to see something of the city."

"That's fine by me," said Tiuri, standing up.

"I'm not in the mood for sitting anyway," Piak said. "I can really tell that I've been sitting all morning... and then some! On a horse! Ardoc's a nice fellow, don't you think?"

"Yes," said Tiuri. "And he seems smart, too."

"You're right," Piak agreed. "He saw straight off that you're a good rider. Do you think I'll ever learn how to ride properly?"

"Of course," Tiuri replied. "If you do it often enough."

They wandered about the square, looking at the goods on sale.

"You want to watch out," said a voice behind them.

Tiuri and Piak looked around to see a dishevelled old man. "You're strangers here, I see," he continued. "Take care! There are pickpockets about. Keep your hand on your purse strings. Dangria's not the city it used to be." He spat disdainfully on the ground and disappeared into the crowd.

"Well, that was odd!" exclaimed Piak.

Along one side of the marketplace was a very grand building made of yellow stone. The side facing the square consisted of a crenellated wall and a tall tower rising up behind. The wall was smooth and plain, with just a few small windows, and a wide staircase of white marble led up to a large gate with a metal-studded door in it.

Piak gazed open-mouthed at the impressive building. "Is that a castle?" he said.

"That is the town hall, and the mayor's residence," said a voice behind them.

It was the same old man who had warned them about pickpockets a few moments before. "The mayor," he went on, "had the staircase built last year. It's very beautiful – and it was very expensive too. But I wouldn't like to set foot on those steps. No, not me!" He looked disapprovingly at the building, sniffed and spat on the ground again. "Oh no, not me!" he repeated. Then he turned around and walked away.

"You know, that old man really is very strange," said Piak.

Tiuri didn't reply but watched the old man walk away until he disappeared behind a stall. Then he laughed and said, "He certainly wasn't keen on those stairs, was he?" But Tiuri was now sure that he didn't want to stay in Dangria for much longer. "Come on," he said. "Let's get going, shall we? There must be a gate to the west as well."

They headed across the marketplace and passed by Ardoc's stall. The farmer himself wasn't there, but Dieric seemed to be doing good business. When he saw them, he gave them a friendly wave, and they stopped to chat with him. Just as they were about to leave, a man in a helmet came over. They recognized him as one of the guards from the gate.

"Ah, there you are," he said. "I've been looking for the two of you. I thought I might find you here. The mayor would like a quick word with you."

"The mayor?" exclaimed Tiuri.

"Yes, he was interested to hear that we had some foreign visitors, particularly young people like yourselves. And he'd like to invite you to be his guests for a short while."

"My, my," said Dieric. "What an honour!"

"Our mayor is most hospitable, as is his city," said the guard. "And everyone knows how fond he is of young people. Would you come with me?" he asked Tiuri and Piak.

"We will," said Tiuri. "But I must tell you we have little time."

"As does the mayor," said the guard, somewhat indignantly. "Less than you, I should think."

"My apologies," said Tiuri. "We appreciate his kindness." He really would have preferred not to go, as it would only mean another delay. But of course one cannot simply ignore a mayor's request.

So Tiuri and Piak followed the guard to the fine building they had so recently been admiring. He led them up the marble staircase and through the large gate.

2   THE MAYOR

The guard took Tiuri and Piak into a large hall, with a red-and-white tiled floor and painted pillars. At the other end of the room, a beautifully carved wooden staircase led up to another floor.

Piak gasped in admiration as he looked around the hall.

Shields and crossed swords hung from each of the pillars and there was a mosaic of coloured stones adorning the ceiling.

Piak whispered to Tiuri, "This mayor must be really rich."

"If the young gentlemen would be so kind as to wait here," said the guard. He walked across the tiled floor and headed up the magnificent staircase, passing a group of a dozen guards in armour, who came clanking down the steps. They raised their spears in greeting to Tiuri and Piak, and headed outside. Two more guards came in through a side door and one of them spoke to Tiuri, "Good afternoon. The mayor will be with you shortly." The guards then headed upstairs, but stopped halfway, on the landing.

"Just look at this place," Piak whispered. "Is King Dagonaut's castle this grand? Does he have a court full of knights and warriors?" He walked around, admiring the hall, stopping here and there to study the shields on the pillars.

Tiuri wanted to follow Piak, but he stayed where he was, because he could see two more men coming downstairs and he suspected that the first of the two was the mayor. He was an imposing middle-aged man, dressed in long red robes with a fur trim and with a gold chain around his neck. Behind him came a pale young man, dressed in black.

Tiuri whispered urgently, "Piak!" But Piak had disappeared behind the pillars on the far side of the hall and seemed not to have heard him.

The man in the robes and chain came over to Tiuri with a broad smile. "Welcome to my fair city of Dangria!" he boomed.

Tiuri bowed. "My thanks, my lord mayor."

The mayor shook Tiuri by the hand. "Yes, welcome, welcome, young man," he said. "You must stay here! As my guest!"

The mayor looked around the hall. "I was told I had two guests to greet," he said.

"Yes, my friend Piak's here, too," Tiuri replied. "He's just admiring the hall. Shall I fetch him?"

"Oh, let him look around," smiled the mayor. "After all, that is one of the reasons I invited you both here. There are so many things I would like to show you." He turned to the young man standing beside him. "My scribe," he said, "will ensure that a good room is provided for the two of you, here at the town hall."

"That is most kind of you, my lord mayor," said Tiuri. "And I appreciate this warm welcome. However, my friend and I are just simple travellers. We would dearly love to see more of your fine city, but sadly we are unable to remain here for long."

"Oh, I am sure you can spare us a couple of days."

"My regrets," replied Tiuri. "Unfortunately, we cannot."

At that point, Piak returned. He looked rather agitated, but Tiuri only realized that later.

"Aha, and here is your friend," said the mayor. "Welcome, welcome. I hear you've been admiring our town hall."

Piak gave the mayor a clumsy bow. "Yes, my lord mayor. It's very beautiful."

"You really should visit the rooms upstairs while you are here. I am sure you must have enough time for that. Come with me."

"But we have to meet Ardoc," said Piak, taking a step backwards. "I... I've left some of my things with him."

"I shall have them fetched," said the mayor. He raised his hand. It was a signal for the two guards to come downstairs from the landing.

"We would be very happy to accept your kind offer," said Tiuri. "But, as I have said, I am afraid we cannot stay for long."

"Why the hurry?" asked the mayor, who was now standing very close to Tiuri. "I really would be very interested to hear some news from the east."

Tiuri was starting to feel uneasy. "We are just boys from the mountains, my lord mayor," he said. "We have no interesting stories to tell."

The mayor tapped Tiuri on the chest with a long finger. "Oh, but I am sure you must have some news from the east for me," he said, almost whispering. "I really must insist that you spend a few days here with me."

"I am very sorry, but that is out of the question," said Tiuri.

"No, that just will not do. You must stay. There is a friend of mine... He is not here right now, but he is most keen to speak to you."

Tiuri's vague feeling of alarm was rapidly becoming a strong suspicion. "A friend, you say? I am afraid I don't understand. Who exactly is this friend?"

The mayor smiled. "You will find out soon enough," he said. "Now come along, young man."

The guards came to stand beside Tiuri. They, too, had smiles on their faces, but their hands were resting on the hilts of their swords. Tiuri was startled to see more armed men appearing between the pillars. He had no time to decide what to do, because then a yell from Piak rang through the hall. He had slipped away and was standing by the door, clutching his hands up to his chest as if he were holding something important.

"Hey, Tiuri!" Piak shouted. "Don't worry! I've got it here! I'll deliver it! I'll deliver it!" And then he turned, pulled the door open and flew outside.

After that, everything happened very quickly. The mayor's welcoming smile became a snarl. "Stop that boy!" he roared. "Grab him! Stop him now!"

The guards ran for the door and disappeared after Piak. The mayor followed them. He hesitated at the door and glared back at Tiuri, but then dashed outside. The door slammed behind him.

Tiuri raced to the exit, but, as he opened the door, two spears came thrusting at him and angry voices ordered him to stay where he was. Then the door banged in his face. He could hear a commotion on the other side, but he had no idea what was happening.

"Oh, Piak!" he sighed, his voice trembling.

Piak had scented danger, so he had pretended he was carrying the letter. The trick had worked, but what was going to happen to him? Should Tiuri tell someone that he, not Piak, was the one who had the letter that the mayor seemed so interested in? No, he couldn't do that. He could never reveal where the letter was. The fate of a kingdom might depend on it. He knew that he had to make use of the chance Piak had given him.

Tiuri ran to the side door, but he could hear voices through that one too. He couldn't go outside; the mayor was sure to have the building surrounded. So he ran through the hall and raced up the staircase, two steps at a time, nearly knocking over the mayor's scribe as he went. He ended up in a large room with doors on both sides, and chose one at random. He found himself running through more rooms and corridors. Behind him, he heard footsteps, and a voice shouted, "Stop that boy! Do not allow him to leave the building!"

As Tiuri ran through the armoury, he stopped to grab a bow and a quiver of arrows. Then he dashed up another staircase. On the next floor, he allowed himself a moment to pause and look out through a window.

He could see the marketplace below, and thought he could make out some kind of disturbance among the townsfolk. Yes, there came the mayor's guards. Four, six, ten... no, there must have been twenty of them! Were they looking for Piak? Tiuri prayed that Piak had escaped. More noises were coming from below, so Tiuri hurried onwards, as quietly as he could. He knew what he had to do.

He raced up another flight of stairs, through yet another exquisitely decorated room, down more corridors and through various chambers and halls until, finally, he entered a room with two big doors and tall, narrow windows. That was where he would make his stand. Tiuri knew he was going to have to put his plan into action soon. The mayor's men were bound to find him.

He was in luck. The door he had come through had a key in its lock. He quickly turned it and bolted the door for good measure. The second door led to a small chamber with no other exits, so he left that one open. Then he pushed a table in front of the main door, thinking to himself, *I hope it takes them a while to find me. And, when they do, they're going to have a devil of a job getting in here!*

Choosing a spot where he could keep an eye on both the door and the windows, Tiuri knelt down, keeping the bow and arrows within easy reach. Then he took out the letter.

The time had come. He had to read the letter and destroy it, so that his enemy would never discover its secrets.

3   The Letter

Tiuri looked down at the letter. Only one of the three seals was still intact. He thought back to the previous time he was locked behind a closed door and had been about to read the letter. The circumstances were so different now.

He broke the final seal and opened up the letter. He was so agitated that the words and letters seemed to dance before his eyes and he could make no sense of them. He closed his eyes, just for a moment. When he took another look, he found that the letters had stopped moving. He focused on the words and read the letter from beginning to end, but still he did not understand. Either the message was in code, or it was some language he had never seen before. He recognized only one word, about halfway down the page: Unauwen. He stared at the words, disappointed that the letter's secret was still a mystery.

The sound of footsteps and voices startled Tiuri and reminded him of the urgency of his task. He had to learn the message by heart, as quickly as he could, and then he could destroy the letter. It was not going to be easy, because he had no idea what the words meant, but he set to work, still half-listening to the sounds outside the room. He heard someone approaching the door, but then the footsteps retreated. Tiuri turned his full attention to the letter, mouthing the words and then closing his eyes and repeating the sentences.

He didn't know how much time had passed when he thought he had finally committed the contents of the letter to memory. Then he wondered if he could manage to remember how to spell the words too. He might be pronouncing the words incorrectly, so he had to be certain that he could write the letter down, not just recite it.

More noises from outside disturbed Tiuri. This time, someone tried to open the door.

"Hello? Is someone in there?" a voice called out.

Tiuri remained silent.

"This door's locked," he heard the voice say. "Go and fetch the keys!"

Tiuri had another couple of minutes to study the letter in peace.

Then he heard a key turning in the lock, but the door was also bolted, so of course it wouldn't open.

"Who's in there?" came a shout. "Answer me this minute!" Tiuri said nothing.

He heard mumbling voices and then footsteps hurrying away. Tiuri repeated the message one more time to make certain that he knew it. Then he walked over to the fireplace. He took out the flints he had found in Ardanwen's saddlebag and banged them together over the logs and kindling in the grate. Eventually, a fire sputtered into life. He held the parchment close enough to the flames that they were licking at his fingers, and then, when it caught light, he dropped the letter and watched it burn. Then he gathered up the ashes, rubbed them between his fingers, and blew them away. All that remained of the letter were the mysterious words in his head. He put out the fire and heaved a sigh. He had done it. He had destroyed the letter. But he was still a prisoner.

"Open this door immediately!" shouted a voice. "Now! Let us in!"

Tiuri said nothing and stayed absolutely still.

"Fetch an axe and break it down," another voice ordered. It was the mayor.

Tiuri took a deep breath and shouted, "I have a bow and arrows. And I will shoot dead the first person who steps through that door!"

There was silence on the other side.

"Break the door down," the mayor repeated. "Come on, you bunch of cowards!"

Tiuri heard muttering and whispering.

"You have been warned," said Tiuri. "I will shoot the first man to enter this room."

He drew the bow and notched an arrow, wondering whether he would really be able to shoot when the moment came. "Yes, I will do it," he swore to himself through gritted teeth. "It's what they deserve."

"What is the meaning of this?" came the voice of the mayor. "How did you ever come up with such a wicked plan, young man? Whatever possessed you to barricade yourself here in our town hall and threaten to kill us? What possible reason could there be for such a foolish, wrong-headed course of action?"

Tiuri didn't answer. He was not going to fall for the mayor's attempts to engage him in conversation.

"What is the meaning of this?" repeated the mayor. "I invited you here as my guest and now you are threatening me in my own town hall! Why don't you come out here? Perhaps you can still put things right."

Tiuri remained silent.

"Won't you at least answer me?" growled the mayor. "You have a lot to answer for, young man, locking yourself up in here like this! And you know you are sure to come off worse." Then, changing his tone again, he wheedled, "Honestly, you have nothing to fear from us. Just so long as you open that door!"

"And will you let me go if I do?" said Tiuri, breaking his silence.

"Well, it's hardly what you deserve, is it?" answered the mayor after a moment. "You have acted most strangely. But I am not the sort to bear grudges. Come along now, young man. We cannot keep speaking to each other through the door."

"I am not the one who is acting strangely," said Tiuri. "And do you know something? I don't trust you."

"How dare you speak to me in that manner?" roared the mayor. "For the last time, come out of that room!"

"No," said Tiuri. "Not until you tell me who your friend is. The friend who wanted to speak to me."

The mayor said nothing.

"Might his name perhaps be... Slither?"

The mayor still didn't answer, but Tiuri heard him muttering. Then came the sound of footsteps retreating, their echoes fading away in the distance.

"Go on then! Just you break that door down!" Tiuri called out in a voice that sounded more confident than he really felt. "My arrow's already aimed!"

Tiuri stood there for a while, bow and arrow at the ready,

waiting to see what would happen. But all was silent. Tiuri realized that they didn't dare to break down the door.

After a while, Tiuri sat down, but he remained ready and alert. Slowly, whatever confidence he had felt began to fade. He had destroyed the letter – and he was certain he had done the right thing – but still he was not free. They didn't even need to break down the door. They could just leave him there, starve him into submission... No! He stood up and walked over to one of the windows. No sooner had he reached it than he felt something whistle past his ear. He leapt back in surprise and saw an arrow quivering in the wall opposite the window.

Very cautiously, Tiuri approached the window again and peeped outside. The windows looked out onto a narrow alleyway and he could see a group of archers standing on the roof of the building opposite. One of them was aiming another arrow. He fired. Tiuri ducked, but the archer's aim was poor and the arrow clattered harmlessly off the wall outside.

"You're not going to get me like that," he whispered.

Tiuri looked around the room; there were plenty of spots where he would be safe. He headed into the small adjoining chamber, which had only one window, but it overlooked the same alley. He took up position, drew his bow, aimed and fired. The arrow narrowly missed one of the archers, startling him.

This time I want to hit someone, Tiuri thought, as he notched a second arrow. *I don't want to kill anyone, just give them a fright.* He pressed himself against the wall beside the window and looked outside.

The archers were shouting and pointing at the windows. *I don't think they've realized I'm in this room*, Tiuri thought. He was almost enjoying himself now. He waited for a good moment before taking another shot. A loud cry told him that his arrow had found a target. One of the archers dropped his bow and clutched his arm. The others let off a few arrows, but none of them even hit the window frame. Then they ran to help their wounded companion. Tiuri sent another arrow flying after them, making them move all the faster. Then he left the window and went back into the other room. He had only four arrows left.

If they decide to break the door down, they've got me, he thought, *even if I manage to shoot the first one or two dead.* What would happen then? Would they torture him to extract the letter's secret? Would the mayor hand him over to Slither? Jaro had described Slither as "the best of spies and the worst of men". Might they even kill Tiuri to make sure the message never reached its destination?

Tiuri had to admit to himself that he was frightened. He hoped something would happen, anything, that they would start banging on the door, or shoot at him across the alleyway. Anything would be better than just waiting. He passed the time by repeating the contents of the letter in his head, a little surprised that he could still remember it word for word. Then he took another cautious peek outside. There was no one around. Even the streets were deserted.

How long had it been since he and Piak had entered the town hall? It seemed like hours, but it was still light outside. Tiuri sighed and wondered where Piak was now. Why had Piak become suspicious before Tiuri? If he ever managed to complete his task and deliver the message, it would all be down to Piak. Piak...

Tiuri took another look outside. He could not escape through the window, as it was too high. And the rope was in Piak's bag. Even if he had had the rope, it probably would not have done him any good, because now he could see two guards patrolling the alley below. He watched them until they disappeared around the corner.

A plan was forming in his mind. Why stay in that room, where he knew he would end up losing? His only hope lay in swift action. The one route of escape was through the door – through the door and then all the way back through the town hall! It sounded like madness, but it had to be worth a try.

Tiuri put his ear to the door. It was still silent outside. Maybe there was no one out there – they probably thought he wouldn't dare to come out. And that was exactly why he had to do it!

4 THE SCRIBE

Tiuri had one fear as he slowly slid back the bolt: the guards might have locked the door from the other side. Very carefully, he turned the key, tried the door... and it opened. He peered around the corner, and saw a guard. He was looking the other way.

Tiuri opened the door wider and whispered, "Turn around and don't say a word."

Startled, the guard turned to look at Tiuri and reached for his sword.

Stepping slowly over the threshold, Tiuri aimed an arrow at him and repeated, "Do not say a word. Lay your sword on the floor. That's right. Now put your hands above your head, and come over here."

The guard did as he was ordered. Tiuri heard voices elsewhere in the building. He saw the guard's eyes flicker with hope and knew that he had to make his escape as quickly as possible.

"In there," he said. "Now!"

As soon as the guard was inside the room, Tiuri locked the door and dropped the key into his pocket. Then he fled down the corridor. He had not gone far when his prisoner started shouting. Tiuri raced back through the long series of passageways and rooms, desperately searching for a place to hide. He knew he had no hope of getting all the way outside without running into trouble. Then he spotted a large closet. He sighed with relief when he found it wasn't locked. He ducked inside, and pulled the door shut. Tiuri heard people running through the room, but no one thought to check his hiding place.

Tiuri waited a while before slipping out to continue his race through the huge building. He reached the second floor without being stopped, and then heard noises both above and below – he seemed to have walked into a trap. He dashed into a side room, hoping to find a window he could escape through, or at least a spot where he could hide for a while.

It was a small chamber that he hadn't noticed before. There was a desk in there, with writing materials on it, and maps all over the walls. He could see a second room through an open door.

As he entered, a pale, dark-haired young man appeared in the other doorway. It was the mayor's scribe.

Tiuri raised his bow again and whispered, "Not a word, or I'll shoot!"

The scribe's large grey eyes grew wide with astonishment. He opened his mouth, but no sound came out.

Voices were echoing throughout the town hall. "He must be somewhere nearby! Search all of the rooms on this floor!"

Tiuri approached the scribe and whispered, "If they want to check this room, you must stop them and say I am not here. Go and stand by the door. And do not forget that I am aiming an arrow at your back."

The scribe did as he was told.

"Now open the door," said Tiuri, "and stand so that they can't see me. Make sure they don't search this room. Do not attempt to leave or I will shoot you dead before you can take another step."

The scribe opened the door. "Hey!" he shouted to someone Tiuri couldn't see. "Over here! I think he went down those stairs. If you're quick, you can stop him in the hall!"

Tiuri heard his pursuers retreating. The scribe locked the door and came over to him.

"How did I do?" he asked calmly. There was even a little smile playing on his lips. "So, what now? You can't go downstairs. They'll be lying in wait for you. You won't even make it to the foot of the staircase."

"Then I'll find some other way," said Tiuri. "No, don't come any closer."

The scribe stayed where he was. He folded his arms and gave Tiuri a searching look. "What now?" he repeated. "Maybe you'd be better off killing me. The longer you wait here, the higher your chances of being caught. Or you could just drop your weapons and climb out of the window. You might be able to escape that way. And I shall do you the favour of holding my tongue until you're out of sight."

Tiuri hesitated.

"Go on, take a chance," said the scribe. "I'm sure you don't trust me, but you can't stay here, not for long anyway. I'd like to remain alive for some time to come and it makes no difference to me whether you escape or not. I have no idea what the mayor wants with you, and I know just as little about why you are behaving in such a barbarous manner, but this is clearly some very shady business, and I would do well to keep my nose out of it."

Someone rattled the door. "Hey, you in there!" cried an angry voice. "Open up!"

"Go into the other room," the scribe whispered to Tiuri.

Tiuri retreated to the doorway and held his bow at the ready.

The scribe turned the key in the lock and spoke to someone outside the room. "What is it now?" he said. "Must you keep disturbing me?"

"Why have you locked this door?" the man asked.

"What? With that young rogue on the loose? I don't relish the thought of being skewered by an arrow!"

"Coward!" the man said, sounding angry, yet amused. "Quill-dippers! You're all the same. But you can't keep hiding away in here. The mayor's sent for you."

"I shall come along presently," said the scribe. "I take it you haven't caught the boy."

"No, but you can be sure we will. He has to be somewhere in the building. The mayor is furious. The town council is meeting later, and he wants this hullabaloo to be over before then. You must help us search for the boy."

"Absolutely not!" cried the scribe. "Such work lies well outside the scope of my duties. I am not required to bear arms, and neither do I wish to. My paperwork is in order, and that is all that matters."

The scribe slammed the door and waited until the sound of the man's footsteps had faded away. Then he turned to Tiuri. "So now do you believe I have no interest in stopping you?" he whispered. "I must say, this is all a very peculiar affair and I do not like it one bit." He paused. "In fact, I am afraid that I may have to give up my position at the town hall. Or would I be wrong in thinking that the mayor is not a good master to serve?"

"You would know that better than I," said Tiuri, surprised by the scribe's words.

"Some of the men here hate him, but he has always been a good master to me. Perhaps, though, that is not enough."

Tiuri ran over to look out of the window.

The scribe followed him. "So who exactly are you?" he asked.

"That doesn't matter," said Tiuri.

They stood at the window, facing each other. The scribe had a curious expression on his face, but Tiuri was still wary.

"The mayor was expecting you," said the scribe. "He ordered the guards at the gate to detain every young man between the ages of fourteen and eighteen who entered the city and to bring them to him."

"Is that so?"

"A carrier pigeon recently brought him a message from somewhere to the east. He would not let me read the letter or store it in the archive."

"Who sent the message?"

"I do not know. Perhaps you could tell me."

Tiuri wondered if it could have been Slither. Had he travelled along the First Great Road? Had he made his way over the mountains? Was it Slither who had asked the mayor to capture Tiuri and hold him until he arrived in Dangria himself? That was certainly a possibility...

"I do not know the mayor," Tiuri said to the scribe, "but I think you might be better off serving another master, at least if you are a loyal subject of King Unauwen."

The scribe gasped. "What?"

"I have to go now."

"Wait a moment. I'll see if anyone's on guard down there."

He leant out of the window and took a good look around. Then he turned to Tiuri and said, "You should go now. It's getting dark. There are guards patrolling, but if you're quick you'll make it. And I wish you better luck than your friend."

"Piak! Did they capture him?"

"Yes, they got him. He is in the dungeon beneath the town hall."

"No!" gasped Tiuri. "I have to help him."

"Then don't wait around here," said the scribe. He looked out of the window again. "Another guard just went past. You'll have to go now. You can only help your friend if you're free. He will not thank you if you manage to get captured as well."

That was true. Tiuri climbed onto the sill and looked down below. A ledge jutted out from the wall beneath. If he stood on it, he would be able to jump down into the street.

"We're at the back of the town hall here," said the scribe. "Quickly! Go!"

"Thank you," whispered Tiuri, as he slipped out of the window.

Down below, a couple of guards were coming around the corner, so Tiuri dashed into a side street and ran away from the town hall as quickly as he could. He heard a shout and wondered if he'd been spotted, but he didn't wait to find out. He raced down the streets and only slowed to a fast walk when he realized people were staring.

He soon reached the marketplace, where he hid in a dark doorway. As he stood there, wondering where to go in this unfamiliar town, which was full of enemies who were searching for him, a man suddenly appeared. "Come with me," he whispered.

Tiuri was startled, but then he recognized the old man who had spoken to him and Piak earlier.

"Let me lean on your arm," the old man said, "and walk with me. I told you going up those stairs would do you no good, didn't I? But you went up them anyway, and what happened? Your friend's in the dungeon and you're running around as if you want to join him."

He slipped his arm through Tiuri's.

"Get rid of your bow and arrows," he said. "You'll attract too much attention."

Tiuri silently obeyed. He didn't know if he was doing the right thing, but he had no better plan.

His new friend walked across the marketplace with him, taking care to keep to the busiest areas. Most of the traders were already starting to pack up their wares and no one paid much attention to Tiuri and his companion. Even so, he still kept looking around, alert and ready to make a run for it.

The old man stopped at a clothes stall. "Tell me," he said to the market trader, "would you have a jacket for my friend? A cheap one?"

"As long as he has the coin to pay for it," said the trader. "I know you certainly don't."

"Oh, he's good for it," said the old man, looking at Tiuri. "I did warn you about pickpockets, didn't I?"

Tiuri rummaged around in the pouch on his belt and took out a few coins.

"Not too much!" whispered his companion. "Here, just this piece of silver. That's enough for a jacket."

"Wants to change his appearance a bit, does he?" said the trader, taking a good look at Tiuri. Then he searched through his goods. "This might do," he said. "Try it on."

"It's not much good for a piece of silver," said the old man. "You're taking advantage because we have no time to bargain."

"A man who's on the run can't afford to be fussy," said the

trader, winking at Tiuri. "Well, it fits you fine. And it makes you look like a true citizen of Dangria too – half a dozen different colours on every piece of clothing. Look, I'll even throw in this hat for free. It looks a bit odd, but it'll serve your purpose."

Tiuri and his helper left the marketplace and walked on.

"So, that's that taken care of," said the old man. "Now let's have something to eat. We'll go to the White Swan. It's safe there."

Tiuri stopped in his tracks and said, "I'm not sure that's a good idea. They know that I came here with Ardoc the farmer, and they also know he was heading for the White Swan."

"Ah, I didn't realize. But that also means they'll probably already have been to the inn to look for you. Tell you what, I'll go on ahead. If they've already searched the White Swan, it'll be fine. They're not likely to check the same place twice. And if they do, the innkeeper will find somewhere to hide you. But I'll go and take a look. You can follow me, slowly. If the coast is clear, there'll be a candle in the window and that means you need have no fear about entering."

He told Tiuri the way to the inn and disappeared without waiting for a reply.

Tiuri stood there for a moment. Then he began walking slowly through the dark streets towards the inn, still surprised at the unexpected help he had received. Finding the inn was easy enough. In the window, beneath the sign of the white swan, a candle was burning.

5   At the White Swan

Tiuri pushed the door open and stepped into the inn. There were no more than a dozen people inside. Most of them were eating. The old man was standing at the counter, talking to the innkeeper. When he spotted Tiuri, he came over to him, followed by the innkeeper, and said, "I've already ordered our meal. But you'll have to pay for both of us."

"Of course," said Tiuri.

The innkeeper laughed. "Iruwen never has any money on him," he said.

"No," said the old man, whose name was apparently Iruwen. "Don't need it."

Before long, Tiuri was sitting opposite Iruwen at a table in a dark corner. The innkeeper brought them their food.

"Enjoy your meal," said Iruwen.

Tiuri looked at him. Iruwen had a straggly beard and his clothes were rather shabby. His eyes, though, were kind and wise.

"I would like to thank you," Tiuri began.

"Ah, hush. I haven't done anything yet that's been any effort for me and would therefore deserve your gratitude."

"Why exactly are you helping me?" asked Tiuri.

But Iruwen shook his head and said, "Let's eat first and then talk."

Tiuri didn't want to start eating until he found out what had happened to Piak.

"Your friend came running out of the town hall," Iruwen told him. "He almost went tumbling down the stairs and the guards were too startled to stop him. When he dashed out into the marketplace, more guards came running outside, with the mayor following after them and yelling, 'Stop that boy! Take him prisoner!' It was quite a commotion. Your friend weaved around the stalls, with the guards running after him. They were knocking things all over the place! I didn't see the guards catch the boy, but later I saw them bringing him back to the town hall. They took him to the dungeon beneath the town hall, and that's probably where he still is."

"How... how did Piak look?" asked Tiuri.

"Oh, a bit ragged around the edges; his clothes were torn. But he didn't show any fear."

"I have to get him out of there!" said Tiuri. "I have to! But how?"

"We'll think about that after eating," said Iruwen. "You're not alone in this city. I want to help you, as do a number of other people. Why exactly was it that the mayor took you prisoner?"

Tiuri was spared from having to answer that question when two men stepped through the door beside the bar. It was Ardoc and Dieric. The farmer looked around the room and said, "Good evening." He greeted Iruwen in particular and then his eye fell on Tiuri.

"Well, well!" he said. "If it isn't young Martin!" He walked over to their table.

Tiuri stood up and said, "Good evening, Master Ardoc."

"Please, don't get up!" said Ardoc. "Enjoy your meal." Ardoc pulled up a chair and joined them.

The innkeeper came to take his order. "Will you be eating at this table?" he asked.

"If they don't mind," Ardoc replied, nodding at Tiuri and his companion.

"Of course not," said Iruwen.

"My thanks," said Ardoc. "Pull yourself up a chair, Dieric."

The innkeeper noted down their order and went back to the bar. Then Ardoc looked at Tiuri. "So where's your friend?" he asked.

Tiuri hesitated.

"He's in the dungeon beneath the town hall, isn't he?" continued Ardoc. "Have you stepped on the mayor's toes? Did you insult him somehow?"

"We've done nothing to him," said Tiuri.

"Nothing? Well, that's precious little reason for a man to be taken prisoner, isn't it? Particularly someone who swears he's never been to Dangria before!"

"It's true," said Tiuri. "It's the first time we've ever met the mayor."

"Really?" said Ardoc. "Then you must be hoping that it's also the last. But what's going to happen to your friend? What a sorry state of affairs!"

Tiuri realized that everyone in the room was looking curiously at him and he felt rather uncomfortable. Ardoc must have noticed, because he said, "Oh, don't be afraid of anyone here betraying you. You're at the White Swan, although that probably doesn't mean much to you. The mayor's men have already been here. And if they return, I'm sure the innkeeper will give you a place to hide. Isn't that right?" he called over to the innkeeper.

"Certainly," he replied. Then he looked at Tiuri and said, "You're not doing much justice to my good food, young man! You must be worried."

"Yes," said Tiuri. "About Piak."

"Your friend?" said the innkeeper. "Well, I'm sure Iruwen or Ardoc will know what to do."

"Perhaps," said Ardoc. "Bring us some wine, would you? And we can drink to finding a solution."

When the innkeeper had gone, Ardoc leant over to Tiuri and asked quietly, "So who are you, then?"

"Who am I?" said Tiuri. "My name's Martin. You already know that."

"What does his name matter?" said Iruwen.

"Oh, your name may well be Martin," said Ardoc, "but you are not who you are pretending to be! You're no boy from the mountains like your friend Piak. You come from a different part of the world, and you've moved in different circles. Your manner could be that of a nobleman. You ride like an experienced horseman. And the mayor must have his reasons for wanting to take you prisoner. So, tell me. Who are you?"

The innkeeper brought over a bottle of wine. Tiuri didn't answer until he'd gone.

"I can't tell you any more than I have already said," he replied. "The mayor may have a reason for wanting to imprison me, but I don't think he would be prepared to tell anyone what it is. And I'm not either. I cannot and will not say anything about it."

"I see," said Ardoc. He opened the bottle and filled the glasses.

"They're strangers here," Iruwen said to him, "but they're not just simple travellers. They are here for a reason."

"Exactly," Ardoc replied. "Travellers from the east rarely visit Dangria just for the sake of it. But what do they have to do with our problems? This Martin says he's never met the mayor before."

"And that's the truth," said Tiuri. "He's the one who summoned us."

"Yes, that's right," said Dieric. "He invited them. I saw it myself."

"He was very friendly at first," Tiuri continued. "He said we were his guests. But then he wanted to keep us in the town hall against our will."

"And your friend escaped," said Ardoc. "He ran out into

the marketplace, shouting something... What was it he was shouting again, Dieric?"

"I've got it! I've got it!" Dieric replied. "That's what he was shouting."

"So what did he have?" asked Ardoc.

"Nothing," replied Tiuri. "I have to get Piak out of that dungeon. He was only trying to help me." He looked at Ardoc, and then at Iruwen. "You have already very kindly assisted me," he said. "Could you help me with this, too, perhaps by giving me some advice? I'm a stranger in Dangria but, if I've understood you correctly, I don't think you're very keen on the mayor. Why is that?"

"Now he's asking us questions!" said Ardoc to Iruwen. "While he plays his cards so close to his chest!"

But Iruwen said, "It is true that many people here in the city regard the mayor as an enemy. And I have always felt that way about him. The rot set in when he took charge of Dangria. He has forgotten that he is only the mayor and that he runs this city in the king's name. He acts like an independent ruler, according to his own whim. Since the rift between the two princes, knights with white shields rarely come to our city. They have to keep watch in the south now. But there are certain people who need their supervision and..."

"Ah," said Ardoc, interrupting him. "Martin doesn't know about all of that."

"Yes, I do," said Tiuri. "Or, at least, I know something about it. I've heard about Unauwen's sons and the conflict with Eviellan."

"But there's going to be peace with Eviellan now," said Dieric.

"So they say," said Iruwen. "Let's hope Unauwen's knights soon return and that the mayor will be ousted."

"Are you rattling on about that again, Iruwen?" said a man at the next table, who had apparently been listening to their conversation.

"Ah, some people don't believe me yet," said Iruwen, standing up and looking around the room. "They're just angry with the mayor because he treats people unfairly or because the taxes he levies are too high. Even here, at the White Swan, there are still people who refuse to see the danger!"

"Danger?" cried the man at the next table. "Danger? I don't like the mayor and his cronies, but I'm not scared of them."

"Iruwen sometimes talks as though the enemy will be at our gates tomorrow," said another man.

"The enemy is among us," declared Iruwen. "Mark my words, all of you here! What has happened in our city today should give us pause for thought. Since when have strangers – no, guests – been treated in such a way in Dangria?"

All eyes turned upon Tiuri.

"But what exactly are these strangers doing here?" someone asked. "I have to say, I don't really understand what's going on."

Tiuri felt that everyone was waiting for an explanation from him. He stood up and said, "And, to be honest, I don't understand it all either. You are clearly dissatisfied with your mayor. So why not do something about it?"

"What can a handful of people do against so many?" said the man at the next table.

"That's nonsense," said Iruwen. "Many people here are dissatisfied, Doalwen, as you well know. You're just too lazy, too cowardly, too comfortable!"

"You can't speak to me like that!" cried Doalwen. "What you're preaching is rebellion, Iruwen, and that's dangerous! I would vote for a different mayor, but I'm not going to rise up and drive him out by force. King Unauwen would condemn such behaviour."

"King Unauwen wishes for justice in his kingdom," said Iruwen. "And he will listen if we ask him to."

"The king has other things on his mind," said Doalwen.

"And maybe we will soon make peace with Eviellan," said the innkeeper, pulling up a chair and sitting down with them.

"We're straying from the subject," said Ardoc, looking at Tiuri.

Tiuri looked around the room and hesitated briefly before saying, "Are you all true subjects of King Unauwen and enemies of Eviellan?"

Everyone stared at Tiuri in astonishment.

It was Ardoc who broke the silence. "Yes," he said. "But why do you ask? We are hoping for peace; we have felt the consequences of the conflict here too, even though we are far from Eviellan. But again, why do you ask that question?"

"Because I believe your mayor is a friend of Eviellan," said Tiuri. "In fact, I'm sure of it!"

His words caused quite a stir. Only Iruwen said, "That does not surprise me at all. It is as I have always suspected and feared."

"But how do you know that?" cried Ardoc.

"Keep it down, keep it down," the innkeeper warned. "This is a grave accusation, not the kind of thing to start shouting about before we know it's true."

"I'm sorry I can't tell you much more than that," said Tiuri. "Most of what I know – and that is little enough – is secret. But what is certain is that the mayor has links to Eviellan, and that he captured my friend and me on the orders of spies who are working for that land."

"But there is to be peace with Eviellan!" said Doalwen, interrupting him.

"Quiet!" called Ardoc. "Let him finish."

"I can tell you that I was pursued through the Kingdom of Dagonaut and attacked by Red Riders," Tiuri continued.

"Red Riders from Eviellan!" whispered Iruwen.

"Yes, Red Riders from Eviellan. They served a Black Knight with a Red Shield."

"A knight of the King of Eviellan," murmured Ardoc.

"But what were they doing in the land of King Dagonaut?" asked another man. "You're not at war with the land in the south, are you?"

"No," Tiuri replied. "They were pursuing one of King Unauwen's knights."

"A knight of King Unauwen? Who? It wasn't Andomar of Ingewel, was it?" asked Iruwen.

"It was a knight with a white shield," Tiuri replied.

"All of the king's knights carry white shields," said the innkeeper.

"It was a knight with a white shield," repeated Tiuri. He had decided not to reveal the knight's identity and not to mention that he had been murdered by the Red Riders. He had, after all, been told to keep his mission secret and he intended to do so, until he could tell the whole story to King Unauwen. "The mayor received certain messages from the east," he continued. "That's why he ordered that all young men between the ages of fourteen and eighteen should be taken to him. It was his own scribe who told me this."

"His scribe?" said the innkeeper.

"Yes, and he helped me to escape."

"Ah," said Doalwen, "so he is on our side, then."

"But why did the mayor want to speak to all of those young men?" asked Ardoc.

Tiuri said nothing.

"Don't you understand? It's a secret," said Iruwen. "He was looking for one young man, or two. And Martin knows the reason, of course, but he isn't allowed to tell us."

"But all that I have been able to tell you is true," said Tiuri. "You must believe me, and you must help me. Please! So much depends on it."

"What would you like us to do?" asked Ardoc.

"I need to get out of this city, as quickly as possible. But first..."

"And what about the mayor?" said Doalwen.

"But first Piak, my friend, has to be freed," Tiuri continued. "I can't abandon him."

"But how?" cried the innkeeper.

"Can't we bribe the guards?" suggested one of the men.

"Bribe them?" snorted Iruwen. "Bribery! Is that what Dangria has come to?"

"So what do you want to do?"

"Let's go to the town hall, all of us together, and demand his release!" said Iruwen.

"That's madness," replied Doalwen. "It's sure to result in fighting and bloodshed! As you say, Iruwen, is that what Dangria has come to?"

"Send an urgent messenger to King Unauwen," said another man.

"No, that'll take too long," Tiuri said. He could hardly tell them he was a messenger himself, on his way to the king! And he had to continue on his journey. But he couldn't bring himself to leave Piak behind in Dangria. Who knew what the mayor and his henchmen might do to him?

Everyone was talking at the same time. But finally Ardoc called for attention.

"Listen, everyone," he said. "Iruwen's idea actually makes some sense to me. I may not be a resident of Dangria, but I'm fairly certain that no one can be imprisoned without reason or charge."

"That's true," said Iruwen. "It's the law."

"And the mayor has no reason for holding the boy, and he can't accuse him of anything, because he can't tell anyone the real reason why he's keeping him in the dungeon. Isn't that right, Martin?"

"Yes," said Tiuri.

"So if we go to him and demand that he releases the boy, he can't refuse," Ardoc continued. "Unless he has a case to make, or he invents one."

"And what if he does invent one?" asked the innkeeper. "Then we're back to where we started."

"What exactly did he do when he tried to take you prisoner?" Ardoc asked Tiuri. "Did he make an accusation? Were there any witnesses?"

"His guards aren't going to testify against him, are they?" said Doalwen.

"His scribe was there too," said Tiuri. "He can swear that neither of us said or did anything to merit imprisonment."

"And your friend escaped immediately?" asked Ardoc.

"Yes. As soon as he saw that the mayor was up to no good."

"Then this is a sound idea," said the innkeeper. "There's a council meeting today. They're always open to the public. We can all go together."

"The mayor will never dare to flout the law so publicly," said Doalwen.

"We must ask Master Dirwin to come along," said another guest. "He's a man of influence and his word carries weight."

"Master Dirwin is the head of the guild of silversmiths," Iruwen told Tiuri. "He used to be on the council, but he resigned because he rarely agreed with the mayor."

"Master Dirwin will need to know what this young man has told us in any case," the other man continued. "About the spies from Eviellan, and such business."

"I still don't understand," said Doalwen. "We were supposed to have peace."

"That's what they claimed," Ardoc said quietly, "but how long has it been since the king's envoys left? We've heard no news since then. And I know that Sir Andomar has not yet returned to Ingewel."

"And neither has Sir Edwinem returned to Forèstèrra," Iruwen added.

"It's not an easy journey, though," said Doalwen. "It's a long way to Eviellan."

"But there has been no message from them. No good news, no bad news... Nothing."

The room fell silent. Tiuri remembered now that he had heard the name of Sir Andomar before. Like Edwinem of Forèstèrra, he had been part of the company that King Unauwen had sent to Eviellan. It seemed almost certain that something had gone very wrong during the peace negotiations.

Then, in the distance, they heard the sound of bells.

"Listen," said the innkeeper. "The eighth hour is striking. The meeting at the town hall begins in half an hour."

"We should be off, then," said another man. "I shall go and talk to Master Dirwin. I hope to be with him at the town hall in thirty minutes."

"And I shall speak to everyone I see," said Iruwen. "I'll head to the marketplace first. There should still be plenty of people around. Will you come with me?" he asked Tiuri.

Tiuri nodded. Then he looked around the room and said, "I thank you all for your help."

"Save that for later," said Ardoc. "Come on. Let's go."

6 RAISED TEMPERS

As Iruwen explained to Tiuri on the way to the marketplace, the mayor and the council held regular meetings at the town hall, and anyone who wished to attend could do so. In the past, there had always been a meeting once a week and every citizen of Dangria had been allowed to make proposals, ask questions and register complaints. However, more recently, the meetings had often been cancelled or closed to the public for trifling reasons. This was one of the objections that people had raised against the mayor.

Tiuri watched in amazement as Iruwen gathered a crowd of people at the market. The old man delivered a fiery speech. He repeated his grievances against the mayor, spoke of the dangers threatening the city, and concluded by announcing that the mayor had deprived two young strangers of their freedom.

"One of those boys escaped and is standing here beside me," he said. "The other is still languishing in the mayor's dungeons. Yes, when the mayor used our money to titivate his town hall, until it was more like a king's palace, he also extended the prison beneath it! Why was that? Did he think he needed to imprison more people? Did he fear enemies? Did he fear us, the peaceful citizens of Dangria, loyal subjects of King Unauwen? Or was his jail intended for innocent strangers?"

Iruwen paused and looked around.

"Certainly a mayor must often be firm," he continued. "And unfortunately that sometimes means locking people up. But a man should never be deprived of his liberty without reason, without accusation! That is our law, and we should hold that law sacred! When such an injustice occurs, people must... *we* must protest. This young man here is about to return to the town hall to demand that his friend is released. Released! Right now! And any person who believes in law and justice must follow him and support his demand!"

The people crowded around Iruwen and Tiuri. Most of them applauded Iruwen's words, but some wanted more explanation and they had plenty of questions for them both. The mayor's guards came over to find out what the noise was all about.

Iruwen shouted, "To the town hall! Anyone who supports us and who would like to have some answers may come with us. This young man is daring to set foot once again on the steps of our town hall, because he has a clear conscience and therefore has nothing to fear... as long as justice still prevails in the city of Dangria!"

A few minutes later, Tiuri entered the town hall for the second time. Ardoc and Iruwen followed him, and many others came after them. Tiuri wondered if Piak would be able to hear the crowd from the dungeon downstairs and if he might suspect that they were there because of him. His heart was pounding. He wasn't scared, but it was the first time since he'd set out on his mission that he'd felt so visible.

In the hall, a large table stood on a platform in front of the great wooden staircase. Ten men were sitting at the table, with the mayor in the middle. Off to one side, sat the scribes, including the young man who had helped Tiuri, and guards with spears and torches lined the stairs and filled the spaces between the pillars. Some townsfolk were already in the hall, waiting for the meeting to start. Iruwen pointed at a man and whispered to Tiuri that it was Master Dirwin, the powerful head of the silversmiths' guild.

When the mayor saw Tiuri, he looked shocked. He and Tiuri stared at each other for a moment and then the mayor leant over to the man on his right and whispered something.

Meanwhile, more and more people were crowding into the hall. If nothing else, Iruwen had at least made them curious.

The man to the right of the mayor stood up and shouted, "Silence! Close the doors!"

A murmur ran around the room.

"This is a public meeting!" someone cried.

"The hall is full!" shouted the official. "There is no more room. Close the doors!"

It was a while before the doors were closed and everyone had settled down.

The mayor leant back in his chair and fiddled nervously with a sheet of parchment. Then he rose to his feet and said, "The mayor and the council of Dangria are gathered together in this place. All who would listen may listen. All who would speak may speak!"

One of the guards on the stairs blew three times on a trumpet.

"I declare this meeting open," said the mayor. Then he sat down.

The official on his right stood up again. "Let the First Scribe read the minutes of the previous meeting," he said.

The mayor's scribe stood up and bowed. He looked around and his gaze rested for a moment on Tiuri. Then he started reading. He read hesitantly at first, as if his mind was elsewhere, but gradually he seemed to gain control of himself.

Tiuri looked at Iruwen and raised his eyebrows.

"Later," Iruwen whispered. "When it's time for questions."

So Tiuri had to wait. He took in nothing of what the scribe said. He looked around the room and saw that the mayor was clearly uneasy and was avoiding his gaze.

When the scribe had finished reading and sat down, the official on the mayor's right said, "This meeting will be dedicated to the improvement of our city's buildings, a subject that concerns us all. So we would ask you to confine your questions and proposals to that subject alone. At the next meeting you may once again address general matters."

"He's done that deliberately!" whispered Iruwen.

Voices were raised in the crowd.

"Silence!" cried the official. "Anyone who is not silent will be removed. You know the rules."

"Yes, we know them!" cried Iruwen. "And we also know the laws, Master Marmuc! Anyone who demands justice may ask for it whensoever he wishes!"

"Silence," barked Master Marmuc. Then he smiled and said, "Of course you may ask for justice. But this evening we shall be discussing the construction of..."

"Why speak about new matters when old matters remain unresolved?" said Iruwen.

Then the mayor spoke. "Silence, Iruwen," he ordered. "There is a time for everything."

"My lord mayor," replied Iruwen, "you speak true. I am certain that you of all people would not approve of an injustice. And surely you would not wish to wait until our next meeting to put right any injustice that may have occurred. Urgent matters must take priority. And now is the time to deal with such urgent matters."

The mayor's face drained of colour.

Some of the crowd followed Iruwen's lead. "Urgent matters must take priority!" they shouted.

"Silence!" yelled the mayor, banging his fist on the table. "If you will not be silent, I will clear this room!"

The murmurs and shouts ceased. Then Master Dirwin rose to his feet.

"My lord mayor," he said, "you can see that many people have come here this evening. It would seem that something important has happened. Let them speak now, as was always the custom in the past."

"Something important!" shouted the mayor, also standing up. "I locked up an impudent boy! Since when have the people of Dangria been concerned about such matters? We are adult men, Master Dirwin, and we know that young people sometimes have to be dealt with firmly."

"My lord mayor," said Dirwin. "No one has yet made any mention of the boy you had locked up. In fact, you are the first to bring up the subject. So it would appear that you believe it to be a matter of import!"

The crowd murmured and whispered. A few people laughed.

The mayor seemed taken aback, but he soon regained his composure.

"Of course I mentioned the boy!" he said. "I can see his friend standing right there! I don't know how he dares to show his face here. He barricaded himself in the town hall today and threatened to kill me. He injured one of my guards. It is I who should be accusing him, not the other way around!"

Everyone looked at Tiuri, and he took a step forward. Again, he and the mayor stared at each other. A tense silence filled the room.

"I asked you and your friend to the town hall as my guests," began the mayor, "but you rewarded my hospitality very strangely! My guards here will testify that you, young man, locked yourself away in this town hall. That you shot at my archers through the window..."

"But if they do so, you will also have to mention that your archers shot at me first," said Tiuri in a loud, clear voice. "And you will also have to say why I felt it necessary to lock myself in one of your rooms. And you will also have to explain why you gave the order for my friend to be taken prisoner. Yes, you really must explain that! My friend has done nothing to you. Nothing! He was running away because he did not want to stay here. Why was it that you wished to keep us here against our will?"

"I didn't want to keep you here against your will!" shouted the mayor. "Why would I do that? I don't even know you! I invited you for hospitality's sake, but you didn't want to stay. You insulted me. Don't you know you can be punished for that?"

"I have come to demand my friend's release," said Tiuri. "He has done nothing to warrant imprisonment. Perhaps the people here will not believe me when I explain what my friend said and did before you sent your guards after him. So why don't you tell them yourself and explain what exactly you are accusing him of?"

The mayor opened his mouth and closed it again. He clearly didn't know how to respond.

"Then let someone else tell the story," Tiuri continued. "Your scribe was there. He can say what happened." He turned to look at the scribe, who flushed and crumpled up a piece of paper with trembling fingers. "Please be my witness," said Tiuri. "What did my friend do to insult the mayor?"

"Were you there, scribe?" asked one of the other gentlemen at the table. "Then speak. What did the boy do?"

The mayor sat down.

The scribe rose to his feet and said, "Nothing."

"Nothing? What do you mean?" asked Master Marmuc.

"Well, nothing," said the scribe. "He didn't do anything. They arrived and I had made a room ready for them, but they said they couldn't stay for long. But the mayor insisted that they should stay. He said he wanted to hear news from the east. Then the other one – the boy who is in the dungeon now, I mean – started shouting. 'Don't worry,' he said. 'I've got it here. I'll deliver it!' Something along those lines. And then he ran outside. And that was it."

"And that is truly all that happened?" Master Marmuc asked the mayor.

The mayor did not reply.

"And what was to be delivered?" asked Master Dirwin, looking in turn at the scribe, the mayor and Tiuri.

"Perhaps you should ask the mayor," said Tiuri.

"I have absolutely no idea," said the mayor. "I know nothing about it."

"You know very well!" shouted Tiuri. "But I can understand why you don't dare to say." He looked around the hall. "And I'm afraid I can't explain either," he continued. "But I do know one thing. Your mayor did not invite us here out of any sense of hospitality. He commanded the guards at the gate to bring to him any young men between the ages of fourteen and eighteen who entered Dangria. Why? You would have to ask him that question. And ask him who it is that sends him messages by carrier pigeon. Ask him who exactly ordered him to deprive strangers of their freedom. Ask him which master he serves, while he governs this city in the name of King Unauwen!" Tiuri fell silent for a moment, suddenly afraid he had said too much. But then he continued, "I am a stranger in your city and I have no involvement in your affairs. All I am asking for is the release of my friend. Right now!"

Tiuri could see the mayor was defeated. His face was ashen and he couldn't utter a word.

The hall erupted. "Set him free!" the people cried.

One of the members of the council rose and ordered the crowd to be silent. "Do you have an accusation to make against this young man or the young man in the dungeon?" he asked the mayor.

"No," the mayor replied, so quietly that it could barely be heard. "No. But everything he said is lies... All lies..." And then, a little more loudly, "It's a misunderstanding, a regrettable misunderstanding, and..."

He could not finish what he intended to say, because the crowd erupted once again. "Set him free."

The gentlemen at the table looked uneasy and whispered together. One of them stood up and spoke to the guards. Then someone called for order again, but it was some time before everyone in the hall had quietened down.

"The meeting is closed for today," declared Master Marmuc.

"Why?" cried a number of angry voices. "We've only just started!"

"The meeting is closed," repeated Master Marmuc. "The boy will be released. Please clear the room and go home."

The guards moved towards the crowd to lend weight to his words. Tiuri looked around, at the seething, unruly crowd and the pale men at the table. He saw Ardoc and Doalwen nearby, but Iruwen had disappeared. Someone tapped him on the shoulder. It was Master Dirwin.

"Your friend will be here soon," he said. "I should like to speak to the two of you."

Before long, two guards brought Piak into the room. He looked surprised to see so many people, but when he spotted Tiuri his face lit up. Tiuri headed straight for him.

He had to push his way through the crowd to reach his friend.

"You're free!" he cried, shaking Piak's hands. "Oh Piak, I..." Then he stopped speaking and just smiled at Piak.

"What are all these people doing here?" asked Piak, after he had enthusiastically responded to Tiuri's handshake.

"They helped to get you released," began Tiuri. He didn't have the opportunity to say anything else because some of the crowd burst into cheers. "Hoorah! He's free!"

The mayor and most of the councillors left their seats at the table and headed up the stairs. It looked rather like an escape.

"Come on," cried Tiuri. "Let's get out of here!"

Later, he could not recall how long it took before he was standing in the marketplace with Piak. There were still people everywhere, talking excitedly and paying no attention to the guards, who kept shouting at them to go home. After a while, Tiuri and Piak managed to sneak away unnoticed.

In one of the streets leading to the square, they bumped into Dieric, Ardoc's man.

"Ah, there you are," he said. "Everyone seems to have gone mad! I've lost the others. Come back to the White Swan with me. I think they'll probably be there."

Dieric was right. They did indeed find most of the people who had helped Tiuri and Piak at the White Swan. The innkeeper poured glasses of wine for them and invited them to drink to their success. Piak and Tiuri had a lot to tell each other, but some parts of the story would have to wait until no one else was around.

Piak told everyone that he was feeling just fine. "Well, you know," he said, "it's not much fun sitting in a dark hole, but it's not that bad if it's just for a short time. If only I'd known it would be over so soon!" And then he wanted to hear exactly how Tiuri had managed to get him released.

"You have all of these people here to thank for that," said Tiuri. And, helped out by Iruwen, Ardoc and some of the other men, he told Piak how the plan had come together.

"Whew!" exclaimed Piak. "That's really amazing! I could almost start to think I'm an important person." Then he turned to Tiuri. "So everything's as it should be?" he said, with a meaningful look.

"Everything's fine," replied Tiuri. He held out his hand again and shook Piak's in silent gratitude.

Then Master Dirwin arrived. He headed straight for Tiuri.

"Good evening, young man," he said. "I thought I'd find you here. I'd like to speak to you. There are many things about this business that still remain unclear to me."

"Oh, he can't say too much about it, Master Dirwin," said Iruwen.

"I'm sure he can tell me more than I know now," said Master Dirwin, stroking his beard. "I have come from the town hall, where I spoke to the council. There is to be an extraordinary meeting, tomorrow morning. The mayor will be required to account for his behaviour." He looked at Tiuri. "There are odd rumours going around the city," he continued. "I have even heard talk of spies from Eviellan! I would like to know how much is true. I would also like to know why the mayor took you prisoner. I feel there is much more to this than you have told, young man. What are your names, incidentally, you and your friend?"

"Their names are Martin and Piak," said Iruwen.

"Well, Martin and Piak, you will have to be present at the meeting tomorrow."

"Why's that, Master Dirwin?" asked Tiuri, even though he knew very well.

"To explain exactly what happened, of course," replied Master Dirwin. "And not only that. We also need to know the reason behind what occurred. You can tell me everything now, but you will have to repeat your explanations before the council tomorrow."

"Tomorrow?" cried Tiuri. "That's impossible! We can't stay here that long."

"Why not?" asked Master Dirwin. "That really is most unreasonable. I, along with many other people in this city, believe that you have been treated badly. That is why your friend Piak was released immediately. But you can't just run away now."

"We're not running away," said Tiuri. "I'm just saying that we cannot stay!"

"Because of you, there was almost an uprising in our city!" said Master Dirwin. "I cannot see what reason might be important enough to prevent you from staying. You have yourself accused the mayor... Oh, not directly, but you've said enough to make it clear that an investigation is required. In the interests of our city, I order you to remain here. I speak not only as a citizen of Dangria, but also as a member of the council!"

"Are you back on the council?" asked Iruwen.

"Yes, after tonight's meeting I was invited to join the council again," Master Dirwin replied.

"Well, that's good news," said Iruwen.

Master Dirwin turned to Tiuri again. "Now, speak," he said.

Tiuri repeated to him everything that he had already told to the people at the White Swan.

Master Dirwin listened in silence, but did not seem too satisfied with what he heard. "It's all very vague..." he said when Tiuri had finished speaking. "But fine, I shall trouble you no longer. I still have much to do. I hope to hear more details tomorrow. For tonight, I command you to remain in the city."

"You can have a room here," said the innkeeper. "I'll show you where it is and then you can go to bed whenever you like."

"I bid you goodnight," said Master Dirwin. "Until tomorrow. I'll come and fetch you. At about eight o'clock. Agreed?"

"Yes, sir," said Tiuri.

Tiuri did not have the opportunity to say anything else, because Master Dirwin appeared to consider the matter closed. He bade everyone goodnight and left. Tiuri sighed. He didn't know what else he could have said.

"Shall we go to bed?" Piak whispered to him.

"Good idea," said Tiuri. "But aren't you hungry?"

"Well, to be honest, yes," said Piak. "I haven't eaten a thing since this afternoon."

"I'll rustle something up for you!" said the innkeeper. "I'll bring it to your room."

"Sleep well," said Ardoc to the two friends. "And you have nothing to fear. Master Dirwin is a wise man, and above all a fair and honest one. You can trust him."

Tiuri and Piak wished everyone goodnight and followed the innkeeper to a small, neat room with two beds. Soon after that, Piak was tucking into a late supper and Tiuri also had a bite or two.

"So," said Piak with his mouth full. "Finally we're on our own."

"And finally I can thank you," said Tiuri.

"You've already thanked me," said Piak. "Do you still have it?"

Tiuri laid his hand on his chest. He could feel Sir Edwinem's ring, but not the parchment and the seals of the letter that he had carried for so long.

"I burned it," he whispered. "But I learnt the message by heart."

"Really?" said Piak, also whispering. He didn't ask what the message was, even though it was thanks to him that it had not been lost.

"It was written in a secret language," Tiuri told him. "I don't know what it meant. Oh Piak, without your trick the mayor would surely have taken the letter. I don't know how to thank you."

Piak looked embarrassed. "Ah, hush," he said.

"But, Piak, how did you know the mayor's hospitality was a trap?"

"Oh, I didn't realize at first," Piak answered. "But I had a funny feeling when I looked at all those shields. Right at the back of the room was one that was as red as blood. I remembered you telling me that the knights of Eviellan have red shields. I thought it might just have been a coincidence. But then I walked past an open door and I heard some guards talking. They were saying they'd have to surround the town hall. Well, I thought that was strange, so I listened in on them. I didn't hear much, but it was enough."

"What did they say?"

"Oh, something about a boy of between fourteen and eighteen, a young man from the east, from over the mountains. And that he mustn't be allowed to escape. It sounded suspicious so that's why I did what I did. And they fell for it!"

"So what happened?" asked Tiuri. "What did they do when they'd caught you?"

"It was so foolish of me," said Piak, "getting caught like that! They took me to that hole beneath the town hall. Well, I say hole... It's actually really big, but nothing like as fine as upstairs. It's so cold and dark. They threw me down on the ground and the mayor came in and he said, 'Give it here!' I played dumb and said, 'Give you what?' He was furious, but he got even angrier when he realized that I didn't have anything with me... at least not the thing that he wanted. No, please don't start thanking me again. Why else did I come with you? To help, of course. Besides, adventures are fun when everything turns out well – and there's a good meal waiting at the end!"

Tiuri smiled but he still felt anxious. "So what do we do now, Piak?" he said. "We're in such a hurry, but we have to stay here to make statements and give explanations. Even though we can't actually explain anything..."

"Couldn't you tell Master Dirwin?" asked Piak.

"I've already thought of that. If he wants to keep us here, I'll have to tell him. But I'd really rather not. My mission's secret. It's awful, but I really can't afford to trust anyone. Even the mayor of this city turned out to be one of the enemy's men. There may be more of them in Dangria, and we've already attracted far too much attention."

"That's my fault," said Piak. "You'd have been better off travelling on as quickly as you could and coming back to help me later."

"No!" said Tiuri. "I'd never have done that. Anyway, it was only thanks to your quick thinking that we managed not to lose the message. But I do wish we could leave right now." He thought for a moment. "You're right. I'm going to tell Master Dirwin the whole story," he said. "And only him. Perhaps I can speak to him tonight."

There was a knock at the door.

"Come in," called Tiuri.

It was Iruwen. "Not in bed yet?" he said, closing the door behind him. "I thought as much."

"Please sit down," said Tiuri. "Now I can thank you again for your help. Piak would never have been released if it weren't for you."

"Yes," said Piak. "A thousand thanks!"

"You're welcome," said the old man, with a smile. He sat down and looked at them. "And now you want to leave the city as quickly as possible, don't you?" he said. "Well, I happen to have a friend who's a guard at the small gate in the northern city wall. And he has the watch from ten until two. So you should be able to leave soon."

Tiuri and Piak stared at him in surprise.

"You're going to help us escape?" asked Tiuri.

"Of course. I understand you're in a hurry. And if you stay here, it could mean a long delay. I know what it's like. Council meetings, questions, answers, more questions, declarations, statements. All very complicated and time-consuming. Master Dirwin is a good man, and I am glad to have him on the council again, but, as I have already said, urgent matters must take priority."

"We are so grateful that you are prepared to help us once again," said Tiuri. "But how do you know our business is urgent?"

"Forgive me for saying so myself, but I have my suspicions," replied Iruwen, "and when I have my suspicions about something, they're usually right. You came here with a purpose and something tells me that it is in all of our interests. And so I must help you to achieve your goal."

"My thanks," said Tiuri. "When can we leave?"

"After you have finished eating," Iruwen replied. "We'll leave by the back door. No one will notice us."

"I'm ready to go," said Piak. "I couldn't eat another mouthful."

"Oh, I almost forgot," said Tiuri. "I still have to pay for our meals. And for this room. Perhaps you would give the money to the innkeeper." But when he reached for the pouch on his belt, he had a shock. It was gone!

"Oh, you fool," said Iruwen. "You didn't look out for the pickpockets."

"I'm so sorry," said Tiuri. "What should I do?"

"It doesn't matter," said Iruwen. "It'll be paid, one way or another. I'll borrow it from somewhere."

"Oh, this is such a nuisance," said Tiuri. "Do you have any money, Piak?"

"Just one brass farthing," he replied.

"Keep it for luck," said Iruwen. "Come now, don't worry about such trifles. I hope I get my hands on those pickpockets though! It must have happened in the crowd. You know, Dangria isn't the city it used to be."

"What was it like before?" asked Piak, standing up.

"It was once as it will be again," replied Iruwen. "Wait until we have a new mayor and the king's knights return. Shall we go?"

"What's Master Dirwin going to say?" said Tiuri, thinking out loud.

"He'll probably be angry. But he won't stay angry for too long. He's far too busy for that. I've heard that he's making all manner of plans. Tomorrow morning, for instance, a messenger will be taking urgent news to King Unauwen."

"They're sending a messenger to the king?" said Tiuri.

Iruwen looked at him sharply. "Yes, a messenger to the king," he said. "Might that perhaps not be necessary?"

"Why do you ask?" asked Tiuri.

"Well, say, if a messenger were already on his way there... Yourself, for example."

"You're right," Tiuri answered quietly. "We're going to King Unauwen."

"Then you must leave at once," said Iruwen. "I'll speak to Master Dirwin tomorrow. You should be able to cover some distance tonight."

Before long, they were walking through the silent streets to the gate where Iruwen's friend stood guard. On the way there, they almost ran into a group of armed men on horseback.

Iruwen signalled to the boys to stay in the shadows, and then stopped the horsemen and spoke to them. They told him that they had been instructed to reinforce the guard on the city gates.

"No one may leave the city," they said. "By order of Master Dirwin on behalf of the council."

When the horsemen had ridden on, Iruwen said, "Come on! Quickly! They'll probably go to the small gate last. We must be there before the reinforcements arrive."

They reached the gate in time, but had to say a hurried goodbye. Piak and Tiuri thanked the old man again for his help and the guard let them pass through. And so Tiuri and Piak finally left the city of Dangria and continued their journey to the west.

7 THE BRIDGE ACROSS THE RAINBOW RIVER

Tiuri and Piak walked all through the night. They wanted to put Dangria behind them as quickly as possible and make up for lost time. All was quiet; they did not hear or see anyone. Occasionally the two friends talked quietly, but as the night wore on they spoke less and less.

They didn't rest until daybreak and still they didn't stop for long, even though they were so tired. Later that morning, they were lucky enough to be offered a ride on a hay cart by a farmer who was travelling to the west. Lying in the fragrant hay, they soon dozed off and they didn't wake until the sun was high in the sky.

"What a couple of sleepyheads!" said the farmer. "If you're heading to the Rainbow River, you'll need to get off here, though. I'm taking a side road."

Tiuri and Piak thanked him and continued their journey on foot through a landscape of low, rolling hills. Tiuri kept glancing back over his shoulder; no one appeared to be following them. Dangria was no longer in sight, but he wouldn't feel comfortable until they were on the other side of the river, in what Ardoc had said was the heart of the Kingdom of Unauwen.

When they came to an orchard, they stopped and gazed up hungrily at the ripe fruit on the branches. "I think I might just help myself to a few apples," said Piak. "Is that so wrong when you have no food and no money to buy food, and you're starving and you're in a hurry and, what's more, you're on a mission of vital importance?"

Tiuri smiled. "Let's risk it, shall we?" he said.

Munching their apples, they continued their journey.

Late in the afternoon, the road led over a ridge and, as they reached its highest point, they saw the Rainbow River lying in front of them. The river was very wide and gleamed in the sunlight. There was a stone bridge crossing the water and a mighty fortress beside it on the eastern bank. Closer to Tiuri and Piak, there were houses and farms, surrounded by fertile fields, and on the opposite riverbank lay a village and the road that led on into the west.

The two friends headed towards the river and found themselves in civilization once again. There were lots of people at work in the fields, and the road was busier, too. They couldn't help but stare at the fortress; the closer they came, the mightier it seemed. The bridge actually appeared to be connected to the building, and a gate built from the same stone as the fortress stood at the end of the bridge.

"Look," said Piak. "There's a barrier."

Tiuri had seen it, too. And there was a guard standing beside the barrier with a helmet, spear, and a shield bearing every colour of the rainbow.

A man on horseback came from a side road and approached the bridge ahead of them. When he had reached the barrier, he leant over and spoke to the guard. The guard raised the barrier and let him pass. Then he lowered it again.

"Oh, that's good," said a relieved Piak. "They're letting people through."

Soon the two friends were standing at the barrier.

"Good afternoon," said the guard. "So you'd like to cross the river, would you?"

Tiuri and Piak nodded.

"And I'm guessing this is your first time across, isn't it?" said the guard. "That'll be three gold pieces each."

"What?!" exclaimed Tiuri. "Can't we just cross?"

The guard looked surprised. "Of course not," he said. "If you want to cross the Rainbow River, you have to pay the toll."

"But why?" asked Piak.

"Why?" repeated the guard. "I've never heard such a strange question in all the time I've been a toll guard and carried the rainbow-coloured shield. Where on earth are you from? How can you not know that everyone who crosses the river has to pay the toll? Do you think you can simply step onto this magnificent bridge and walk across to the other bank?"

"But," said Tiuri, "what if we can't pay?"

"Then you can't cross," replied the guard.

Tiuri looked at the river. It was even wider than he had thought at first and the current seemed very strong. He doubted that he would be able to swim to the other side. But perhaps he could get hold of a boat somehow...

"Any person who wishes to cross the Rainbow River – by whatever means – must pay the toll," said the guard. He must have guessed what Tiuri was thinking. "Whether you walk over the bridge, or go in a boat, or swim across, you pay the toll. But I wouldn't advise swimming."

Tiuri looked at him. "We need to get to the other side," he said, "but all we have is one brass farthing. Why is there a toll on the river here?"

"That's something you'd have to ask the toll master," said the guard, pointing at the fortress. "He is the one who enforces the toll, by the orders of King Unauwen."

"But we can't pay it!" cried Piak. "This is so unfair. It means poor people can never reach the heart of the Kingdom of Unauwen."

"That is not true," said the guard, angrily. "Everyone, rich or poor, may cross the river. The toll must be paid, but the toll master gives everyone the opportunity to earn the money. You can work on his land and receive a gold piece for every week that you work. After three weeks, you'll have the gold pieces you need."

Tiuri and Piak looked at each other.

"So what do you say to that?" asked the guard. "You see there's no need to be miserable. Just go to that big farmhouse over there and ask the steward what work needs to be done. You should be able to start tomorrow."

"We don't have time to work for three weeks," said Tiuri. "We're in a hurry."

Another guard came out of the castle and walked over to them.

"You're in a hurry, are you?" said the first guard. "Lots of people say that."

"But it's really true," said Piak.

"What's true?" asked the guard who had just arrived.

"These young men have no money to pay the toll, and they say they don't have enough time to work for the money."

The second guard studied the two friends.

"Three gold pieces in three weeks is quickly earned," he said.

"Yes, and I'm sure the lord of this castle has no shortage of labourers," muttered Piak.

The guard looked at him with a mixture of surprise and anger on his face.

"What are you trying to say?" he asked. "Three gold pieces in three weeks, that's good pay."

"Not if you have to hand back those gold pieces to pay the toll," said Piak.

"But the point of working is to get to the other side."

"I want to go to the opposite bank now, not later," said Piak. He turned to Tiuri and said, "Have you ever seen anything like this? People not being allowed to cross a river?"

"Never," replied Tiuri.

"I realize you're not from these parts," said the second guard. "Otherwise I'd have lost my temper with you by now.

Now I'd like you to tell me, young man, have you ever seen a river with a bridge like this over it? With seven stone arches, in such a strong current? Have you ever in your life seen such a fine bridge?"

"No," said Tiuri, "I admit that I have not. But I'd be just as happy to cross to the other side in a boat. Isn't that allowed?"

"Of course it's allowed," said the first guard. "If you pay three gold pieces. That's the rule. And whether you like it or not, that's the way it is and that's the way it's staying. If you can't pay and you don't want to work, you're not getting to the other side."

But the second guard added, "If you're truly in a hurry, you can speak to the toll master. I remember once he let a woman through because her son on the other side was very ill. If you have a valid reason for your haste, you should go to the toll master yourself, and ask him to let you through without paying. He's the only one who can make that decision."

Tiuri and Piak looked hesitantly at each other.

"The toll master is out inspecting his properties at the moment," the second guard continued. "He's usually back at around six, so he should be here soon. You can go to the main gate and wait for him there."

"Thank you," said Tiuri.

Tiuri and Piak said goodbye to the guards, but the first one stopped them for a moment. "I'll warn you," he said. "Don't do anything foolish. It could cost you more than three weeks. Offenders are dealt with severely."

"What now?" whispered Piak, as they slowly made their way to the main gate.

Tiuri sighed. "I don't know," he said.

Ask the toll master? But then he'd have to reveal his secret, and how could he know if the toll master was to be trusted?

The very fact that he charged this toll made Tiuri inclined to dislike him.

The main gate was open and some guards were sitting in the passageway. Tiuri and Piak stopped a short distance away. They didn't say anything else to each other but somehow knew that they should wait for the toll master to return. Maybe, after they had seen him, they would be able to make a decision. *But I really shouldn't tell him*, thought Tiuri. Sir Edwinem had said, "Tell no one." *Yes, Piak knows, but that feels just the same as knowing about it myself...*

Then Piak nudged Tiuri. "This must be him," he whispered.

The sky in the east had become quite dark; it looked as if bad weather was on the way. And sharply delineated against that sky, a man on a white horse was swiftly approaching. His long black cloak fluttered out behind him as he rode, revealing an azure blue lining. He raced past, a lord who inspired respect, with a pale complexion and a face that was handsome but stern, his dark hair streaming in the wind. He rode through the gate without looking at them, and the guards greeted him as their master.

Tiuri and Piak turned and walked away from the fortress, as if by agreement.

"What do you think of the toll master?" asked Tiuri after a while.

"I didn't get much of a look at him," Piak replied, "but he seems like a great lord, a powerful man. I wouldn't like to fall out with him."

"Stern and unapproachable," murmured Tiuri. No, the toll master did not appear to be the kind of man who would be easy to lie to, or who would open the bridge without a valid reason. And Tiuri dared not reveal his reason for wanting to cross so urgently.

Tiuri and Piak walked back past the bridge. Only the first guard was there now and he raised a mocking eyebrow. They headed along a path that ran alongside the river. A short, steep slope ran down from the path to a narrow strip of pale yellow sand, with water lapping onto it. Tiuri and Piak stopped and gazed longingly at the opposite bank. They could now see the bridge in all its glory: seven perfect arches on pillars that stood strong and firm in the rushing water.

"What should we do?" Piak whispered.

"I'm still thinking," replied Tiuri. "I'm wondering if I can swim to the other side. The river's wide and the current's strong, but there's a small island. I could pause there to catch my breath."

Piak peered at the island, which was no more than a large rock. "Maybe," he said doubtfully. "I couldn't do it. To be honest, I can't swim. But don't let me hold you back."

Just then, a soldier approached them. It was the second guard, who had spoken to them earlier. "So," he said, "I see you're looking at the opposite bank. I do hope you're not thinking of trying to swim."

Tiuri and Piak both looked at the man without responding.

"You can get that idea out of your heads," the guard continued. "As far as I remember, there have been three attempts. The toll master sent a boat to save one man from drowning and then threw him into prison for attempting to avoid the toll. The second man reached the other side – his body washed up on the opposite bank days later. And the third was never seen again."

"Couldn't they swim?" asked Piak.

"They were all good swimmers," the guard replied. "It's just that the current here is so treacherous. Particularly around that little island. It's full of eddies, even though you wouldn't think so to look at it from here."

"Fine," said Piak, "then we won't try swimming."

Tiuri pointed at the opposite bank. "I can see some boats over there," he said. "Does anyone ever cross the river in a boat?"

"Of course," said the guard. "There are ferries from one bank to the other, and fishing boats, and ships that come from the north and south with goods to trade. But everyone who wants to go from this side to the other has to pay the toll. The first time you pay three gold pieces, the second time you pay two, and the third time you pay one."

"And what about after that?" asked Piak. "Don't you have to pay anymore?"

"Exactly," said the guard. "But you're strangers here, so you'll have to pay the toll. Let me give you some good advice. Don't try to get out of paying it! The toll master's men are already keeping an eye on you. If someone can't pay or won't pay, the security is tightened. Just take a look at the bridge."

The friends looked and saw two guards slowly patrolling the bridge.

"And there'll be men standing guard on the other side, too," he added.

"So we'll just have to go and work on the land, then," said Tiuri. He didn't mean a word of it, but the guard didn't need to know that.

The guard smiled. "That's very wise," he said.

A man at work in a nearby field had kept looking over as they talked. He stuck his spade in the ground now and came over to them.

"Hello there, Ferman," said the guard. "Earned your bread for the day?"

"By the sweat of my brow," replied Ferman, wiping his forehead. "Good evening," he said to Tiuri and Piak. "Wanting to get to the other side, are you?"

"I've already told them not to do anything foolish," said the guard.

"And you are right," said Ferman, "as always, wise Warmin, Watchman of the Toll." He pointed to the northwest and said to Tiuri and Piak, "If you want to go that way and try crossing there... You can forget it! There's another toll. And there's one to the south, too, the Rainbow Mountain Toll, and then upstream there's the Toll of Vorgóta."

"Is there nowhere you can just cross the Rainbow River?" asked Tiuri.

"No," said Warmin, the guard. "The toll masters guard the entire Rainbow River. And there's a toll fortress on the Silver River, too."

Piak pulled a face, but he kept his opinions to himself.

"Come on," said Warmin. "I'm going back to the castle. It'll be dinnertime soon. The two of you should head off and talk to the steward. If you go there now, he'll give you food and a place to sleep, as an advance on your labour. Will you walk with me, Ferman?"

"Yes," Ferman said, but he stayed where he was and looked at the two friends.

"Come on, then," said Warmin. He turned to Tiuri and gave him one last piece of advice. "Even if you were to get a boat," he said, "it's still dangerous to sail on a river you don't know." Then he said goodbye and walked off, with Ferman following him.

"So," said Piak, "now we know! We're not allowed to swim, we're not allowed to sail, and we're not allowed over the bridge. And we can't ask the toll master either. Could we borrow the money? But who'd give us three gold pieces when they don't know us? Could we go back to Dangria and try there? No, we were in such a hurry to get away from there... So what now?"

"Shhh," said Tiuri. He was silent for a while and then said, "It's strange but I feel there's another way to get over the river... I just can't think what it might be."

"Shhh," said Piak back to Tiuri. "Someone's coming. I think it's that Ferman again."

It was indeed Ferman. He waved and came over to join them. "The sun's going to set soon," he said. He paused and added in a mysterious tone, "Fog to the west, rain to the east... Yes, it'll be a dark night for sure. We won't see any stars or moon tonight."

The two friends looked at him quizzically.

Ferman took a quick glance around and then whispered, "I have a boat, just a little one. It's not too far from here."

"Do you mean..." said Tiuri. "You'd lend us your boat?"

"Ah, I might just do that, but you can't tell anyone. It's forbidden and I could be punished for helping you. I know you don't have three gold pieces, but I'm not asking for much. What do you have to pay me with?"

"This," said Piak, holding up his brass coin. "This is all we have."

Ferman shook his head and said, "Ah, that's not much." Then he took the coin from Piak's hand, mumbled something and threw it on the ground. He bent down to pick it up and said, "Heads."

"And what does that mean for us?" asked Tiuri.

"I tossed the coin to see what I would do. You can't pay me anything, but I could still help you. So I decided that if it was heads, I'd do it. And it was heads, so you can have my boat. If you want it." Ferman gave Piak his brass farthing back.

"So we can borrow your boat?" whispered Tiuri eagerly.

"Yes, if you like," replied Ferman. "Do you know how to row?"

"Yes," said Tiuri.

"Good, then you can give it a try, but it's at your own risk! I'll show you where my boat is, later, when it gets dark. You can't leave before then."

"Thank you so much," said Tiuri.

"Hush!" said Ferman. "Don't thank me. If the coin had landed differently, I wouldn't have done it. Just one thing: don't tell anyone the boat belongs to me. I've already been to prison twice and I don't want to go through that again. And if you get caught I won't help you. The risk is your own. You saw the boat sitting there and you decided to take it. Got it?"

"Absolutely," said Tiuri.

"I'm leaving now," said Ferman. "Come back here after the clock's struck twelve and make sure no one sees you. Follow the current downstream. I'll be waiting for you. And if I can give you some advice, you should go to the farm over there now and ask the steward for work. Once you've done that, the toll master's guards will stop keeping such a close eye on you. And you might get some food as well."

8 SINK OR SWIM

Tiuri and Piak headed to the farm and the steward promised them work for the next day. He also gave them some bread and milk and a place to sleep in an empty barn, where they waited until they heard a clock strike twelve. Then they slipped outside and cautiously made their way back to the river. Ferman had been right; it was a very dark night. It was chilly too. Tiuri and Piak were shivering, and not just from the cold. They reached the river without incident and walked along the narrow strip of sand on the bank, following the current downstream, as Ferman had instructed. Gradually their eyes became used to the darkness, but there was not much to see. Everything was so quiet; all they could hear was the river. They could barely make out the bridge, but there were still lights at a few of the castle windows.

The two boys jumped when Ferman came looming up out of the darkness.

"Ho, there," he said quietly. "Come with me. It's not far."

Warily, they followed him. "Here," said Ferman and he stopped.

Tiuri and Piak could just about see the outline of a small boat on the riverbank.

"The oars are inside," whispered Ferman. "So you can leave right away."

"But the boat's so small," said Piak. "It won't tip over, will it?"

"Any boat can capsize," replied Ferman. "But let me just remind you that it's your own risk. You can tie up the boat on the other side. I'll make sure I get it back. To be honest, though, I wouldn't do it if I were you, not now and not tomorrow. If it were me, I'd rather work for three weeks. But that's for you to decide."

"So why are you letting us take your boat?" asked Piak.

"Well, I tossed the coin and that's what happened. Why? Perhaps because I can understand someone wanting to avoid the toll. I've tried it myself. I've no need to do it now, because I've been to the other side more than three times. So, what are you going to do?"

"I'm going," said Tiuri. "But you don't have to come with me if you don't want," he said to his friend.

"Of course I'm coming," said Piak. "As long as I'm not a burden, I'll stay with you."

"But..." Tiuri began.

Piak interrupted him. "Quiet. Shall we just get in and push off? You can row."

"It'd be best if one of you rows and the other keeps a lookout," said Ferman. "Even if you can't see much. I can't exactly tell you what to look out for, can I? Row quickly, with long strokes. After about thirty strokes, you'll need to be careful. You'll be close to that little island that you'll have noticed earlier. The current swirls around in every direction at that point. Make sure not to get too close; you could run aground on one of the rocks beneath the water. It's a nasty spot to cross, but one of the toll master's guard posts is down that way, so there's a good chance you'd be spotted. It's the same closer to the bridge. Once you're past the island, there's not much to worry about, at least not from the river itself. So, are you ready?"

Tiuri nodded. "We're ready," he said. His heart was pounding. He realized that the crossing would be dangerous, but he'd done plenty of rowing before, on the Blue River.

"We're ready," echoed Piak.

Ferman sighed. "Well, best of luck," he said. "I'll help you to push the boat out and then you're on your own."

Soon they were in the boat, Tiuri at the oars and Piak sitting opposite him. Tiuri couldn't see Piak's face. "You can still get out if you want," he whispered to him.

"No!" said Piak.

"Sssh!" hissed Ferman, as he pushed out the boat.

Tiuri raised the oars.

"Good fortune be with you," said Ferman. "Row firmly and evenly. Yes, like that! Don't wave the oars around and rock the boat."

Tiuri felt a little out of practice, but after a few strokes it came back to him. Now he could feel just how strong the current was. The beach and Ferman, who stood watching them go, were just vague outlines, and the darkness soon swallowed them up. Tiuri focused all of his attention on the boat, which was rocking and spinning.

"Look out for the island," he said to Piak, "and warn me the moment you see anything."

"Can't I help with the rowing?" asked Piak.

"No," gasped Tiuri. "One of us has to keep an eye out. Can you see anything on the riverside or on the bridge?"

"No, nothing," said Piak. "There are still lights inside the castle. I'm sure they can't see us. I can hardly see anything myself. No rocks. And no sign of the opposite bank."

Tiuri glanced around. Piak was right. It was as if they were floating on a vast expanse of water that had no beginning and no end. He stopped rowing for a moment. The boat immediately twisted off course, so he tugged on the oars again. Downstream, he spotted a light on the riverbank. Was it the guard post Ferman had mentioned?

"My feet are getting wet," said Piak.

Now Tiuri noticed it too. There was water in the bottom of the boat. Had it been there when they climbed in? Or was the boat leaking?

"We're not sinking, are we?" said Piak. He sounded anxious.

Tiuri stopped rowing again. "Sssh!" he whispered to Piak. "I can see a light over there. They might be able to hear us."

"I don't think so," said Piak. "The water's making too much noise."

"See if you can find something to bail with," said Tiuri.

"To do what?"

"To scoop out the water. Is there a bucket or anything like that in the boat?"

As Piak moved, the boat rocked.

"Be careful!" whispered Tiuri. He knew for certain now that the boat was a rickety old thing – and probably leaky. He looked back over his shoulder. It seemed even darker back there. Were they near the island yet? He started rowing again. Drops of water splashed up at him and he could feel beads of sweat on his forehead.

Piak searched around on the bottom of the boat. "There's more and more water coming in," he said. "Hang on. I've found something! A bowl."

"Start scooping the water out," said Tiuri. "But move as gently as possible."

The boat was definitely leaking. If Piak kept on bailing out the water, they would make it to the other side. But he was supposed to be watching the river! Piak looked around. Nothing in sight. Or was there something? A darker patch standing out against the darkness? A wave suddenly hit the boat and turned it around.

Piak gasped. "Look out!" he whispered.

"Watch the river," said Tiuri. "We can't be far from the island now."

The river was bouncing them around in every direction. Tiuri had to struggle to keep the boat heading in what he hoped was the right direction.

"I can hear something!" said Piak.

He was right. There were voices in the distance.

"Nothing we can do about that," said Tiuri.

"But look! I can see something!" said Piak. "The island, the island! It's close. Row! This way."

Tiuri rowed with all of his might. Piak forgot to bail out the water, until Tiuri reminded him.

"We're nearly there," panted Tiuri. His hands were sore from pulling on the oars and he could feel the pain of his recently healed injury again. The river was tugging the boat in every direction. The toll guards had not been exaggerating. The water really was treacherous.

Piak divided his attention between bailing the water and watching the island. "We're nearly there," he said, repeating Tiuri's words. He seemed to have got over his anxiety.

Suddenly it happened... A jolt, a crack... They had run aground on a rock! Tiuri made a desperate attempt to free the boat... And it worked!

But then... "We're sinking!" whispered Piak.

Everything happened so quickly that Tiuri had no time to think. The boat may have been free from the rock, but water was streaming in and it seemed certain that they would sink. Then they hit something else and the boat rocked wildly. A stifled gasp from Piak was followed by a splash. He was in the water!

Tiuri lowered the oars. For a second, he felt paralysed. What if Piak drowned?

A moment later, Tiuri was in the water too and shouting out, without even worrying that anyone might hear. "Piak, Piak! Piak, where are you?"

He swam a few strokes, dived, and fumbled around. Where could Piak be, in this dark, wild water? But then, thank God, he heard a faint cry. It was Piak.

"Piak!" he called out again. "Where are you?"

"Here," came a weak voice.

Tiuri reached out into the darkness and found his friend.

"Keep yourself afloat," he panted. "No, don't hold on to me. I can't swim like that." Then a wave hit Tiuri and silenced him. But his grip on the floundering Piak was firm and he held on. The boat, where was the boat? Probably at the bottom of the river. He had to reach the island. It was their only chance. If they weren't dashed against the rocks...

"Try to lie on your back!" he called out to Piak. "I'll pull you."

He wasn't sure Piak had understood, but he stopped struggling. Then Tiuri started swimming towards the island, pulling Piak with him. They were anxious and exhausting moments, but finally Tiuri felt solid ground beneath his feet. They were on the island.

Tiuri felt battered and bruised and he was gasping for breath. Piak was lying beside him, very still. Tiuri leant over his friend.

"Piak!" he said, shaking him.

Piak groaned, lifted his head and coughed. "So much water," he whispered, so quietly that Tiuri barely heard him. Tiuri felt like singing and dancing for joy, but he had to settle for slapping his friend on the back.

"Where... where are we?" asked Piak, trying to sit up.

"On the island," said Tiuri. "Please, just lie there."

But Piak sat up and said, "Where's the boat?"

"I think it sank," replied Tiuri.

"It was a useless boat," said Piak, his teeth chattering.

"Well, at least we didn't sink with it," said Tiuri. "How do you feel?"

"I thought I was about to drown," said Piak, "but it must take longer than that. Did you drag me here?"

"Yes, what else could I have done?"

"Well, you could have taught me to swim," said Piak. "But I don't think swimming's for me. I don't like all that water. Have we really lost the boat?"

Tiuri stood up and peered into the darkness. He even waded some way into the water, but there was no sign of the boat.

Piak called him back. He sounded anxious. "Please don't

start swimming again," he said. "I won't be able to rescue you if anything happens."

Tiuri went back and sat beside his friend. "We'd never have made it anyway," he said. "The boat was wrecked as soon as we hit that rock."

"Ferman's not going to be pleased," said Piak. "Serves him right! What was he thinking of, lending us a leaky old boat like that?!"

"At our own risk," said Tiuri, quoting Ferman.

"Yes, but he didn't mention that it had a leak!"

"Everyone warned us about the current here, including Ferman."

"So what do we do now?" asked Piak. "Ugh, I feel sick. And it's so dark."

"Do you feel really ill?" asked Tiuri.

"No," said Piak. "Honestly, I'm fine. I'm just wet and angry. Aren't you?"

Tiuri sighed. Now they were halfway across the river, without a boat. When morning came, the guards would most likely spot them. But they couldn't escape. Yes, he could of course try to swim the rest of the way, but that was dangerous and probably foolish. And he'd have to leave Piak behind; it would be impossible to take him.

"You're not thinking of swimming, are you?" Piak said, interrupting his thoughts. "You'd be mad to swim. You'll drown, and your message will drown with you. And I'm not just saying that for my own sake. I really don't care if I have to stay here. The toll master can throw me into jail tomorrow morning, but I'm used to that now. And anyway, I know he'll release me before too long."

"But if I stay here, the message will never reach the king," said Tiuri.

"That's true," admitted Piak.

Neither of them spoke for a while.

What now? Tiuri found himself wondering, yet again.

Then, suddenly, he knew the answer.

"You fool!" he said out loud.

"Huh? Why am I a fool?" asked Piak.

"I was talking to myself. I don't know why I didn't think of it before!"

"What?"

"The toll! Paying the toll! I don't have any gold, but I have something that's worth far more than that!"

"You do?" said Piak. "Where is it?"

"On a cord around my neck."

Sir Edwinem's ring, the ring with the stone that shone in the dark! Tiuri had never seen the ring as his own, but as something that he was guarding, an object he respected. Perhaps that was why it hadn't occurred to him before to offer it as payment for the toll. But Sir Edwinem would surely have done just that. The message for the king was more important than any jewel might be. Tiuri pulled out the ring and showed it to Piak.

"It's like a star," Piak whispered.

"I should have thought of it straightaway," said Tiuri. "Now we've wasted even more time. It was so unforgivably stupid of me."

"But the ring is worth far more than three gold pieces, or even the six that we'd both have to pay."

"Plus maybe a fine on top of that," added Tiuri. "I think this ring must be priceless, but I'm only planning to use it as a guarantee. Later, on the way back, perhaps I can claim it back. I'd be happy to work for weeks if that's what it takes."

"Do you think the toll master would agree?" asked Piak.

"I hope so," said Tiuri. "I..." He faltered. He thought of the Grey Knights who had pursued him. What if the toll master knew the ring too, and recognized it? Sir Edwinem had been a famous knight, especially here, in the Kingdom of Unauwen. What if the toll master asked Tiuri how he had come by the ring?

Tiuri stood up again. Should he try swimming after all? He knew it was dangerous, maybe even irresponsible, with an arm that might fail him halfway across, and in the dark as well. But if he waited until it was light, the guards would see him. What was the best course of action?

"What are you going to do?" asked Piak's voice behind him.

Tiuri sat back down beside his friend and shared his thoughts.

"I think our only option is to pay with the ring," said Piak. "I don't like the idea of swimming. But you're the one who has to decide."

Tiuri thought for a moment. "I know one thing for certain," he said. He lowered his voice and continued, "How are you feeling, Piak? Well enough to remember if I tell you something?"

"Of course," Piak replied. "If it's something important."

Tiuri whispered a few words in his ear.

"What did you say?" asked Piak.

"It's the start of the letter. I'm going to tell you the message, word for word. You need to know it too."

"I do?" whispered Piak.

"I already thought about telling you, because you're right, my task has become yours too. You need to know the message, so that you can take over if anything happens to me."

"Oh..." sighed Piak. Tiuri's words seemed to have made quite an impression on him, but he promptly added, "Fine, at least it'll give me something to do until it gets light. Tell me the message. I just hope I'll never have to take over your task."

Word by word, Tiuri told Piak what was in the letter and his friend repeated the words after him.

"Do you understand any of it?" asked Piak after a while.

"No. Do you?"

"No, not a thing. Is it a secret language? Never mind, go back and start again at the beginning, until I know it by heart."

"Make sure you never let anyone see you know the message too," said Tiuri.

"That goes without saying," said Piak. "Hey, look. It's getting light in the east. We need to hurry. I want to know all of the message by the time the sun comes up."

9 ALARMING NEWS

"Rainbow River," muttered Piak, as the night slowly gave way to the greyness of dawn. "Ha! When I think of rainbows, I picture something beautiful, but this river is so cold and unfriendly."

Tiuri looked around, hoping that, against all odds, he might see the boat. But there was no sign of it. He realized that they were closer to the eastern riverbank than the west. People were walking across the bridge. The toll master's men?

"They're bound to spot us soon," he said to Piak.

"The sooner, the better," Piak replied. "I don't want to stay here too long." Then he sneezed three times. "Sneeze thrice, weather's nice," he said with a grin. "So at least it's going to be a fine day."

The two friends sat side by side, shivering in their wet clothes, and waiting for it to get light. There were people on both banks of the river now; some of them even pointed at Tiuri and Piak.

Then a horn sounded; it seemed to come from one of the towers of the castle. Tiuri wondered if it had anything to do with them.

"Look! Over there!" Piak cried a little later. He pointed towards the castle. "A boat!"

The boat slipped through one of the arches of the bridge, moving quickly towards them, beautiful and sleek, with a team of rowers working in perfect time. A guard with a rainbow-coloured shield stood in the stern. The rowers' shields adorned the sides of the boat.

"One of the toll master's boats," said Piak. Then he sneezed again.

Anxiously, the two friends watched the boat. Yes, it was heading for the rock. It soon reached them and the man in the stern called over to them, "Wade towards us and climb on board. We can't come any closer."

They did as they were told. Hands reached out to pull them on board.

"Attention!" called the man in the stern, who seemed to be in charge. "Oars to starboard!" When the boat was safely underway again, he turned to Tiuri and Piak. They recognized him as Warmin, the guard they'd spoken to on the riverbank the day before.

"You are now the toll master's prisoners," he said sternly. "You have attempted to evade the toll and will be punished." Then, more kindly, he said, "Why didn't you listen to my advice? I was concerned that you wouldn't, but I hoped you'd have more sense. You borrowed that old wreck of Ferman's, didn't you?"

"Oh, no," lied Tiuri.

"No?" repeated Warmin. "So you swam all that way in the middle of the night? You're more capable than I thought."

Piak started to say something, but he sneezed instead.

"If you have a cold, it's no more than you deserve," said Warmin, but he took off his cloak and wrapped it around Piak's shivering shoulders. Then he told the two friends where to sit and paid no more attention to them.

The boat headed back towards the bridge, but it was upstream, so it took longer, even though the oarsmen were working very hard. As Tiuri saw the bridge and the castle coming closer, his heart started beating faster. He turned to Warmin and said, "I should like to speak to the toll master."

"Speak to the toll master?" repeated Warmin. "You should have thought of that yesterday. It's too late now to request an audience just so you can express your apologies."

"Apologies?" snapped Tiuri. "I'm not interested in apologizing. Yes, I'm sorry I didn't manage to get over the river, but I'm not sorry that I tried."

"Why doesn't that surprise me?" Warmin barked back at him.

Tiuri persisted. "It really is very important that I speak to the toll master."

"Why?"

"That's something I can explain only to him."

Warmin frowned. "Really?" he said. "We shall have to see about that."

By then, they had reached the bridge. Tiuri looked up and saw a man peering down at them over the stone balustrade. He was wearing a wide-brimmed hat and the shadow almost completely concealed his face. As the boat came closer, he leant forward. Tiuri couldn't stop looking at the man, even though he had no idea who he was. Then he heard him laugh, a mocking, triumphant laugh. It was still echoing in his ears as they passed under the first arch of the bridge. He glanced at Piak to see if it had spooked him too, but Piak sat huddled beside him, staring straight ahead.

When they emerged on the other side of the arch, Tiuri saw that the castle came right up to the edge of the water. There was a small landing with a set of stairs leading directly into the building. As they were mooring the boat, a man appeared at the top of the stairs. With a start, Tiuri recognized him as the toll master himself. He just stood there, watching them.

Warmin was the first to jump ashore and he saluted his master with his sword. Then he ordered his prisoners to follow him. He did not head up the stairs, however, but walked towards a small gate at the far end of the landing.

Tiuri didn't move, but said, "I wish to speak to the toll master."

"We shall see about that," Warmin said. "Follow me."

"I want to speak to the toll master," repeated Tiuri. "Now." He was sure the toll master, standing at the top of the stairs, must have heard him, but the man did not react.

Warmin paused for a moment and then went up the stairs and spoke to his master. Tiuri saw the toll master shake his head and Warmin came back downstairs. The toll master turned away and disappeared into the castle.

"Come with me," barked Warmin.

"Can't I speak to the toll master?" asked Tiuri.

"I'm sure you know the answer to that question," came the reply.

"But I have to speak to him," said Tiuri. "It's important. Really."

"That may well be the case," said Warmin, "but it won't

be that easy now. I've asked him and he said no. And that's the end of it."

Warmin remained silent as he led Tiuri and Piak through the gate and into the castle. He took them along a passageway and down a flight of stairs into a dark, vaulted room. A portly man came over to them, with a lantern in one hand and a bunch of keys in the other.

"Prisoners," Warmin said. "Tried to evade the toll." He took his cloak from Piak's shoulders and was about to leave, but Tiuri stopped him.

"Sir," he said, "you have been so kind to us. And I would ask you for one more kindness. Would you please speak to the toll master on my behalf? It's vital that I talk to him as soon as possible. I can explain to him why I tried to avoid paying the toll."

"Yes. Why did you do that?" asked Piak. Back on the island, the two of them had agreed that Piak should act as if he knew nothing. It seemed the best way to keep it secret that Piak now knew the message too.

"That is something I can tell only to the toll master," said Tiuri, as they had agreed.

Warmin looked at Tiuri, then Piak. "Hmm," he said. "We'll see."

Then he turned and walked away.

"Come along," said the large man. "I'm the jailer. And you're my responsibility until they let you go."

He opened a door and told them to go through. They found themselves in a bare cell with no windows and just a pile of straw in one corner.

"How long do we have to stay here?" asked Piak.

"You could have worked for three weeks, outside in the sunshine," replied the jailer, "and you'd have earned your toll money. Now you'll have to sit around in the dark for three weeks, doing nothing, and when you get out you still won't have a farthing to help you pay the toll."

"Is there no way they can just let us go now?" asked Piak.

"No," said the jailer with a look of satisfaction. "Because I'm your guard and I'm not letting you out. Unless someone comes to pay the three gold pieces for you, that is... That's the fine for getting you out of jail. And if you still want to cross the bridge, it'll cost you another three gold pieces. But you didn't have any gold pieces, did you?"

Tiuri and Piak didn't reply.

"Well then," said the jailer. "I'll be off. You're lucky you're in here together. At least you've got someone to talk to. And if I can give you some advice: take off those wet clothes. You're better off with no clothes than wet ones. The straw's dry. I put some fresh stuff in only yesterday."

Then he left and locked the door behind him. The cell was plunged into darkness.

"I don't know what's worse," said Piak. "The cold or the dark."

"Let's hope," said Tiuri, "we won't be in here too long."

They followed the jailer's advice and got undressed and curled up on the straw. But there was no way they could sleep. They were far too agitated. Tiuri slipped the ring onto his finger and held up his hand. The light of the stone was faint, but clear, and it gave them both some comfort.

When they heard a key turn in the lock, they had no idea how much time had gone by. Tiuri slid the ring from his finger and hid it in his hand.

The jailer came in. He held up his lantern and said, "Which one of you wanted to speak to the toll master?"

"I did," said Tiuri, standing up.

"Then you must come with me."

Tiuri quickly pulled on his clothes.

"Shouldn't your friend come too?" asked the jailer.

"No," said Tiuri. "Just me." And when the jailer wasn't looking, he winked at Piak.

"You're not leaving me alone in here, are you?" Piak said, pretending to be scared.

"No," said Tiuri. "I just need to ask the toll master something. You'll be fine!"

Tiuri followed the jailer through the vaulted room and back up the stairs. Another of the toll master's servants was waiting to lead him up into a higher part of the castle.

"Here we are," said the servant finally, opening a door. "Go on in. The toll master is expecting you."

Tiuri went through the door. He couldn't help blinking at first, because it was so bright. Then he looked around. It was a large room with two windows on the opposite wall, which looked out over the river. At the far end was a large table with a man sitting at it. It was the toll master. Tiuri hesitated for a moment and then started to walk towards him. The toll master's voice stopped him.

"Go to the window," he ordered, "and look outside."

Tiuri did as he was told. He stood beside one of the windows and looked out at the river. Now he realized where its name came from; in the sunlight, the water glinted with every colour of the rainbow. The bridge was directly beneath him. He saw people walking across it, and a rider and a horse-drawn cart. The sky had cleared up, and he could see a long way.

Tiuri turned to look at the toll master, who had stood up and come to join him.

"Have you taken a good look at the bridge?" he asked. His voice was very different than Tiuri had expected. It was a low, melodic voice, the kind of voice you had to listen to, whether you wanted to or not. "It looks smaller from up here," continued the toll master, "but you get a better impression of the width of the river it spans. This bridge was constructed long, long ago, and building it took a great deal of hard work and effort. Lots of work and lots of money. That is why every person who used it had to pay. Because the bridge was built for everyone. Paying the toll made a person a partial owner of the bridge, even if it was just one stone. This bridge linking east and west now has thousands of owners."

"But," said Tiuri quietly, "hasn't it been paid for by now?"

He looked up at the toll master, who stood beside him, his arms crossed and his hands hidden in the wide sleeves of his long robe. He was looking out at the bridge, with an expression that was both thoughtful and serious. Then he turned to Tiuri. He had dark eyes, which looked sad rather than stern.

"If you want something, you have to be prepared to pay for it," he said.

Tiuri was surprised by this man, who was so different from what he had expected and feared.

The toll master looked through the window again. "This bridge, like the others, was built to connect the Kingdom of Unauwen to the world beyond," he continued. "The Rainbow River was once the country's border. Many people came from the east, longing to get to the other side of the river and prepared to pay for the crossing. There have also been difficult times, times of danger, of raids from the north, east and south. Back then, the toll masters were the guards of the river, the defenders of the heart of Unauwen's kingdom. In later years, the land all the way to the Great Mountains came under the rule of Unauwen, but the tradition remained: anyone who crossed the Rainbow River owed a toll to the king. The king himself appointed the toll masters. This is still the case, although nowadays anyone who crosses more than three times no longer has to pay the toll. And this will probably long remain so. Although I hope the toll masters will never again have to be defenders of the kingdom, the stern, unrelenting lords that many people think we are."

Tiuri didn't know what to say, so he remained silent. The toll master looked at him again and said briskly, "So, now tell me who you are and why you wish to speak to me."

"My lord," Tiuri began, "I wish to cross the Rainbow River, but I have no money to pay with and no time to work for the gold. I..."

The toll master interrupted him. "What is your name?"

"Martin," replied Tiuri, after a brief moment of hesitation.

"You come from the other side of the mountains. I can tell from your accent," said the toll master. "Is your name really Martin?"

"Yes, my lord," said Tiuri. "That is... what I call myself."

"Fine, so on this side of the mountains you are Martin. You have attempted to cross the Rainbow River without paying. That is a punishable offence and one that I never pardon. Why did you not come to me yesterday?"

"Because..." Tiuri squeezed the ring he was holding in his hand.

"My lord," he said then. "I had no gold pieces to pay with, but I have something else, a jewel that is worth far more. I could use that to pay the toll, and the fine for both my friend and myself."

"I see. What kind of jewel is it? And why did you not mention this before?"

"I am reluctant to part with it, my lord. Not only because it is valuable, but also because it is dear to me. I have no wish to sell it either. I wish to leave it as a guarantee. I should like to reclaim it later, and work for it for as long as you require."

"A guarantee?"

"Yes, my lord. As proof that I will return. Do you agree to my request?"

The toll master narrowed his eyes and did not reply. "Why exactly are you in such a hurry?" he asked.

"It's hard to explain," Tiuri replied.

"Just start at the beginning."

"My lord," said Tiuri. "I really cannot tell you."

Once again, the toll master turned his penetrating gaze on him. Tiuri waited anxiously for his reply.

Finally the toll master spoke. "You and your friend owe me two times three gold pieces," he said, "and another two times three gold pieces to get out of jail. If your piece of jewellery is worth twelve gold pieces, I will do as you ask. Show it to me."

The toll master held out his right hand, his palm facing upwards. Tiuri placed the ring in it. The toll master stared at the ring, closed his fingers around it, and looked back at Tiuri. Before the toll master had even spoken a word, Tiuri knew that he recognized the ring!

"How did you come by this ring?" the toll master asked sharply. He opened his hand again and said, "This ring does not belong to you! So how did you get it?"

"My lord," said Tiuri, "I see that you recognize this ring. And indeed it does not belong to me, although it was given to me..."

"Given to you?" said the toll master. "Given to you? By whom? There are only twelve such rings. Look!" He held out his left hand and showed Tiuri the ring he was wearing.

Tiuri gasped. "It's the same!" he said.

"Not exactly. Only two of these rings are identical. King Unauwen gave them to his sons. He gave five to his knights and five to the lords of the bridges and rivers."

Tiuri remembered what Sir Evan had said: "King Unauwen gave these rings to his most faithful paladins."

"So how did you get this ring?" the toll master asked again.

His faithful paladins! And the toll master was one of them!

"Sir Edwinem gave it to me," replied Tiuri.

"Edwinem," repeated the toll master. "Where, when and why did he give you his ring?" Then he asked quietly, "Is Edwinem dead?"

"Yes," Tiuri replied.

The toll master's face showed no sign of horror, grief or even surprise, but his hand closed so tightly around the ring that his knuckles turned white. "Tell me more," he ordered.

"I can tell you but little," said Tiuri. "He was murdered by the Red Riders and their master, the Black Knight with the Red Shield."

"Murdered?"

"Lured into a trap."

"Where?"

"In the forest close to the City of Dagonaut."

"In the Kingdom of Dagonaut? Not in Eviellan?"

"He rode from Eviellan," said Tiuri, "and he was on his way here."

The toll master walked back to the table and sat down. He pushed aside the book that lay open on the table and placed Edwinem's ring in front of him. He beckoned Tiuri closer. Tiuri stood beside the table and told the toll master about the slaying of Sir Edwinem, and how it had come to pass. But he mentioned nothing about the letter.

"I gather from your words that it is he who sent you here," said the toll master, when Tiuri had finished.

"Yes, my lord," said Tiuri.

"He gave you the ring to carry with you."

"Yes, my lord."

"And you are on your way to the king."

"Yes, my lord."

"Is that all you can say?"

"Yes, my lord."

"And you wanted to hand over this ring – Sir Edwinem's ring – as payment for the toll."

"Yes, my lord. As a guarantee that I will return."

"It does not belong to you. How can you give something that does not belong to you?"

"Sir Edwinem would have done the same. I... I am travelling in his stead."

"To King Unauwen."

"Yes, my lord."

The toll master picked up the ring and looked at it again. "You bring alarming news," he said. "One of Unauwen's knights has been murdered by riders from Eviellan. Such a death cannot remain unavenged!" He put down the ring and rose to his feet. He looked just as Tiuri had imagined him to be when he had seen him the previous afternoon: stern, unrelenting, a man who was to be feared by his enemies.

"Knights have ridden out to avenge his death," explained Tiuri. "They call themselves the Grey Knights. They have already defeated many of the Red Riders."

"Grey Knights. And who are they?"

"Their leader is Sir Ristridin."

"Ristridin of the South? I know his name. He was a friend of Edwinem's."

"And Sir Bendu, and Arwaut, and Sir Evan of this land."

"Evan's with them? Good. But you, Martin, or whatever your name might be, what do you have to do with these matters? What you have told me has surprised me, but much is still unexplained."

"I cannot say any more," said Tiuri. "What remains to be told is for your king alone."

"And that is why you're in such a hurry?"

"Yes, my lord."

"You are the first messenger to have brought me this news. Do you know anything else about the company that was sent to Eviellan? About Sir Argarath and Sir Andomar of Ingewel?"

"No, my lord," said Tiuri. "It was actually by chance that I met Sir Edwinem... or perhaps not chance... I don't know. But Sir Ristridin did tell me that Sir Edwinem fled Eviellan for some reason."

He gave the toll master a brief summary of what he had heard from Sir Ristridin.

The toll master thought for a moment. Then he handed the ring to Tiuri. "Take the ring," he said. "You should give it only to the king. You may cross the bridge. But you must promise me that you will come here on your return and pay me what you owe me. No one may cross the river without paying the toll."

"I promise, my lord," said Tiuri. "And my friend..."

"Your friend?"

"Yes, he has to come with me."

"Fine, he may go too. When do you wish to leave?"

"At once," said Tiuri.

The toll master banged a gong that stood beside the table. "You may leave directly, king's messenger," he said.

"My lord," said Tiuri, "please do not call me that. My mission is secret; no one may know of it."

The toll master nodded. The door opened and two servants came in.

"Fetch the other boy from the cell," said the toll master to one of the men. "And bring him to me."

The servant bowed and left.

The toll master turned to the second servant and said, "You have something for me?"

"My lord," replied the servant, "a messenger has come for you from the east." He handed the toll master a letter.

The toll master broke the seals, read the letter and then asked, "Where is this messenger?"

"He is waiting in the hall below," the servant answered.

"I shall come down," said the toll master. He looked at Tiuri and said, "Wait for me here. I will soon return." He left the room, with the servant following him.

When Tiuri was alone, he started pacing the room. He was relieved that everything had turned out well, and eager to continue on his way. He looked out of the window again and thought about what the toll master had said. Then he walked back to the table. He hoped the toll master would return quickly. And Piak, faithful Piak. Tiuri's eye fell on the book on the table, which the toll master had been reading. It was a big, thick book, and it was open at a page with beautifully drawn letters and a single golden initial, which was decorated with colourful flowers and tendrils. Tiuri walked around the table to take a better look. He recognized the letters, but the words themselves were unfamiliar, the words of a language he didn't know. As he looked for longer, the words started to seem more familiar, and he realized that he had seen some of them before. In the letter for King Unauwen! Was this book written in the same language? If the toll master knew this language, he would understand the message. If only Tiuri could ask him!

Footsteps outside the room startled Tiuri. He stopped looking at the book and walked towards the door. It opened and Piak came in, accompanied by the servant.

"My master will be with you soon," said the servant and then he left them alone.

"Free!" said Piak. "Is everything all right?"

"Yes," replied Tiuri, "we'll be able to leave soon." He was about to start explaining, but before he could begin, the toll master returned, still with the letter in his hand.

"Ah, so here's your friend," he said. "Your name's Piak, isn't it?"

"Yes, my lord," replied Piak.

"A messenger just arrived from Dangria," said the toll master, "sent by Master Dirwin, on behalf of the town council."

The two friends held their breath.

"This probably comes as no surprise to you," the toll master continued. "The letter refers to two young men who caused a commotion in the city, before leaving against the express wishes of the council."

"But we couldn't stay!" protested Tiuri.

"Master Dirwin has asked me to question you and to keep you here if I deem it necessary."

"My lord," said Tiuri, "I have told you everything I could. We cannot wait; we have to travel on, to the king. I have already told you more than I should, but you are wearing a ring just like Sir Edwinem's so I felt that I could confide in you. Please let us go!"

"Oh, I shall," said the toll master and, for the first time, he smiled. "You dared to trust me and now I shall do the same for you. Just one thing: you are in a hurry, but are you planning to go on foot?"

"We have no other means of transport," said Tiuri.

"And no money either. Well, you can both borrow a horse from me. You'll reach Ingewel by this evening, where you can leave the horses in the care of the landlord at the Inn of the First Night."

"Oh, thank you," said Tiuri.

"The innkeeper may give you fresh horses if he has them. Then you can ride on to the inn in the Hills of the Moon. And as for the toll, I have already said that I expect to see you back here as soon as possible."

"Yes, my lord," said Tiuri.

"Then you may leave," said the toll master.

Tiuri and Piak bowed, but he shook both of them by the hand and kindly wished them a good journey.

As they were walking through the hall downstairs, a man leapt to his feet.

"So it is you!" he cried. It was Doalwen, whom they'd met at the White Swan. And it turned out that he was the messenger from Dangria.

"Well, well," he said. "You've certainly given us plenty of trouble!"

"We have?" said Piak. "But we got out of Dangria as quickly as we could."

"That's just it," said Doalwen. "Iruwen helped you, didn't he? He always gets involved in things that are none of his concern. When Master Dirwin came to fetch you, Iruwen told him you'd already left for the town hall. But of course you weren't there. The morning was half gone by the time they realized you'd flown. Iruwen had a long discussion with

Master Dirwin, trying to convince him that you were right to leave. Are you coming back to Dangria with me?"

"No," said Tiuri. "We have our own road to follow."

Doalwen looked surprised. "I see," he said. "Well, we all have our orders to follow. Anyway, your escape is old news by now. The mayor made an escape attempt of his own. What a thing! But they managed to catch him and now he's back safe and sound in his fine house on the town square."

"Pah!" said Piak. "They should have thrown him into the hole beneath the town hall!"

Doalwen laughed. "It's a shame we have to say goodbye again," he said. "Now I have to ride back on my own. Did you see the messenger they sent to King Unauwen? He should have passed through here already. He left Dangria yesterday morning. You know him, actually. It was the mayor's scribe. Turns out he's not just a quill-dipper, but a good horseman too!"

Tiuri and Piak would have liked to talk to Doalwen for longer, but they knew they had to be on their way. So they said farewell and headed outside.

The barrier at the bridge was already up and they found Warmin waiting with two horses.

Tiuri spoke to him. "It was you who ensured that I could speak to the toll master so quickly," he said. "My sincere thanks."

"Oh, don't mention it," said the guard, looking at them curiously. "I see you obviously had a good reason for wanting to cross the river as soon as possible."

The two friends climbed onto the horses. This time, Piak looked as though he'd done it a thousand times before.

"You'll find a few useful things in your saddlebag," said Warmin. "Good journey!"

The two young men rode through the gate and over the bridge. *Click, clack!* went the horses' hoofs on the stone surface, and the water on both sides sparkled in the sunlight.

"Maybe the Rainbow River is the right name after all!" Piak called out to Tiuri.

And so they set off on the final part of their journey.

PART SEVEN

TO THE WEST OF
THE RAINBOW RIVER

1 THE FOREST OF INGEWEL

A wide, well-kept road ran from the Rainbow River through a flat expanse of fields, meadows and orchards. The friends rode quickly. Piak was already quite at home on his horse.

"With a bit of practice, you'll make a good horseman," Tiuri predicted.

"Phew!" said Piak, when they stopped to rest for a moment. "I'm so stiff. But what a lot of new things I've done! I've ridden horses, and I've been in a boat. I've nearly drowned, I've been in prison twice – although I could have done without that new experience – and I've met so many people. And the things I've seen! A city, a castle, a big river... But it all must seem so normal to you."

"Not really," said Tiuri. "I've seen a city, a castle and a big river before, but they weren't the same as these."

"I wonder what else we'll see and do on our journey," said Piak. He looked westwards. "Do you see that forest over there?" he said. "Could it be the Forest of Ingewel already?"

"I think so," replied Tiuri. "We've made good progress."

Inside the saddlebags they found bread, a bottle of wine and a pouch of silver coins.

"How kind," said Piak. "The toll master was so much nicer than I'd expected. Strange, isn't it, how some people turn out to be very different than you thought at first?"

"Yes," said Tiuri, thinking about what Piak had said. "That's what happened with the toll master and when I met the Grey Knights, too." Tiuri was in good spirits and he could hardly imagine that they might encounter any more difficulties.

Piak felt the same and, as they rode on, he started singing happily. He sang one song after another, and eventually it turned into a melody without words, a tune that Tiuri didn't know. It sounded strange: quick at times, and then slower, sometimes lively, sometimes soft and mysterious. Piak hummed the tune over and over again, changing something about it every time until he seemed to find a melody that he liked. Then he looked at Tiuri and said in a quiet voice, "Do you know what I'm singing?"

"No," said Tiuri.

"It's a tune to the words that only we know. I'm not allowed to say them out loud. Why don't you sing them along with me, in your head?"

Piak started humming again, and Tiuri realized that it was true: he could sing the letter's message to the tune that Piak had devised. Tiuri hummed along and, singing without words, the two friends rode into the Forest of Ingewel.

The forest was like no other forest Tiuri had ever seen. The grass was greener, the trees were more beautiful, the climbing plants more unusual than anywhere else. The road surface was made up of thick, springy moss. But the most amazing thing about the forest was the flowers that were blooming everywhere; they grew along the roadside and climbed up the tree trunks and whole clusters of them hung down from the branches.

When they had been riding for a couple of hours, they came upon three men resting by the side of the road, dressed in green and brown. Bunches of flowers lay beside them, which they had clearly just picked.

"Good afternoon, boys!" one of them called. "You know, you're riding far too quickly!"

Tiuri and Piak reined in their horses.

"Why's that?" asked Piak.

"Well, what do you think of this forest?" said the man.

"It's the most beautiful forest I've ever seen," Piak replied.

"And that is the only correct response," said the man. "But you shouldn't hurry through the Forest of Ingewel. We don't appreciate haste in these parts. Come, sit with us a while and listen to what the birds are singing. And have one of my apples. Or would you prefer a plum, or a wild cherry? No fruit tastes better than the fruit of Ingewel. In fact, the king won't eat fruit from any other place."

Tiuri and Piak climbed down from their horses. It was about time they stopped to rest anyway. They took the man's advice, lay down on the grass, and ate some of his fruit.

"Ah," sighed Piak. "That's so good."

"Strangers here?" asked one of the other men.

"Yes," replied Piak.

"We've come to take a look at your country," Tiuri added.

The men thought this a most praiseworthy enterprise and asked all kinds of questions about where Tiuri and Piak came from and where they'd been on their travels. Then they told them some stories about their own land and about Ingewel in particular.

"You must return for the flower festival," said one of them. "We adorn ourselves with flowers and sing and dance through the forest. And in the evening we gather by Lake Ingewel; that's the lake that the area's named after. We go out in boats and throw flowers at each other until the water has disappeared and all you can see are the flowers floating on the surface."

"There was no flower festival this year," another of the men said sadly, "because Sir Andomar wasn't here. Sir Andomar is the lord who governs this area; there's no other man like him! He went away at the beginning of this year when the king sent him on a mission to Eviellan. It's a dangerous place; don't ever go there."

"But we are to make peace with Eviellan," said the third man. "That's why the king sent his best knights there. And who better to choose than our own Sir Andomar?"

"But he has still not returned," said the other man.

The men fell silent and so did Tiuri and Piak. Tiuri wondered if these kind people would ever see their lord again, and if Sir Andomar would return to celebrate the flower festival with them.

When Tiuri felt rested, he stood up and said it was time to move on.

"So soon?" cried the men. "You're in such a hurry."

"We want to reach an inn before nightfall," said Tiuri. "The Inn of the First Night."

"You should sleep out in the open air," said one of the men. "But the First Night is good too. It's in the village, beside Lake Ingewel. If you follow this road, you'll come to it."

The two friends said goodbye to the men and rode on. They spoke little. Tiuri was thinking about Sir Andomar. He didn't know him, but he had been a companion of Sir Edwinem's. Having spoken to the men, he suddenly realized that worry and fear lay concealed behind the apparent peace and contentment of this pleasant part of the world. And he thought about the letter that he, a stranger, was bringing to this land. What consequences would it have for the people who lived here?

*

It was almost dark by the time they reached the village, which was also called Ingewel and which lay on the lake, close to the western edge of the forest. The lake glinted in the evening light, tranquil and mysterious. White water lilies hugged the banks, which made Tiuri think of how the lake must look during the flower festival. To the south, they saw a few towers pointing up above the trees; they later heard that these were the towers of Sir Andomar's castle.

They soon found the Inn of the First Night. It was a large building and the only inn in the village. The innkeeper gave them a warm welcome. He made sure the horses were taken care of and said they could have two fresh horses to continue their journey.

"You're in luck," he said. "I have only two horses that are well rested. The best horse isn't here right now. I gave it to a man who came through from the east this afternoon. But he was a messenger, on his way to the City of Unauwen."

Tiuri realized it must be the messenger from Dangria, and he said, "Oh? And when did he leave?"

"Let me think. He got here at about four," the innkeeper replied. "He had something to eat and rested a while. And he left over an hour ago, at about seven."

Then he asked Tiuri and Piak what they wanted to eat.

"We don't really mind," said Tiuri. "But first let me show you what we can pay. We don't have very much money."

"Oh, that's not a problem," said the innkeeper. "You've come from Lord Ardian, the toll master of the Rainbow River, and so you would be welcome even if you had no money at all. I'll give you a room for tonight as well. Travellers who are coming from the toll fortress always sleep here the first night. That's how my inn got its name."

The two friends tucked into their dinner. There were

not many people at the inn, just one other traveller and a few villagers. After dinner, the innkeeper's wife took them to their room.

Piak dropped down onto the colourful patchwork quilt and sighed. "Oh, that's wonderful. You've no idea how tired I am. I can really feel that I've been in the saddle all day. But now I can lie on my stomach and have a lovely sleep." He gave a loud yawn, and then looked at Tiuri and started laughing.

"What is it?" asked Tiuri.

"Oh, it's just that this room looks so beautiful, but I can't say the same about you! That jacket of yours is quite a sight; all of the colours have run into each other!"

Tiuri laughed too. "Yes, my bargain from the market in Dangria," he said. "But you don't exactly look very elegant either."

"We're both so scruffy. Pity about this lovely bed, isn't it?" said Piak. "Oh well. I don't care. I'm just going to keep on lying here."

Tiuri became serious again. "But not for too long, eh?" he said.

"Why? Do you want to be off again soon?"

"Yes, I want to reach the City of Unauwen as soon as possible. We'll have fresh horses, so..."

"You're right," said Piak, holding in a sigh.

"I'll go and tell the innkeeper that we'd like to leave soon," Tiuri continued. "Not right away, though. Let's say an hour."

He went back downstairs. The innkeeper promised to have the horses ready in an hour. He didn't seem to be the curious type, because he hadn't said a word about the appearance of his young guests, nor did he ask a single question about their business.

When Tiuri went back to the room, he found Piak asleep. Tiuri lay down on the bed too, but he didn't sleep. It was strange, given the peaceful, friendly surroundings, but he felt the need to hurry more than ever before, as if there were no time to lose.

2   An Eventful Night

"You can stable the horses at the Inn of the Hills of the Moon," said the innkeeper as Tiuri and Piak were preparing to leave.

"The Hills of the Moon?" said Piak, pulling himself into the saddle with a pained expression.

"Yes, they're called that because they look best by moonlight. It's no longer full moon, but they'll still be beautiful enough."

"How far is it to the inn?" asked Tiuri.

"About a day's journey," replied the innkeeper. "So, eleven, twelve hours. You can ride quickly across the Hills of the Moon and it's a clear night. If you need to travel onwards, you can keep these horses, unless you find new ones at the inn. I'll get them back in due course. Have a good ride!"

Tiuri and Piak thanked him and said goodbye, and then they set off. The horses trotted through the silent village and then moved more swiftly through the forest. Before long, they had left the forest behind and were heading into the hills.

They entered a wondrous landscape, a place straight out of a fairy tale, with low, grassy hills, grey boulders and just the occasional clump of bushes or a twisted tree. The road looked almost white and all of the colours were soft, dreamy shades, except for the deep black of the shadows. Perhaps it was the effect of the moon, which shone brightly in a sky full of small, wispy clouds. It was so quiet, but when they reined in their horses for a moment, they heard a constant sound in the background: the chirping of crickets in the grass. The hills appeared to be uninhabited; they saw no houses or any other signs of people.

Tiuri and Piak rode on in silence for some time. The quietness all around was affecting them, too. Gradually, though, the character of the landscape began to change. At first they hardly noticed it, but then they realized that the hills had become higher, the road was narrower, the undergrowth was thicker, and the trees were even more gnarled and twisted. The whole landscape seemed wilder and more desolate. And something else seemed to have changed. The silence felt ominous, and the light was ghostly; everything somehow seemed to have become sinister and frightening. At least that was what Tiuri thought, although he didn't mention it to Piak. But Piak was apparently feeling the same way; he kept looking back over his shoulder, and at one point he started singing quietly, perhaps in an attempt to chase his fears away. But his voice sounded strange and too loud in the quietness of the night, and then it faltered and died away.

It came as a surprise when they heard another sound. Tiuri immediately reined in his horse.

"Did you hear that?" he whispered.

"Y-y-yes," said Piak. "What was it?"

"I don't know. Quiet, there it is again!"

Neighing!

"A horse," said Tiuri.

Then the horse appeared over a ridge. It ran across the road and paused for a moment before darting away and disappearing.

"There was no rider," said Tiuri. "How strange!"

"Could it have been a wild horse?" asked Piak.

"But it had reins and a saddle," said Tiuri.

"Ah, yes," Piak replied.

They stood there, staring at the ridge where they had seen the horse appear.

We should go and see if something's wrong, thought Tiuri. But perhaps the horse had simply run away. Why should anything bad have happened? Even so, he rode slowly as he headed to the ridge, with Piak alongside him.

As they got closer, Tiuri had a growing feeling that something wicked was nearby, something hiding in the shadows of the hills or lurking behind the motionless bushes.

"This is where it came from," he whispered.

"Are you going to take a look?" Piak whispered back.

"Yes," said Tiuri, steeling himself.

He climbed down from the horse and Piak did the same. They stood and looked down into a narrow valley, where they saw a track heading off into a thicket. They listened hard, but all they could hear was their own breathing and the chirping of the crickets. So they cautiously started to walk down into the valley.

After just a few steps, Tiuri stopped. "Stay with the horses," he whispered to Piak.

"No," Piak replied. "I'm coming with you."

"No, don't. If there's anything... dangerous out there, it's better if we don't both go. You know the reason why!"

Without waiting for Piak's reply, Tiuri quickly walked on, overcoming his fear and heading into the dark thicket. Very soon, he came upon a clearing. There, on the ground, was a body. Tiuri stopped. He had been expecting something like this but still he hesitated before going closer and kneeling down beside it. What he saw made him gasp. He was looking at the face of the scribe from Dangria. He seemed to be

sleeping, but there could be no doubt about it. He was dead...
shot through the heart by an arrow.

A noise from behind startled him and he looked around.
It was Piak, who had followed him after all. His face was pale
and aghast, and his lips were moving but no sound came out.

"He's been killed," said Tiuri.

Piak let out a trembling sigh and repeated, "Killed?"

Neither of them spoke for a while.

"But why?" Piak mumbled finally.

"I have no idea," replied Tiuri. He looked back at the face
of the young man who had helped him so recently, the messenger who had been sent to Unauwen by the town council
of Dangria. A messenger carrying a letter for King Unauwen!

Shaking, he took the dead man's hands and folded them
on his chest. "Let's pray for his soul," he whispered.

The two friends did so. Then they stood up and looked
helplessly at each other.

"What now?" whispered Piak. "Do we have to leave him
here like this?"

"I don't know," Tiuri said. The scribe's murder had been a
terrible shock. And he had the strange suspicion that it was
somehow connected to his own mission. The scribe had also
set out with a message for King Unauwen...

A pouch lay on the ground beside the body. Tiuri looked
inside, but there was no letter. After some hesitation, he
searched through the dead man's clothes, but he found nothing there either.

"What are you doing?" whispered Piak.

"Looking for the letter," Tiuri replied. "But it's not here."
Then he stood up and added, "He can't have been dead for
long."

"But who do you think he is?" asked Piak.

"Ah, yes! You never actually met him," said Tiuri. "He is, he was, the mayor's scribe, the messenger that Dangria sent to King Unauwen."

"The messenger!" whispered Piak.

They looked at each other again. Piak was the first one to speak.

"Do... Do you think whoever murdered him is still nearby?" he whispered.

Tiuri didn't reply. Now that he had time to reflect, the thought that this murder had something to do with his own mission was not so strange. After all, the scribe had been sent to the king to inform him about what had happened in Dangria... and those events were closely connected to his task. And then a dreadful thought occurred to him. Might this murder have been a mistake? Had it happened because of a different letter, another message... the message he was carrying? Was the murderer Slither?

Tiuri gasped as Piak grabbed his arm and pulled him back into the thicket.

"What is it?" he whispered.

"I... I think I saw him," Piak whispered back.

"Who? Where?"

"It was just a movement. Over there. The tree." Piak pointed to the west.

Tiuri looked where he was pointing.

"On that hill over there. Do you see the tree?"

"Yes..." whispered Tiuri. Could he see something moving in the bushes beside it?

The two friends peered intently, but they saw no more movement. Had they just imagined it, or was there really someone nearby? Tiuri was certain someone was close. And if it was the murderer, they were in grave danger. He could have been spying on them and they knew he was armed with a bow and arrow. They had no weapons themselves, except for the small dagger in Tiuri's belt.

"Come on," Tiuri whispered.

They crept through the bushes until they were back at the road. Their horses were still there, waiting for them.

"What are we going to do?" Piak asked.

Tiuri put his finger to his lips. He peered through the bushes to see if he could see any sign of danger. But everything looked perfectly calm in the white moonlight.

"If he's here, our lives are at risk," he said. "But I don't think he's close enough to hurt us."

"The murderer?"

"Yes."

"He won't attack us, will he?"

"I'm afraid he might."

"Why?"

Tiuri didn't reply. He took another good look around. They couldn't stay there.

"Do you think... Do you think... Do you think it might be Slither?" Piak whispered in his ear.

"Sssh!" said Tiuri. Suddenly he really didn't want to hear that name.

They stood there silently for a short while, side by side.

Tiuri quickly considered their options. *We could carry on riding*, he thought, *until we reach an area with people around. Or we can go back to Ingewel. But he might follow us there. No... I know what to do.*

And he said, "We have to get out of here. One of us should return to Ingewel and the other will ride onwards."

"No!" whispered Piak. "We should stay together."

But Tiuri knew his plan was the best idea. If someone

was lying in wait, he could follow only one of them, and the other would be sure to get away. "I'll ride onwards," he decided. "And you can go back. Go to the inn and tell them about the murder. Get some armed men, and ride back here with them."

"And what about you?"

"I just told you. I'm riding onwards."

"But Tiuri, you can't! Not alone! I'm coming with you."

"No," said Tiuri. "Don't you get it? We can't stay together. We have to split up to improve our chances."

"But there's more chance that you'll be... What if you run into him? And you're on your own?"

"Shhh!" said Tiuri, interrupting his friend. "You don't know that. Now go!"

"No," said Piak. "I don't want to."

"Well, if you don't want to, I'll just have to order you!" Tiuri whispered hurriedly. "You promised you would obey my every command."

"But if it's Slither..."

"That's exactly why we have to do it this way!" Tiuri replied. He continued, almost angrily, "Piak, you have to do as I say! You can't think of yourself... or me."

Piak didn't say anything.

"Will you obey me?"

"Yes," Piak whispered unhappily.

Tiuri walked over to the horses. Piak slowly followed him. The horses were a little restless, but there was still no sign of anyone around.

"This is it, then," whispered Tiuri, holding out his hand to Piak. Piak reached out and shook Tiuri's hand, but then he stopped and looked around.

"Listen!" he said.

"I can't hear anything," replied Tiuri, pulling his hand away.

Piak put his finger to his lips.

Tiuri listened. Then he heard it too, very quiet and very far away. It took him a moment to recognize the sound.

Hoofs!

He knelt down and put his ear to the ground. Then he stood up and pointed eastwards. "They're coming from that direction," he whispered.

They looked back down the road, but they saw nothing... not yet.

"Should I go now?" asked Piak.

"No," said Tiuri. "Wait for a moment." It felt as though all of this had happened before, and suddenly he remembered a night that seemed so long ago, the first night of his adventure. That time, it had been the Red Riders who were riding through the night. Who were the horsemen who were approaching now? Were they friends or enemies?

He took his horse by the reins and beckoned to Piak. They hid some distance away from the road, close to the place where they had found the dead scribe.

The sound of hoofs grew louder; the horsemen would reach them soon. Yes, there they came! Fast shadows moving closer... They looked like guards and were carrying lances or spears. As they galloped by, Tiuri saw that there were about ten of them and that they were not dressed in red. He considered stopping them, but thought better of it. The horsemen had not gone far beyond the point where Tiuri and Piak were hiding when one of them shouted an order. They stopped to talk, but Tiuri couldn't hear what they were saying. Then they turned around and started to go back the way they'd come.

Involuntarily, Tiuri and Piak grabbed hold of each other. The men were coming back! Some of them had climbed down from their horses and were leading them by the reins. Slowly they headed down the road towards Tiuri and Piak's hiding place.

"You see," came the clear voice of one of the riders. "They didn't ride beyond this point. There are the tracks they left."

They're looking for us! thought Tiuri. He had to do something – and fast!

He leant over to Piak and whispered, "Go! Now! Ride to Ingewel! Quickly!"

Piak stared at him and shook his head.

Tiuri gave him a push. "Quickly!" he whispered. "Remember our mission. I'll hold them up if..." He fell silent. The men were so close now that he didn't dare say anything else.

Fortunately, Piak did as he was told. He made his way over to the horses, which were standing nearby, took his by the reins, and started to sneak away.

Tiuri looked back at the horsemen.

"Well, they must be here somewhere," said the same voice. It was a voice that sounded familiar. Its owner was now standing very close to him, holding his horse by the reins, but Tiuri couldn't make out his face. The man spoke again. "Hey," he said, "is someone there?" And then he shouted, "Martin, Piak! I'm looking for Martin and Piak! Are you out there?"

Tiuri held his breath. He could hear branches cracking and undergrowth rustling behind him. He glanced over his shoulder, but there was no sign of Piak now. Another man came closer, still riding his horse.

"Sshh!" the man said. "I can hear something!"

Tiuri and the guards all stood in silence. He could clearly hear the noise that they too must be able to hear, which was of course the sound of Piak making his way through the undergrowth. He had to give Piak the chance to escape!

Before the horsemen could start moving again, he said in a voice that trembled only slightly, "Who's there?"

"Is that you? Martin? Piak?" called the man who stood nearest to him. Then he walked over to the bushes where Tiuri was hiding.

"Stop!" shouted Tiuri. "Stay where you are! I am armed. Do not come another step closer!"

A murmur passed through the men. The one who had spoken to him – probably their leader – took a step back and said in a surprised voice, "What's all this? My good friend, you have nothing to fear!"

"Stay where you are!" shouted Tiuri. "I have a bow and a quiver full of arrows here. And I will shoot! Don't come a step closer. Stand still, don't move, any of you!" He drew his dagger so at least he would have a weapon of sorts.

The leader of the horsemen began to say something, but Tiuri interrupted and spoke over him. "Stay where you are! I will shoot the first man who moves. I'm warning you: I will shoot!" He spoke loudly, quickly, repeating his words several times. Piak had to be far away by the time the horsemen realized Tiuri didn't have a bow and arrows at all!

"But, friend!" called the leader, when Tiuri finally stopped for a moment. "We mean you no harm! Is that Martin, or Piak?"

"I think there's only one of them out there," said another man.

"We're both here," said Tiuri. "Who are you? And what do you want from us?"

"Don't you recognize us?" called the leader. "We were sent to catch up with you."

"Who sent you?" asked Tiuri.

The man came a step closer. "The toll master," he said.

3 A Shepherd
and a Messenger

This news came as a great surprise to Tiuri. But he was still suspicious.

"The toll master?" he repeated. "Why? And how do I know you're telling the truth?"

"You've met me before. It's Warmin!" shouted the leader. "Look, I'll throw down my weapons so that you can see I'm a friend." And he did just that.

It certainly sounded like Warmin's voice.

"The toll master sent us," he continued, "to protect you from danger. It seems he had good reason! I can tell you something that will prove you can trust us. Let me come closer."

"All right," said Tiuri. Still cautious, he added, "But only you."

Warmin – if it was Warmin – told his men to stay where they were and he walked over to the bushes. "Where are you?" he asked.

"Here," replied Tiuri, taking a step forward. He looked at the other man. Yes, he recognized the guard's rugged and trustworthy face.

"Hello, Martin," he said. Then he leant closer and whispered, "The toll master sent this message for you: 'By the jewel we both know, I would ask you to accept my men's aid.'"

Tiuri's hand went to his chest and touched the ring. He sheathed his dagger and said, "Thank you, Warmin. But what made the toll master decide to send you?"

"He heard something that worried him. If you trust us, please accept our help. And tell your friend he can come out, too." Warmin held out his hands to show he was unarmed.

Tiuri let go of his last objections. He reached out and shook Warmin's hand. "Forgive me," he said, "but something has happened that led me to fear there were enemies nearby."

"You don't even have a bow and arrow!" Warmin exclaimed.

"No," said Tiuri, "I was just pretending. I... I am glad they did not prove necessary."

He breathed a sigh as the tension left his body. The other riders came over and stood around Tiuri and Warmin.

"Where's your friend?" one of them asked.

"He's not here," replied Tiuri.

"You're alone?" said Warmin. "What on earth happened?"

"Wait a moment," said Tiuri. He cupped his hands around his mouth and called, "Piak! Piak!"

"So I was right. I did just see him," said one of the men.

"Piak!" Tiuri called again. "Come back!" His friend couldn't have gone far and he might still hear his shouts. In the silence that followed, Tiuri started to worry. What if something had happened to Piak? "Piak!" he shouted again.

"Over here!" came the reply. "I'm coming, I'm coming!"

Piak emerged from the trees surprisingly quickly. He stopped a short distance away and shouted over, "Is that really you, Tiuri?"

"That's right, Piak," said Tiuri. "You should never be too trusting! Come on over. We're among friends."

Piak rode over and dismounted. "It didn't take you long to get back here," Tiuri said.

"I wasn't that far away," replied Piak. "As if I'd ride off and leave you all alone! I was just over there, on the other side of that boulder. And I'd made a big pile of stones just in case... in case..."

Warmin laughed. "Well, well," he said. "It seems we've escaped a grave danger!"

"Warmin!" cried Piak.

"The very same, at your service," replied the guard.

"Phew!" sighed Piak. "What a night! I think I saw him again, Tiuri. Along the road. I think he was heading westwards."

"Who?" asked Warmin.

"The... the..." Piak paused.

"What on earth happened here?" Warmin asked again, looking at each of them in turn. "And there's a strange thing! He called you Tiuri. But I thought your name was Martin."

Piak slapped his hand over his mouth.

"And that's true," Tiuri replied calmly. "I mean, my name here is Martin, even though I'm also called Tiuri." He gave Piak a nod to let him know it was all right. It really didn't matter if people knew his real name now.

"Aha," said Warmin.

"We found someone nearby," Tiuri told him. "Dead. Killed by an arrow."

"Killed?" said Warmin. "Who?"

"The messenger who was sent to King Unauwen," said Tiuri. He walked over to the place where the body was lying. The others followed. Warmin looked down at the dead man. "The messenger from Dangria!" he exclaimed. "Why did this happen? And why here, of all places? Was it robbers?"

"I think that only the letter is missing," said Tiuri. He turned to Piak. "You saw him again," he said. "So perhaps we can still catch up with him!"

"The murderer?" asked Warmin.

"He can't have gone far," said Piak. "There was nothing we could do. He would have... He was going to..."

"I understand the situation better now," said Warmin. "But we shouldn't waste time talking." He ran to his horse. "Where did you see him?" he asked Piak.

Piak pointed at a hill to the southwest.

"Shall we go after him?" Warmin asked Tiuri.

"Yes," Tiuri replied, climbing onto his horse.

"But be careful, Ti... Martin," Piak said to his friend.

"Stay close together," Warmin ordered the men. "And keep the youngsters in the middle."

And they set off. But Tiuri was thinking: *If the murderer's really Slither, I'm afraid we're not going to find him.*

The hours that followed were not anxious ones now, but full of feverish excitement. They found a trail of flattened grass and followed it until it disappeared into a stream. Then they rode across the hills for some time. But they might as well have been chasing shadows, because they found no one. The night was well advanced by the time they returned to the road, not far from their starting point.

"Are you sure you didn't imagine it?" Warmin asked Tiuri and Piak.

"It's possible, of course," said Tiuri, "but I don't think so."

"I'm sure we didn't," said Piak firmly.

"If it's the man I fear it is, he won't be easy to find," said Tiuri.

"And who's that?" asked Warmin.

"I can't tell you," Tiuri replied. "I know hardly anything about him."

Warmin looked surprised. "Well, that's mysterious," he said. "Might he perhaps be dressed in brown, with thin, blond hair and a hat with a wide brim?"

Now it was Tiuri's turn to be surprised. "What makes you say that?" he asked. Then he remembered something. The man who had leant over the bridge and laughed...

"Yes, I still need to tell you about that," said Warmin. "But what are we going to do now? We can't just leave the dead man lying here. And the murderer must be caught, if not now, then tomorrow. We need to notify Dangria and the king – but firstly, Ingewel; that's the closest town and there's sure to be a messenger there. Sir Andomar's men can help to look for the murderer. He may have headed to Ingewel, don't you think?"

"You're right," said Tiuri. "But we can't wait. We have to travel on."

"I know," said Warmin. "We are to accompany you for as long as you wish. But shall I tell some of my men to go to Ingewel and make sure the dead man's taken care of?"

"Yes, that's a good idea," said Tiuri.

Warmin gave instructions to three of his men, who set off on the road to Ingewel. Then he turned to Tiuri and Piak. "Now I'll tell you why the toll master sent us," he said. "What shall we do? Ride on or rest a while?"

"A little rest would be welcome," said Piak, and Tiuri agreed.

They sat down by the roadside and Warmin said, "What I have to tell you will not take too long. The messenger from Dangria – God rest his soul – arrived at the toll bridge yesterday evening."

"Did you know he was a messenger?" asked Tiuri.

"He had no reason to keep it a secret," said Warmin. "He needed a fresh horse, and a messenger may ask for a fresh horse wherever he stops. So he swapped horses and went on his way immediately. He said he wanted to cover more distance before he rested. That's all I know about him. Imin had better tell you the rest. He had the morning watch."

One of the other men took over. "Yes, I had the watch this morning," he said. "Or yesterday morning, as it is now. The first person to reach the bridge was that foreigner – at least I think he was a foreigner, judging by his accent. He paid the toll, three gold pieces, as it was the first time he'd crossed the river. Then he struck up a conversation with me. We talked about all kinds of things, about the weather, about the crops, and then he asked me if a young man had crossed the bridge recently. He said it might have been two boys. One was about sixteen years old, with dark hair and light eyes. He didn't say anything about the other one. I told him there had been two young men – I meant the two of you, of course – who had been unable to pay the toll and who must still be on the eastern side of the river. The stranger seemed to find that amusing. Well, maybe that's a bit strong. He just said, 'Fancy that,' but I could swear he smiled. I couldn't see his face very well. He'd pulled his hat down low and it had a wide rim..."

"Did you get much of a look at him?" Tiuri asked.

"Not really. He had blond hair, which stuck out from under his hat, and just ordinary clothes, all brown... and he... but I'll come to that. Anyway, then we spotted you on the island. Warmin was ordered to go and fetch you. And I forgot all about that business with the foreigner. I thought he'd ridden on. But I was standing with another guard on the bridge, watching them fetch you from the island, and suddenly he appeared beside us. 'So those are the boys you were talking about, are they?' he said. 'Shame on them, trying to avoid paying the toll!' He asked us what the punishment was and he seemed to like the reply. He leant over the bridge to look and he laughed. The way he laughed made me shudder. I thought you deserved your punishment, but I didn't like that fellow at all. Then we went back to the barrier because people were waiting to cross the bridge. Later on, Warmin came over to us."

"Yes," said Warmin. "I told Imin you'd asked to speak to the toll master."

"And the foreigner was still hanging around," Imin continued. "He said the two of you belonged in jail. Then I said, 'You almost seem to be wishing it upon them! You know those boys, don't you?' But he said he didn't. 'Really?' I said. 'You were asking about a boy with dark hair and light eyes, weren't you?' 'There are plenty enough boys who match that description,' he said. 'I don't know that young man. The one I asked about is a friend of mine. He was supposed to be crossing the river with me, but he must have been held up. He's coming from the east, from Dangria.'"

"When he said that," Warmin chipped in, "I told him about the messenger who had passed through the previous evening. He too had dark hair and light eyes. Perhaps I shouldn't have done that, but I had no reason to suspect anything untoward. When the man heard that, he looked shocked..."

"Oh, yes. He was shocked all right," said Imin. "He lifted his head and he just stared at us. And that was when I had a proper shock – it was those eyes of his. It was like looking at a snake! And then, suddenly, he was in a hurry. He raced over the bridge as if the devil himself were chasing after him!"

So it's as I feared, thought Tiuri. The man must have been Slither; it was almost certain. At first, the spy had believed – correctly – that the boy he was looking for was safely locked up, but when he heard about another young man who had ridden westwards, a messenger for King Unauwen, he had started to doubt himself and had gone chasing after him. The poor scribe had been killed by an arrow that was meant for him, for Tiuri! But Slither must know by now that he had made a mistake and murdered the wrong man. He had stolen the letter and read it, so he must have realized it wasn't the letter he was looking for...

Warmin continued the story, "Later, after you'd gone, I spoke to the toll master. He seemed to be concerned about something that the second messenger from Dangria had told him. He asked me if you'd already left and then he said, half to himself, 'I wonder if it was wise to allow them to travel alone.' 'Why, my lord?' I asked. 'They might be in danger,' he said. Then I told him about the man on the bridge. It wasn't much, but it seemed to alarm him. 'Warmin,' he said, 'do you think you can still catch up with those young men? Then saddle your horse and take ten armed men with you. Find them, ride with them and guard them with your own life if necessary. Maybe you'll even be able to catch up with the messenger from Dangria. Perhaps I'm overly concerned, but I sense danger, particularly for the two boys.' That's what he said, and so here we are." Warmin looked at the two friends. "So," he said, "will you accept us as an escort? Or was the toll master unnecessarily concerned, and are you not in danger?"

"I'm afraid that he was right," said Tiuri.

"Does the murder of the messenger from Dangria have something to do with it?"

"Yes," said Tiuri. "I met him before. He helped me in Dangria. And now... now he's dead, and I'm still alive..."

Warmin looked at him with a question on his face. "Do you think he mistook...?"

Tiuri sighed and shook his head. "Talking about it won't help."

Warmin shrugged. "My master told me not to ask any questions," he said. "So I shall simply do as I was told and assist you with men and with weapons."

"My thanks," said Tiuri. "Shall we get going?" He stood up and realized that his legs were shaking with exhaustion. But, even so, he was soon back in the saddle.

And so Tiuri and Piak continued their journey, guarded by the toll master's men.

At daybreak, they encountered some shepherds who were grazing their sheep on the slopes. Warmin told them about the crime and gave them a description of the murderer, and asked them to keep an eye out for him.

The morning was almost over when they came to a small village and the inn where they intended to rest. Before long, they were sitting together at a table and the innkeeper was placing a meal in front of them. Warmin told him they had come from the toll master's castle and asked if he had any fresh horses.

"Not for your entire company," said the innkeeper. "I don't have that many horses."

Warmin looked at Tiuri. "What do you think?" he asked. "It seems that the best course of action would be for us all to stay here for a while, so that our horses can rest, and then travel on together. We could do with some rest ourselves."

Tiuri nodded. "Fine," he said. "But I don't want to stay here too long."

Warmin looked more closely at him. "You certainly look like you need some rest," he said. "And so does your friend. Look, he's already fallen asleep."

And indeed Piak had dozed off. His head lay on the table beside his half-eaten lunch. Tiuri could feel now how tired he was himself, so tired that he could hardly eat anything. His companions' conversations were muffled and distant, and not even the fear that Slither might be nearby could keep him awake.

Warmin laid his hand on Tiuri's shoulder. "Hey, how do you feel?" he asked. "How long is it since you last had a good sleep?"

How long had it been? Tiuri's memory of recent days was of almost constant travelling, of tiring days and sleepless nights. "I don't know..." he mumbled.

"The two of you are going to bed this instant!" cried Warmin. "Or would you rather fall asleep on your horse later and roll out of the saddle?"

His loud voice woke Piak, who sat up, blinking.

Tiuri rose to his feet. Warmin was right. He needed to rest for a while and gather his strength for the final part of his journey.

"How far is it to the City of Unauwen?" he asked.

"Two and a half days' ride," replied Warmin.

"And what time is it now?"

"Past midday," replied the innkeeper.

"Do you have a bed for these two young men?" Warmin asked him.

"Of course," said the innkeeper. "Come with me."

"Fine," said Tiuri. "But I want someone to wake me at four."

He wouldn't go with the innkeeper until Warmin had promised to wake him. Before long, he and Piak were in bed and fast asleep.

*

Warmin kept his promise and came to wake them at four. "We can stay longer if you like," he said. "Why not spend the night here and travel on tomorrow?"

"No," said Tiuri, stifling a yawn. "It's another two and a half days and I want to get there sooner if possible."

"I have news of the murderer," said Warmin.

"Slither?" cried Piak.

Warmin smiled. "Ah, so he's called Slither, is he?" he said.

"What news?" asked Tiuri.

"Oh, there's no need to be afraid of him anymore," said Warmin. "He'll be caught soon enough. Come downstairs when you're ready. I've asked the innkeeper to serve up a decent meal." And with those words, he left the room.

"Oh, I'm such a fool!" said Piak, when Warmin was gone. "I keep opening my big mouth."

"Don't worry," said Tiuri. "Why shouldn't Warmin know that our enemy's name is Slither?"

"But I'm still a fool," said Piak with a sigh. "I wasn't quite awake, that's why. You're right, though. It doesn't matter if Warmin knows. It's no real help to us either. We know so little about the man."

Warmin's news had removed any lingering drowsiness, and the two friends couldn't get downstairs quickly enough. They found Warmin and three of his men waiting for them. While they were eating, Warmin told them that a frightened horseman had arrived at the inn an hour before. It was one of the shepherds from the hills to the east.

"The shepherd told us he'd been alone with his flock," said Warmin, "when a man came riding up. He got off his horse and asked the shepherd if he had any food to spare. The shepherd saw that he matched the description of the murderer that we'd given him... dressed in brown, with long, thin, blond hair and a wide-brimmed hat. He was scared and the murderer realized that he'd recognized him. The man threatened to kill him if he called for help. So the shepherd did the best thing he could have done: he jumped on the man's horse and rode off! The murderer shot an arrow after him but luckily he missed."

"The arrow's still in his hat," added one of the other men.

"So where's this shepherd now?" asked Tiuri. "Why didn't you wake me?"

"There was no need," said Warmin. "You were sleeping so soundly. But we've sent out a group of armed men to the spot where the shepherd met the murderer. Four of my men went with them and the shepherd's gone to show them the way. He acted quickly and cleverly by taking the horse. The murderer's not going to be able to go anywhere far or fast now."

"That's true," said Tiuri. And yet he would have liked to have spoken to the shepherd himself. He wanted to know more about the man whose evil presence he had felt time and again since they had left Dangria. There was no doubt that it was Slither. But so many people were looking for Slither now, he had lost his horse, and they were some way ahead of him. He and Piak just had to make sure they didn't lose their advantage.

He looked at Warmin. "Perhaps, Warmin," he said, "we no longer require your escort. I don't think he's such a threat to us now."

"As you wish," Warmin replied. "But it would be little effort to ride some of the way with you. The road through the Hills of the Moon is a lonely one. And the toll master has ordered me to protect you. I should be most upset if anything were to happen to you after we had parted."

Tiuri smiled. "I am very grateful to you and to the toll master for your help," he said. "Without you, this might have ended badly."

Finally they agreed that Warmin and his three remaining men should accompany the two friends at least as far as the end of the Hills of the Moon. And then they could decide what to do next.

By half past four, they were on the road again, and they made quick progress. The moon was already high in the sky when they spotted a castle on a hill in the distance.

"That is the Castle of the White Moon," said Warmin. "The home of Sir Ivan. The innkeeper said we'll be able to spend the night there."

"So I'm going to get to sleep in a castle," said Piak, "and not in a dark dungeon this time! It looks beautiful from here."

"It's very old," said Warmin. "But the toll master's castle is even older. Sir Ardian was once a knight-errant without a home, but now he bears the ancient title of toll master and resides in the fortress beside the Rainbow River."

"Isn't the castle at the toll his ancestral home?" asked Tiuri.

"No. The title of toll master is not passed on from father to son. The king himself appoints the toll masters and he selects the best of his knights to do the job."

"The knights with the white shields," said Piak.

"Yes. But the lords of the toll may also bear the seven colours of the rainbow."

"How many knights does your king have?" asked Tiuri. "And what are their names?"

"Oh, there's no quick answer to that question! You know

some of the names already, don't you? There's Ardian, my master, and Wardian, his brother, and Sir Ivan, whose castle you can see there, and Sir Ivan's sons, who are still young. And then there's Andomar of Ingewel, and Edwinem of Forèstèrra, also known as the Invincible, and Marwen of Iduna... Oh, I could list many more names and tell tales of their deeds. My master could do it better than I, though; he has big books that are filled with the history of our land."

Tiuri remembered the book he'd seen when he was waiting for the toll master.

"Hey, Warmin," he said, "your language is almost exactly the same as ours. Don't you think that's strange?"

"What's so strange about it?" said Warmin. "I think it's stranger when someone who looks just the same as me speaks a language I don't understand, just because he comes from a different country. But the language we speak here is not our only language. There is another language, which is very old... so old that most people don't know it these days. It's just the king and the princes, the scholars and some knights who can still speak and understand that language."

"Does the toll master know it?" asked Tiuri.

"I believe so," replied Warmin. "He's very learned, and he can read books. I used to have to draw a cross whenever anyone asked me to write my name, but he taught me my letters."

As they carried on talking, they drew nearer to the castle. A narrow road, flanked by stone walls, wound its way up the hillside to the gate.

Although it was late, the guards let them in straight away. Both the riders and the horses received a warm welcome, with food and a place to sleep for the night.

*

Very early the next morning, Tiuri stood in the courtyard with Warmin and Piak, ready to set off. One of the castle servants came over and said to Warmin, "You're the leader of Sir Ardian's knights, aren't you? Sir Ivan would like to speak to you. Would you come with me?"

Warmin pointed at Tiuri and said, "This young man should come too."

"Is that necessary?" asked the servant. "My master wanted to speak to the leader."

"In that case, he definitely has to come," said Warmin.

The servant looked puzzled and stared at Tiuri. He clearly thought he looked too young and shabby to be of any importance. But then he nodded and led them inside. Tiuri frowned. He wished Warmin had not drawn attention to him. *If only we had got up earlier*, he thought, *and then we would already be on our way*. He glanced at Piak, who gave him an encouraging wink, and then followed Warmin.

They were taken to a large hall, which was still in semi-darkness. The lord of the castle stood waiting for them beside a table with two candles on it. Sir Ivan was no longer a young man. His hair was white, but his back was as straight as a lance. He looked from one to the other and then asked Warmin, "Are you Warmin, the leader of Sir Ardian's men?"

"Yes, sir knight," said Warmin with a bow.

"I heard a man was killed last night in the Hills of the Moon," Sir Ivan continued. "A messenger, on his way to King Unauwen. Is that true?"

"Yes, sir knight," replied Warmin.

"Why was I not immediately informed?" asked the knight. "The western Hills of the Moon are within my territory – and the eastern part is also under my protection, until Sir Andomar returns."

"We sent word to Ingewel, sir knight," said Warmin. "And everyone in the area was warned to look out for the murderer."

"Why have you not gone in search of him yourself?"

"The toll master has sent us on a mission to the west, sir knight, so we had to continue. But I have sent back some of my men. More than half of them, in fact."

"Good," said Sir Ivan. He looked at Tiuri. "Might you," he asked, "be one of the young men who discovered the body?"

"Yes, my lord," Tiuri replied. And he thought to himself, *I hope he doesn't start asking all kinds of questions. It seems like everyone I meet is trying to hold us up.*

Tiuri's fears were unfounded. Sir Ivan asked no more questions but said, "Well, I can tell you that the murderer has been caught."

"What? Really?" said Tiuri and Warmin.

"Yes," said Sir Ivan. "He is at this moment being held at the Inn of the Hills of the Moon, until I decide what is to happen to him. He was captured in my lands, so I am the one who shall pass judgement on him."

"When did this happen?" asked Warmin.

"Yesterday evening, shortly after you left the inn. A messenger brought me the news early this morning. He'll be able to tell you more. He's still here."

Only then did Tiuri realize that there was someone else in the dimly lit hall. Sir Ivan beckoned the man and he came over and bowed. He looked like a farmer, but he was wearing chainmail over his clothes and a helmet on his brown hair.

"This messenger came with a letter written by the landlord at the inn," said Sir Ivan, "and he also has his own tale to tell."

The messenger bowed. "The innkeeper paid my fee," he said, "but the message I have brought is also from the toll master's men. It is sent for Sir Ivan, lord of the White Moon, for Warmin, leader of the guards, and for the two young men who are travelling with him."

"Please continue," said Sir Ivan.

The messenger bowed again and told his story. "Yesterday evening, some men from my village, assisted by the toll master's men-at-arms, captured the man who matched the murderer's description. He called himself by a strange name... what was it again? It's in that letter I gave you, sir knight."

"Slither," said Sir Ivan.

"Slither..." Tiuri repeated quietly.

"At first he denied that he was the murderer," said the messenger, "but after we had caught him, tied him up and locked him in a room at the inn, he started ranting and raving. He cursed us and he cursed this land and then he cursed those two young men. He cursed them with all of the wicked names under the sun."

"And why was that?" asked the knight.

"That's the strange thing about it," said the messenger in a hushed tone. "He didn't say why. He just cursed them... in a way that was enough to send shivers down your spine! I was there myself and I heard everything. He called one of them by his name. 'Curses on you, Tiuri,' he said. 'May the devil and all his black powers break your neck!'"

Then the messenger fell silent and Tiuri felt his blood run cold, as if he himself had been there and heard Slither cursing him. But that feeling didn't last for long. Slither had been captured, after all!

"And who is this Tiuri?" asked Sir Ivan.

Warmin glanced at Tiuri, but said nothing.

"Are you Tiuri?" the knight asked him.

"Yes, my lord," Tiuri admitted.

"And why exactly does this Slither wish you harm?"

Tiuri thought for a moment before answering, "I think it's because I'm one of those who are to blame for him being captured."

Sir Ivan looked at him thoughtfully. Tiuri realized that he reminded him of someone he knew, but he couldn't think who it was. Then the knight turned back to the messenger and asked, "Do you have anything else to report?"

"No, my lord," said the messenger. "Just what's in the letter. That the toll master's men have asked their leader to return to the east as soon as possible, together with the men who are still with him. But only if the two young men can spare him, of course."

"Why must I return?" asked Warmin.

"They didn't tell me that," said the messenger.

"Do you have anything to add?" asked Sir Ivan. And when the messenger shook his head, he said, "Then you may go. My servants will make sure you're fed. I'll give you a message to take on your return."

The messenger bowed deeply and left the room.

"Who are you?" the knight asked Tiuri.

"You already know that, my lord," he said. "My name is Tiuri."

"Where are you from?"

"From the east, my lord."

"So you're not one of the toll master's men?"

"No, sir knight, he's not," said Warmin. "But the toll master ordered me and my men to accompany him and his friend. They need to go to the west and they are in a hurry."

"That's right, my lord," said Tiuri.

Warmin took something from under his chainmail and handed it to the knight. "Here is the proof that I am acting on the toll master's orders," he said. "His glove."

"Yes, I recognize it," said the knight. He returned the glove to Warmin and continued, "Although order and peace appear still to prevail, events are occurring that make me uneasy. Sir Ardian will not have sent out his men for no reason! I shall not hold you up, now that I have told you what you needed to know. As for Slither, he will remain my prisoner, and I expect you to return and testify in the case against him. That applies to you, too, Tiuri."

"Yes, my lord," he replied. Suddenly, Tiuri felt happy and relieved. Slither had been captured! Now he had nothing left to fear. They would reach the City of Unauwen by the evening of the following day. His journey was almost over. He turned to Warmin. "There is no need for you to travel on with us," he said. "Slither can no longer harm us."

"Who exactly is this Slither?" asked Sir Ivan.

"I don't know him," replied Tiuri. "All I know is that he is dangerous, and wicked."

"That much is clear," the knight said wryly. "But surely you must know more about him than that!"

"He is from Eviellan," said Tiuri.

This answer seemed to shock the knight. "From Eviellan!" he repeated.

Warmin was also clearly surprised by this news.

"My lord," said Tiuri. "By your leave, I wish to depart immediately. Perhaps you will soon hear more about this business than I can tell you now."

"You are a most puzzling young man," said the knight. "If my ears do not deceive me, you come from the other side of the Great Mountains. Is that correct?"

"Yes, my lord," said Tiuri.

"Have you then by any chance..." the knight began, but he didn't finish his question. He shook his head and then said, "I trust the toll master implicitly and shall abide by his decision. Go in peace! You, Warmin, must decide for yourself if you wish to travel on or to return to your men in the east. Farewell."

Tiuri and Warmin bowed and returned to the courtyard, where the others were waiting impatiently.

"What did the knight have to say?" Piak asked his friend.

"Good news!" said Tiuri. "Slither's been captured. A messenger brought the news."

"Captured? Really?" whispered Piak.

"Yes," said Tiuri. "Apparently so."

Piak looked at him with gleaming eyes. "That's excellent news," he said. "Now I won't have to keep jumping at every shadow and looking behind every bush."

Warmin came and stood beside them and cleared his throat.

"What is it?" asked Tiuri.

"So, then. What should we do?" he said. "Shall I come with you or not?"

"You may leave us with a clear conscience," said Tiuri.

"Well, if you say so..." said Warmin. "You see, I've been wondering why my men asked me to return so quickly. And if you no longer need our help, I'd like to go and see where it's needed. Something is amiss in this country. Trouble seems to be brewing... But," he continued, "if you want me to, I'll gladly come with you. I now see you as my commanding officer, no matter if that sounds foolish, as you are so much younger than I."

Tiuri held out his hand and said, "I thank you for your help, Warmin. And please thank the toll master for us. We shall do so ourselves when we return to the Rainbow River."

"Fine," said Warmin. "But I won't let you go until I'm certain you're properly armed. It might not be needed, but it can't hurt. An imaginary bow and arrows won't do you much good! I'll find you some real ones, and I'm sure they can spare some chainmail from the armoury here."

It took some time for the equipment to be gathered together and handed over to the two friends. "Phew! Do I really have to wear this thing?" asked Piak, after he'd put on chainmail for the first time in his life. "I'd prefer an ordinary shirt."

Warmin smiled. "You'll get used to it," he said. "It's good protection, so it's worth wearing."

"Then I'll keep it on," said Piak with a sigh. "But I really have no need for that bow. I couldn't hit a mountain, even if it was three feet away." Then he changed his mind. "No, give it here," he said with a grin. "It might look good with the chainmail."

The two friends said goodbye to Warmin and his men and headed along the road to the west.

"So now it's just the two of us again," said Piak. "So, what do you think? Do I look a bit more like a squire now?"

4 THE BEGGAR AT THE GATE

And, of course, Tiuri had to tell Piak exactly what Sir Ivan had said to him.

"Well, I'm glad he let us leave so soon," said Piak. "I was a bit worried that we'd be held up again. Perhaps we should have disguised ourselves. A couple of old men with beards maybe?"

Tiuri laughed. "And where were you hoping to find these beards?" he asked.

"I don't have to think about that now," replied Piak, "since it's no longer needed." Then he looked around at the landscape and said, "You know, these hills are a bit like the mountains, and it's true enough that they're beautiful, but I'll be glad when we're away from here. How about you?"

"Me too," said Tiuri.

Tiuri and Piak would always associate the Hills of the Moon with those hours of anxiety, the threat of the wicked Slither and, above all, the young scribe who had died there.

To their relief, they had soon left the hills behind and entered a region that looked completely different, with rolling fields of golden corn and green meadows and horse paddocks, interspersed with dark patches of woodland. They saw lots of people, and villages and farms and, now and then, the distant towers of a castle.

In the afternoon, it started to rain, but that didn't spoil their mood or slow them down. They even rode on for some time after the sun had gone down. The weather was dry by then and the pale light of the moon lit up their path and gleamed in the puddles on the road. Frogs croaked in the ditch by the side of the road and crickets chirped in the long grass.

"We could just keep going all night," Piak whispered.

But Tiuri shook his head. He looked over his shoulder at the Hills of the Moon, where they had left the danger behind. And yet he was still on his guard, as if he were travelling through a hostile land. Why was that? He hadn't felt that way during the daytime. So why did he now feel as if they were being followed and spied on again? It was foolish! He decided not to mention his feelings to Piak, but to find a safe place to sleep as soon as possible.

When they came to a barn, they decided to spend the night there. But no sooner had they led their horses inside than a dog started barking. Then they heard footsteps, and a deep voice called out, "Who's there?"

Tiuri peered around the door to see a man with a lantern in his hand. A large dog was jumping around his legs. Tiuri hesitated as he considered how to respond and Piak didn't reply either. The dog left its owner and ran towards the barn, wagging its tail.

"Look, Parwen," the man called to his dog. "It seems I have guests in my barn! Well, that's fine, just as long as I know who they are."

Having heard that, Tiuri dared to venture outside. Piak followed him. "Good evening," Tiuri said to the farmer. "May we stay the night here?"

"Certainly," said the man. "But you're welcome to come to the house with me if you prefer. There's an empty bed and you're sure to get a better night's sleep there. And maybe the wife can rustle up some food for you."

The friendly farmer was so insistent that he persuaded Tiuri and Piak to accept his invitation. Soon they were sitting with the farmer and his wife in the kitchen, eating bacon pancakes.

"Our thanks for your kind hospitality," said Tiuri.

The farmer smiled. "You're welcome," he said. "It's late to be out and about. Are you on your way to the city?"

"You mean the City of Unauwen?" said Piak.

"Yes, which other city would I mean? Although there are, of course, other cities and..." Then the farmer paused and said, "Listen. Parwen's barking again. I'll just go and see who's there." He picked up his lantern and headed outside.

"Where are you two boys from?" asked the farmer's wife.

"Oh, from far away," replied Tiuri.

"From the Great Mountains to the east," Piak said.

"Really?" she exclaimed. "Then you have travelled a long way! Have you been to Dangria? And did you cross the

Rainbow River? Did you pick flowers in Ingewel and see the moon shining on the hills? Such beautiful sights... I'll tell you something, though. The king's city is the most wonderful sight of all."

"Do we still have far to go?" asked Piak.

"Oh, no. Not far. You could be there by tomorrow afternoon if you wake up with the chickens."

Then the farmer returned and said, "I couldn't see anyone out there. It's strange, though. The dog doesn't normally bark for no reason." He turned to the two friends. "I don't know what time you boys want to get up tomorrow," he said, "but I think it's about bedtime."

"Yes, you look tired," his wife agreed. "Come with me. I'll show you to your bed."

"These people are so kind," whispered Piak, when they were in bed.

"You're right," agreed Tiuri.

Outside, the dog started barking again and Tiuri wondered what it was barking at, but then he smiled and thought, *Let the dog bark! We're lying safe inside, behind closed doors.*

Piak soon dozed off and the dog settled down, but Tiuri lay awake for a long time, staring into the darkness, before finally falling asleep.

At the first cockcrow, the two friends got up, thanked the farmer and his wife again and set off on their way. The weather was good; there was a strong westerly wind, but the sun was shining. At first, they rode through a landscape that was similar to the countryside they'd seen the day before. Later, the road led through a forest and up a hill and when they reached the top... they saw the City of Unauwen lying there in front of them.

It was a large city; there were so many towers, nothing but towers in fact, white and silver, glinting in the sun. They reined in their horses and stood there for a moment, just gazing at the city. The end of their journey was in sight!

Then they urged on their horses and galloped swiftly onwards. The road became much busier at that point, with other byways joining it, and they soon realized that they were not the only travellers heading to the capital. They still had quite some way to go, and they did not spare their horses. The closer they came to the city, the more they longed to be there.

The City of Unauwen was built on gentle hills, and it was not grey and enclosed by a high wall, but light and open. It spread out over a wide area, and had low walls and lots of gates and steps, and towers with gold weathervanes glinting on top. A gleaming river flowed into the city from the south; Tiuri knew it must be the White River. In the distance, to the north, there were higher hills, which glowed red in the sun, and more hills rising up behind them like a rainbow and vanishing into the mists. Many roads led to the city, all good, wide roads like the one the two friends were riding along.

"That," said Piak, "is the most beautiful thing I've seen on this journey."

"I agree," said Tiuri.

"Does the City of Dagonaut look like that?"

Tiuri shook his head. "No," he said. "This is more beautiful."

"It must be the most beautiful city in the world," said Piak.

Tiuri repeated the words of his message to himself and sang them quietly to Piak's tune. Piak hummed along with him as they continued towards the city. But as they came closer and the sun hung in the west above the city, they both fell silent.

Grassy bridleways and paved paths and stone steps split off from the main road and headed to different gates on the eastern side of the city. The gates were open, but intimidating guards stood at each one, with colourful shields and feathered helmets. Guards were posted along the low white walls as well.

The two friends looked at each other and grinned from ear to ear.

"We're here! We've done it!" whispered Piak.

"Almost," Tiuri added.

Tiuri and Piak kept to the main thoroughfare and, without thinking about it, they slowed their horses to a walking pace. There was so much to look at. Along the roads and paths were stone columns, decorated with carvings and strange symbols.

Then they spotted a person who looked somewhat out of place in those beautiful surroundings. An old beggar sat on the ground near the city gate, leaning back against a column. He was wrapped in a torn and tattered cloak with a hood, and all they could see of him was his nose and his long grey tangled hair and beard. A walking stick lay beside him, and he held out a begging bowl. He called out to the friends and asked for alms.

Tiuri took out the pouch of coins that the toll master had given him. He had little money left, but he threw all of it into the beggar's bowl. Piak also gave everything he had: his brass farthing.

The beggar mumbled his thanks and Tiuri and Piak were about to ride on. But the beggar's voice stopped them. "You know, I would rather not thank you!" he shouted.

"And why is that?" exclaimed Tiuri, who was closer to him.

"You sit so high up there on your horse, traveller," said the beggar. "From that height, it's easy to toss me a coin, without even looking at my face! And now you will ride on and forget about me. I see you're impatient and that you find me a nuisance. And you are right. I am only a beggar, who has caused you delay, but who fortunately is soon passed by."

Tiuri looked down at the beggar, not knowing quite what to say. And yet he couldn't find it in his heart to ride on, no matter how much he longed to do so. The old man's voice had sounded so sad, so bitter and without hope.

"What are you waiting for?" said the beggar. "Ride on, stranger. This is the City of King Unauwen, the city where poverty does not exist. Enter the city and forget me, just as everyone forgets me. Why should you dismount and stoop to talk to a wretch like me?"

"Do not be angry with me!" said Tiuri. "I did not intend to insult you. I am sorry that I forgot in my haste to pause with you for a while. I have given you all the coins I had, and I would like to help you if I could."

"Ah!" said the beggar. "I thank you! You would like to help me... if you could. I am happy enough with that. I need no more. Farewell. May you achieve all you deserve and receive all that I would wish for you. Yes, farewell!" He turned away, picked up his stick and started struggling to his feet.

Piak put his hand on Tiuri's arm and whispered, "Come on!"

But Tiuri couldn't take his eyes off the beggar. He felt very sorry for him and he was suddenly certain that he didn't want to enter the city until he'd looked this man in the face. Ignoring Piak's whispers, he jumped down from his horse. He held out his hand to help the beggar and said, "I am in a hurry, but not so much that I can't stop to prove to you that I do want to help you and to know you better."

The beggar allowed Tiuri to assist him to his feet. He stood before Tiuri, huddled over his stick, his face almost entirely hidden by his hood and his hair. "Thank you," he said quietly. "You are just as I hoped you would be. I thank you – not for your coins, but for standing before me now."

"Would you look at me?" asked Tiuri.

The beggar bowed more deeply and did not reply.

"Would you look at me?" asked Tiuri again. His heart had started to pound. He didn't know why, but he knew he couldn't take another step until he had looked the beggar in the eye. Only later would he come to understand exactly what he had felt at that moment. His compassion had given way to curiosity. And added to that was a strange sense of tension, as if it was vitally important that the beggar looked at him, as if a lot depended on this moment.

Then the beggar responded, "Very well. I shall do so... Fool!"

And Tiuri suddenly knew he was in danger. He wasn't shocked when the beggar lifted his face; he knew whose eyes would be looking at him... those cold, mean eyes, like a snake. Slither! Finally, he was facing the enemy he had feared for so long!

The man pulled something from his stick and thrust it at Tiuri. A dagger! But Tiuri was ready. He parried the jab and received only a small scratch. Then he forced him to drop the dagger. But the man immediately closed his hands around Tiuri's throat. Behind him, Piak gasped, "Slither!"

Tiuri struggled with Slither. The man was stronger than him, but Tiuri was not afraid. He freed himself from the clutches of those clawing hands and fought to overpower his enemy. Then help arrived: first Piak, and then some guards and passers-by. Slither let go of Tiuri and made a run for it.

"He's getting away!" yelled Piak. "Get him! Catch the murderer!"

The guards drew their swords and ran after Slither. Piak turned to take care of his friend. "Are you all right, Tiuri?" he asked. "You're bleeding!"

Tiuri wiped his forehead. "It's nothing," he said, still panting from the exertion.

"You gave me such a fright," said Piak. "I saw that dagger and I thought, I thought..."

"I could feel it coming," said Tiuri. "When he looked at me, I knew who he was... no... even before that, I think..."

He watched the guards chasing after the fleeing Slither. Yes, they had him! Only then did he notice all the people standing around him, asking what was going on, with expressions of surprise and fear on their faces.

The guards returned, bringing the beggar with them. "And now," their leader said, "we'd like to know what is the meaning of this behaviour!"

"As would I!" shrieked the beggar. "What have I done to be treated in such a way?"

"You tried to murder him!" cried Piak.

"That is not true!" shouted the beggar. "He attacked me!"

"Liar!" Piak yelled furiously. "Look, your dagger's still there on the ground. And you murdered the messenger too, the messenger from Dangria."

The beggar tried to move, but the guards had a firm hold on him. "I don't know what you're talking about!" he said.

"You know very well!" Tiuri said, calmly. "You've been following us for a long time, Slither!"

The beggar threw him a look of hatred. He started struggling again and, for a moment, it seemed as if he might pull away, but he did not succeed. Then he said, "Curses on you, Tiuri! Go into the city and take your important message to the king. Be proud that you have carried out your task so well!

But know that you cannot change the fate of this country. May strife and discord come upon this land, and fire and blood rain down upon this city!"

Tiuri shivered, not so much because of the words themselves, but because of the tone they were spoken in.

"Silence!" called one of the guards, sounding both angry and shocked. Then he turned to the two friends, "Who are you? And who is he? How do you know him?"

"He is a spy," replied Tiuri, "a spy from Eviellan."

"Well, now you are our prisoner," the guard said to Slither, "the prisoner of King Unauwen. And you will accompany us into the city."

"Then I refuse to speak another word," said Slither.

The guard looked back at Tiuri and Piak. "I shall ask again," he said. "Who are you?"

"We have come from the Kingdom of Dagonaut," Tiuri replied quietly, "with a message for King Unauwen."

The guard seemed surprised and concerned. "Then follow me," he said. "Some of my men will escort you to the palace."

5 KING UNAUWEN

Finally, the two friends passed through the gate and entered the City of Unauwen. Slither was led away and was soon out of their sight. Then, escorted by two guards, Tiuri and Piak were on their way to the palace.

Tiuri noticed hardly anything about the houses, the streets and the people around him. He sat up straight on his horse, his eyes fixed on the guard who was riding ahead of them, and he could think only about the message. Soon he would have completed his task and kept his word. When he glanced over at Piak, he saw that the expression on his friend's face was a serious one, too.

Tiuri started to pay more attention to his surroundings as they reached the White River, which flowed through the middle of the city; it was beautiful, with clear, silvery water, but it was not as wide as the Rainbow River. King Unauwen's palace stood on a hill on the opposite bank. It was built of grey and white stone with low walls around it, and terraced gardens running down to the water's edge.

They rode over a wooden bridge, went through one gate and stopped at a second, where some soldiers stood guard. The men accompanying Tiuri and Piak asked to be let through.

"Who goes there?" asked the leader of the guards.

"Two messengers for King Unauwen."

"You may pass," came the reply.

At the next gate, they had to dismount. There were guards there too, who opened the gate for them after a brief exchange with their escorts, who then took their leave of the boys and rode back to their post.

"We'll look after your horses," said one of the palace guards. "Go inside and report to the captain of the guard."

Tiuri and Piak entered a large, bustling courtyard. A wide staircase led up into the palace. A young knight with a white shield approached them and introduced himself as the captain of the guard. "What is your request?" he asked.

"We would like an audience with King Unauwen," said Tiuri.

The knight studied them with a somewhat puzzled expression. "Why?" he asked. "Who are you?"

"Our names are Piak and Tiuri. We have brought a message for King Unauwen. A message of great importance."

"Who sent you?"

"Sir Edwinem of Forèstèrra."

The young knight seemed surprised, but all he said was, "Follow me." He led them up the stairs and into a large hall. "Wait here," he said, "and I shall announce your arrival to the king. What is the message?"

"I can tell that only to the king himself," replied Tiuri. "And I need to do so as soon as possible. Right away!"

"I see," said the knight. "I shall inform the king. But first you must tell me..."

Tiuri pulled out the cord from around his neck and showed him the ring. "Here is the proof that I was sent by Sir Edwinem," he said, interrupting the knight. "Now please let us see the king immediately!"

For a moment, the knight stared at him wide-eyed. "Fine," he said. "Come with me."

They walked through a series of rooms and finally the knight stopped at a door. He knocked and went in. He soon reappeared and said, "King Unauwen bids you enter."

Tiuri was about to enter, but saw that Piak wasn't following him. He stopped in the doorway and whispered, "Come on, Piak!"

Piak shook his head.

"Now!" said Tiuri.

"No," said Piak.

"You have to be there!" said Tiuri impatiently.

"No," repeated Piak. "You should go alone. Really, it's better that way."

"King Unauwen bids you enter," the knight repeated.

"Go on!" whispered Piak. "You can't keep the king waiting!"

Tiuri had no choice but to go in alone, but he was disappointed that Piak didn't want to come with him. As he stepped through the doorway, he realized his legs were shaking. The door quietly closed behind him.

The room was not a large one. Tiuri had enough time to notice that it was white and blue with a row of columns on either side – and then he was standing before King Unauwen.

The king rose from his seat and looked at Tiuri. He was an old man with a silvery-white beard and hair. His long robe was also white and he wore no adornments except a slim band of gold on his head. But no one could have doubted that he was a king: his posture was regal and his face was noble and wise. He reminded Tiuri very much of Menaures; his eyes in particular were like those of the hermit.

"Step closer, messenger," said the king. His voice, too, was the voice of a king. Tiuri walked over to the king and knelt, as he had often done before King Dagonaut. For a moment, his voice failed him. Then he said, "Your Majesty, I bring you a message from Sir Edwinem with the White Shield. But first I must tell you that Sir Edwinem is dead. Before he died, he gave me a letter to deliver to you, and his ring... Here it is."

King Unauwen took the ring. "Rise," he said.

Tiuri obeyed.

The king stared silently at the ring. Then, slowly, he said, "You bring sad tidings, messenger. How did my knight die?"

"He was murdered, sire," replied Tiuri. "By Red Riders from Eviellan."

"Sir Edwinem... murdered... by riders from Eviellan!" repeated the king. "And I fear there is more bad news to come. Give me the letter, messenger."

"Sire, I no longer have it," said Tiuri. "Sir Edwinem ordered me to destroy it if I feared it might be taken from me. And I had to do just that. But I have learnt the message by heart."

The king looked at him intently and then he asked an unexpected question. "Who exactly are you, messenger?"

"My name is Tiuri, sire."

"Well then, Tiuri, tell me your message. I am listening."

Tiuri opened his mouth but then, to his horror, he realized that he did not know what to say. He couldn't remember a word! Not one single word of the message he had repeated to himself so often... But that was impossible. If he kept calm and thought about it, it would surely come back to him. Tiuri closed his eyes and thought frantically. But his mind seemed to be empty. A shiver ran through his whole body. Tiuri had forgotten the message!

He opened his eyes again and looked at the king. Did the king seem impatient? Tiuri hung his head and felt his face flush with shame. He had to remember... He had to!

Then he thought of something. Piak knew the message too! He had even written a tune for it. The tune... Tiuri began to hum it, and the words immediately came back to him. He raised his head and saw King Unauwen looking at him with a puzzled expression.

He wanted to explain that his friend Piak had written a tune to go with the words. But first the message! He took a deep breath and then spoke the mysterious words, slowly, but clearly and without any hesitation.

Tiuri could see the impact of what he said on the king. He thought he saw shock in his eyes, and horror, then grief, finally followed by fury. When Tiuri stopped speaking, the king turned away. He suddenly looked much older. For a brief moment, the room was very silent.

"Repeat what you just said," the king ordered. Tiuri did so. King Unauwen listened to his words, still with his face turned away. Then he stood motionlessly for a while, with his head bowed, as though lost in thought.

Tiuri didn't dare to say anything. He didn't even dare to look at the king. The silence seemed to go on forever. He started to wonder if the king had forgotten about him. Should he leave? But at that moment, the king raised his head, as if he had come to a decision. He looked at Tiuri and said, "Forgive me, Tiuri. I had to allow this news to sink in. The message you have brought me is a grave one, and of great importance for this land and its people. Are you able to write down the words, too, as they were in the letter?"

"Yes, sire," said Tiuri. "I... I don't know what they mean, but I learnt them by heart, including the spelling."

"Good," said the king. "Now tell me how Sir Edwinem came to charge you with the task of delivering this message. Come." He laid his hand on Tiuri's shoulder and led him to a corner of the room, where there were some chairs and a table. He sat down and asked Tiuri to join him. "Now tell me," he repeated.

So Tiuri told him. He told him about the old man who had knocked on the door of the chapel at night, and how his request for help had led to the dying Sir Edwinem giving him the mission.

"And so then you set off," said King Unauwen, "across the Kingdom of Dagonaut, and over the mountains, through this land, all the way to my city. That was a long journey, and a dangerous one too, I should warrant. The enemies that killed Sir Edwinem must have pursued you as well."

Tiuri nodded.

The king smiled at him, a kind, heart-warming smile. He shook Tiuri's hand and said, "Thank you, Tiuri."

Tiuri felt a wave of happiness and gratitude wash over him. He had completed his mission! Then he remembered Piak.

"Sire," he said. "Would you perhaps thank my friend Piak too? He has done just as much as I. Without him, you would never have heard the message. He is, he has..."

He fell silent as the king banged a gong that was beside the table. At this signal, the young knight entered the room. He bowed and said, "What does my king wish?"

"The other boy," said the king. "Send him in."

A moment later, Piak appeared, looking very timid. The young knight left the room. King Unauwen stood up, walked over to Piak and held out his hand. But the boy knelt and said, "Greetings, Your Majesty."

The king smiled again. "Stand up, Piak," he said, "so that I may thank you for what you have done."

Piak did as he was told; the king's words seemed to have touched him. Tiuri also felt quite emotional and could hardly believe his task was now completed.

The king invited Piak to sit with them, and asked the two boys some questions. He wanted to know how long it had been since Tiuri had started out on his journey and asked him to tell him everything he knew about what had happened to Sir Edwinem. He also wanted to hear why the letter had to be destroyed. The two friends answered his questions as well as they could and then Tiuri wrote down the contents of the letter.

When Tiuri had finished writing, the king said, "Later I will want to hear more about your adventures, Tiuri and Piak. But now there are matters that must take priority. I have a great deal to do."

He banged the gong again and said to the young knight, "Sir Ivan, soon all those who carry the White Shield, the councillors and the lords and dignitaries will come together in the great hall to hear the news that has been brought from the east. Have the senior councillor and my friend Tirillo sent to me immediately. As for these two young men, they are my honoured guests. Will you take them to Lady Mirian and tell her to look after them? And then return to me."

The knight bowed and Tiuri and Piak did the same. King Unauwen stood upright; he seemed great and stately now, strong and invincible.

"Until we meet again," he said.

The two friends followed the young knight.

Piak whispered to Tiuri. "Don't you think King Unauwen looks like Menaures?"

"Yes," said Tiuri. "I thought the same."

"Finally our job is done," said Piak with a sigh.

But Tiuri realized that he still didn't know what was in the message he'd delivered.

6 Sir Ivan and Tirillo

The young knight took them to a small cloistered court-yard, and into a room where an old woman was sitting at a spinning wheel.

"Lady Mirian," he said. "I bring you guests, honoured guests of the king."

The woman stood up and walked over to them. She was dressed simply in grey, with a large bunch of keys on her belt that jingled with every move she made. An intricately folded snow-white headscarf framed her friendly face.

"The king asked if you would take care of them, milady," asked the knight.

He turned to Tiuri and Piak. "I have to return to the king now," he said. "But you'll see me again later. I will leave you in the care of Lady Mirian."

"Such haste, Sir Ivan!" said Lady Mirian. "You have not even introduced our young guests to me. What are their names? Where have they come from?"

"Their names are Tiuri and Piak," answered the knight. "They are messengers and they have travelled a long way."

"Welcome, Tiuri and Piak," said the woman warmly. "I hope that you have not brought us ill tidings."

"May God forbid," said the knight. "But we shall hear soon enough." He bowed and then left the room. Tiuri watched him go. So his name was Sir Ivan, like the lord of the castle in the Hills of the Moon. Was he perhaps a member of the same family? It was possible; he certainly resembled the lord of the White Moon – but he looked even more like someone else...

"So, you're Tiuri and Piak," said Lady Mirian. "And where do you come from?"

"From the land of King Dagonaut, milady," Tiuri replied.

"Well, you are a long way from home," said Lady Mirian. "But don't let me bombard you with questions. Look at the state of you! You must feel exhausted after such a long journey."

"Yes, milady," said Piak. "And also... somehow... odd... strange... overwhelmed... I don't quite know..."

"We'll soon put that right," said Lady Mirian. "Come with me."

She organized a bath for Tiuri and Piak and then brought fresh clothes: grey breeches for each of them, and white shirts with embroidered doublets over the top.

"Good," she said, when they were dressed. "Now you look just like the squires we have running around here."

Piak smiled and looked at Tiuri. "A squire," he whispered.

"See for yourselves," said Lady Mirian, and she took them to a mirror made of polished metal. Tiuri was a little surprised to see his reflection. It was a long time since he'd last seen himself. He seemed to have changed – he was thinner and his face was browner, but his eyes also looked different... more serious somehow.

Piak's eyes widened. "Oh dear," he said. "This is the first time I've ever been able to take such a good look at myself. And I think I look rather silly, especially in these clothes. Maybe they don't suit me after all."

They turned away from the mirror and followed Lady Mirian into the cloister, where they sat down on a bench. The garden looked delightful; white daisies and blue larkspur were blooming, and a fountain splashed away in the centre of the courtyard.

Piak sighed. "This all feels like a dream. Are we truly in King Unauwen's palace?"

Lady Mirian laughed. "Yes, you truly are," she said. "And Sir Ivan has asked if you would like to dine with him. I'm sure you'll feel better after that."

"Sir Ivan..." said Piak. "There are other knights called Ivan in this land, aren't there?"

"Yes," replied Lady Mirian. "This knight is the young Sir Ivan. He's a son of Sir Ivan of the Hills of the Moon. Look, here comes his squire to fetch you."

The two friends stood up and thanked Lady Mirian for her hospitality.

"There's no need to thank me," she said. "I'll have a room made up for you, and then you can go to bed whenever you choose. Enjoy your dinner."

As the two friends followed Sir Ivan's squire, Piak whispered, "I keep wondering how Slither managed to reach the gate before us... if he was captured in the Hills of the Moon."

"Sssh!" said Tiuri. Slither's name sounded so wrong in these surroundings. And besides, at that moment he didn't care how the spy had reached the gate before them. Slither had been caught and defeated. And Tiuri would have been happy if that was the last he ever saw or heard of him.

Sir Ivan was waiting for them in a large room with red-brown wood panelling and big windows along one side. The knight had removed his helmet and Tiuri realized who it was that he reminded him of: Sir Evan, the youngest of the Grey Knights.

The knight greeted them warmly and invited them to sit at a table by the windows. The table was laid with a white linen cloth, with elegant crockery and fine glasses. They could see the palace gardens through the window, sloping down towards the White River. The squire brought in dishes of food, filled the glasses and then left the room. Sir Ivan sat with them, but he did not eat. He was a gracious host, but he appeared to be concerned about something.

"I have heard the news," he said after a while. "Sir Edwinem is dead. The Invincible has been defeated by treachery. Many here will be sad to hear of his passing."

He asked the friends no questions and Tiuri wondered if he already knew more about the matter than they did. After all, they didn't even know what the message was about. He suddenly felt so empty and downhearted.

"You must be tired," said Sir Ivan. "I heard you had a difficult journey. All the way from the Kingdom of Dagonaut!" He paused before continuing, "You may have no desire to speak about your journey, but there's something I would like to ask you. You have come from Dagonaut's land, and..." He hesitated.

"Whatever it is, please feel free to ask," said Tiuri.

"I... have a brother. Some time ago, King Unauwen sent him to your land with a message of friendship for King

Dagonaut. He was to arrive there before midsummer's day and return as soon as possible. But we have heard nothing from him since he left."

"Sir Evan?" asked Tiuri.

"Yes, that's his name! How did you know?"

"You look so much like him," said Tiuri with a smile. "Or he looks like you."

Then he told him that Sir Evan had joined the Grey Knights, who had sworn to avenge the death of Sir Edwinem. As he told the story, he forgot his sadness for a while.

Sir Ivan listened attentively and wanted to know all about the Grey Knights and the circumstances of Sir Edwinem's death. "I am happy to hear that my brother is well," he said, "and our father will be too. Now at least I understand why Evan has not yet returned."

At that moment, the squire came back. "Sir Ivan," he said, "King Unauwen requests your company."

The knight stood up. "I must excuse myself," he said to Tiuri and Piak, "but I shall return as soon as possible. You may view the palace as your home. If there is anything you need, please ask Lady Mirian. Your arrival here has caused quite a commotion. There is much to be done. I shall see you later."

After he had left, the two friends sat at the table for a while, looking out of the window. The sun was setting and everything was bathed in a beautiful orange glow. They noticed some signs of the commotion that Sir Ivan had mentioned. Knights were riding across the bridge in both directions. In the palace too, they heard the sound of footsteps coming and going, and a murmur of voices, and people shouting orders.

"What do you think was in that letter?" Piak asked.

"It's still a mystery," said Tiuri with a sigh. "I think it was something about a threat from Eviellan, some kind of betrayal. But I don't know what exactly."

"What should we do now?" asked Piak. "Shall we go for a walk around the palace? I'm sure I won't be able to sleep."

"The garden's a better place for a walk," said a voice behind them.

Startled, they looked around. At the other end of the room stood a slender boy, who was clothed in every colour of the rainbow. He must have slipped in silently.

"The garden's wonderful," he continued. "You can sit on a wall and watch everything happening around you without having to get involved." As he spoke, he came closer and they heard a soft jingling. Now they saw that he was not in fact a boy, even though he was so small and slight. His age was impossible to guess; he could have been anywhere between thirty and fifty years old. He had a merry, pointed face with dark, twinkling eyes and he wore a white cap with bells on it. "Good evening," he said with a bow. "I am Tirillo, court jester to King Unauwen – the folly that serves wisdom so well! Now is not the time for jokes or banter," he continued, "but I would invite you to accept my company and to sit with me in the garden and to talk or to be silent, whichever you prefer."

He walked to an open window and nimbly leapt through it. Tiuri and Piak followed him and they walked together through the garden to a low wall, where they sat in silence and watched the river flowing past and the hustle and bustle on the opposite bank. Slowly, it grew dark. Here and there, lights were coming on already.

Then the jester moved, and the bells on his cap jingled. "There was once a man who saw a rainbow," he said, "a beautiful rainbow. It stood in the sky like a high, arched bridge, with its ends touching the earth. The man said to himself, 'I shall journey to the end of the rainbow. And then I can follow the bridge to the other side of the world...'"

"I always wanted to try that when I was younger," said Piak. "What happened next?"

"He set off on his journey," said the jester, "and he travelled for a long time. He passed through cities and villages, through fields and deserts, over rushing rivers and through thick forests. And, all that time, he kept looking forward to what he was going to see. He knew the place where the rainbow ended must be magnificent, beautiful... The closer he came to his goal, the more he longed to see it. But when he got there, the rainbow had vanished, and the place where it had touched the earth looked just like anywhere else. And the man was very sad. But then he thought of how many beautiful things he had seen on his journey, how much he had experienced and learnt. And he realized that what mattered was not the rainbow itself, but the search. And he returned home, with a happy heart, and he said to himself that there would be plenty of other rainbows in his future. And indeed, when he got home, there was a rainbow right above his house."

"Is that the end of the story?" asked Piak.

The jester smiled and nodded.

"Why did you tell us that particular story?" asked Tiuri, who thought the jester must have chosen it for a reason.

"Ah, just because," said the jester. "It's an old, well-known story. But that's what we jesters are like. We always tell the same old tales."

All three of them fell silent once again. Then the jester started quietly humming. Tiuri recognized the tune. Lady Lavinia had once sung it to him at Castle Mistrinaut.

Sir Edwinem the brave rode out
from Forèstèrra in the west.
Of all the knights of Unauwen,
he surely was the best.

The jester stopped humming and said, "Now you feel strange and a little bit lost, because your job is done and you have no other new task as yet. And you are wondering what the message might be about, after carrying it for so long. But the meaning of the message doesn't matter! It matters only that you delivered it safely, true to your promise, and acted with courage and determination, in spite of the dangers."

Tiuri looked at him. He was surprised to realize that the jester was right. Now his feeling of emptiness lifted, and he became calm.

"Hmm," said Piak quietly. "I think I'll be able to sleep now."

The jester hopped down from the wall. "That's the best thing you could do," he said. "You may well be busy again before long. Go and sleep. I shall take you to Lady Mirian."

They walked back through the darkening gardens to the palace.

"What is Lady Mirian's position?" Piak asked the jester.

"She runs the household," he replied. "She makes sure that there is food on the table and that the beds are made. That makes her, without a doubt, the most important person in the palace."

In the courtyard, they met Sir Ivan. "I was just looking for you," he said to the friends. "I see you have been in good company. I have come to wish you farewell for the time being. The king has sent me on a mission to the south. I am about to set off."

"To the crown prince?" asked the jester.

"To the crown prince," replied Ivan with a nod. He turned to Tiuri and Piak. "So farewell," he said. "If you see my brother before me, please give him my greetings. And to you too, Tirillo, my best wishes."

"And let us hope that your best wishes are good enough," said the jester. "That is not always the case! But jesting aside, Ivan, my good wishes go with you, and may the sun shine on your white shield."

Sir Ivan left and Tirillo took the friends to Lady Mirian. She looked as if she had been crying, but she didn't say a word about her sadness.

"Your room is ready," she said. "Please come with me."

Tirillo wished the friends goodnight and Lady Mirian took them to their room. Soon they were curled up beneath snow-white sheets on a soft bed, and sleeping soundly.

7   A Final Confrontation

The next morning, in the city's cathedral, a solemn service was dedicated to the memory of Sir Edwinem, the lord of Forèstèrra. Tiuri and Piak were both invited to attend.

They had breakfast afterwards in the palace with Lady Mirian, Tirillo and other members of the king's court. Grief at the death of one of the king's most valiant paladins filled the palace and mingled with the atmosphere of anxiety and unrest. Tiuri and Piak heard rumours about Eviellan's deceit, but no one seemed to know the full story or to want to discuss the matter.

After breakfast, the two friends went for a walk around the palace. There were so many beautiful things to see; even King Dagonaut's palace was not as impressive, Tiuri told

Piak. Some rooms had ornate columns and blue ceilings with gold stars, while others had stained-glass windows and walls painted with images of heroes and saints. There were floors of coloured mosaics, and marble stairs, and statues of wood, bronze and stone. What was most astounding was that all of those exquisite things fitted together perfectly, and nowhere did the opulence seem excessive.

Sometimes one of the palace residents would come over to talk to them, but it was never for too long; everyone was so busy. People were still busily hurrying in and out of the palace: messengers, knights and men-at-arms.

After a while, the two friends headed into the garden and sat down on the wall where they had spent the previous evening with Tirillo. They looked out at the sloping garden terraces, with their trees and flowers, steps and fountains. They watched people riding over the bridge to the palace. There were lots of knights among their number, with their white shields and coloured suits of armour. Piak couldn't stop staring at them.

"Look at that!" he cried out at one point, as a knight came riding up on a white horse that seemed almost too spirited to be ridden. Almost... because the knight had the horse under control and he flew over the bridge like a hurricane, bareheaded, with a white shield on his arm and his cloak like a rainbow streaming out behind him.

"His locks as red as the sun in the west, his eyes as blue as the sea," came a voice from behind them. It was Tirillo.

"Who is that?" asked Piak, following the knight with his gaze until he leapt down from his horse and disappeared into the palace.

"Marwen of Iduna," the jester replied. "His horse is called Idanwen, and it is one of the finest horses in this kingdom.

Sir Edwinem rode a brother of that horse: Ardanwen, or Night Wind."

Tiuri realized that Sir Edwinem must have seemed just as impressive when he rode through the City of Unauwen on Ardanwen. He actually looked nothing like Sir Marwen, and yet the two were somehow very similar.

"But I didn't come here to tell you that," said the jester. "I have three things to say. The first is that the king would like to see you later."

Tiuri was pleasantly surprised. He and Piak had seen King Unauwen only briefly that morning in the cathedral. So he had not forgotten them.

"And I am to greet you on behalf of Warmin, a guard from the toll fortress at the Rainbow River," Tirillo continued.

"Warmin?" said the two friends.

"Yes, he arrived here last night, with some long and complicated tale about a messenger who told lies to Sir Ivan in the Hills of the Moon. I'm sure you'll hear all about it. He would have liked to speak to you himself, but the king sent him back with a message for the toll master this morning before dawn."

"That's right," said Piak. "Why did that messenger tell us Slither had been captured when we found him waiting here for us?"

"Slither!" said Tirillo. "That's the third thing I had to tell you. You're to report to the sheriff and tell him exactly what you know about Slither. You'll have to make a statement and... You don't look too keen," he continued, after one look at Tiuri's face, "but it has to be done. And right away."

"We shall do as you ask," said Tiuri.

"Excellent," said the jester. "You know, I think I'll take you there. The sheriff's court and the prison are on the other side of the river, on the main square. It'll give you a chance to see more of the city."

The streets were rather busy and people kept stopping them to talk. Everyone seemed to want a word with Tirillo, and he certainly stood out in his rainbow-coloured costume and his white cap with bells on.

"The king's jester!" people cried. "Do you have news for us, Tirillo? But it surely cannot be good!"

"And why not?" said the jester. "Look around and tell me: isn't the city beautiful today? In fact, you'll notice it's more beautiful than usual. That's because you feel it may be in danger. It's only when something's threatened that you realize just how much you love it."

"Is it true, Tirillo, that there's a war coming?" someone asked.

"You'll hear what you need to hear when the time comes," the jester replied. "It's true that we have an enemy, but I don't want to name that enemy as yet."

"Eviellan," came the whispers.

"Have faith in our king," said the jester.

"Go on, Tirillo, sing something for us," cried one of the crowd. "Our hearts are heavy. Give us some cheer!"

"I cannot take away that sadness," said the jester. "Sometimes you need to be sad so that you can appreciate joy all the more. Just as rain must fall between sunny spells. Farewell."

He led Tiuri and Piak to a large building on a beautiful square. "Go inside," he said. "I shall wait for you."

Tiuri and Piak did as they were told and were immediately admitted to the sheriff, who proved to be one of Unauwen's knights. He was expecting them and he already knew all that they'd told the king. He asked what else they knew about Slither. Tiuri and Piak answered his questions and when that was done, the sheriff said, "I thank you. This Slither refuses to say a word. But perhaps he will speak when he sees you. I shall send for him."

Slither was brought in. He was not chained or tied up, but he was accompanied by two armed guards. He no longer looked anything like the old beggar; his grey locks were gone and he had short, light-brown hair. But his eyes still gave him away. When he saw the two friends, his face twisted into a snarl.

"Pah!" he spat. "Isn't it enough for you that I'm a prisoner? Do you have to come and gloat at the sight of a vanquished enemy?" He looked at Tiuri. "Oh, I bet you feel like quite the man," he said. "Oh, oh, such a valiant knight, successfully completing such a perilous quest! And what exactly was your task? Taking a letter to King Unauwen! Travelling many miles, risking your life... and for what? What is in that letter that is so important? Something King Unauwen didn't already know? Well, good for you! Messengers come to him every day, a whole procession marching in and out, and they all think they're bringing a special message. It's hilarious. Ha, ha!" And he laughed his mean and spiteful laugh.

Tiuri was taken aback and didn't know how to respond. Worst of all, there seemed to be some truth in Slither's words. Because Tiuri still had no clue what was in the letter...

"You're just a bad loser!" shouted Piak. "Of course that letter was important. Why else did you chase after us all that time and try so hard to stop us?"

Slither stopped laughing and gaped at him. Tiuri could have thrown his arms around Piak. He was right! And besides... he remembered what Tirillo had said: the letter itself had not been the most important thing for Tiuri, but keeping his promise to Sir Edwinem.

Then Slither found his vicious tongue again. "Oh yes," he said. "Oh yes, you're not wrong! I too had a job to do, a task for my master, the Black Knight with the Red Shield."

At that point, the sheriff interrupted him. "And who," he asked, "is the Black Knight with the Red Shield?"

Slither sneered. "Who is he?" he said. "I don't know. And if I did know, I wouldn't tell you. But you'll get to meet him soon enough when he comes with his knights with their red and black shields to conquer this land."

"Your words are foolish and spoken in anger," declared the sheriff.

"Not foolish," replied Slither. "But they are indeed angry. I am angry!"

He turned to Tiuri and Piak. "I did not accomplish my mission," he said. "But I should have succeeded, because I am stronger and better than you! Yes, it's true. Who are the two of you? A squire who neglects his duty and runs away when he should be keeping his vigil on the eve of his knighting ceremony. A shepherd boy who has done nothing in his life but climb up and down mountains. I don't know how you managed to shake off Jaro; it was obviously him who betrayed my name to you. The devil take him! I suspected he wouldn't manage to stop you, Tiuri. He is weak, even though he thinks himself better than me. That's why I took the First Great Road over the mountains and sent carrier pigeons to my friend and ally, the mayor of Dangria. He was to hold you prisoner until I arrived. But when I got there, you and that friend of yours had fled and Dangria was in turmoil. That's what happens when you rely on other people! But I did the rest by myself. I saw you captured by the toll master's men when I was on the bridge over the Rainbow River. And yes, I went after the wrong man, but he is no great loss!"

Tiuri and Piak glowered at him.

"I should have had you!" Slither continued, rattling away faster and faster. "I was more intelligent than all of you! I was the shepherd who said he'd ridden away on the murderer's horse; I was the messenger who told Sir Ivan the murderer had been caught! And I did what I set out to do: your escort, those stupid servants of the toll master, abandoned you and headed home. That was what I wanted: you were to be alone and unprotected. I followed you, but everything conspired against me, blast it! There were people in the fields and I preferred not to kill you in broad daylight. And at night you slept at a farmer's house, and he bolted his doors and his dog barked at me. Not that I let that deter me. I rode on and I was ahead of you, and I was waiting for you in the guise of an old beggar. It should have worked. I'm so much stronger than you. You felt sorry for a poor old beggar, didn't you? Well, that was weakness! Pah!" He spat on the floor before finishing his speech, "So, now you know everything you wanted to know. But I'm warning you. Don't feel too high and mighty, too good, too strong! That could prove your downfall. And one last word to you, Tiuri, son of Tiuri! Do you know what you have done by running off and throwing away your chance to become a knight? Do you think perhaps that King Unauwen will make you a knight? Well, that's folly. This is not your country, and he is not your king. I hope King Dagonaut treats you as you deserve, and that you never carry a sword and a shield!"

"Silence!" cried the sheriff. "That is enough!" He ordered the guards to take Slither away. "He will get the punishment that is coming to him," he said to Tiuri and Piak. "Don't waste any more thoughts on him. You are free to leave. And many thanks for your help."

When they were back outside, Tiuri heaved a sigh of relief.

"Phew!" said Piak. "What a villain! The sheriff's right. I certainly won't waste any more thoughts on him!"

But Tiuri doubted he would ever forget Slither's snarling face and vicious words.

8   SWORDS AND RINGS

It took Tiuri and Piak some time to find Tirillo. He was standing in the middle of the square, with a crowd of people around him. As he sang for them, he moved his head and hands so that the bells on his cap and gloves formed a jingling accompaniment to his song. When he saw Tiuri and Piak, he stopped singing and came over to them.

"Don't go, Tirillo!" the crowd called. "Please, sing another song for us!"

"Not now," said the jester. "I must take these young people to the palace and the king is expecting me."

Everyone turned to look at Tiuri and Piak. "Who are they?" someone asked.

"They come from the land of King Dagonaut," said Tirillo, "and they could tell you a great deal. But they shall not do so, as they are coming with me." He linked arms with Tiuri and Piak and walked back to the palace with them. "I just sang for them a little," he whispered. "One of the few things I can do to help."

When they were back at the palace, he took them to the king, who was not alone this time. Sir Marwen was with him. King Unauwen introduced Tiuri and Piak to the knight and kindly invited them to sit. Tirillo poured five glasses of wine and joined them, sitting at the king's feet. Tiuri saw that Sir

Marwen was wearing a ring like Sir Edwinem's and realized that he too must be one of the king's most faithful paladins.

"I sent for you," said Unauwen, "so that I could talk to you once again and hear more about your adventures. Do not be shy. Please speak freely."

And the two friends told their tale, first in brief, but then in greater detail. The king listened attentively and asked plenty of questions. He heard more of their story than they would later tell anyone else. They also talked about the old man who had called Tiuri out of the chapel. It had, of course, been Vokia, Sir Edwinem's squire.

King Unauwen asked Tiuri to try to find Vokia once he was back in the Kingdom of Dagonaut. "Be sure that Vokia receives everything he might wish for," he said. "I hope he will be capable of travelling back here or to Forèstèrra. But I fear that his age and his grief at his master's death will have weakened him."

Then he said, "I thank you once again, Tiuri and Piak. I would like to reward you for what you have done, but there is no suitable gift I could give you."

"Oh, but that is not necessary, sire," said Tiuri.

The king smiled. "I am aware of that," he replied. "But I intend to give you a token as a reminder, although I am sure you will never forget your experiences. Sir Marwen, would you pass me the swords?"

The knight handed two very fine swords to the king.

"One for each of you," said the king. "These swords have been in my family for many centuries."

"They are over a thousand years old," said Sir Marwen, "but they are still just as sharp as the day they were made."

The king presented the swords to the friends. "Use them only for a righteous cause," he said. "And here is a ring for each of you... just a small, simple ring. Not the kind of ring my trusty paladins wear; you are still too young for that. I give these rings to all my men after they have been knighted and even though you are not my knights, you too shall receive one."

Tiuri and Piak thanked him.

"One more thing," said the king. "You told me, Tiuri, that Ardanwen has accepted you as his master. So from now on he shall be your horse."

"Thank you, sire," said Tiuri, delighted.

"You need not thank me for that," said the king. "I cannot give Ardanwen away. That horse chooses his own master. Is that not so, Sir Marwen?"

"Yes, sire," he replied. "Just like Idanwen, the Dawn Wind, my own horse and Ardanwen's brother." He gave Tiuri a friendly nod.

King Unauwen stood up. Tiuri realized the conversation was over and he also rose to his feet. Piak followed his example.

"Is there anything you would like to ask me?" said the king, looking at Tiuri.

How did he know? Tiuri thought.

And then, somewhat hesitantly, he said, "Y... Yes, sire."

"What is it?"

"Sire, what was in the letter I brought to you?" asked Tiuri. He immediately regretted his words. It felt disrespectful to ask about something that was clearly a secret.

But the king did not seem angry. "I do not wish to talk about that as yet," he said in a most serious tone. "But you shall know soon enough. Perhaps even tomorrow."

"A sword!" said Piak, gazing at it in awe. "A real sword! And what a sword!"

"It's magnificent," said Tiuri. "Look, it has figures engraved on it, and the name of King Unauwen."

"To be honest, I think it's a bit of a creepy thing to have," said Piak. "I don't know if I like the idea of going around with a sword myself. It seems more like something I might hang above the bed and look at every now and then. But I shall always wear the ring."

They were sitting together on the edge of the fountain in the small courtyard.

"What do you really think of all this?" Piak asked Tiuri.

"Why don't you tell me what you think, Piak?"

"Oh, it's wonderful, beautiful, but still I don't feel entirely at home here. Maybe it's all just too much for me. All those knights with their white shields and sparkling rings. And then there's the king himself! What do you think of him?"

"He is a great king," said Tiuri slowly. "He is old, and yet he is strong and valiant, a powerful ruler but still with a ready smile, a man who inspires awe, and yet who is not at all proud or arrogant."

"He still reminds me so much of Menaures," said Piak. "That's why he doesn't make me feel shy. Otherwise I'm sure I would have been."

"Yes," said Tiuri. "The hermit certainly looks a lot like him, or he looks like the hermit."

"Is King Dagonaut like King Unauwen, too?" asked Piak.

"No," Tiuri replied. "King Dagonaut's younger. He is a warrior and he is stern, but just. He is, I think, perhaps not as... not as wise as King Unauwen. But it is hard to judge such men. Dagonaut is my king, my country's king. I love him, I respect him, and I wish to serve as his knight."

"Well, you'll be able to do that soon, won't you?" said Piak.

Tiuri thought back to what Slither had said, but he kept quiet.

"Would you like to be a knight of Unauwen," asked Piak, "and carry a white shield?"

"Yes," replied Tiuri, "I would. But if I become a knight, I would have to be a knight of Dagonaut; his kingdom is my home."

"I don't know if I would want to be a knight," said Piak, thinking aloud. "I'm just an ordinary boy. I feel so clumsy in chainmail and I look ridiculous with a sword in my hand. But perhaps, as Warmin said, you get used to it."

At that point, they spotted Tirillo coming towards them.

"I have come to take you out," he said. "Something different from this palace full of knights and lords for a change." He gave Piak a wink.

Tiuri wondered if Tirillo was a mind reader or if he had heard their conversation.

"I can read minds," said the jester. "You should watch out; I am a dangerous man. So do you want to come? Then take your swords to your room. You may wear them tomorrow. That is when King Unauwen is planning to address his priests and his paladins, his knights and his councillors. The two of you are also expected to attend."

"Where do you want to go?" asked Piak.

"Out on the river for a while."

Piak frowned.

"Oh, the White River's nothing like the Rainbow River!" Tirillo laughed. "And my boat doesn't leak. Come with me. The sun's shining and there's a fresh wind from the west, a sea breeze. I asked the kitchen to make a lunch for us; we can eat it on the water."

A short time later, the friends stepped into Tirillo's boat. It was a beautiful boat, painted in bright colours.

"I shall row downstream," said Tirillo. "You can row back upstream later. You're sturdy young lads, strong and muscular, and I am just a puny jester."

He pulled off his gloves and started rowing. Tiuri held the rudder. The jester told Piak he didn't need to do anything until he got over his fear.

"I'm not scared at all!" said Piak indignantly. "I think it's wonderful."

And it *was* wonderful. The water gleamed in the sunshine and the wind blew through their hair. Tiuri felt light and happy, far from all responsibility and duties.

The river looped around the palace and to the west. They saw another bridge ahead, with a gate beyond it.

"The White River flows through that gate and out of the city," Tirillo told them, "and then onwards to the sea."

"To the sea..." murmured Piak. "I've never seen the sea. What does it look like?"

"Water," said Tirillo. "Salty water. Waves as far as you can see, and beyond, until the end of the world. If you floated along with the current, you'd end up at the sea. But it'd take you a couple of days."

Tiuri thought that he would rather like to do that. He had never seen the sea before either. Sir Edwinem's castle, Forèstèrra, was by the sea...

He looked at Tirillo and suddenly noticed something: a ring on his left hand. The stone sparkled as he moved the oars. Surprised, Tiuri leant closer and said, "You have one of those rings... the kind that Sir Marwen and the toll master wear, and Sir Edwinem!"

Tirillo smiled. "That's right," he said. "When King Unauwen

gave it to me, he said, 'One does not need to carry a sword and a shield to be a knight.'"

"Yes," said Tiuri. "Yes, of course."

It was true. Why should a jester not be among the king's most faithful paladins? Tirillo was worthy of such a ring. He knew how to cheer people up when they were downhearted, and that was a gift few people shared.

9 KNIGHTS AND KINGS

The next day, more and more knights came riding over the bridge to the palace. They had all been called to the capital by King Unauwen. Tiuri and Piak heard the king was waiting for a message from the City of the South, where his eldest son, the crown prince, had his residence. It was said the crown prince himself would come, but that might not happen for some days yet.

Among the knights who came was a man whom Tiuri had met before: the lord of the White Moon, the father of Ivan and Evan. Tiuri had a long conversation with him, and they talked a lot about Sir Evan.

At midday, the knights and lords gathered in the largest room of the palace, where King Unauwen would address them. Tiuri and Piak were permitted to attend, and they felt most insignificant among all those powerful people. They saw the king in his full regalia for the first time, wearing white and purple, with a golden crown and sceptre. Not all of his knights were present; many were still in other parts of the land, not to mention those who had been sent to Eviellan. But there was a good number of knights, with gleaming helmets, white shields and rainbow-coloured cloaks. There were councillors and wise men in long robes and tall, pointed hats. Only Tirillo looked as he always did, with his fool's cap and bells, and the glittering ring on his finger.

King Unauwen rose from his throne and welcomed everyone. Then he said, "Friends, knights, subjects, hear now what I have to say. You know that two young men have brought us news of Sir Edwinem's death. Tiuri and Piak have travelled through many dangers from the Kingdom of Dagonaut to our city..."

Tiuri did not take his eyes off the king, but he could feel that many people were staring at him and Piak.

"In addition to this sad news, they brought me a message," the king continued, "from a letter that Sir Edwinem had passed on to Tiuri before his death. This letter came from Eviellan, but the ruler of that land did not want us ever to read it. As you know, the King of Eviellan has asked for peace, and in the spring I sent a delegation of knights to him. You also know that Sir Edwinem fled from Eviellan and that he was attacked and killed by Red Riders in the Kingdom of Dagonaut. So you will already have realized that Eviellan did not truly wish for peace. Messengers have been sent to the south for more information but it will be some time before they return. And yet I have news for you, a message that will be painful, although now it may not come as such a shock. Sir Andomar of Ingewel will never return to our land either. He was killed in the Southerly Mountains by men from Eviellan!"

A deathly hush fell upon the room. Every face bore an expression of pain, horror or fury.

"He was a valiant knight," said the king softly, "a true paladin. May heaven have mercy on his soul."

Everyone in the room bowed their head to remember the valiant knight who would never return to Ingewel. Tiuri could picture the beautiful forest, and the village on the lake. His own anxious forebodings had been correct. Had the offer of peace been a trap to lure the knights to Eviellan?

Then the king spoke again. "I received this news an hour ago," he said. "It was brought by carrier pigeon from the City of the South in a message from the crown prince. The message was brief, but I hope to hear more soon. My son himself is to come here. Sir Andomar was killed but his squire escaped and reached the City of the South on the same day as Tiuri and Piak arrived in our city. His adventures may well have been similar to theirs. Sir Andomar was on his way to our land, perhaps with the same news as Sir Edwinem..."

A quiet murmur went around the room, but as the king started talking again, everyone fell silent.

"So, now for the message," said King Unauwen, "the letter that Sir Edwinem gave to Tiuri. I did not want to reveal its contents until the crown prince had been informed, as the message primarily concerns him and his brother, the King of Eviellan. Sir Ivan took the message to him immediately and the crown prince has now heard the news." He paused for a moment, his face troubled.

"I have already told you that my younger son – because yes, the King of Eviellan is also my son – did not truly desire peace," he continued. "And yet I tell you that he certainly wanted to sign a peace declaration! And if Sir Edwinem had not been there, we should be at peace now!"

Another murmur rippled around the room. Tiuri looked wide-eyed at the king. What did it all mean? Surely the king did not doubt Sir Edwinem!

"Sir Edwinem fled from Eviellan," the king continued, "dressed in black, with a black shield. But the white was concealed beneath the black. He had discovered something...

454

we do not know how, and we shall never know, because he can no longer tell us. A knight and riders from Eviellan killed him to prevent him from telling me what he knew. But the letter he wanted to bring was saved. Or rather, its contents were. It was written in the old tongue that is known to only a few adepts. My younger son also knows that language."

The king paused again.

"I shall tell you what would have happened," he said, "if Sir Edwinem had not been there and if the message he wanted to bring had been lost. We would have made peace with Eviellan. My younger son would have been reconciled with me and with his brother and he would have returned to his fatherland and his ancestral home. And we would all have been delighted, not suspecting what danger threatened us, what misfortune awaited us. We would have welcomed the enemy inside our borders. And what would have happened? Before long the crown prince would suddenly have died! Do you understand? My younger son was planning to kill his brother, or to have him killed, at a time when we no longer suspected him of any wrongdoing... so that he could get what he wanted: power over this kingdom! After the death of the crown prince, he would be the heir apparent. And that is the treacherous plan that lay concealed behind his request for peace! Eviellan is not enough for him; he wants to rule this land too!"

King Unauwen looked around the room. Sadness was in his eyes, but his expression was stern as he said, "Now you know that the King of Eviellan is still our enemy. He must never rule this kingdom, for he is wicked! He is my son and I love him, but he is a wicked man. Sorrow would come to this land if he were ever to become its king!"

So that was the message, thought Tiuri. He looked around and saw expressions of horror, fury and disgust. Then he looked back at the king. He was clearly angry too but, more than that, he looked sad.

King Unauwen spoke again. "We know now about his evil intent," he said, "so he shall never be able to carry out his cunning plan. He shall soon become aware that we know about it, if he does not realize already. He has already killed two of my knights so that his murderous plans would not be revealed. We do not yet know what has become of the others – of Sir Argarath, of Marcian, and Darowin – but I fear the worst. But, gentlemen, we already know enough. The King of Eviellan has failed; he will not ask for peace again. I fear that he will now attempt to achieve through violence what he can no longer gain through deception! I am afraid he will take up arms again. So we must prepare to defend ourselves."

The king concluded, "The news I have brought you is sad, but there is one stroke of good fortune: we now know where the danger lies. And, if needed, we shall face it together. Who among you is ready to fight?"

The knights unsheathed their swords and the room became a forest of gleaming blades. And they all cheered their king.

Then there was a discussion of how best to prepare the country's defences. Tiuri and Piak were excused, as those matters did not concern them.

The two friends left the palace and headed into the city. They stopped on one of the bridges over the White River and talked about what they'd heard. After a while, they ran out of things to say and, lost in thought, they both gazed down into the clear water.

Tiuri thought about the young squire who had brought back news of Sir Andomar to the Kingdom of Unauwen. It was strange to think that he had not been alone. Another young man had been charged with the same kind of task as

Tiuri and had perhaps known the same fears and the same satisfaction. Had the other messenger also found a friend as loyal as Piak? Tiuri looked at his companion. Piak was looking down the river towards the west.

"Just think," he said. "The sea's over there. You know, I really would like to sail down the river to the sea."

"Me too," said Tiuri. "If we had more time..." As he spoke the words, he realized that he had no time at all. He couldn't stay any longer: King Dagonaut was surely expecting him to return. Nothing was preventing him from going back now. His job was done.

"If we had more time," he repeated, "but I need to get back to King Dagonaut."

"I understand," said Piak. "When do you want to leave?"

"I have to go, so it might as well be as soon as possible," replied Tiuri. "Tomorrow."

"Fine," said Piak, "then we'll go tomorrow."

"Would you like to stay longer?" asked Tiuri.

"I'm going with you," was all that Piak said.

They stood in silence for a while and then Piak asked, "Do you want to go back?"

"Yes and no," said Tiuri. "I'd like to remain here for a while and get to know the city and the people better, but I'm also longing to return home. It's funny, eh?"

"No," said Piak. "I feel the same way. Part of me wants to stay here and another part of me wants to go back to the mountains."

"The Kingdom of Dagonaut seems so terribly far away," Tiuri continued. "Sometimes I feel that everything will have changed when I get back there." How long was it since he had left? Not even a month. Yet he'd seen so much in that time!

Piak turned in a circle, waving his hand. "Farewell then, City of Unauwen," he said.

"No," said Tiuri. "Not farewell. Let's say, 'Until we meet again.' I'm certain we will return."

When they went back to the palace, the meeting was over and they found Tirillo surrounded by knights and squires.

"So, Tirillo," called one of the knights, "you chide us for daring to think about the great deeds that we will perform. But are you not accompanying us when we ride out?"

"Most certainly," replied the jester. "Someone has to keep an eye on you!"

"And which weapons will you be taking, Tirillo?" asked another in a gently mocking tone.

"His fool's bauble to rap our knuckles," said Marwen of Iduna, "and his jests to save us from pride." Although he said this with a smile, he was clearly being serious.

"That's right," another knight agreed. "If we are to combat evil, Tirillo's presence is required."

"Well said, sir knight," said the jester. "As long as you remember that fighting evil doesn't necessarily make you good! Good and evil are each other's enemies, but they are often found close together. Never forget that our crown prince and the King of Eviellan are brothers, the two sons of one father." Then he spotted Tiuri and Piak. "Aha," he said. "Here come our two friends. So, do you feel at home in our city?"

"Yes, Tirillo," said Tiuri.

"But now, sadly, you must leave us," the jester continued.

"That's right," said Tiuri. He was no longer surprised when the jester guessed his thoughts. "Do you think we could speak to the king today?" he added.

"Come with me," said Tirillo, "I'll take you to him. I'm sure he has a moment."

Tiuri and Piak followed him and Tiuri thought, *Now I understand even better why Tirillo wears that sparkling ring. Not only because he is both wise and cheerful, but also because he makes sure the knights never become too conceited.*

Tiuri and Piak told King Unauwen that they had decided to begin their return journey as soon as possible.

"You are right to do so," said the king. "You are subjects of King Dagonaut. And Tiuri, now that you have kept your promise and completed your mission, you must tell your king everything. This time you shall be my messenger. I shall give you a letter for King Dagonaut. No, do not fear. It is, of course, an important message, but there are no dangers involved this time."

Tiuri smiled. "I am at your service, sire," he said.

"And what about you, Piak?" asked the king. "How far do you intend to accompany your friend? To the Great Mountains?"

"N-no, sire," said Piak. "We have agreed that I will travel on with him, to the City of Dagonaut."

"But I imagine you will be returning along the same route, will you not?" said the king. "When you see the hermit Menaures, please give him my regards."

"Do you know him, sire?" asked a surprised Piak.

"Yes, I know him," said the king. He smiled at the two boys and continued, "I am sorry you must leave, but I hope and expect to see you here again. Though your home and your duty lie in the Kingdom of Dagonaut, you will forever be allied with my own country too."

PART EIGHT

—

BACK TO THE CITY
OF DAGONAUT

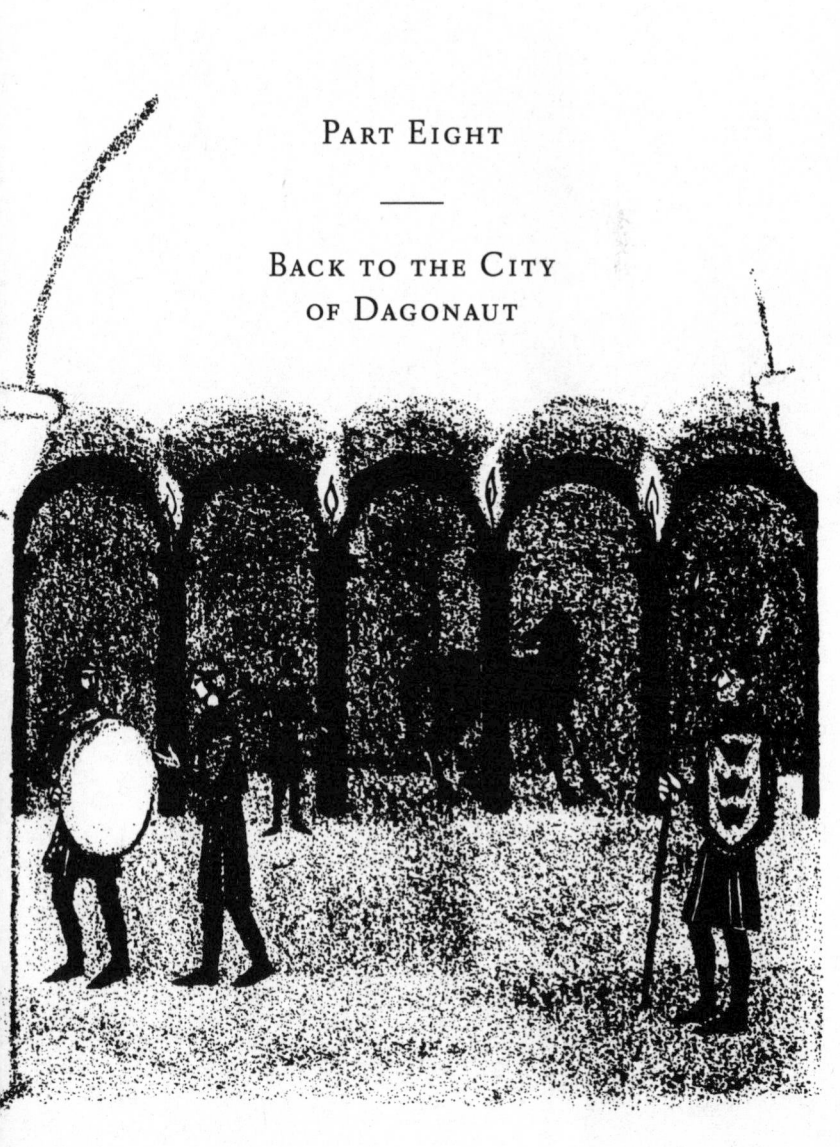

1   BROTHERS AND FRIENDS

The next morning, the two friends left the City of Unauwen. They had taken their leave of the king and the other people they had met, and rode towards the rising sun. The sky ahead of them blushed purple, pink, red and gold but, as they rode slowly on, they often looked back at the city, wondering when they would see it again. When the city was finally out of sight, they urged on their horses, and the greater the distance from the city became, the faster they rode.

"Now I just want to get home as soon as possible," Piak remarked.

Tiuri felt exactly the same way. So they rode quickly, even though they were sometimes hit by a pang of longing for what they agreed was the most beautiful city in the world.

They spent the first night of their journey home in the open air and the second at the castle of the White Moon. The day after that, they rode through the Hills of the Moon, this time in sunlight. It was already quite late by the time they reached Ingewel, where they returned the horses to the innkeeper at the Inn of the First Night.

The innkeeper offered them fresh horses to ride to the toll fortress. He seemed to regard them as personal friends of the toll master and important servants of the king.

This time, there were many villagers gathered at the inn. They were not there for the company, but to discuss the shocking news that had just reached Ingewel. Sir Andomar's death had, of course, hit them particularly hard.

Tiuri and Piak listened to their conversations without joining in but, when the innkeeper told his other guests that the two boys had just arrived from the City of Unauwen, they were bombarded with questions. Was it true that the King of Eviellan himself had killed Sir Andomar? And that the lord of Forèstèrra had also been defeated? What was the latest news from the city? Had they seen the king? Had he said there was going to be a war? Was the crown prince really going to challenge his brother to a duel?

King Unauwen had told Tiuri and Piak that there was no need for them to keep any secrets now. So they answered all of the questions as well as they could but, as if by unspoken agreement, they remained silent about their own role in the events.

The next morning, when they headed outside, where the innkeeper was waiting with their horses, they saw a small procession of riders approaching along the lakeside. They soon drew level with the inn and the villagers stopped what they were doing and stood at the roadside, bowing respectfully. The first rider was around the same age as Tiuri; his expression was sad and grave, but his bearing was brave and proud. He was dressed in grey, as a sign of mourning, and he carried no weapons. A number of men-at-arms followed him. "Andomar of Ingewel," said the innkeeper, when the procession had passed by and was heading to the west.

"Sir Andomar?" repeated Tiuri, rather surprised.

"His son," said the innkeeper. "He shares his father's name and he also resembles him. He is now on his way to the City of Unauwen. I believe the king will knight him, so a new Sir Andomar will soon be lord of Ingewel. You see, when a man dies, there is always another to take his place."

"Always another to take his place," repeated Tiuri thoughtfully.

"It's true, though, isn't it?" said the innkeeper. "So we must not be too downhearted."

As the two friends rode through the Forest of Ingewel once again, they were both silent. The flowers were blossoming just as magnificently as before, as though nothing had changed. *I so hope*, thought Tiuri, *that nothing will happen to destroy this beautiful forest.* But then he realized that, even if it did, other flowers would come to take their place. These were strange thoughts, ones that had never occurred to him before...

After they left the Forest of Ingewel, it was not far to the Rainbow River.

They rode over the bridge and asked to speak to the toll master. Tiuri had received some money from the king, so that he could pay the toll fee they still owed.

The toll guards didn't recognize the friends at first; it was only when Warmin came up and greeted them warmly that the other men realized who they were.

"I hadn't expected you back so soon," said Warmin. "I must announce your arrival to my master." He led them into the castle. "I know what you were up to now," Warmin said to them. "You were taking important news to the king. I haven't heard the details yet, but my master has recently started new training drills with his guards. He says his castle may soon become a real fortress again, as it was hundreds of years ago. My lord's spirits are low. In the evening, he stands on the bridge and peers down into the water, without saying a word."

However, the toll master showed no sign of sadness when he welcomed the two friends. There was indeed sorrow in his eyes, but that seemed to be part of his character. It was the melancholy of a man who knows and understands a great deal, and so cannot be light-hearted. He greeted them warmly and treated them as honoured guests, refusing to accept the money for the toll, as he said it had already been paid. Tiuri suspected the toll master had paid it himself. He asked Tiuri and Piak to tell him the news from the City of Unauwen, although he already knew most of it, including Tiuri's real identity. After dinner, they sat with him for a long time in the room overlooking the bridge and the river. The toll master asked Tiuri if he was related to Tiuri the Valiant, and Tiuri discovered that the toll master knew the Kingdom of Dagonaut well, as he had been there a number of times, years ago, before he had become toll master. But he knew far more about his own land, of course, and, at the friends' request, he told them all about the Kingdom of Unauwen. He talked about the different regions, rivers and castles, about King Unauwen and his knights, and about the two princes.

"It's so strange," said Piak, thinking aloud, "that the two brothers are enemies. Twins should love each other all the more."

"I agree," said the toll master. "And it could have been so different. King Unauwen also had a brother, who was born on the same day and who was just like him. But that prince never laid claim to the throne. He even rejected his royal title and set out to explore the world instead. Later he withdrew to the mountains and became a hermit."

"A hermit?" repeated Piak, staring at him with wide eyes.

Tiuri too was surprised. He couldn't help but think of Menaures, the hermit at the source of the Blue River.

"Is the brother... the hermit still alive?" asked Piak.

"Yes, he's still alive," replied the toll master.

"And what is his name?"

"When he renounced his royal title, he also took on a new name," said the toll master, "and I am not sure if I should say what it is. He lives on the other side of the Great Mountains and has not been here for many years. But knights and pilgrims have often passed through here on their way to visit him in the mountains. Perhaps you have met him yourself; after all, you come from the mountains, don't you?" He smiled and looked at Piak.

"Yes, yes," Piak replied. "Perhaps I have..."

Later, when the friends were in bed, Piak said to Tiuri, "What do you think? Do you think Menaures could be King Unauwen's brother?"

"It's possible," said Tiuri.

"Possible?! He has to be! Never in my wildest dreams... And yet somehow it's not such a surprise. Didn't I say that Menaures and the king were alike?"

Although the friends had had a late night, they got up early the next morning, because they wanted to reach Dangria the same day. After a warm farewell from the toll master, they rode away on the horses he had loaned them. Warmin and another man rode out with them. They were to accompany Tiuri and Piak to Dangria and then return with the horses.

As they looked back at the bridge for the last time, Piak said suddenly, "Oh, there's something we forgot to do!"

"What's that?" asked Tiuri.

"I wanted to go and have a word with Ferman about that boat of his."

Tiuri laughed. Piak still seemed rather upset about his soaking in the Rainbow River.

Warmin laughed as well. "So I was right. It was that wreck of Ferman's!" he said. "Thank goodness the thing's finally sunk."

That afternoon, they were back in Dangria's marketplace. It looked just as it had before, packed with colourful stalls, merchants and customers.

"It's like we never left," said Piak, as they stood looking at the town hall.

"And yet so much has changed," said a voice behind them. It was Iruwen, of course. He smiled and continued, "There have been so many changes! Master Dirwin is now mayor. As soon as the permission comes from the king, he will be officially installed." He walked over to stand between Tiuri and Piak and added in a hushed voice, "They asked me first if I wanted to be mayor. But I didn't fancy the idea. I want time to wander around the city and to keep my eyes and ears open. And Master Dirwin really will be a good mayor. But," he continued, "I haven't even asked yet if you had a good journey. In any case, I can see just by looking at you that you have done what you set out to do. I am keen to hear the stories you have to tell." He pointed at the town hall. "Perhaps you'd like to say hello to Master Dirwin first?" he said. "He is the mayor, after all."

"Yes," said Tiuri. "King Unauwen told us to convey his greetings to Master Dirwin and to pass on the news."

"Ah," said Iruwen. "We have heard about the death of the good knights, and of our poor scribe. Messengers from the capital have already been here. But more news is always welcome. I always said that Eviellan was our enemy, in spite of their request for peace."

Iruwen accompanied the two friends as far as the steps to the town hall.

"Will you come to the White Swan later?" he asked. "Ardoc will be there too. He happens to be in town today, which is fortunate. I shall go and tell the innkeeper that you're coming. See you later!"

The friends did as Iruwen had asked, and after their visit to Master Dirwin they went to the White Swan, where they found Iruwen, Ardoc, Doalwen, and some other acquaintances. They ate dinner together and exchanged news. It was indeed fortunate that Ardoc was in the city, as he said they could ride with him next morning to his house in the shadow of the Great Mountains.

2   A Broken Promise

So the next morning the two friends rode on with Ardoc, this time sitting up front beside him on the cart.

"So do you think it's really going to come to war?" said Piak.

"We are far from Eviellan here," said Ardoc, "and it will likely be some time before we notice any signs of it. The raids in the south will probably begin again soon. But even if Eviellan's armies do invade our country, they will never pass beyond the Rainbow River, not as long as the toll masters are there. And they won't take Dangria either. The city has withstood many a siege in the past and, if necessary, it will do so again. The danger within the city's own walls has been discovered and the mayor who is now in place is a stalwart and trustworthy man." Ardoc turned to look at Tiuri and Piak. "I could never have anticipated any of this when you rode with me last time," he said, shaking his head. "Do you remember when I said to you about discovering things for yourselves? You already knew so much more than I ever suspected."

"Well," said Piak, "we didn't really know all that much ourselves. We've found out so much more since then."

"And yet you played an important role in recent events," said Ardoc. "You were the first to bring news of Eviellan's deceit."

Piak looked at the mountains, which were getting closer and closer. "Soon we'll be home," he said with a sigh. "I can hardly believe it! I'm going to take off my chainmail and leave it behind. Don't you think that's a good idea, Tiuri? We already have enough weight to carry – like our swords, for instance. I've never climbed a mountain with a sword at my side before!"

"I do hope you don't intend to leave your sword behind," said Tiuri.

"Oh no, never!" said Piak.

"It would be a great shame if you did," said Ardoc. "Many a knight would envy you such a sword."

They rode onwards and, after a while, Ardoc pointed ahead with his whip. "Look. You can already see my house up there," he said. "You will stay until tomorrow morning, won't you? Then you can meet my children and my grandchildren. I have a large family; there's never a dull moment!"

Tiuri and Piak gladly accepted his invitation.

The next morning, they said farewell to the last person they knew to the west of the Great Mountains and began the climb upwards.

"Ah, now I'm back on familiar ground," said Piak the next day, after they had passed Filamen. "Oh, it's all been wonderful, but I still feel most at home here."

Of course they paid Taki and Ilia a visit, who greeted them warmly, but with some surprise.

"Well, I never!" said Taki to Piak. "What have you been up to and where have you been? You've come back with a sword at your side like a real knight."

Piak laughed. "Far from it!" he said. "But my friend here's a knight."

Tiuri shook his head and said, "Not yet, Piak."

"You look like you've been through all sorts," said Taki. "I hope you'll be able to tell us all about it this time. I'm just saying that for Ilia's sake, of course."

"If you're going to start calling me nosy again, you won't be getting any bread pudding later," threatened Ilia.

Taki laughed. "Then my lips are sealed," he said.

"And we can tell you the whole story now, aunt," said Piak. "For about the hundredth time. Phew! Now that I'm here, I can hardly imagine that it all really happened."

Piak repeated those same words a couple of days later when he and Tiuri were standing on his lookout tower taking one last look back at the Kingdom of Unauwen.

"How long is it," said Piak, "since we were last here?"

Tiuri thought about it. "About three weeks," he said.

"And we had no idea at the time what would happen to us when we were down there and what everything would look like from close up."

"And we've been even further than we can see," Tiuri added.

They stood up there for a while, gazing out over the Kingdom of Unauwen, before resuming their journey.

"We're travelling at the right time," said Piak. "Soon the autumn rains will begin, and then it'll be hard to cross the mountains."

A day later, they reached the pass and, the night after that, they slept in the cave beneath the seventh crag. It wasn't too far to the hermit's cabin from there. The weather was good – much better than the previous time – and most of the path was downhill.

Piak was delighted to see familiar places. However, the closer they came to their destination, the quieter he became. Tiuri was a little puzzled. His friend didn't seem to be tired...

It was already dark as they headed down to the cabin, but there was a light to guide them. Menaures had placed a lantern outside.

The hermit came out to meet them. He had obviously been expecting them.

"All day, I've had the feeling that you were coming," he said, "and look, here you are. Welcome!"

Soon the two friends were sitting at the table with the hermit and telling him about their successful journey.

"I am glad to hear you succeeded," said the hermit, "and I am also pleased you have become such firm friends. I hoped that it might happen."

"Did you expect me to travel on with Tiuri?" asked Piak.

"Yes," replied Menaures. "I was not surprised when you did not return."

Piak opened his mouth and closed it again. He looked silently at the hermit for a while and finally said, "King Unauwen asked me to send you his regards."

Menaures bowed his head. "Thank you," he said.

Again, there was silence. Tiuri looked at the hermit and then at Piak and wondered if Menaures really was the king's brother. He certainly looked like King Unauwen. But Tiuri didn't dare to ask him directly.

Piak seemed to feel the same way, because the next question he asked was simply, "Do you know King Unauwen?"

The hermit smiled. "You know that I do," he said.

"Um, but do you know him well?" Piak asked.

"I do," said Menaures. He was still smiling and there was a twinkle in his dark eyes.

"So why did you not ask us to pass on your regards?" asked Piak.

"My brother knows I think of him often," the hermit replied. "Yes, that's right. My brother! That is what you wanted to ask, isn't it?"

"Yes, yes," said Piak, blushing.

"You could have asked me," Menaures continued. "I don't know how you found out, but now that you know, I shall not deny it."

"You look so much like the king!" said Piak.

"But you should continue to see me just as you have always seen me," said Menaures. "As a hermit in the mountains – not as some prince or ruler."

Even so, Tiuri thought there was definitely something regal about the hermit. His simple clothes and his lean build did nothing to disguise it.

"Now tell me about your journey," said Menaures.

The two friends did so, with Tiuri doing most of the talking. In fact, Piak was very quiet. Tiuri kept glancing over at him, wondering if something was troubling his friend.

A little later, as they were making their bed of straw and blankets on the ground, Piak suddenly said, "Did you miss me, Menaures?"

The hermit smiled. "I certainly did," he replied.

"You know, Tiuri told you that I'm going with him to King Dagonaut. But if you can't manage without me, obviously I'll stay here."

"Missing you doesn't mean I can't manage without you,"

said Menaures. "It would be wrong if that were true. So you may leave with an easy heart. You would not have stayed with me forever anyway."

"I..." Piak began. Then he stopped himself and asked something else. "Did anything happen here while we were away?"

And Tiuri said, "Do you know what Jaro decided to do? Did he come to see you?"

"Yes," said the hermit. "We talked for a long time. I think, Tiuri, that Jaro will no longer serve the King of Eviellan." And that was all he said.

Soon after that, Menaures wished them goodnight. He didn't go to bed himself, but disappeared outside and left the door ajar, as he had done the previous time.

Tiuri was tired and he soon dozed off. Then he thought Piak was leaning over him and whispering a question, but when he opened his eyes, he saw Piak lying there beside him, perfectly still. Tiuri turned over and had almost fallen back to sleep, when he heard Piak quietly getting up. He looked and saw him going outside. Then he heard his friend talking to the hermit. He couldn't make out what Piak said, but Menaures's answer was loud and clear.

"You do not have to go, Piak," said the hermit. "If you would rather stay in the mountains, then that is what you must do."

Tiuri was immediately wide awake.

Piak was mumbling at first, but his voice became louder and Tiuri heard him say, "But I promised him, Menaures. I promised I'd go with him. I even asked to go myself! And I really wanted to go at first. I wanted to be a squire. But now that I'm back in the mountains, I feel that this is where I belong."

"No person truly belongs in any place on this earth," said the hermit. "But I know what you mean. You feel that your place is here."

"I'm not even certain about that," said Piak with a deep sigh. "I don't think I know what I want! Sometimes I think I'll never feel at home in the mountains, not the way I did before. Not now that I know what it's like down below. But I don't know if I would want to live anywhere else. And I don't know if I really want to go to the land of King Dagonaut and become a squire."

Tiuri listened to all that Piak said and he understood why his friend had been so quiet; this was what had been bothering him. Piak was regretting his decision to accompany Tiuri to the City of Dagonaut.

"What should I do, Menaures?" asked Piak.

Tiuri suddenly felt guilty for listening to words that had not been intended for his ears. But on reflection he felt that it was good that he had heard what Piak had said. Piak would probably never have confided in him.

"That's something you'll have to decide for yourself, Piak," came the hermit's reply.

"But that's exactly what I can't do," said Piak. "I know what I have to do, though. I gave Tiuri my word."

"Tell me honestly, Piak," said the hermit. "Would you rather stay in the mountains?"

It was silent for a while. Then, quietly, Piak said, "Yes." And he continued, "But I asked Tiuri if I could go with him. And I don't want him to think I'm abandoning him because..."

"Because?" the hermit asked calmly.

"He's scared that King Dagonaut won't make him a knight now," said Piak, "and he might think that's why I don't want to go with him..."

"Of course he won't think that," said the hermit.

No, of course not, Tiuri thought to himself.

"But that's not the problem," said Piak. "It's... well... it's what I already told you. I was so happy to be back here that I knew I really wanted to stay. And yet – and this is what's so strange, Menaures – I know I'll still be longing to go down the mountain. I feel miserable at the thought of having to say goodbye and I may well regret it. But if I go with Tiuri, I'll just miss the mountains again."

"Yes," said Menaures, "there will always be something that you miss, whether you leave now or stay here. All throughout our lives, we must keep saying goodbye. But if you would prefer to stay here, if you think that this is your place, you must be honest with Tiuri. He will not hold it against you."

Of course I won't, thought Tiuri. Imagine being angry at Piak for his honesty! But he was sad. He was going to miss his friend. Was it true what the hermit had said, that you had to keep on saying goodbye?

When Piak came back to bed, Tiuri pretended to be asleep. But he lay awake thinking for a while, even though he already knew what he was going to say to his friend the next day.

3   GOODBYE

"So, Piak," Tiuri said the next morning. "I know that you'd rather stay in the mountains."

"What makes you think..." Piak began, but Tiuri didn't let him finish.

"Whether you come with me or not," he continued, "we'll still be just as good friends. You belong in the mountains, and I belong in the Kingdom of Dagonaut. That's just the way it is. I'm not going to stay here for your sake either, am I?"

"But," said Piak, "I was going to be your squire!"

"That was what you wanted, yes," said Tiuri, "but I'm not angry with you for changing your mind. And I have to confess... I heard what you said to Menaures last night."

Piak hung his head. "Oh," he said. "Well, now you've heard it all, I've no need to say anything else. I feel really awful about it, Tiuri, but it's true. I'd rather stay here."

"Why do you feel awful?" said Tiuri calmly. "I understand."

"No, you don't," said Piak. "The thought of not going with you makes me feel terrible too. I'm sure I'll long for the City of Dagonaut, even though I've never been there, and it can't be as beautiful as the City of Unauwen. But if I were there, I'd be longing to be back in the mountains. It's just that... I probably wouldn't feel at home with all those knights and squires. But you do. That's where you belong."

"You'd get used to it," said Tiuri. "But of course you shouldn't feel that you have to come with me."

Piak sighed. "I wish I knew what I wanted to do," he said. Sadly, he looked around at the valleys and mountaintops.

"You belong here," Tiuri said firmly. "That's all there is to it. And so you should remain here. What could be simpler?"

Then Menaures called them for breakfast.

"So the two of you have spoken?" he asked. "Have you made your decision, Piak?"

"Yes," said Tiuri, answering for his friend. "Piak's staying here, in the mountains."

The hermit looked from one to the other, with an enigmatic smile on his face. "Fine," he said, "so that's decided. And when are you leaving, Tiuri?"

"You could stay for another day, couldn't you?" said Piak.

Tiuri shook his head. "No," he said, "I'd better not. I'll go after breakfast."

The hermit nodded.

Piak gave a sigh and said, "You don't mind if I come a short way with you, do you?"

"Of course not," said Tiuri.

Tiuri said goodbye to Menaures, who gave him his blessing. Then he left, accompanied by Piak, and took the path along the Blue River. The two friends did not speak much, as they were both feeling miserable about having to say goodbye.

Just after the gorge that Jaro had almost fallen into, Tiuri stopped. "Piak," he said, "isn't it about time for us to say farewell? You need to get back before dark."

"Yes..." said Piak, but he didn't sound too certain. "I could walk on with you for a bit longer," he said, "even to the City of Dagonaut."

"No, you mustn't do that."

"Why not?" asked Piak.

"It's better for us to say goodbye now than to keep putting it off. You can always visit the City of Dagonaut later, but that's different. And I plan to come back here to visit you. You can be sure of that!"

Piak looked a little happier. "Yes," he said, "you must."

"I certainly will!"

The two friends stood there for a moment, looking at each other, and then they both looked away, in opposite directions.

"Well then," said Tiuri finally. "All the best, Piak. I can't thank you enough for everything you've done for me."

Piak smiled. "Oh, be quiet!" he said.

"All the best," Tiuri repeated. "I don't really want to say goodbye. It sounds so final."

"No, please don't," said Piak.

So they shook hands and said, "Until we meet again."

Then Tiuri turned and strode off down the hill. After a while, he looked back and saw that Piak had climbed up onto a rocky outcrop and was waving at him. Tiuri couldn't make out his face, but he wondered if Piak had tears in his eyes as well. He waved back at his friend.

The next time he looked over his shoulder, there was no sign of Piak.

Now Tiuri was on his own again, and he felt lonely and downhearted. He walked on quickly, but sometimes he wondered what he was hurrying for. He wasn't longing to see the City of Dagonaut at all now, or his home. What could be waiting for him there that was worth the effort? The king would most likely refuse to knight him and, even if he did, what then? But he had one very good reason to make haste: he had to explain everything to his king and give him the letter from King Unauwen. And that was exactly what he planned to do.

In the afternoon he passed the crucifix, and soon after that he stopped at the spot where he had heard Ristridin's horn for the last time. He looked down at the First Great Road, and saw two riders heading west. As he walked on, he thought about the Grey Knights. Had they caught up with the Red Riders and punished them? And what about the Black Knight with the Red Shield?

The sky clouded over and looked as gloomy as he felt. Even the babbling of the Blue River sounded mournful. He realized just how many weeks he had been away from home. Before long, it would be autumn.

The road beside the Blue River felt long to Tiuri, perhaps because he was travelling alone and on foot instead of on horseback. But he reached the Inn of the Setting Sun in three days. The innkeeper didn't recognize him and he had a new manservant. Tiuri didn't ask him what had happened to Leor. And he didn't enquire about the Grey Knights either. He'd be sure to receive news of them when he reached Castle Mistrinaut.

4   A Warm Welcome

Tiuri set off on his way before sunrise. He wanted to reach Mistrinaut that same day, and this time he was not riding the fleet-footed Ardanwen. He begged a ride on a farmer's cart, but it was dark by the time he reached the castle. The rain was falling and he had put on his monk's habit for protection.

"Good evening, reverend brother," said the guard who opened the gate. "Are you very wet?"

Just like the last time! thought Tiuri. *And it's the same guard too.*

In the room beside the gate, the same scene awaited him: the other guard was staring at a chessboard, deep in thought.

Tiuri forgot for a moment that he was tired, wet and gloomy, and he started to laugh.

"Reverend brother," said the first guard, "what has amused you so much?"

"Is that still the same game?" asked Tiuri.

"What do you mean?" asked the guard, as he took out the big book and gave his companion a nudge.

"You were playing chess last time I came here, several weeks ago," said Tiuri.

The other guard looked up and said, "Now that you mention it, reverend brother... you do look familiar."

"I am Brother Tarmin," said Tiuri.

"Brother Tarmin," repeated the guard. Then the first one said, "But then you're not Brother Tarmin, are you? Brother Tarmin wasn't a monk and his name wasn't Tarmin."

"That's right," said Tiuri, throwing back his hood.

"Yes, I recognize you!" cried the first guard. "Welcome to Mistrinaut. There's been a lot of talk about you here. Actually, it was more like whispers, because we weren't supposed to know anything about you. So what's your real name?"

"My real name," said the young man, "is Tiuri, son of Tiuri."

"I shall write it down in a moment," said the second guard. "I think our master will be pleased to see you." He moved one of the pieces on the board. "My knight," he said with some satisfaction. "That reminds me, Tiuri, son of Tiuri. You're the one with the horse, aren't you? The black horse that the Grey Knights brought here?"

"Ardanwen!" Tiuri exclaimed. "Is Ardanwen here?"

"Yes, he certainly is," said the first guard. "What a magnificent creature! We've let him out to run every day, but no one could ride him. Come with me," he continued. "I'll take you to the lord of the castle. I'm sure you'll want to bring him your greetings."

The guard took Tiuri to the great hall, where many people were still gathered, even though dinner was over. The lord was standing beside one of the tables, talking to some squires. His wife was embroidering beside the fire. Lady Lavinia was sitting at her mother's feet, sorting out tangled balls of coloured yarn. It was a warm and cosy scene.

The guard announced Tiuri in a loud voice, "My lord, my lady, here is a guest you know."

The lord walked up to Tiuri with his hand outstretched. "Welcome back!" he said.

They gave Tiuri a very warm welcome. Lavinia dropped all of the balls of yarn onto the floor and Tiuri knelt to pick them up.

"Stand up, stand up!" cried the lord. "Is that any way to welcome an honoured guest?"

Someone pulled up a chair for Tiuri. The lord invited him to sit and looked at him inquisitively. He was not the only one; all eyes in the room were on Tiuri. "It is some time since we last saw each other," he said. "Are you on your way home? Oh, but I won't ask you any questions if you do not wish me to."

Tiuri undid the rope around his waist and as he removed the habit he said, "You may ask anything you like, Lord Rafox; I have no secrets to hide now. I am indeed on my way home or, to be more accurate, on my way to see King Dagonaut."

"And where have you been?" asked Lavinia.

"To see King Unauwen," said Tiuri.

"Oh..." she said, looking at him with wide eyes.

"Then you have come a long way," said the lord. "But," he continued, "it is not polite to start by questioning you like this. Have you eaten?"

When Tiuri shook his head, one of the servants was told to bring him a good meal as quickly as possible. Tiuri gave them a brief version of events and filled in more of the details as he ate.

The lord also had news of the Grey Knights. "They left the horse behind and asked us to take care of him until your return," he said. "It is a shame you did not arrive a couple of days ago. Then you could have spoken to Sir Evan and his squire."

"Only Sir Evan?" said Tiuri. "What about the others?"

"The company of the Grey Knights has disbanded," the lord told him. "Sir Evan has returned to his own kingdom. Did you not meet him on the First Great Road?"

"I travelled by a different route, over the mountains," said Tiuri. "But why have the knights parted company? Have they captured all of the Red Riders?"

"Most of them, if not all," replied the lord, "but they have not found the Black Knight with the Red Shield."

"Have they given up looking?" asked Tiuri.

"They had to," the lord told him. "But not forever. They have only interrupted their hunt. The trail of the Knight with the Red Shield led them back towards the east. They stopped on the way and left Ardanwen here. I heard the most recent news from Evan. He said they did not find the Black Knight with the Red Shield and feared that he had fled to Eviellan. They were planning to go there, but King Dagonaut gave them a new mission that meant they had to delay their search. But it is no more than a delay; the Grey Knights will come together once again to complete their revenge."

"But why the delay?" asked Tiuri.

"The king had need of the most experienced of his knights-errant," said the lord, "especially Ristridin. The king's mission was more important than the task the knights had set for themselves. I know little else about it. Evan said that he wanted to travel to the south himself to continue the search for the Knight with the Red Shield. But on reflection he felt it was better to report to King Unauwen first. He had already stayed away longer than agreed, and a journey to Eviellan would take even more time. He needed to account for his long absence, and finally to bring his king news of Sir Edwinem's death, as he could not be certain that you would arrive in the City of Unauwen before him. He only suspected that was your destination. And that is how he came to journey back to the west and stay here for a night as our guest."

"It is indeed a pity that I did not see him," said Tiuri. "I met both his brother and his father in the Kingdom of Unauwen."

Tiuri had to tell his own story yet again as well; Lavinia in particular asked him lots of questions.

"You know, a minstrel could write a song about your adventures," she said.

Tiuri smiled. He felt slightly embarrassed, but also a little proud. Then he told them all about Piak and the songs that he knew and how he'd made a tune for the words of the letter. Ah, Piak! Tiuri still missed him, but his gloom had vanished in the halls of this friendly castle.

Although it was late, he still wanted to go and say hello to the horse Ardanwen. His horse! The lord agreed to take him to the stables and the black horse recognized Tiuri straightaway. It was a happy reunion. Tiuri rubbed the loyal horse's nose and found himself looking forward to the journeys he would enjoy on Ardanwen's back. He would be a knight-errant – yes, a knight! – and he would wander far and wide, with King Unauwen's sword at his side.

Tiuri already felt almost like a knight as he rode away on Ardanwen the following day. He was a little sorry that he could not stay longer at Castle Mistrinaut, as he had been invited to, but he had to return to King Dagonaut as quickly as possible. The lord and Lavinia rode with him for some of the way, to the point where the forest began. There was a small inn there, where they rested for a while and ate together before saying farewell.

"You must promise that you will come to visit us again," said the lord.

Tiuri promised. Then he took his leave of Lavinia. As he

held out his hand to her, she dropped her glove. He picked it up and was about to return it, but then he changed his mind and said, "May I keep your glove, Lavinia?"

"Why?" she asked.

"To wear on my helmet at the next tournament," replied Tiuri. "If I ever become a knight..." Then he fell silent and felt himself blushing.

Lavinia blushed too, but she said kindly, "Of course you will be a knight. Everything will be fine, Tiuri."

Then they realized that Lavinia's father was watching them and they both blushed again. He looked at each of them in turn and smiled into his beard. "Well," he said, "perhaps we shall make a journey to the capital in the summer when the tournaments are held. So it's 'until we meet again', Tiuri, and all the best to you."

And soon Tiuri was riding eastwards again. As he looked at Lavinia's glove, he could picture her standing there. He hoped she would come to the city in the summer. He knew that he wanted to see her again and he would pay another visit to Castle Mistrinaut as soon as he could. The people who lived there had become his friends – not least of all Lady Lavinia.

I have found so much friendship on my journey, he thought a little later. Here, and in the Kingdom of Unauwen. He gave a sigh. He was alone again now; he had said goodbye to everyone. Even Piak, who had been through so much with him, was no longer by his side. Then he patted Ardanwen's neck. "But I still have you, Night Wind," he said, "and I'm sure I shall see the others again."

5   In the Forest

The road that Tiuri was now travelling along was new to him. On the journey to Unauwen, he had avoided the Great Road. With Ardanwen, he would be able to reach the city in around six days. The weather was beautiful, with a faint scent of autumn in the air and a red-golden haze already shimmering around the trees. It was very quiet; he saw hardly anyone.

On the afternoon of the third day after his departure from Castle Mistrinaut, he came to one of the wooden shelters that stood on the roadside here and there to provide accommodation for travellers and horses. There were very few inns in that sparsely populated area. Tiuri rode up to the hut and considered whether to spend the night there or to travel on. It was still early and he could stop later to sleep in the open air. There were already travellers inside; he could hear the sound of horses in the stable, and a shield was hanging beside the front door. That meant a knight must be staying there. Tiuri was trying to remember which of Dagonaut's knights had a shield that was silver, grey and green, but before it came to him a voice called out, "Ho, there! Is that not Tiuri, son of Tiuri?"

He turned around and saw a knight standing on the road. When the knight came closer, Tiuri recognized him as Ristridin of the South. In his light chainmail and green cloak, he looked very different from the Grey Knight he had been before. They greeted each other warmly and Tiuri decided to stay so that he could talk to Ristridin and hear his news.

"Have you seen Evan on your travels?" asked Ristridin.

Tiuri told him that he hadn't.

"You almost missed me too," said the knight. "I'm waiting for Arwaut and his men. When they get here, we're going to ride into the forest together. I was expecting them to arrive a while ago. I just came out to take a look and see if there was any sign of them."

"And where's Sir Bendu?" asked Tiuri. "I heard from the lord of Mistrinaut that the Grey Knights had disbanded."

"It is true," said Ristridin. "But we shall reunite to punish the one man who remains unpunished: the Black Knight with the Red Shield. But first you must tell me your news. Or are you still obliged to secrecy?"

"Not any longer, Sir Ristridin," said Tiuri. "I did as Sir Edwinem requested and took a letter to King Unauwen. And that is all."

"So few words to describe such a long journey," said Ristridin with a smile. He looked intently at Tiuri. "But whatever adventures you have experienced," he added, "have clearly done you no harm and much good, Tiuri, son of Tiuri! I spoke to your father in the City of Dagonaut. You have been on his mind a great deal, but he has complete faith in you. Your mother has been very worried, and she does not want to return home to Castle Tehuri before you are back in the city."

"Sir Ristridin," said Tiuri, "you must tell me everything!"

"Certainly. I shall answer all of your questions," said the knight. "But let's go inside and have something to eat. I am here with my squire and some men-at-arms. Look, here comes Ilmar now."

Ilmar too was surprised to see Tiuri. "I see you have Ardanwen again," he said.

"Yes, he is my horse now," said Tiuri proudly.

"And did our trick help?"

"Yes and no," replied Tiuri. "Not entirely. But it all ended well."

"I had gathered as much," said Ristridin. "But you must tell me more! I want to hear what news there is from the Kingdom of Unauwen, and about the land of Eviellan."

Sir Ristridin also had stories to tell Tiuri. Tiuri heard that the Grey Knights had caught up with the Red Riders and punished them, and that they had followed the trail of the Knight with the Red Shield to the east, close to the City of Dagonaut. When the king heard that the Grey Knights were in the area, he had called for them, as he had need of his knights-errant.

"Bendu and myself, in particular," Ristridin told Tiuri. "We are older and experienced and we were already planning to go to the Wild Wood anyway."

"To the Wild Wood?" asked Tiuri.

"Yes," said Ristridin. "King Dagonaut said he had heard strange rumours about the Wild Wood, about robbers who shun the daylight, about wild hunters and Men in Green. And he wants us to investigate and find out which of those rumours are true. He is concerned about dangers lurking in the Wild Wood that might threaten the kingdom, so we need to head there immediately. After that, we may continue our quest for vengeance. As the king said, the interests of our kingdom must take priority. I cannot help but admit that the king is right, even though I am sorry that we have not yet found the Knight with the Red Shield. The king said one of our number could continue the hunt. So Bendu has headed south, as we believe the Knight with the Red Shield has now fled to Eviellan. And I am on my way to the Wild Wood.

Arwaut will be here soon, with his men, to accompany me. We are to travel through the Robbers' Wood and across the Green River to our goal."

"Did you choose to go to the Wild Wood yourself?" asked Tiuri.

Ristridin nodded. "Yes," he said. "I remembered something Edwinem once said to me: 'You must do as you have planned: head into the Wild Wood. A knight should know his own land.'" Ristridin paused for a moment and then added, "We have built a mound upon Edwinem's grave, close to the Yikarvara Inn, with a cross on it, and his white shield. Another grave lies beside it, that of Vokia, his squire. We saw him again in the City of Dagonaut, but he died shortly afterwards. The shock of his master's death proved too much for him."

"The stranger outside the chapel..." said Tiuri. After a moment's silence, he asked, "When do you think you will see the others again?"

"The four of us have agreed to meet at Castle Ristridin in the spring. Bendu may have news from Eviellan. The plan was initially for Evan to go with Bendu, but he decided it would be better to go to his own country first and to report to his king."

"And so you parted company," said Tiuri.

"Yes, Bendu went to the south, Evan to the west, and Arwaut and I to the Wild Wood. It is a shame you have to go to King Dagonaut or you could have accompanied us."

"I should have liked that," said Tiuri.

"Then join us at Castle Ristridin in the spring... or sooner, if the weather allows."

"With great pleasure," said Tiuri. "If I am able."

"Of course, it is possible that King Dagonaut might give you another task," said Ristridin. "He'll be sure to reinforce the patrols on the southern border when he hears your news. The attention of the King of Eviellan is now focused on the Kingdom of Unauwen alone, a country whose king and crown prince he detests, and which is perhaps a worthier conquest than our own land. But the Grey River is all that separates our land from Eviellan, and that makes us an easier target."

Then he raised his head. "Listen," he said. "I hear hoofs in the distance. That will be Arwaut and his men."

It was indeed Arwaut, and so Tiuri was able to greet him too. Tiuri had to take his leave of the knights the next day, but he hoped to see them again, the following year, at Ristridin's brother's castle.

Tiuri continued his journey without any further incidents or encounters, but as he was approaching the City of Dagonaut, he remembered a promise he had made. A promise to Marius, the Fool in the Forest, the first person who had helped him on his journey. He had promised the Fool that he would visit him on his way home to tell him about his adventures on his journey to the place "where the sun goes down". He obviously could not disappoint him.

Tiuri left the road when he spotted a side path, but he could not find the place where he had first met the Fool. He wandered around for a while and was starting to think he might not be looking in the right area when he heard a shout, "Ho, there, fine horse and rider! What are you looking for?"

It was the Fool. He emerged from the bushes, twirling the curls of his beard, and looked very pleased to see Tiuri. "Rider, traveller and fine black horse," he said. "Who are you seeking and where are you going? Do you remember me?"

"I am looking for you, Marius," said Tiuri, climbing down from his horse. "I promised I would return and talk with you about where I'd been, didn't I?"

"I know where you have been," said the Fool. "To where the sun goes down. But I told no one. Not a soul. It was a secret. Riders in red came and so did knights in grey and they all asked about the secret. But I didn't tell them. And I didn't tell my mother either, or my brothers."

"I thank you, Marius," said Tiuri with a smile.

"And now you have returned, traveller, and you are different and yet you are the same. Will you come with me to the cabin now and talk with me?"

"Of course," Tiuri replied.

The Fool stroked Ardanwen's nose and looked happily at Tiuri. "And you have come to visit me!" he said. "You are my guest! My mother will cook food for you. And I shall say to my father and my brothers, 'He's here to visit me. He's a stranger to you, but he's my friend. He has been to where the sun goes down.' Tell me, friend, where does the sun go down?"

"I didn't travel that far," Tiuri said. "But I've heard it goes down in the sea."

"The sea? What's that?"

"It's made of water."

"Like a stream, or a spring?"

"No, much bigger."

"Like a river? Like a lake?"

"Much bigger even than that," said Tiuri. "The sea is so big that there's nothing but water, as far as the eye can see. Water and more water, all the way to the end of the world."

"And that's where the sun goes down?"

"Yes."

The Fool thought for a moment. "That's good," he said. "Then the sun can cool down, after shining so brightly all day long. The sun goes down in the sea, in the water.

I shall tell my brothers, because they don't know. Or is it a secret?"

"There are no more secrets now," said Tiuri, as he walked to the cabin with the Fool.

The Fool stopped and wrinkled his brow. "No more secrets?" he said. "They call me the Fool, but I don't believe that there are no more secrets left."

Tiuri looked at him with new respect.

"Yes," he said. "You're right. I am free to tell my secret now, but of course there are still lots of other secrets. The secrets of the Wild Wood, for instance, and all kinds of other mysteries. Some of them we have never even heard about. And others we shall never understand."

"I'm not sure I know what you mean," said the Fool.

Tiuri smiled at him. "Take me to your cabin," he said, "and I shall talk to you for as long as you want."

"We shall talk together," said the Fool. "I waited for you every day. I knew you would return. And now you are travelling to where the sun comes up. Do you know where the sun comes up?"

"No," said Tiuri, "I don't know that. So you see that you're right, and that there are still more secrets out there."

6   ACCEPTANCE

T iuri stayed overnight at the Fool's cabin and travelled on to the Yikarvara Inn the next day. Along the way, he also paid a brief visit to the graves of Sir Edwinem of Forèstèrra and Vokia, his squire.

The innkeeper recognized Ardanwen and so he also remembered Tiuri.

"You are the young man who wished to speak to the Black Knight with the White Shield, heaven rest his soul," he said. "So how is it that you have returned on his horse?"

"The horse belongs to me now," said Tiuri.

"Really?" said the innkeeper, studying him suspiciously. "Who are you? Riders in red and knights in grey came here, looking for you. It has been a few weeks, but I remember it very well."

"I am a messenger," said Tiuri, "on my way to King Dagonaut with a letter from King Unauwen." The innkeeper would have to make do with that explanation.

Tiuri slept at the inn that night – or rather, he lay on a bed, as he slept hardly a wink.

It was just a short distance from the inn to the city and it was still early in the morning as Tiuri approached his destination. He felt rather peculiar. It seemed somehow strange that his king's city still looked exactly the same. He gazed at the chapel where his adventure had begun over a month and a half ago and looked at the towers rising up above the city walls; the royal standard was flying on the towers of the palace, showing that Dagonaut was in residence.

Tiuri thought about Piak and wondered what he would have said now. Would the City of Dagonaut have disappointed him, as Dangria had at first? The city did, after all, look rather like Dangria, even though it was larger.

Tiuri reined in his horse, took the old habit from his bag and put it on. He wanted to remain unnoticed as he entered the city, where so many people knew him, and to speak to no one until he had seen King Dagonaut. As he rode to the western gate, a group of riders came in the opposite direction: two knights, followed by squires and archers. The knights were young and they looked magnificent, with their gleaming weapons, coloured cloaks and falcons on their wrists. Tiuri was startled to recognize them as his friends Arman and Jussipo. They galloped past without paying him any heed, and he watched them go until they disappeared over a hill.

I could have been with them, thought Tiuri. *If I hadn't listened to that voice, maybe now I would be going out hunting with my fellow knights in the Royal Forest.* But he knew he did not wish for things to be any different. He would not have wanted to miss out on his adventures.

The guards let him through the gate, but not without remark.

"Your horse is finer than your habit, monk!" one of them called out.

"I am no monk," said Tiuri. "I am a messenger with news from the west for King Dagonaut."

He rode through the familiar streets and soon came to the square where the palace stood. Opposite the palace was an inn, with a shield of blue and gold hanging beside the door, the shield of Tiuri the Valiant. Tiuri hesitated for a moment. Should he go inside and greet his parents? No, he should go to the king first. That was more important.

The palace guards asked him who he was.

"A messenger for King Dagonaut," he said again.

"Who sent you and what is your name?"

"King Unauwen sent me, and Tiuri is my name."

The guards recognized him then and allowed him to enter. Tiuri left Ardanwen in the care of a couple of grooms in the courtyard and soon found himself in the great hall, where the king's visitors had to wait. He hoped the king would be able to receive him soon.

A knight entered the room and, when he spotted Tiuri, he cried out.

Tiuri looked up. "Father!" he cried.

They ran towards each other and embraced.

"Father!" repeated Tiuri.

Sir Tiuri smiled at him joyfully. "Is all well with you, my son?" he asked.

"Yes... Oh yes, Father."

"Are you the messenger from King Unauwen?"

"Yes, Father," said Tiuri. "How are you? And how is Mother?"

"Everything is fine," said Sir Tiuri. "The king wishes to see you now. I'm to take you to him." However, he still showed no sign of doing so, but stood there, studying his son. "You're taller," he said. Then he placed his hand on his son's shoulder. "Come," he said. "I'll take you to the king. We shall talk again later."

A few moments later, Tiuri was standing before King Dagonaut and looking into his familiar face. It was a strong face, with bright, sharp eyes, framed by thick brown hair and a short beard. The only other person in the room was Tiuri's father, who had stepped back and was standing beside the door.

Tiuri bowed to the king and handed him the letter from Unauwen. Then he said, "Sire, I would also like to explain why I ran from the chapel on midsummer's eve."

"I am sure you would," said King Dagonaut. "I have already heard some of the details from Sir Ristridin, but I wish to hear the whole story from you. You left with no warning or explanation and were absent for a long time. Although it was not so very long for a journey to the Kingdom of Unauwen."

He studied Tiuri as closely as his father had done. "Have you greeted your father?" he asked.

"Yes, sire."

"And your mother?"

"No, sire," said Tiuri.

"That is good." The king broke the seals on Unauwen's letter, which consisted of many closely written sheets of paper. He gave the letter a cursory glance and then looked up at Tiuri. "I wish to hear your story and your explanation, Tiuri, son of Tiuri," he said, "but first I shall read what the great king in the west has written to me. Go now with your father and return to me in an hour."

Tiuri bowed once again and said he would obey.

He accompanied his father to the inn, where he was reunited with his mother. The hour was soon over and Tiuri had not come close to finishing his story when he and his father had to return to the palace. This time he was admitted to the king's presence on his own.

Tiuri explained to the king why he had run away from the chapel instead of keeping his vigil until seven o'clock in the morning.

"The stranger asked me for help," he said, "and I could not refuse. And after I had sworn to Sir Edwinem that I would deliver the letter, I had to keep my promise."

"That is true," said King Dagonaut. "And was it difficult to complete your task?"

"At times," said Tiuri. "But I was helped by many people."

The king tapped the letter, which he was holding in his hand. "King Unauwen mentioned you in his letter," he said. He took another long look at Tiuri. "You have won a sword, a ring, and a horse," he said, "but still you are not yet a knight."

"N-no, sire," said Tiuri, not sure what to make of the king's words. Did King Dagonaut approve of his actions? He had such a peculiar smile on his face.

The king did not speak for a while. Tiuri, too, was silent.

"Well," said the king finally, "is there nothing else that you would like to say to me or tell me?"

"No, sire," said Tiuri. What else could he say? He had told the king everything that he needed to know.

"And nothing to ask, Tiuri, son of Tiuri?"

Yes, there certainly was something that Tiuri wanted to ask!

"S-sire," he stammered. "You just said that I am not yet a knight. Would you... will you make me a knight?"

King Dagonaut rose from his throne. "Make you a knight?" he repeated slowly. "You chose, of your own free will, to run away before I was to knight you. Do you think that now, over a month and a half later, I should act as if nothing has happened? Midsummer's day is long gone. Why should I make you a knight now?"

"I-I had hoped you might still do it," Tiuri said.

"Once every four years, young men are chosen to be knighted," said the king. "They are tested beforehand and have to abide by many rules. It is their duty to spend the night before the ceremony in reflection and vigil, and not to heed any voices from outside. If they cannot or will not obey, they have broken a rule and proven that they are not prepared to do whatever it takes to become a knight. And that is what happened in your case, Tiuri."

"But..." Tiuri began. He couldn't speak another word. What he had wanted to say was, "But I could not have reacted any differently..."

"Tell me honestly, Tiuri," the king continued. "If you had the chance to spend another night of vigil in the chapel and, once again, someone called out and asked for your help, what would you do?"

Tiuri looked at him. He suddenly felt very calm.

"I would do the same," he replied.

King Dagonaut nodded. "Exactly," he said. "You would do the same, even though you know what the consequences would be. And you shall have to accept those consequences."

Tiuri raised his head. "Yes, sire," he said, loud and clear.

"Even though that means you will not be knighted."

"Even though that means I will not be knighted," repeated Tiuri firmly.

King Dagonaut nodded again and said, "You may leave now, Tiuri. I expect to see you back at the palace this evening. You still owe me obedience, not only because I am your king, but also because you are in my service as a squire."

Tiuri bowed and took his leave of the king.

He left the palace and returned to the inn, where his mother was waiting for him. His father arrived a little later. They made him tell them more about his adventures, but his mind was elsewhere. He was still thinking about his conversation with King Dagonaut. He realized now that, over the past few days, he had been counting on the king knighting him. Slither's curse had come true.

"Is something troubling you?" asked Tiuri's mother, as he paused between stories.

"Tiuri must be tired," said his father. "He has been through so much in such a short time and he still needs to get used to being back in the city and with us."

Tiuri wondered if he should confide in them. He wanted to tell them his worries, because he knew that his parents were proud of him. Maybe they would sympathize and feel that the king had acted unfairly – although he wasn't sure about his father, who had a very high opinion of Dagonaut and considered his word to be law. But Tiuri decided not to say anything. First he wanted to get his own confused and contradictory thoughts in order. Anyway, his parents would find out soon enough that he would not become a knight, or at least not for a while yet.

That afternoon, Tiuri became restless and needed to get some fresh air. He saddled Ardanwen and went for a ride outside the city, so that he could think everything through calmly.

He did not regret running away on midsummer's eve, and he would do it again if it came to it. King Dagonaut was right: he had to accept the consequences. He had to reconcile himself to the thought of not becoming a knight. He reflected upon King Dagonaut, whose attitude had disappointed him. Would King Unauwen have reacted in the same way? But he knew that he must not think that way. Dagonaut was his king and he was duty bound to obey him. Dagonaut was stern, but not unfair. It was quite possible that Dagonaut approved of his actions but still felt that Tiuri should bear the consequences.

Tiuri reined in Ardanwen and gazed at the city. The afternoon was drawing to its end and he had to return. The ride had done him some good; he felt he could accept the disappointment now. As he rode back into the city, Tirillo's words echoed in his thoughts: "One does not need to carry a sword and a shield to be a knight."

"Exactly!" he said to himself. "It doesn't matter if I am a knight or not. I am still Tiuri, and I can still do good whenever it is needed."

7 A Knight with a White Shield

Tiuri's parents were waiting impatiently for him at the inn. King Dagonaut was holding a feast at the palace and they were expected to attend. All of the knights who were in the city would be there, along with their ladies and their squires.

"The king wants you to be there too," Sir Tiuri said to his son.

"I know," Tiuri replied.

"Wear your sword," said the knight, when they were ready to leave.

"I'm not entitled to wear a sword to the palace," said Tiuri. "You do know the king is not going to knight me, don't you?"

"I know," his father said calmly. "But you are still to buckle it on; those are his orders. Here, and take my shield."

"May I become your squire again, Father?" asked Tiuri, accepting his father's shield.

"That is for the king to decide," his father replied.

"Which of the knights will be there this evening?" asked Tiuri. "I saw Arman and Jussipo this morning."

"They are the only ones among your friends who are still in the city. Wilmo is back on his father's estate and Foldo has been sent to the south. And only a few of the older knights are still in the city. Your mother and I also intend to leave soon. We kept delaying our journey back to Tehuri because we hoped to receive news of you."

Castle Tehuri! Suddenly Tiuri longed for his ancestral home, where he had not been for over a year. He wondered what would happen to him now. Would he have to stay and serve the king as he had done before? Then he felt a longing for somewhere else... If only he were still in the City of

Unauwen, the most beautiful city in the world, on the White River, close to the sea in the west!

At the palace, tables had been laid in the smallest of the halls that were used for gatherings of the king and his knights. It was still a large enough room, though, and was surrounded by a beautiful series of columns. The shields of the knights who were present that evening hung on the columns. Tiuri placed his father's shield in its place and stepped into the background, but he was soon spotted. Arman and Jussipo came over, dressed in their full armour, as befits true knights. But their young and cheerful faces had not changed at all.

"We heard you were back," they said, shaking Tiuri's hand, "but we didn't know if it was really true. How are you?"

"I'm fine," said Tiuri with a smile. "I don't need to ask you that question, do I?"

The young knights looked at him with a mixture of curiosity and embarrassment.

"You've travelled a long way, haven't you?" said Arman. Then he added, "I saw you sneaking out that night, you know."

"Why did you do that?" asked Jussipo.

"Why did I leave?" said Tiuri.

"Yes. It was really rather foolish of you."

"I'm sure he didn't do it without a good reason," said Arman, a little angrily.

Tiuri smiled again. Arman had always been his friend.

"You're right," he said. "There was a good reason."

Then the lord steward asked the guests to take their seats. The king was about to arrive.

"Come and sit with us," said Arman to Tiuri.

Tiuri shook his head. Only the knights and their ladies sat at the main table at such occasions. His place was still with the squires and the servants. He walked over to join them and to greet some old friends. But the lord steward stopped him and said, "Tiuri, son of Tiuri, your place is there."

"At the main table!" exclaimed Tiuri. "No, Sir Muldo. That can't be right!"

"Your place is at the main table," repeated the lord steward, "between Sir Arman and Sir Jussipo. Those are my orders."

Tiuri could no longer protest, because the sound of trumpets announced the arrival of the king. So he stood with the knights and their ladies at the main table, which was arranged in the shape of a horseshoe. He bowed when the king entered and waited for him to welcome his guests and take his seat. Only then would everyone else be allowed to sit down.

However, King Dagonaut remained standing and he looked around the room at those present. His gaze rested on Tiuri, who felt rather uneasy, as he believed he had no right to be standing at the main table as if he were a knight.

The king welcomed his knights and their ladies. And then he said, "You will have noticed that a young knight has joined us for the first time... the youngest of you all. I would like to welcome him in particular. Greetings, Sir Tiuri, son of Tiuri!"

Tiuri stared at the king in amazement. King Dagonaut started to laugh. "See how he looks at me!" he cried. "Sir Tiuri, I bid you welcome! Step closer, so that we may better greet each other and I may perform the appropriate gesture to lend force to my words."

Tiuri obeyed. "Your Majesty!" he said, when he stood before the king. "Forgive me, but I thought..."

"You thought I would not knight you!" said the king, laughing again. Then he became serious and said, "You misunderstood, Tiuri, although I must confess that I deliberately misled you. I wanted you to realize that you would have acted as you did, no matter what the consequences."

"Oh," said Tiuri quietly.

"However, there is another reason why I said I would not make you a knight," the king continued. "It was, in fact, no longer necessary. If you had not listened to that plea for help, you would be a knight by now. But, having heeded it and successfully completed your mission and kept your promise to Sir Edwinem, does that mean that you are not a knight? You may not have been knighted in a ceremony, but you have proven yourself a knight. You have knighted yourself, Tiuri, and my tapping you on the shoulders with a blade will not make you any more of a knight than you already are!"

A murmur went around the room. Tiuri looked at the king, feeling full of emotion: he was astonished, bashful, proud and happy, all at the same time.

"Give me your sword," said the king.

Tiuri did so.

"Kneel," the king ordered.

Tiuri obeyed. The king tapped him on both shoulders with the flat of the blade and said, "Arise, Sir Tiuri!"

When Tiuri had stood up, King Dagonaut buckled on his sword for him, and kissed him, as was customary. Then he beckoned one of his servants, who brought him a shield as white as snow.

"Sir Tiuri," said the king, "you are about to swear your loyalty to me. But at the request of King Unauwen I am to give you a white shield, as a sign that you will also be Unauwen's servant, and as a reminder of the knight whose task you performed."

Tiuri took the shield and, with trembling voice, he spoke the oath that every young knight must promise and keep.

"I swear as a knight to serve you loyally, as I will all of your subjects and those who call upon my aid. I promise to use my sword only in the service of good, against evil, and to use my shield to protect those who are weaker than myself."

Then all the people in the room cried out, "Long live Sir Tiuri with the White Shield!"

And Tiuri bowed his head because his eyes were full of tears.

Now the feast could begin. Servants and squires carried in dishes of food and filled glasses to the brim. Tiuri saw many happy, surprised and curious faces looking in his direction. He did not sit down, however, but turned to the king and said in a whisper, "Sire, may I ask you something?"

"What is it, Sir Tiuri?"

"May I have your permission to leave the feast?" asked Tiuri, so quietly that only the king could hear him.

"Why?" the king whispered back.

"Sire... I have not yet completed my vigil..." Tiuri began.

The king immediately understood.

"Then go, Tiuri," he said kindly. "I shall see you tomorrow."

As discreetly as possible, Tiuri left the hall and headed outside. He climbed up onto Ardanwen's back and rode through the silent streets to the city gate.

Tiuri knelt on the stone floor of the chapel, staring at the pale flame of the candle in front of him. Everything that he had seen and done seemed like a dream. He felt certain that he would turn around and see that his friends were there, too: Arman, Foldo, Wilmo and Jussipo. And then he would know that he had just imagined the voice that asked him to open the door, and all of the adventures that followed.

But when he looked around, he was still alone, and his white shield hung above the altar.

So it had really happened. The Tiuri who was keeping his vigil now was a different person from the Tiuri of all those many days ago. Only now did he realize what it meant to be a knight. And still he was only at the beginning of his life in the service of his king and his country. Everything that he had been through could be seen as a test. He thought about his experiences, the people he had met, the friends he had made. He also reflected upon the future and promised himself that he would try to be a good knight.

And that is how Tiuri spent the night. He did not rise to his feet until the first rays of sun shone through the windows of the chapel, making them glow and gleam.

8   SUNRISE

Tiuri left the chapel and headed outside to where faithful Ardanwen had waited patiently for him. The sun hung behind the towers of the city, which looked magnificent in the morning light – almost as beautiful as the City of Unauwen. Tiuri climbed onto Ardanwen and slowly rode downhill.

When they had almost reached the bottom of the hill, Tiuri saw a boy coming along the road from the west, shabbily dressed, but with a sword at his side.

He looks like Piak, he thought. And then he realized with a jolt that it *was* Piak!

The boy stopped to look at the city, shielding his eyes with his hand. He had not seen Tiuri. Tiuri shook the reins and raced towards his friend.

Piak didn't recognize him at first and he leapt back, startled.

"Piak," said Tiuri. "Piak!" He jumped down from his horse.

"Tiuri... it's you!" Piak exclaimed.

The two friends shook hands and slapped each other on the back.

"It really is you!" said Piak. "I thought you were a knight. Wait... are you a knight now?"

"Yes, yes," said Tiuri. "But what are you doing here?"

"I changed my mind," replied Piak, suddenly looking shy. "I want... I'd like... I realized I'd rather be your squire."

"My squire!" exclaimed Tiuri. "My friend, travelling companion, guide and – who knows? – maybe one day a knight of the king!"

"That's asking too much!" cried Piak. "All I want is to be your friend and squire. At least, that's if you still need a squire."

"You are the only squire I want," said Tiuri.

"You're an impressive sight!" said Piak, looking him up and down. "I didn't even recognize you at first. Am I still allowed to call you Tiuri?"

"I'll clip you around the ears if you call me anything else," said Tiuri, laughing.

"And you have a white shield! How did that happen? I thought only Unauwen's knights had white shields."

"I'll tell you all about it later on," said Tiuri.

"Is this your black horse?" asked Piak, cautiously stroking Ardanwen's nose.

"Yes, this is Ardanwen and he belongs to me now," said Tiuri. "I'm sure he won't mind if you ride him too, though.

But tell me, how did you get here so quickly? When did you change your mind, and why?"

"I regretted it almost immediately," said Piak. "I was walking up the mountain, back to Menaures, and with every step I took, I thought, *The distance is getting longer, and longer, and longer...* And when I was back up there, doing the usual chores, and I had more time to think, then I knew for certain. I really regretted my decision! Finally I told Menaures and he just smiled and said, 'I knew you would. Go on, then. Go after your friend, as quick as you can.'"

"Why didn't he say that before?" asked Tiuri.

"I asked him the same question. Do you know what he said? 'Because now you know for certain that you want to be with Tiuri, no matter how much you miss the mountains.' He was right. You see, since you left, any doubts I had were gone. So, I said goodbye to Menaures and I started running down the mountain. Phew, did I hurry! It took me a day or so to reach Castle Mistrinaut. I remembered that you'd told me about it, so I decided to stop there. And, of course, I asked if they had any news of you, which they did. They all came to talk to me, the lord, his wife and his daughter. She seems very nice and, of course, she's really pretty too. You know, I think she likes you." Piak gave Tiuri a mischievous grin. "Do you like her too?" he asked.

"Yes, I do," said Tiuri, blushing a little.

Piak grinned again. "They were very kind to me," he continued. "They even lent me a horse. A squire rode with me some of the way and took the horse back with him. I only had to walk the last part of the way." He paused. "So here I am," he finished. "And now you have to tell me all about your journey and what King Dagonaut said to you."

"All in good time," said Tiuri. "First come back to the city with me. Then you can meet my parents, and Dagonaut's knights, and the king himself."

"And then?" asked Piak.

"And then we'll see what happens next," said Tiuri. "I'm sure there'll be something for us to do."

Then Tiuri, leading Ardanwen and with Piak by his side, walked slowly eastwards, back to the City of Dagonaut.

The Adventures
continue in...

'FANS OF *THE LETTER FOR THE KING* WILL BE DELIGHTED WITH ITS SEQUEL'
SUNDAY TIMES

'ACTION-PACKED DRAMA'
DAILY MAIL

The Secrets of the Wild Wood

TONKE DRAGT
INTERNATIONAL BESTSELLER
PUSHKIN CHILDREN'S

TONKE DRAGT writes and illustrates books of adventure, fantasy and fairy tales. She was born in 1930 in Jakarta. During the Second World War, when she was twelve, she was imprisoned in a Japanese camp, where she wrote her very first book, using begged and borrowed paper. After the war, she moved to the Netherlands with her family and eventually became an art teacher. She published *The Goldsmith and the Master Thief* in 1961, and a year later this was followed by her most famous story, *The Letter for the King*, which won the Children's Book of the Year Award and has been translated into twenty-six languages. She was awarded the State Prize for Youth Literature in 1976 and was knighted in 2001. *The Goldsmith and the Master Thief*, *The Secrets of the Wild Wood* and *The Song of Seven* are also published by Pushkin Children's Books.

LAURA WATKINSON studied medieval and modern languages at Oxford, and taught English around the world before returning to the UK to take a Master's in English and Applied Linguistics, and a postgraduate certificate in literary translation. She is now a full-time translator from Dutch, Italian and German, and has translated Tonke Dragt's *The Goldsmith and the Master Thief*, *The Letter for the King*, *The Secrets of the Wild Wood* and *The Song of Seven* for Pushkin Children's Books. She lives in Amsterdam..